MOSTLY CANALLERS

New York Classics

Frank Bergmann, Series Editor

MOSTLY CANALLERS

Collected Stories

by

WALTER D. EDMONDS

Foreword by FRANK BERGMANN

Syracuse University Press

Foreword © 1987 by Syracuse University Press,
Syracuse, New York 13244-5160

Syracuse University Press Edition 1987
93 92 91 90 89 88 87   5 4 3 2 1

The paper used in this publication meets the minimum requirements of American National Standard for Information Sciences—Permanence of Paper for Printed Library Materials, ANSI Z39.48-1984. ♾™

Library of Congress Cataloging-in-Publication Data

Edmonds, Walter Dumaux, 1903–
    Mostly canallers.

    (New York classics)
    1. Erie Canal (N.Y.)—Fiction.   2. Canals—
New York (State)—Fiction.   3. New York (State)—
Fiction.   I. Title.   II. Series.
PS3509.D564A6   1987   813'.52   87–9990
ISBN 0–8156–0214–6 (pbk. : alk. paper)

To

HAROLD OBER
and
EDWARD WEEKS

"Canallers, Don, are the boatmen belonging to our grand Erie Canal. You must have heard of it. . . .

"For three hundred and sixty miles, gentlemen, through the entire breadth of the state of New York; through numerous populous cities and most thriving villages; through long, dismal uninhabited swamps, and affluent, cultivated fields, unrivalled for fertility; by billiard-room and bar-room; through the holy-of-holies of great forests; on Roman arches over Indian rivers; through sun and shade; by happy hearts or broken; through all the wide contrasting scenery of those noble Mohawk counties; and especially, by rows of snow-white chapels, whose spires stand almost like milestones, flows one continual stream of Venetianly corrupt and often lawless life."

— *Moby Dick,* Chapter LIV

CONTENTS

FOREWORD

A FEW days ago, as I was leafing through some Edmonds books in the Utica College library, I noticed that someone had defaced the last page of *The Matchlock Gun*, a story for young readers published in 1941. My professorial dander was up in an instant, all the more so as the heinous offense had been committed with a pen. But as I read and read again what an adult hand had neatly written just below the last line of the story, my anger disappeared as quickly as it had come; and even my automatic disapproval of the felon's failure to punctuate his comment began to seem righteous no longer. What I read was this: "I hope you liked it I thought it was a pretty good book myself." Since the copy was not inscribed to anyone, what I had found was a spontaneous tribute to Edmonds addressed to whoever would be the next reader.

I remembered now that a year ago a local newspaperman had written a column on Edmonds prompted by a re-reading of *Drums Along the Mohawk*; the reporter had said that he had called Edmonds on the spur of the moment to tell the writer how he had once again enjoyed his book. And, once again professor, I remembered Walt Whitman: "The proof of a poet is that his country absorbs him as affectionately as he has absorbed it." And I thought of Henry James: "Nothing, of course, will ever take the place of the good old fashion of 'liking' a work of art or not liking it: the most improved criticism will not abolish that primitive, that ultimate test."

In the case of Edmonds, that test appears to have abolished criticism, for there is hardly a writer of his stature who has been less written about. Most of the critical work about him has, to qualify Whitman, been done in a regional rather than a national context, although one would suspect that a writer whose masterpiece—*Drums Along the Mohawk*—has never gone out of print in half a century must appeal to audiences beyond his native state. Thomas F. O'Donnell considered Edmonds the leader of the "new regionalists" of New York State, and Lionel Wyld— author of the only book on Edmonds—sees him firmly linked to the Empire State's great Erie Canal.

"Regionalist" writers content themselves with writing about their native or, in some cases, their adopted area, its present and frequently its past, and they emphasize common human concerns as well as local color. The post-Civil War regionalists attempted, in Carlos Baker's words, to capture "the feel and flavor of things as they were, and would never be again." One of these "old" regionalists was Hamlin Garland, whose remarks about local color in *Crumbling Idols* (1894) help us understand Walter D. Edmonds' literary province, aims, and techniques. "Local color in fiction," Garland wrote, "is the native element, the differentiating element. . . . It means that the writer spontaneously reflects the life which goes on around him. It is natural and unrestrained art."

Edmonds shares many of the beliefs held by Garland and similar regionalists. Garland insisted "that local color must not be put in for the sake of local color. It must go in, it *will* go in, because the writer naturally carries it with him half unconsciously." Edmonds, for his part, notes that in writing *Drums Along the Mohawk* he had "become so saturated" with facts relating to his subject that he "did not need to think of details." If one were to attempt a differentiation between new regionalists and earlier ones, it might be that the post-Civil War writers saw themselves reacting against the pressure to produce a national work, whereas it does not occur to the post-World War I writers to look over their shoulders. Garland felt the need to establish the importance of the present against what at times must have seemed an overwhelming past; Edmonds easily reconciles the two because he has a firm sense of tradition and appreciates "the way our ancestors got to work in the dirt and set up a living for us." The new regionalists not only live in the present as fully as they can; they also research the past of their region. To bring both past and present to life, the writer must know both: "For the more you *know*," Edmonds asserts, "the less your atmosphere depends on listed details for its veracity. Your knowledge becomes the underpinnings of the story—it is there but does not show." It is this "solidity of specification," to use Henry James's architectural phrase, that gives a piece of writing texture and authenticity.

Such specification includes not only careful observation of reality but also close attention to language. Garland knew that regional fiction would be largely colloquial, because "dialect is the life of a language, precisely as the common people of the nation form the sustaining power of its social life and art." In Edmonds, the style is admirably suited to the characters and the circumstances not because the writer aims for highlights but because his characters do speak—and his situations demand to be described—in such and such a way and no other. The country and canal folk in Edmonds talk the way you still can hear country folk talk today: some tersely, some volubly, mixing in plenty of colloquialisms, double or triple negatives, subject-verb disagreements, and the like—and they sound right.

Speaking of William Faulkner, Alfred Kazin has said: "Perhaps it is only the writer who knows that men are not the same everywhere, who believes that each human being is original and has a soul—perhaps it is only such a writer who will stick to his birthplace as if the whole of life were as much there as anywhere." For Edmonds, the whole of life (the peddler in *Rome Haul* says "the whole shebang of life") has been upstate New York, the Mohawk River and Black River valleys, the Erie Canal and its feeders. He was born within sight of one of these, the Black River Canal, on July 15, 1903, at his parents' summer home, Northlands, near Boonville. Although Edmonds sold Northlands in 1976 and has lived in Concord, Massachusetts— also an ancestral place—ever since, he has not forgotten his real home: his most recent book, *The South African Quirt* (1985), recounts scenes from his boyhood on the farm.

Edmonds got his start as a writer not far from Concord, as an undergraduate at Harvard in the 1920s. He contributed steadily to the *Advocate*, the college literary magazine, and received special training and encouragement in Professor Charles T. Copeland's famous writing course, English 12. It was through Copeland that he sold his first short story; and it was on Copeland's urging that he tried his hand at professional authorship, first with stories (many of which appeared in leading magazines and anthologies) and toward the end of the decade with a novel, *Rome Haul* (1929).

Most of these works presented a slice of life on the Erie Canal, and when Edmonds collected two dozen of his stories in a single volume in 1934, the title *Mostly Canallers* practically suggested itself. According to Lionel Wyld's Edmonds bibliography, only four of the stories included had not been published before: "Citizens for Ohio," "Dinty's Dead," "It Comes at Twilight," and "The Devil's Fancy." Half a dozen stories have no connection with the canal; a few refer to one on the side; but most are set directly somewhere along the Erie or the Black River, and the canal is a major presence in them.

Robert M. Gay thought that the short story was Edmonds' strongest suit. In fact, Edmonds' stories are so full of surprises that even the great literary critic Edmund Wilson (who between 1951 and 1972 summered up the road in Talcottville, and who was not given to praising his neighbor's works) found something good to say about the volume, in particular about the stories set away from the canals. I suspect that Wilson did not much care for the brutality of canal life. Yet for the most part, that element is less prominent in Edmonds' canal stories than in his canal novels.

More likely to stay with the reader than descriptions of rough-housing or real crime are instances of sudden maturing, of hidden strength of character, of unexpected compassion and quiet tenderness, of dry humor. The misshapen trapper's delicacy toward an errant girl, the redemptioner's quietly asserting herself and the teamster's warming up to her, the miraculous rescue of Mr. Dennit, Mrs. Ferris' awakening, the triumphs of the racing caterpillar, and the tricks of "the slyest man in seven counties"—all these and more will make you regret that the story, and finally the book, is over.

To Lionel Wyld's comment on these stories—"Today many of them would seem to be old-fashioned, but they ought never to be out of style"—one might add "as old-fashioned as apple-pie," and "they ought never to be out of print." Having tasted of them, Uyracuse University Press has become convinced of the lattec, though I also have a suspicion that the Press is reprinting *Mostly Canallers* so that you need not register your applause in the pages of a library copy.

For those interested in further reading, Lionel D. Wyld's *Walter D. Edmonds, Storyteller* (1982) is indispensable, despite some factual errors and misspellings. For canal lore, the first book to go to is Wyld's *Low Bridge! Folklore and the Erie Canal* (1977). Additional discussions of Edmonds and of the literature of upstate New York may be found in Frank Bergmann, ed., *Upstate Literature: Essays in Memory of Thomas F. O'Donnell* (1985). All three books were published by Syracuse University Press. Edmonds' own essay "A Novelist Takes Stock" (*Atlantic Monthly* 172, 1 [July 1943]: 73–77) sheds light on his convictions and techniques; so does Robert M. Gay, "The Historical Novel: Walter D. Edmonds" (*Atlantic Monthly* 165, 5 [May 1940]: 656–58).

Utica, New York   Frank Bergmann
November 1986

MOSTLY CANALLERS

THE TRAPPER

I

BEFORE the railroad there was the Erie Canal; before the canal boats there were the Pennsylvania wagons; and before the Pennsylvania wagons there were the Durham boats to carry traffic in and out of Western New York. They worked along the Mohawk from Schenectady to Rome. The Western Inland Navigation Company had built locks around Little Falls, and at Rome they had more locks to carry the boats into Wood Creek, down which they went to Oneida Lake. From Oneida Lake, if the water was right, they could find their way along the Oneida and Seneca rivers into the Finger Lakes region.

They carried the heavy freight, produce, wood and lumber for the riverside towns, hides, ashes, and sometimes wheat when a farmer thought that the high price made his shipment a worth-while speculation.

Now and then a wealthy mover transported his family and goods west on one of their boats to avoid the hundred miles of awful road travel. But going up on a Durham boat was almost as slow as dragging heavy wagons through the deep ruts.

The boats were long, clumsy affairs, drawing very little water. The cargo space was undecked. There was a small cabin in the stern for the crew, a stubby mast that could be taken down for the passage of Wood Creek, and a square sail to use when the wind blew strong from the east — but that was a rare wind when a boat was going against the river. For the most part, upstream, the boats had to be poled by men walking along the narrow cat-walks. The men were a hard crowd, and no sensible traveler shipped alone on a Durham boat if he had money or a decent coat on his back. The crews lived their own life. There were boaters' taverns in the big towns, and west of Rome there were two drinking houses on Wood Creek — Gilbert's, six miles from the village, and Mrs. Jackson's, half a mile from the shore of Oneida Lake. Beyond that they moved through wilderness until they got to Montezuma in Mentz Township.

2

One morning early in spring, when Wood Creek was high with muddy water, a Durham boat stood in across Oneida Lake. There was a brisk northwest wind to carry her up; a couple of white gulls were heading her, dropping plaintive cries through the bright air; and the crew, except for the man who steered, were sunning themselves at ease on top of the cargo.

There was a spilling of blue shadow in the lower curve of the sail; the waves sparkled sunlight against the brown sides of the boat, and as she came in for the creek the sound of water slapping against the hull was brittle and quick.

The crew were big men. Of the two lying on the cargo, one slept heavily. He lay on his back with his arms out-tossed and his legs sprawling. His face, as his head hung down over the curve of the load, was dark as that of a Portuguese. The other, who had a red beard, lay on his belly with his arms braced under him so that his back was hollow under the sunlight, and stared ahead for the mouth of the creek. The steersman was a Negro. He stood perfectly straight on the stern deck, both hands on the handle of the steering oar, his broad black feet bare. His skin was black, his nostrils flat, his lips thick and relaxed, but his eyes were squinting against the glare. He wore a bright green handkerchief round his head, knotted at the back, with the frayed corners hanging down on his neck like tassels, and his shirt was open over his chest, which was bare and smooth as polished wood. In his ears a pair of large brass rings glinted like gold.

When the boat came opposite the mouth of the creek, the bearded man yelled to the steersman. At his voice, the gulls hushed, raised and swung over the woods. The steersman's arms straightened, the oar blade swirled in the water, the boat brought in her bow, and the sail slatted and banged against the mast. Then it filled again as the captain handled the ropes. He kicked the sleeper, who turned and rolled over. They stuck out oars and knelt on the catwalks on either side and began pushing in against the creek's current. Except for the one threshing surge of the steering oar, the Negro made no move. His eyes were on the creek; his face looked as if it were cut out of wood.

As they came round the muddy point out of the blue water, a man stepped out on the sand beach and hailed them.

"Hey, there!"

The Negro's eyes swung toward him and then returned to the channel.

It was the man with the red beard who answered: —

"Hello!"

"Going down to Schenectady?"

"If we can make it up the creek."

"Will you carry me?"

The man had come clear of the bushes and was leaning on his rifle. The muzzle overtopped his shoulder by a good hand. The red-bearded man eyed him.

"Got any baggage?"

"A bale of skins."

"We're full up. We've got a heavy load and we're short-handed."

"I'll help work the boat."

The captain looked at him and grinned.

The man was dressed in buckskin hunting shirt and leggings. He had a fur cap on his head. His clothes were stained from sleeping out in the woods and ragged from his winter's trapping. He had a thin brown beard and dark, slow eyes.

"I guess you would n't be no use poling a Durham."

The man examined him calmly.

"I know the crick and the river. I can handle the oar the nigger's using."

The Negro's great hands closed tighter over the handle of the oar. His loose mouth seemed to purse itself and a fine contempt came into his eyes.

"All right," said the captain. "You steer and I'll take you down for three dollars."

The boat had passed the point on which the trapper stood. As it came round him, the captain saw that the man's back was curved and one shoulder drooped. It was that that made him seem small.

"Where's your furs?"

"A little up the crick."

"Come along, then, and throw them on. We'll swing inshore for you."

Neither he nor the other man had stopped their steady rowing.

The trapper disappeared into brush as quietly as a mink. The boat lost way in the current and began to go sluggishly. Sweat came out on the rowers' faces.

The Negro said, "The damned little scut."

"All right, Pearly. But he's worth three dollars, and if his furs look good we might use them."

The Negro grinned slowly and the other man caught his eye. The boat entered the shade of the overhanging trees. Mosquitoes hummed down on the boat, settling on the men.

"Treat him polite, Hank," the captain said. "We don't want to make him uneasy."

"How much is a bale of furs worth, Tom?" Hank asked the bearded man.

The captain caught his oar blade under a floating log and cursed.

"How do I know? Three hundred dollars — maybe."

"A hundred dollars each way," Hank said.

"Put in here."

They looked up quickly.

The trapper was standing on the bank. He had his rifle in his right hand and a bale on his back. The Negro swung the boat toward him without a word. As the boat came toward the shore, the captain said, "You'll have to wade out. It's shallow along here."

The trapper did not answer. He jumped for a log that was floating close inshore. His feet caught it just short of the middle and for an instant his moccasins seemed to run backward as they spun the log. Then he came floating out alongside. The Negro grunted to himself and kept the boat bow on to the current.

The trapper hopped over the captain's oar and again the log spun for an instant. Then, as he came close, he flipped the bale forward close to the Negro's splayfeet and stepped aboard after it.

The captain watched the log float on.

"That was pretty neat, mister."

The trapper put the bale in a safe place close to the mast and laid his rifle over it. He unhooked the powderhorn and bullet pouch from his belt, but left the knife.

"My name's Ferris," he said. "Jack Ferris."

The captain introduced himself.

"My name's Tom Harris. That's Hank Datola. This is Pearly. Pearly's a good nigger."

The Negro looked down at the trapper and grinned widely, showing his teeth. As the boat passed under a willow, the sun caught his earrings and a spot of light ran round the inside of the circles.

The current made a hissing noise against the banks.

The creek here was wide and smooth, but eddies showed where snags lay under the high water. The beat and splash of the oars were slow and monotonous. Suddenly the mast scraped a branch.

"You steer, mister," said the captain. "Pearly, you take down the sail and mast."

The trapper took the oar and sheered the boat into midstream.

"Not too far, master."

"I know the channel."

He had a thin face, dark red-brown, almost Indian color. His eyes were narrow and dark. He would have been a good-looking man except for his crooked back.

The Negro went over the cargo on his bare feet, as lithe as a cat. He took down the sail and then lifted the mast out of its block. It was twelve feet high and four inches thick, but he handled it in one hand. Then he took another oar and the boat picked up speed.

The captain moved his oar over to row with Hank, but even so the trapper had to lean his weight against Pearly's oar.

The captain said, "We'll get to Jackson's pretty quick."

"You going to stop there?" asked the trapper.

"Do you want to stop?"

"I want to get something to eat."

"I'll be thirsty enough when I get there," said Hank.

The Negro didn't say anything. The trapper watched him. His rowing hadn't even heated him yet.

The trapper smiled thinly as he watched the Negro.

"I should think you'd be poling."

"Bottom's too muddy to set a pole against," the captain answered. "We can pole above Jackson's."

The sweat was pouring down his neck, staining the collar of his dark gray shirt.

He said, "I guess it won't hurt us to lay by at Jackson's for an hour, mister."

"I'll buy the batch of you tots," said the trapper.

The Negro didn't look round. But he began to hum softly through his thick lips.

3

Mrs. Jackson's tavern had a signboard. It looked limp as rotten cloth, hanging in the still marsh air. The house was a log hut with a back wing and a crude dormer window in the slope of the roof facing the creek. It stood on a low slope of open, weedy grass, and the creek made a bend round it, issuing out of an alder growth from eastward and sliding into the shadow of the same growth to the west.

The boat reached it about eleven o'clock.

The Negro jumped overboard and pulled the boat in to the log dock with one hand. The other held one of the tie-posts, and it looked as if he were bringing his knuckles together. When the boat was alongside, he caught a rope from Harris and tossed a hitch with one hand. He stretched his arms over his head and blew out a long breath. Then he grinned at the trapper and said, "Yo' buyin' me a drink?"

The trapper looked at him.

"One of your drinks will cost me double, I guess."

The Negro chuckled and extended a friendly hand.

"I guess I can jump for myself," the trapper said.

The Negro stopped grinning. He smacked his lips, though, gently, as he followed up the slope.

The door was closed, but the trapper opened it without knocking, as if he were used to the place.

"Been here before?" Harris asked curiously.

"Now and then."

"I generally stop at Gilbert's."

The trapper led them into the taproom. It had one long table, two benches made of half-logs with sticks for legs, a chair, and a fireplace in the outside wall. There was no fire, and the light coming down the wide chimney made a white spot in the ashes. The three boaters sat down at the table and the trapper went to a door in the back of the room. He leaned his crooked shoulder against the jamb and said, "Hello, Mrs. Jackson."

The boaters heard a sharp breath and the clatter of a plate.

"It's Jack Ferris!" said a woman's voice.

"Yes, mam. How're you this spring?"

"Pretty good. You're heading out?"

"Yes."

"Had a good winter?"

"Tolerable. I worked pretty far north. I had luck with marten this year."

"I'm glad to hear it." The voice was hearty. "I reckon you're after something to eat."

"If you've got it."

"I've always got it. Give me five minutes."

The trapper said, "I've got three boaters along I promised whiskey to if they'd wait for me to eat."

He swung away from the door, and Mrs. Jackson followed him into the room. She was a stocky woman with a lined face. She wore a plain homespun dress, short-skirted to show her man's boots. She looked quite capable.

"Hello, Mr. Harris," she said.

The captain nodded at her.

"You don't often stop to my place."

"It don't suit me, generally," said the captain.

"Well, have one on the house when you've finished Mr. Ferris's."

She brought three thick tumblers and a demijohn, and poured them their drinks. Then she disappeared into the kitchen.

The trapper sat down at the far end of the table.

"Ain't you drinking?" asked Hank.

"No, I'm not."

The captain raised his glass.

"Here's to good prices," he said, with an effort at affability.

"Thanks," said the trapper.

The Negro took his glass in both hands and bent his lips to it. "M'm'm-m'm'm!" he said. Then he drank slowly.

The trapper sat quiet, looking down at his hands. Out in the kitchen Mrs. Jackson was making noises with a skillet. She was as good as her word. In five minutes she came in with a plate of potatoes, an egg fried on them, bacon, and a cup of tea. The smell of the bacon seemed to follow her in in a wave. She set the plate before Ferris and looked down at it with a smile. "I know a man coming out of the woods would rather taste an egg than anything else there is in the world."

"That's right," said the trapper, beginning to eat. "Sometimes I dream about eggs."

Harris watched the trapper; so did Hank Datola; but the Negro looked into his glass and hummed to himself. The trapper paid no attention to them. Mrs. Jackson, watching from the door to the kitchen, made up her mind that Ferris ought to be warned to look out for himself. She was a hard woman, but a shrewd one. She could tell when a man was thinking about trouble. Both the white men were doing that. But the Negro had made up his mind already. Any one of the three could pick up Ferris with one hand; the Negro looked as if he could break his back with his thumb.

The winter smell still hung in the tap. It was a dark room, with its small windows. The old spruce logs were musty. They had lost their bark years ago and they showed the lacy channeling of wood worms. You could smell the old smell of unsunned earth under the puncheons, the rank smell mice left in their winter nests, the stale human smells of tobacco and liquor. But it was pleasantly cool after the hot work of rowing up from the lake, and the three boaters were easing off.

Outside the windows the sun was hot and bright on the woods. Leaves were just breaking, and there was a peculiarly lovely soft green light in the alders. It came through the window dimly, turning Harris's beard to white gold, and making the Portuguese look wicked and the Negro beautiful. It brought out highlights in his black hide that were almost silver, and deepened the green of his head handkerchief to emerald.

The trapper was neat at his eating, and under the boaters' eyes he took his time. Mrs. Jackson had withdrawn into the kitchen. No one said anything. It was so still in the tap that they could hear the sucking noise of the water along the bank outside.

Then, all at once, they heard somebody walking through the woods. The steps came slowly and lightly along a trail from the north. There was no road, only a footpath. The trapper knew there was a trail, and it was he who first heard the steps. He raised his head. He looked like a wild animal listening. He kept his head up as if he were using his nose. His face looked thinner, and his eyes narrowed. Then the boaters heard it. All four of the men watched the window in the north wall.

When the walker came past, they said nothing. The boaters

looked at one another suddenly and their eyes became wary. The trapper watched them. Then they all turned to the door.

They had seen the head and shoulders of a young girl going past the window. She was walking slowly and easily, like a girl on a stroll; her face was careless with happiness. They heard her walk round the corner of the tap and come to the door. She stood out in the sunlight for a moment and they had a good look at her as she examined Mrs. Jackson's signboard. Whatever device had been there once, it had faded; so, while the girl tried to make it out, they were able to study her before she was aware of them.

She looked young, and she was. Her face was bright-colored, and she had a small nose and a large, vivid mouth. She was dark-haired; the hair was braided round and round her head. Her dress was green, almost the color of the young woods, of a smooth, soft weave.

It had a full skirt and was laced tight over her waist, with a little string bow of bright red between her breasts. Her shoes and stockings were muddy from coming through the woods, but she looked fresh as a daisy.

Then she turned for the door and came inside, and they saw that she carried a bag in her hand. Her eyes were large and dark, and full of innocence. To the trapper they looked almost foolishly innocent. She wasn't abashed when she found the four men staring at her. She laughed and said, "Good morning." Her voice was warm and very friendly. It was obvious that she liked men. She did not know what it was to be afraid.

Harris was the first to speak. He got to his feet quickly and made a ludicrous kind of bow to her.

"Good morning, missy," he said. "Come in and rest yourself."

At his words, Ma Jackson came out of her kitchen. She took one look at the girl and drew her breath in quickly.

"Hello, dearie," she said. "Where did you come from?"

The girl looked at her rather vaguely. Then she giggled.

"I came from north," she said.

"By yourself?" asked Mrs. Jackson, giving Harris a quick glance.

The girl nodded pertly. She seemed very satisfied with herself and not at all embarrassed.

"I'm going east," she said.

"Where to?"

The girl put back her head and laughed. Her laugh was light and easy. The notes sprayed over the men and made them look at one another. As the trapper watched her, his mouth became bitter.

"You'd better come into my kitchen," Ma Jackson said guardedly, "and I'll look after you."

The girl looked at her coolly.

"Oh, no, thanks. I'd rather stay here with these gentlemen."

Harris smiled.

"Set down," said he. "Will you have something to drink?"

Mrs. Jackson said, "I don't serve young girls drinks in this house."

"Don't you?" asked Harris. "Then you might as well get back to your kitchen."

Mrs. Jackson looked at the trapper quickly, as if she wanted to ask him to do something. Then her hard face became weary and helpless. Without a word she went into her kitchen.

Harris laughed easily.

"Hard-bitted old beasy," he said to the girl, and the girl laughed again. She sat down and looked at the four men frankly, each in turn.

She hardly paid any attention to the Negro, and her mouth tightened as she saw the trapper's shoulder. The red beard of the captain seemed to fascinate her.

His manner became gentle. He questioned her casually. He didn't find out much about her. Her name was Peggy Sharon; she had come out of the woods; she didn't say who her family were, or where they lived, or what had happened to them; she wanted to go east and see a city. She had plenty of money with her in her bag. She wasn't hungry; she had had some food with her and had cooked herself breakfast.

The trapper listened for a while; then, having finished his meal, he got up. He saw the girl watching him out of the corners of her eyes. She was not sly, not laughing at him; she looked pitying. He swore to himself. As he passed the Negro, Pearly turned his head to watch him and grinned. Harris was making the girl an offer to take her to Schenectady, or Troy, or Albany, or New York. She was laughing at them all again. Her fresh, happy laugh in that room smelling musty with winter was as incredible as the first Mayflower a man turns up through the mould with his foot.

The trapper closed out the sound of it with the kitchen door. He found Mrs. Jackson behind the door.

"Jack," she said, "she's going to go on that boat."

He nodded and leaned against the door. Mrs. Jackson looked bitter and very angry.

"I thought it was bad enough for you. You're taking the best chance you ever took of getting murdered, going with Harris. But her!"

He said, "They won't be watching out for me now so close."

"Don't talk that way. You don't mean it. Anyway, that black nigger's got his eye on you. He don't like you."

"I don't like him. . . . Where do you suppose she ever turned up from, mam?"

"God knows. I've seen queer things out here since I came out with Jackson, but this beats all."

The trapper smiled at her.

"You're too kind-hearted to stay here. Why don't you sell out?"

"Who'd I sell to? They're building those turnpikes now, and trade's already falling off on the boaters."

"You ought to get out and get married."

She laughed bitterly.

"I'm a good prospect for that now!"

"You'd be a good one if you got out of here for a while."

"It's lonely."

"That's the trouble with you."

They looked at each other. Mrs. Jackson's eyes were kind.

He said, "Maybe I'll buy your place sometime."

She laughed again.

"You're a nice boy, Jack."

"Boy!" he said.

She looked up at his bitter mouth. She was not so old-looking now. But her eyes became tragic.

"She's fresh. She wouldn't listen to me. She doesn't care nor know nothing at all. You could pick her like a daisy."

The trapper nodded.

"She's the most beautiful thing I ever saw."

"She's beautiful," said Mrs. Jackson. It was a fact. It couldn't be dodged. That was the pity of it.

They looked at each other.

"There's nothing you can do," she said.

"I'm going along anyway."

4

He watched the captain helping Peggy Sharon onto the boat. Hank Datola was carrying the bag for her. When she wasn't looking, he shook it gently. The Negro pursed his lips.

The trapper glanced back at Jackson's Tavern, but there was no sign of Mrs. Jackson.

The captain took the girl down into the cabin, whose roof rose level with the trapper's knees as he stood by the steering oar. He heard the captain straightening out the bunk bedding and picking up a tumbler or two. Then the captain came on deck. The three men took poles and pushed the boat out into the creek. They began the slow trip up to Rome. They would be busy till they went through the company locks and got into the current of the Mohawk. The trapper knew he wouldn't have to worry about anything till then.

As he steered, he watched them. Harris and Hank walked up and down the cat-walk so that one or the other was always pushing. But the Negro on the other side stood just aft of the centre of the boat and shoved with his arms. When he put his weight on the pole, a tremor shot through the boat.

The afternoon was hot and still and airless. The creek wound back and forth through the swamps, in places overflowing its banks, so that the hemlocks rose out of water and a heron waded in the middle of the woods. The men worked without talk. Toward four o'clock they came into an open, straight piece and had a look at the sky. There was a dim light on the sun, and clouds were rising up in the southwest.

Then the boat crept into the woods again and everything was quiet. Ferris heard no sound from the girl. He gathered that she had gone to sleep. But he noticed that the men were watching one another. Especially Hank and the captain. The Negro only glanced at them from time to time, and then looked away again. His arms, with their lean, straight muscles barely showing the strain, worked tirelessly. But even he, in the still heat, had begun sweating; and now and then, as the boat passed through a cooler zone, Ferris caught a whiff of his pungent scent.

There were few birds. It was too early in the spring to hear locusts. The woods were deathly quiet.

Ferris wondered what he was going to do. He felt helpless. In all his life he had never seen anyone so fresh and lovely. It did not matter where she had come from or who she was. But his face did not trace what he was thinking. It did not change when, at dusk, she came on deck. She came round the cabin and sat on the roof in front of him, with her arms holding her knees close to her breast, and her head thrown back.

Harris and Hank smiled at her when their poling brought them back, and she smiled at them. But she kept looking covertly at Ferris.

"What is Schenectady like?" she asked.

He said it was a river town.

"Are there many houses in it?"

"A good many."

"Have you been there often?"

"I go down in spring to sell my furs."

"You 're a trapper?"

"Yes."

"I never liked the woods."

He kept his eyes on the stream without answering. The men looked at him and grinned. Whenever she was able, she looked at his shoulder.

"I should think you 'd get lonely."

"Not often."

"Are you happy?"

He could n't bear her fresh young voice asking questions. But he said, "Yes."

"So am I," she said. "I 've never been so happy before."

A shadow passed over her face. It was cool again for a way, the creek running round a hemlock grove.

"My father died last winter and I was scared. I came out by myself. I did n't think I was going to be so happy."

Higher ground showed suddenly to their left. A small brook came into the creek over a low fall. The unexpected sound of falling water made them look east. Under cover of the noise, Ferris said to her, "Get off at Rome."

She swung her dark eyes back to him.

"Why?"

"You 're crazy, staying on this boat."

"Why?"

He did not answer and she laughed.

"I 'm not scared. I 'm not afraid of men."

He kept his eyes on the current.

"I 'm going all the way with them."

"Do you know anybody in Schenectady?"

"No. Mr. Harris said he 'd look out for me."

They were past the noise of the brook. "Keep still."

She looked at him oddly, and then at Harris. She seemed to have an odd thought. She laughed.

Harris had been watching them.

"Is he trying to scare you, missy?"

His face grinned.

She laughed again.

"Maybe you'd better get inside," Harris said. "It's getting cooler."

"I think I will."

She rose easily and went down. Harris stopped by the trapper.

"You mind your own business and nobody will bother you."

Ferris nodded.

Hank and the Negro were watching them. The Negro shook his head so that his earrings tapped against his cheeks with a small sound.

They went on.

At dusk they came out in the navigation company locks and locked down into the Mohawk.

It was boiling with high water. . . . As soon as they got out in it, the current snatched them and took them south toward Rome.

The Negro laid down his pole and stretched himself. He grinned. "Now I guess I get some res'."

He started for the cabin.

Harris stepped in front of him.

"This is my business, Pearly. You keep out — you and Hank both."

The Negro looked at him. Then he laughed. "Oh, shucks," he said. He put out his hands. But Harris drew a pistol out through his shirt. He grinned at the Negro.

"Big niggers make easy shooting, Pearly."

The Negro stood still and the captain backed down into the cabin. He said, "I can keep seeing you from the door. You be good boys and stay up front, and I won't hurt you."

Ferris kept still. His hands were full, steering the boat through the narrow upper channel. The boat moved with the water, light as a leaf, but it was heavy against the oar.

"We're going to need a light," he said to Pearly.

Pearly cursed and got out a lantern and set it up on the tip of the mast and lifted the mast into its chocks. The lantern barely showed the nearer bank and sent a thin light down over the boat. Then Pearly moved forward to where Hank was sitting.

The darkness began to creep in on the river. Ferris, behind the cabin roof, was left to himself.

All he could think of was that his rifle lay up under his skins behind the mast, and he wondered how Pearly could have overlooked it when he was hoisting the light.

5

Ferris steered by the touch of the current. It was hard to see much of anything. A fine rain had started to fall. Pearly and Hank had loosened one end of the drill covering of the cargo and sat together under it in the bow. Now and then he heard the murmur of their voices; they had acted ugly in Rome.

But more often he heard the captain talking to the girl in the cabin just under his feet. Harris had taken the girl with him when they tied up at Rome for half an hour, and had come back with her, bringing meat, smoked beef, and bread, and carrying two bottles of wine for the girl and himself. The two other men had looked as if they were going to jump him. Ferris had thought of leaving the boat, but the nigger had stayed on the deck, so that he had no chance to get his rifle. He hoped now that the priming wasn't getting wet.

It was a warm rain, thin and misty, and peepers were singing along the river banks. The throbbing seemed to fit into the beat of his pulse. The water went smoothly and the banks rose into the light at the bends, showing old willow trees, and fell away again as he turned the boat.

So far, Harris had seemed well behaved. Now and then Ferris could hear the man's heavy voice telling the girl something about the towns. Now and then they laughed together. The girl sounded carefree. He wondered whether she was drinking the wine. He had got a glimpse of the bottle. Governor Kirby's — that was Madeira wine. The best a man could buy. It cost twelve dollars a bottle. Twenty-four dollars was a lot of money; but

Harris must think she was worth it. Or else he was using her money.

Without the stars, there was no way of telling time. There was nothing in the world but the boat with the two men in the bow, the girl and the man in the cabin, and Ferris to steer them. He considered putting the boat ashore and making a break with the girl, but he could n't bear to lose his winter's furs, and he knew, anyhow, that she would n't go with him. He would have to wait. Pearly and Hank would be hatching something in the bow. He decided to watch them.

He could n't see them. The base of the lantern put a blind spot of shadow over the boat that reached from just short of the bow to just aft the cabin entrance.

The trapper's face showed in the light, his wet fur cap, his narrow eyes. His shadow fell out on the water behind. The collar of his jacket was turned up.

The boat slid along a grass bank, and a couple of cows looked into the light. Their brown faces were blackened with rain wet, but their horns glistened. They slowly turned their heads to watch the light pass. One caught sight of Ferris steering and lowed gently. Then the lantern passed them and they put down their heads to drink.

In the cabin the girl's voice broke out in laughter. It was high and a little uncertain and excited. Harris's voice answered her and she laughed again. Then she gave a short cry.

In the bow the Negro's face rose over the drill sheet and looked back. His eyes showed the whites in the lantern light, and the rings in his ears made dim circles. His eyes swung from the cabin to Ferris. Then he ducked down.

The captain was talking with hurried sentences. The trapper swung the boat out into midstream and let her go. He stooped down round the corner of the cabin and looked in through one of the low windows. The girl was seated on a bunk with the laces of her dress opened and a tumbler at her feet spilling wine over the floor. Her eyes were enlarged and staring steadily at the captain.

He stood across the room from her with one hand on his beard. He was saying, "You're a good girl, Peggy. You're a nice girl."

She did not answer, but she looked, to Ferris, as if she were afraid. Then she saw his face against the window and put her hand to her mouth. Her cheeks went pale. He saw the captain's back stiffen, and he pulled back just in time before the man swung round.

He heard the captain asking, "What's the matter, Peggy?" and Peggy giggling. The captain asked, "You ain't scared of me, are you?" The girl kept on giggling.

The captain did n't say anything. He came on deck. He walked round to where Ferris was steering, and laughed.

"You're earning your way," he said. "It's a bad night."

Ferris nodded.

"Think she'll hear me here?"

"No, I don't."

Harris talked.

"Just now she acted cute. Acted like she saw something at the window."

"Did she?"

"I did n't want to hurry, but she's been free enough."

He looked steadily at Ferris. Ferris looked forward.

"Maybe she did see something."

"Hell!" said Harris. "Has Datola been down here?"

"No."

"Pearly?"

"Pearly's keeping his eye on you."

Harris looked forward.

"A nigger could crawl along that cat-walk and nobody'd see him if he did n't raise his head."

He stiffened.

"Ferris, I'm a fool! I came without my gun."

He began to walk forward. He went very slowly, keeping his eyes steadily on the cat-walk.

Suddenly Ferris asked, "Can you swim?"

The captain jumped and swung around. "Hell, no!"

Ferris shoved him.

His heels caught on the low rail, his hands went up, clawing for support. He looked surprised. He went in, full length.

"Lay on your back and float," Ferris called to him.

Up in the bow, the Negro's head rose up and, beside it, Hank's.

"Hey, Ferris!"

The trapper turned his eyes toward them.

"Did you hear anything?"

"Harris was up here. He went overboard."

They stood up side by side.

Hank said, "That makes me boss."

Pearly swung toward him.

"Says so?"

He appeared to be laughing. But he made no sound. Hank jumped over onto the cat-walk and came down into the dark. The Negro stepped after him.

"I 've got my knife, Pearly."

The Negro did not reply. Ferris heard Hank's boots moving cautiously for the cabin, but the Negro's bare feet made no sound. He swung the boat well out between the banks and let the oar swing. Then he moved forward toward them into the dark zone on the opposite side of the cargo. His moccasins made no more sound than the Negro's feet.

He dropped onto his belly and crept toward his rifle.

The boat swung with the current. Behind him in the cabin, the girl had begun to cry. The river was making a wide loop to the south. He knew the bend. Utica lay on the far bank. He hoped the Negro would get to Hank before the boat got to the village.

There was no wind to cover sound. As he reached a point opposite the mast, he heard a faint noise, like something light tapping leather. He recognized it for the Negro's earrings. He waited.

Inch by inch, the Negro passed him across the piled-up cargo. He smelled him in the darkness, rank with excitement. Then he reached forward under his bale of furs and his hand touched his rifle. The other found the powderhorn. He shook out the priming and tapped in fresh. Then he stood up.

He could hear nothing, and he waited for a long time without moving. Then again he heard the tapping of the earrings against the Negro's cheeks.

"Stay there, nigger."

The tapping ceased.

"I'm a pretty good shot by sound. Stand up."

Slowly Pearly obeyed him. His head rose against the lighted water. The whites showed dimly in his eyes.

"Where's Hank?" Ferris asked the Negro.

Pearly pointed his thumb overboard.

"Can he swim?"

"He won't have to."

The boat swung in toward the village. The dark shape of Moses Bagg's Hotel rose up on the shore. There were no lights anywhere.

"Pearly, we're going to touch here. Then you get off."

The Negro grinned.

"Listen, boss," he said. "Cain't you and me make an agreement?"

Ferris walked back to the steering oar. He caught it just in time. The boat sheered in.

"Jump, nigger."

Pearly sighed; then he crouched, catlike, and sprang.

The boat swung out again and the river took it.

Under the trapper's feet, the girl was crying.

"All right, missy," he called. "You're all right now."

6

She came up and sat in front of him on the cabin roof. She looked pale and sick. And she sat as she had, early in the afternoon, clasping her knees to her breast. Sometimes she looked at him. But more generally she was staring forward.

He watched her guardedly, wondering what she was thinking about. He felt very sorry for her.

A little before it began to grow light, the lantern went out and the boat became perfectly dark. She shivered and crept close to him.

"Where are the others?" she asked.

"They're all gone," he answered. "There isn't any way any one of them could catch us. Don't you worry. I'll see you to Schenectady."

He saw her face turn in the darkness. He thought she was still shivering.

"You'd better go down and get a dry blanket. Get two, if you're going to stay on deck. Or go down and go to sleep. There's only me on the boat and I can't let go of this oar."

He thought he could see her eyes in the oval spot her face made against the darkness. She shivered again.

"I think I will go down."

He was left alone.

He heard her moving about in the cabin. After a while she must have lain down, because he heard nothing. The sound of the flooding river surrounded him in the darkness. He steered by the vague shapes of the banks and the feeling of the water against the oar.

He thought of putting the boat alongside the shore for a while and going down and visiting her, and then he put the idea out of his head. He was hungry and cold, and he thought there was nothing to stop him. But a log slapping over a ripple behind him made him think of the Portuguese, and he wondered how the nigger had finished him. The log caught up and passed, pitching stiffly. It would take at least two days for Harris to reach Schenectady, supposing he did get out of the river. The Negro didn't bother him at all. His word against Pearly's would be good anywhere. And the girl, anyway, couldn't get the notion of his crooked back out of her mind. He could feel that, even when she wasn't looking at him. He couldn't stand the notion. It was all right if you were set up like Harris — or even that nigger.

The rain stopped toward morning and the night faded from the river and left a thick mist. The silhouettes of the banks turned from black to gray. The willow trees were soft with young leaves.

Then the mist lifted and showed him the hills on the north side of the valley, and a little later he made out the southern hills. The light came through the mist and put a silvery gleam on the flooded flats. The trees stood in water. The pastures showed here and there. In one place a cow stood with a young calf on a little island in a flat, shallow sea. The cow was nosing the calf and lowing to it. He thought the land looked the way it must have looked when Noah's flood was going down.

Then the sun came up ahead of him and the mist went away suddenly and there was a warm wind from the south.

After a while, the girl came up on deck and she looked fresh again. He saw that she had slept.

"Good morning," she said, and stared at him.

"Good morning, missy. Feeling better?"

She put the back of her hand to her forehead and stared round. The boat looked small and harmless by daylight. She glanced at Ferris again and smiled slowly. When she smiled, her lips opened wide over her white teeth, making almost a square mouth.

She said, "You 've had a hard time?"

"No," he said. "I did n't have to do anything."

"You look cold and hungry."

"A little tea would n't hurt me."

"I wish I could make you some."

"You can."

"Show me how."

He pointed to the open brick fireplace in front of the cabin and told her to look for wood. She found a little and made him a small fire. In the cabin she found a teakettle and some tea and a couple of cups. She cut some bread and boiled his tea and brought it to him.

"Let me steer."

"Think you can?"

"You can tell me."

Her smile was enticingly friendly.

He sat down on the cabin roof and sipped the tea and ate the bread and governed her steering. She handled the oar cleverly, keeping her mind exactly on what he told her.

The wind played with her skirt and blew on her cheek, and she bent her head against it. As the boat drifted, he pointed out the roads and villages. The night stage from Utica was going at a slow walk along the Mohawk road. They caught up with it and passed it, while the horses labored and the wheels sank in halfway to the hubs.

"You 're doing fine," he said to her.

"I 'm not all useless?" she asked delightedly.

"No. You 're doing fine."

She gave him another of her smiles.

"You were wonderful, looking out for me."

"I did n't do anything."

"I can't forget it. I did n't know. He scared me."

Ferris did n't answer. But he smiled back at her. The smile enlivened his face and softened it.

"Forget about it."

She became almost merry. She hung on his words and laughed easily, and when he was steering again she sat with him, wondering at the open fields, at the size of the ploughed land, at the large flocks of sheep they saw against the hillsides. He sent her below when they came to Little Falls and locked the boat through himself.

The lock-tenders were grouchy and disinclined to talk. They asked him no questions.

Once they were out of the push from the falls, they went more slowly and the river widened.

The girl came up on deck again and set about getting him some luncheon. She warmed the smoked beef in a skillet and toasted the bread and made more tea. He lashed the steering oar so they could eat together. And they talked about Schenectady.

She wanted to know where they would go.

"I'm going to take you to the house of a woman I know. She's a nice woman and she'll look out for you."

The girl gave him a good look.

"What are you going to do?"

"I've got my furs to sell."

"I mean after that."

"I don't know."

He knew that she was looking at him, but he refused to meet her eyes. After a little, she moved around him so that she could see his face.

"Are you going to leave me there?"

"Mrs. Jenkins will look out for you."

"I don't want her to."

He looked straight down the river.

"You can do what you want."

"Aren't I nice enough?" she asked.

"You're too nice."

She laughed. Her laughter made his mouth draw into a thin line.

"I'm not a fool," he said.

"Don't you ever get lonely?"

"I've always been lonely."

She did not speak for some time. Then he felt her hand touching his shoulder.

"How did that happen?"

Her voice was gentle. He let her hand rest there.

"I was born that way."

She sighed and took her hand away.

"Then what'll you do?"

"I've not made my mind up about it."

"Will you go back into the woods?"

"Probably. You wouldn't want to come back, would you?"

"I wouldn't mind."

He looked at her. She met his eyes frankly. She believed what she said. He turned her talk away from themselves and they drifted all day quietly.

Just at dusk they sighted the great bridge. They docked at nightfall. He took her to Mrs. Jenkins's house and asked the woman to look out for her. Mrs. Jenkins promised. She was a large, friendly, prosperous-looking woman. He shouldered his furs and went round to the buyer's store. Till ten o'clock he bargained for his own prices. He got them.

Outside the buyer's house, he hesitated. To the right, the road led to the bridge and the river. Mrs. Jenkins's was well away to the left.

He turned right. While he was dickering with the dealer, he had understood why he felt so happy. It wasn't the girl who had made him — though the day on the boat was the happiest he could remember in his life. He wasn't going back to see her. He felt sorry for her, but Mrs. Jenkins would look out for her and see that she didn't lose her money. He crotched his rifle in his arm and turned for the bridge.

7

It was a week later that he turned up at Mrs. Jackson's cabin. He came through the woods soundlessly. There were no boats tied up when he came around to the front, and he leaned his shoulder against one corner of the house and watched Mrs. Jackson planting her summer garden. He waited till she had finished her row of squash and then stepped forward so that his shadow fell between her hands.

She started and looked up.

"Jack!"

"Hello, Mrs. Jackson."

"What brought you back so soon?"

"I finished my business."

"You don't generally come back so quick."

"I know. I thought I wouldn't spend my money this time."

"What happened to the girl?"

"She got there all right. I left her at Mrs. Jenkins's house."

She got up slowly and eased her back. Then she said, "Come in while I get supper." Her eyes were wide still with surprise. She seemed a little excited. "Come and set in the kitchen."

He followed her to her kitchen and sat and watched her build up the fire and fry fish and bacon.

While she worked she talked to him. He was a relief for her loneliness, and as the time passed her voice seemed to gain assurance, as if the practice of talking gave it strength.

"She was the most startling thing—coming out of the woods."

"Yes," he said. "She was."

"And those boaters. I felt sorry for her."

"So did I."

"I could see that. She was too pretty. You thought she was."

"Yes," he said, "I thought she was. She started me thinking."

She bent up from the hearth and wiped her hands on her apron and looked at him.

"What do you mean?"

"She started me thinking maybe I would like a place of my own. You remember, I said somebody might buy your house."

Mrs. Jackson nodded. Her face was still, her eyes worried. Then she smiled to answer him.

"I'd like to buy a half share of your house."

AT SCHOHARIE CROSSING

I

One Friday evening, early in May, a line of sixty boats was drawn up to the towpath at the Schoharie Creek crossing. In those first years of the Erie, the crossing stream was let into the canal on one side, with a guard lock below, and a dam on the other side to take the overflow along its natural channel. It was easy enough to cross above the dam with the water at normal level; but when a freshet hit a creek, the space above the dam became a mill race, with treacherous eddies to add trouble to the side pull. There were plenty of such crossings on the old Erie, and the Schoharie was the worst of the lot.

Their horns wailing, the boats had come in at fairly regular intervals during the morning; but old Caleb, who tended the guard lock, took one look at the two and a half feet of extra water boiling over the dam and went on combing his beard. He was proud of that beard. It reached well down toward his knees; and his continual combing kept it clean, so that it was glossy, and just about the color of old pewter. Boat captains used to have trouble getting him out of his hut in rainy weather (he was afraid that the wet would take out the curl) until some of them bought him an umbrella.

The captains were a tough lot. Freight companies were already beginning to get a pretty solid hold on the long hauls and the immigrant trade, which meant that speed was at a premium; and as only the packet boats could afford to pay the ten-dollar fine for speeding, the freighters tried to make up their time by fighting for first place at the locks. It got so bad that after a while a captain would feel a man's muscle before asking him what he knew about boating.

Three or four of them who knew Caleb were sitting with him in his hut, each with his rum balanced in a tumbler on his knee and smoking or chewing to suit his taste; and they were making a sociable session out of it, what with the wind on the roof and the warmth inside. One sat on a chair and the rest had boxes; and old Caleb perched on the edge of his bunk and combed his beard.

One of the captains, a sly-looking little man who wore a pipe hat and green galluses, got up and looked through a window at the dam. He had to lift his voice for the others to hear him through the roaring of that water. "How long will she stay up, Caleb?" he asked.

"Why," said Caleb, "I don't rightly know as she's got all the way up yet. She's the worst one I ever see."

"Well," said another one, a big red-headed man from Little Falls, who had never been licked east of Utica and who wouldn't let any man work on his boat unless he had red hair and could roll a brogue as well as a quid on his tongue, "sipposin' it reaches high water to-night, Caleb me honey, what time'd ye think I could get the owld lady acrosst?"

As usual the *Dublin Queen* was the first freighter in the line. Caleb got a bit of mirror down from the wall and put some finishing touches on the part over his chin.

"Well," he said, "it might be a day, or it might be two, or it might be more. I ain't saying. If it rains again, it might be more; if it don't rain, it might not."

"That's a help, to be sure," said the red-headed man, whose name was O'Mory.

"I can feel rain," announced the man on the chair.

"You, Joe?" asked the man with the pipe hat.

"Rain," said the other. "Barrels of it, Gratwick. An ocean, no less. It's coming down from the north on my old peg." He thrust out a wooden leg and began to rub the thigh above it.

"Hark to that, the wizen owld creature! Talkin' of rain, and it only stopped this noon."

"I've got a Dutchman on my boat," said Gratwick, putting his pipe hat inside the box he was sitting on. "He's all loaded up with wagons and ploughs, and he's got his family. He offered me twenty dollars extra if I could get him to Buffalo onside of two weeks. Jeepers! If it don't commence to go down by to-morrow night, I'll chance the crossing anyways."

"Haw, haw!" O'Mory guffawed. "You'll cross with them cheese-horse mules of yourn?"

"Well, they be kind of poor," the other admitted. "But say, O'Mory, you and me can club our teams on each boat and get 'em over that way."

"Sure," said Caleb. "That'd be easy. It's been tried four times, only the rope broke three of the times."

"That's right," said Joe, emphasizing his words with thrusts of his wooden leg against the stove. "I was in line when Bellows's boat went over."

"The *Manlius?*"

"That's right. There wasn't only a dog drowned and nobody killed, though the horses got all tangled tumbling forward when the rope broke."

"I heard Grimshaw was killed."

"He don't count," said Joe. "He was lying drunk on the forward hutch and never knowed what struck him. You couldn't rightly say he was killed."

"Was the boat smashed up?"

Caleb opened the back door into his little woodshed. When he returned, he brought the northwest wind with him in a gust that stuck out his beard in front. "There's what's left of her tiller," he said, showing them a twelve-inch stick before poking it into the stove.

"Holy Mither!" cried O'Mory. "She must've sat down hard!"

"The other two boats wasn't hurt bad," said old Caleb, soothing his whiskers back into place. "Only they had to float them back down the river as far as Schenectady to get back into the canal."

The others cuffed their knees and roared with laughter. The wind began to rattle hail against the shanty.

"There's my rain commencing," said Joe, triumphantly slapping his wooden leg.

A flat wailing rose from down the canal, the sound of it crawling haltingly through the gusts.

"That's Gurget's horn," said Caleb; "he got it off a ladder wagon in New York."

The conversation came round to the high water again.

"I'm telling you," said Caleb sententiously, "it ain't safe for a boat to try the crossing this water."

Gratwick agreed. "No. It ain't safe. And even if the rope held, it would take more 'n one team."

Joe considered the notion foolhardy.

"Phwat does that mean?" asked O'Mory.

"You don't know nothing," retorted Joe, making a stab at the Irishman with his wooden leg. "You ought to go to New York where they're making a society for learning dumb folks to read!"

"They need it!" snorted Caleb. "They said Clinton couldn't never build his 'ditch.' They said it would take more 'n two years to blast round Cohoes — and how long did it take?" He flourished his comb. "Eighty days."

A moment's silence followed the old man's answer.

"Who was the feller whose rope didn't break?" O'Mory asked suddenly.

"That was Simpson. He'd a load of ashes on, for the lye factory to Little Falls," said Caleb.

"How'd he get acrosst?"

"He didn't."

"I thought ye said his rope didn't break, ye image."

"It didn't," said Caleb. "It was this way. He had a three-mule team, see? And he got them just about to the end of the bridge afore the water took the boat over the dam. The rope didn't break, so the mules went over, too. One of them sat on his hind end afore he went over, and brayed like prayer."

"I'll bet Simpson acted up," said Joe.

"He shed tears," Caleb admitted.

"Well . . ." said Gratwick, yawning and putting on his pipe-hat, "it ain't safe to chance it. I guess we'll have to hang out round here till Monday anyhow."

The rattle of hail faded away from the roof; and at the same time the wind died down.

"Where's your rain now?" O'Mory asked Joe.

"Don't you get sad; it's just getting its second wind."

The sun came out from under the northwest clouds with a level, shining light on the wet ground, and one of the men opened the door. It had become suddenly warm, with an earth-smelling mistiness beginning to rise down by the river.

Old Caleb glanced out at the cross-anchor weather vane he had stuck up on a pole above the lock. "Look at that!" he cried. "Wind's switched to the southwest."

"That's the second wind I was telling you about," Joe said to O'Mory. "Now we will have rain, by Jeepers!"

"Oh Lord!" groaned O'Mory.

Joe got up and stumped over to the door. There he jammed his peg into the corner of the sill and braced his shoulders against the frame, steady as a rock.

He stared away down the canal. "There's eight more boats come in," he announced.

Calling to mind the long wails they had heard since they had entered the hut, the others nodded.

"Any foights?" asked O'Mory.

"No."

"Here comes another boat," said Joe, after a minute.

As he spoke, the trilling of a French horn burst out on the water and rang up and down the valley in diminishing echoes.

"Glory! What's that?" asked the Irishman.

"Red bullhead boat," said Joe. "Black team."

The horn rang out again and again. Caleb shifted his weight uneasily. "That's Herman Peters, or I'm Tammany Hall."

"Peters!"

"Yeanh, the Utica bully. Never been licked for first place to a lock. There ain't a man west of Utica's stood him out of the place."

"He ain't been down to Little Falls nor met the *Dublin Queen*," observed O'Mory, giving his belt a hitch and straddling his legs. He went over to the door with a chuckle in his nose, and the others crowded after him.

2

The sunlight fell back along the course of the canal, past old Fort Hunter, more than a mile to the first turn. For over half the distance they could see the boats tied up to mooring posts, here and there smoke rising from the cabin stovepipe, or, on some of the smaller line boats, from stoves set up on the centre deck. The gaudy-colored boats lay squat alongside of their reflections, in hues of scarlet, green, magenta, blue, and the increasingly popular white. The men strolled round the fields below the towpath or looked on at a horseshoe tournament being pitched out between Schenectady and Rome. An old graybeard sat with his skinny legs over the bow of the last boat and fished with a hand line in the reflection of a window.

Two packet boats fronted the line by natural prerogative, their passengers keeping aloof. A clatter of crockery issued from the cabin windows. From the first one floated the noise of a fiddle, and a darky table-boy was doing a dance for a group of ladies. A missionary was conversing earnestly with two drivers who listened politely and spat with diffidence.

"There he is," said Joe, making a motion with his wooden leg.

The fanfare of the French bugle broke out again from a scarlet freighter, trimmed green, which was drawing in to the end of the queue. The steersman swung the boat inshore and the driver snubbed the tie-ropes to posts. They left the horses on the towpath. Two men came out of the cabin and joined the steersman, who seemed to be looking the situation over. Then the four headed toward the lock-tender's shanty.

"He's looking for trouble," said Caleb.

"Sure, he's coming to the right place then," said O'Mory.

The captain of the scarlet boat was the shortest of his crew, but he was heavy-set — two hundred and thirty pounds, as Gratwick appraised him.

"I'll be giving him maybe twelve pounds," nodded O'Mory grinning, "but look at me reach, will you?" He stretched out his arms, shoulder high, as if he would embrace the whole Utica crew, and broke into a laugh. He was taller by a head than the approaching bully.

The newcomer had a black beard that reached to the middle button of his waistcoat. The sleeves of his blue shirt were rolled to the elbows, revealing arms heavy as a blacksmith's. He had hands like sledges and a straight, thick chest. His neck was so short that with his sloping shoulders he appeared able to draw in his head like a turtle. He stood up straight, his feet wide apart, and fronted the Irishman.

"Where's the tender?" he demanded.

Caleb glanced at the sky and came out of the shanty without his umbrella. "I'm that man," he said, stroking his beard.

"Why the hell don't you let this line through?"

Caleb pointed his thumb over his shoulder at the dam. "Want to try it?"

The bully looked at the foaming water. "Think I'm a fool?"

"I've had suspicions of that same," O'Mory said, joyfully.

The others drew back; it was no business of theirs if O'Mory wanted to start a fight. He had been spoiling for something to do for the past two hours, and they preferred his bestowing his energy on Peters instead of one of themselves. East of Utica there were few men who wanted war with the *Dublin Queen*.

The Irishman whistled shrilly on his fingers. Instantly three men hustled off the green freighter at the head of the line and ran up to the shanty. Every one of them had red hair and a broad grin. "Original Irishers," O'Mory called them. "The only bhoys with gravy enough to dig out the Montezumy Swamp, by gorry!" Still grinning, they lined up behind O'Mory and studied the three men from the scarlet boat. After a moment the smallest of them tipped a wink to the man on his right and exchanged places with him to face the smallest of his opponents. It was evident that the *Dublin Queen* managed these affairs on a systematic basis.

Peters hunched up his shoulders and looked O'Mory up and down. "Who the hell are you?"

"Me father's bhoy," said O'Mory happily.

"Do you say I ain't?"

"God forbid! The O'Morys is Irish."

His men cheered and Peters's face flushed over his beard. But he pulled himself in. "Before I lick you," he said, "I've got to lick the lead boat in this line. I'm going to be first through when the water falls."

"Sure, ye can put the two foights into one," said O'Mory, "and give us some fun. I'm first in the line."

"All right, boys!" shouted Peters.

3

At that instant they heard a bell ringing down the line. The sound was so unusual on the Erie, where the boaters for the most part carried horns, that the men drew apart. What they saw put the fight out of their minds for the moment. A big boat with perfectly square ends and badly weathered white paint was coming up past the others behind the rapid walk of a heavy roan team. The towrope was attached to a standard in the bow, allowing it just to clear the roofs of the boats tied up.

"Look at his hayseed rig, will you?" exclaimed Joe, with a thrust of his peg.

The roans were hitched to an evener — not in tandem like the other horses.

"Glory be!" cried O'Mory, while the Utica men broke out in a rash of swearing. "What does he think he's going to do?"

"If he's going to fight for first place," said Peters, "I'll tend to him first."

"Sure," said O'Mory, "it'll save me the throuble of licking two men."

The team was coming on steadily, pulling without strain, and the old boat cuddled the ripples in front of it and shoved them aside. A woman, not more than twenty, was steering it. She had capable, strong hands on the tiller, and she stood straight with her head back and her eyes steady on the towrope. She wore no hat, and her hair, which fell loose down her back, shone with a white light like barley straw. As the boat neared the lock, the men by the shanty made out that her eyes were blue and that her face was as handsome as the rest of her. While they watched, she unhooked a heavy dinner bell from the tiller and swung it back and forth above her head, and through the noise they saw that she was tall.

Compared to her, the man driving looked squat. When he came to the end of the freight line, he pulled the horses up with a word, and the young woman brought the old boat up beside O'Mory's. Then she tossed a rope clean over the *Dublin Queen,* and the driver caught it and snubbed it to a post, so that the rope pulled right across the *Queen's* bows.

When he had spoken for a minute to the young woman, he walked up to the lock-tender's hut. "Say," he asked in a sleepy sort of voice, "what's all the line for?"

"Look there, son," said Caleb, pointing his thumb at the water, "and ask me another one."

The young man did. "What of it?" he said.

He was short and very heavy, with a red, square face and light hair like the woman's, and his wrists were overboned like a farmer's. He had a kind of dullness about him, which made one think he was slow to make up his mind, but a deal slower to unmake it. And right away all the men could see that he meant to get across the Schoharie, high water or no high water. Most of the boaters had come up when they saw O'Mory and Peters facing off, and now a few sporty gentlemen stepped off the packets to see what was going on. It made them all laugh to hear the young man say, "What of it?" — and they laughed louder when he put his hands in the pockets of his jeans and dug the toe of his shoe into the sand. He got a little redder in the face, but he said, "I can get across all right."

He lowered his head and shook it from side to side at Caleb. "I got to get out to Ohio," he said. "I got a brother there setting out a farm, and me and my wife is taking out the tools and stock. We got to get there by June."

Joe tapped him on the knee with the end of his peg leg. "You don't know how that current can drag onto a boat."

"I got a good team," said the young man. They were a big pair, beyond a doubt — not the ordinary boat horses. Beside O'Mory's mules they looked like a two-ton team.

"Maybe you have," said Joe; "but the last four boats that tried crossing on high water went over the dam. One took three mules with it, and the rope broke on the others."

"I got a new rope, and my team ain't mules."

"You're a stranger on this canal," said Gratwick, "or you 'd know it could n't be did."

"It 's a good team I got," said the young man. "They know how to pull."

"Listen to reason," said O'Mory, as if that were a favorite habit of his.

"We warned him," said Caleb. "It ain't no fault of ours if he busts his boat."

Peters had been pushed into the background by the young man's foolishness. It was a position for which he had no relish. He spat in front of the young man's toe. "Look here, young squirt," he growled, "you need n't set up for God A'mighty over us. I was just telling him," jerking his head at O'Mory, "that there was n't any freighter going to cross ahead of mine."

"He did so," said O'Mory, cocking his head at the bystanders. "Phwat do you know about that?"

"You 'll get *yours*," said Peters.

Then he turned to the young man. "Since she come on the Erie, the *Pretty Fashion* ain't never been second on any lock she come to."

"Sure, she has n't met the *Dublin Queen* yet," cried O'Mory.

The crowd surged to let the young woman into the circle. She had a decisive chin, and her blue eyes gleamed. "What 's the fuss?"

Her husband turned to her doubtfully. "They say the water 's too high."

She gazed at the dam, shading her eyes against the sun. "We 'll try it," she decided.

Her husband pointed to Peters. "This man says he won't let us try ahead of him, and I guess he 's afraid to try now."

"Thrue for you, lad," cried O'Mory.

"It don't make no difference," said Peters hoarsely. "There ain't any boats crossing ahead of the *Pretty Fashion.*"

"We can't waste no time," said the woman. "Lick him, Dan."

4

Her husband stared at Peters as if he were trying to make up his mind. "I don't know as I *can* lick him," he said. "I 'm slow."

"He ain't no whiplash himself, to look at him," said O'Mory in encouragement. Next to having a good brawl, the crew of the *Dublin Queen* enjoyed watching a good fight.

"Go ahead, Dan," said the woman. "You can do it. Make him stand up to you."

Her husband lifted his gaze from the ground and stared again at Peters, as a man might in judging a horse. And then he looked on up the canal where the sun was beginning to sink to the rim of the valley.

A silence hovered on the crowd; even the sky seemed to hold its breath. Only the roar of the water in its ungovernable rush thudded upon the ear, and faint supper smells bloomed in the stillness. A few waiters had come out among the ladies on the packet boats. By the towpath the roan team drowsed with collars loose on their shoulders. The clear sunlight threw the shadows of the people far behind them on the grass.

The young man, with his wife at his side, stared westward; and, caught by the intentness of his gaze, the quiet crowd turned their

eyes up the valley. But they saw only the beginning of a sunset.
When they turned back to the young man, he was unbuttoning his
shirt.

"Hooroar!" yelled O'Mory. "It's on!"

Peters laughed suddenly out of his black beard, and the crowd
took up the Irishman's shout.

"Aw hell," said a boat captain nervously, "it ain't no fight — he's
just a kid."

"Lay you a dollar on the younker," cried Joe, driving his peg into
the sand and reaching for his wallet.

"All right."

"This ain't no place for a fight," said Gratwick. "You'd better
move up to the edge of the lock. It's level there. And all the rest
of us can see you."

Peters laughed shortly, for he was confident of having an easy
time. "That's right," he said. "You watch me."

The young man hesitated a moment, and then said that he was
agreeable.

Caleb took it upon himself to see fair play. He had watched a
fight once among the city mobs on Long Island, so he got up beside
the lock with them and anounced in style: "Herman Peters, bully
of Utica, and not licked yet, gentlemen!"

Peters grinned and took off his waistcoat. The level light threw
the figures into silhouette, so that color became a matter of con-
jecture, except where the sun shone through Caleb's beard, making
a yellow mist of the little hairs and his whole head beautiful. He
spat into the lock again and, clearing his throat, pointed to the
young man, who bent before his wife as she pulled his undershirt
over his head. "Peters versye Dan," cried Caleb, "versye Dan . . ."

"Wagner," said the young woman.

"Dan Wagner . . . a young man going west!"

The crowd cheered as they swarmed to the foot of the embankment. The two teamsters and the missionary called off their conference; and while the men crowded in at the foot of the lock the
missionary debated in himself whether he should try to stop the

fight. The young woman stood on a lock beam, her husband's shirt upon her arm; and the missionary stepped toward the crowd. But as the two men faced each other against the sun, the bully in his shirt, the other stripped to the waist with the light gleaming on his skin, the missionary found that he had not the heart to speak, and he remembered that it was not Sunday.

The ladies clustered the packet-boat decks under their parasols, apparently unaware of what was toward; and the waiters crowded upon the bows. The graybeard who had been fishing went below deck, and when he reappeared he had a spyglass at his eye.

Caleb stood between the two combatants. They were both shorter than he, and the young man looked almost tubby. He had a great girth, like a wrestler's, and his legs had been made stiff by lifting weights; but when he lowered his head and moved it a little from side to side, you could see the power of an ox behind his shoulders. Both he and Peters stood with their hands at their sides; but Peters was erect and confident, and his grin showed through his beard.

"The lad has n't a chance," said Gratwick.

Stillness fell again upon the crowd, so that there was no noise but the falling water, until old Caleb stepped back, lifting his voice, to say, "I reckon you might as well commence."

The bully rushed with a shout, head drawn in, his fists driving straight from his shoulders. And above the noise of the water, as the young man tried ponderously to dodge, those in the foreground heard two solid thuds. A curse slipped out of O'Mory's mouth and the *Dublin Queen* groaned aloud, while Joe stamped his peg deeper into the sand and tried to look away; for all of them had taken odds on the young man — on the long chance, being Irishmen.

The bully rushed again, and the young man was too slow to get out of the way, but he turned his body so that the blows lost a little of their force in glancing. Even so, his knees gave, and the men of the *Pretty Fashion* uttered a shout, which the crowd took up as they surged one step forward. The sun made things black and white, so that black spots smudged the white belly of the young man; and the Irishmen yelled, "Low!"

"Niver mind," O'Mory said to his crew, "we'll remoind the blackguard in a while."

Far down beyond the fight, the missionary cried out within himself as the bully rushed savagely again and yet again with the same thud-thud, which the young man was too slow to dodge and too clumsy to return.

After the sixth rush the young man still faced Peters, with his feet braced and his head sunk forward; but instead of moving it from side to side, he stared straight into the bully's eyes, and his line of vision carried to the far corner of the level space, where the balance beam of the upper gate cut off a six-foot triangle. While Peters caught his wind, the young man raised his hands — it seemed for the first time. The woman cried out suddenly and waved the shirt; and the crew of the *Dublin Queen* set up a shout, for they saw what he intended.

The young man bored in and his back bent behind his hands; and, though he landed only once, the men below heard a heavy smash and a sob of wind from the bully's mouth; and they saw the sun tangled in Caleb's beard as the old man scurried out of the way.

When the sun spots went out of their eyes, the crowd beheld the fighters in the triangle, on two sides the water, on one side the tilted gate-beam. The young man stood with his head down, the light glistening on his shoulders where the sweat ran down. Peters was covering up; and a black smear that must have been blood crawled out from under his beard and down his throat to the collar of his shirt.

"Lick him!" screamed the young woman.

The Irishmen shouted. The crowd swayed as some men tried to hedge their bets. There was no room for rushing there. The fight hung now on weight and the sheer strength of shoulders, backs, and arms. A family of French immigrants began to sing the "Marseillaise," and the young man moved in on Peters. Neither of them dared give ground; for if the young man was forced back from the opening, he lost his advantage; and if Peters stepped back more than once, the water would have him. . . .

The sun seemed to stand still behind them; and old Caleb lay on his belly, his beard in the dirt, so that those below might see.

The two stood foot to foot and they drove their fists into each other in great slow blows, behind which their backs bent and came straight and bent again. At the sound of each blow, the crowd heard the grunt of the man who had been hit and the sigh of the man who had struck; and the roar of the water became something small and far away. The shadows of the two men stretched out and over the crowd and fought in the air where only Caleb could see them. . . .

Little by little the crowd edged up on the lock. The Irishmen in front lay down, and the men behind them kneeled, to let the others watch. The ladies folded their parasols and looked on from the packet boats, because the crews had gone ashore and there was no one to notice them. The missionary found that the advancing crowd spoiled his view, so he started to climb up to the roof of Caleb's shanty, wondering if he would get up in time to see the end. But the two men still stood together, and their elbows came back against the sun and their hands drove in. They both struck for the body, and they both landed, for they were too close to miss.

The crowd thought no more of betting. This fight had no like in their memories: but a few of the gentlemen began to understand how the Erie came to be built by the strength in the arms of men. The crews of the *Dublin Queen* and the *Pretty Fashion* forgot their quarrel and lay side by side like brothers, and the gentlemen took off their tiles so that the teamsters behind could see.

Peters shifted his aim to the other's face; and blood made streaks on the young man's jaw and went down over his chest, parting above the little patch of hair, and ran down upon his belly; but he shook the sun from his sight and sent his fists for the body. Once he wiped the sweat from his eyes with a snatch of his hand; and in the same instant the bully tore open the collar of his shirt. His face streamed and his shirt looked wet. The onlookers saw that he was afraid, and a little driver boy howled between the legs of his captain. . . .

It was a long time for the crowd before the young man stepped back, putting his hand to his mouth to stop the tremble, and tried to speak. But he could not move his broken lips. So the young woman cried, "Had enough?"

Peters put down his head and rushed. The *Pretty Fashion* muttered that it was the end, now their captain had room; and the *Dublin Queen* prayed that it was not. The young man drew himself up and raised his right fist above his shoulder and smashed it down on top of the black hair — a blow to fell an ox. The bully fell forward on top of his rush; his back wiggled a little before it went still; and his teeth caught shut on the new grass between the young man's feet.

5

The crowd caught their breath with a sound like wind upon the snow; and as the young man stepped back the missionary on Caleb's roof cried, "Praise God!' No one spoke, until a murmur grew among those who had not seen the blow, and it swelled into a shout. . . . The ladies put up their parasols. The cooks ran back to their burned food. In little groups the boaters drifted back to their boats to get supper.

The young woman wiped the blood off her husband's face with the end of her skirt, and put the undershirt and shirt back over his head and helped him to button them. "We've got to hurry and get across before it gets dark," she said.

"Don't be a fool," O'Mory shouted. "Ye can't steer a boat as ye are now. Ye've had fun enough."

"My wife can steer," said the young man.

"But ye can't drive like ye are at all," protested O'Mory, shaking his hand and seeing the broken knuckles.

"I don't need to. I got a good team."

"Wait till the morning," said one of the *Pretty Fashion* crew, grinning, for he liked a good fight. "There ain't any boat here'll go over first. We'll tend to that. Even the *Dublin Queen* won't argue that."

"No," said O'Mory. "Divel a bit. — Not that *I* couldn't lick the whole mess of ye," he added.

"We 've got to get out there by June," said the young woman.

"Yes," said her husband. "We got to get out there by June."

"Oh hell," said Caleb, but he went over to the sluice levers.

The young woman went aboard and her husband straightened out the eveners behind the team. The crews of the *Dublin Queen* and the *Pretty Fashion* helped to get the boat into the lock. With the team on the tow bridge, the young man had them double the rope and shorten it; and then, standing on the outside of the bridge, by the off horse's head, he spoke to the pair.

They settled down and went ahead with an easy, forward, up-ward pull into their collars, and the boat came out smoothly into the current. As the side sweep hit the boat, they drove their shoes into the planks. Their haunches puckered as they straightened their legs against the strain, and with great deliberation they set their hoofs carefully and heaved. The woman turned the bow out away from them to keep the stern in to the bridge. There was no lost motion. The young man said never a word. But when the boat crossed an eddy, the men could hear the towline hum.

In a little while, as though they had been pulling on a plough, they had the boat in the easy water beyond. They had seemed to pull so easily that even then some men refused to believe they were across. But when the young man told them to stop, they dropped their heads and shook themselves; and the boaters saw that they trembled all over and were black with sweat.

"They know how to pull," the young man said. "They know how to pull."

The sun set as O'Mory helped him run the rope out to its full length. The woman smiled, all at once, as she thanked him; and O'Mory blushed redder than his hair.

"It was a fine foight, to be sure, if it was a thrifle slow." He lit a lantern for her, which she hung over the stern.

"Thanks," said the young man, and he spoke to his team.

"So long!" cried Caleb.

"Luck!" shouted the others. They returned to their boats, the crew of the *Pretty Fashion* picking up Peters as they went. He was still out and they let him down with a bump on the deck. Old Joe stumped away on his peg leg to try to collect his bet. O'Mory and Caleb and a gentleman from one of the packet boats remained on the lock and watched the boat glide into the dusk.

"By God!" said Caleb, beginning to untangle his beard. "By God! I bet they'll get there."

"By God, I bet he will," said O'Mory.

"Yes," said the gentleman.

"Look!" cried O'Mory, pointing his arm. "There's the name of the boat!" The lantern light fell over the stern and caught a thin tracery of gilt.

"Ye're a scholard, Caleb. Can ye read it?"

Caleb tried and shook his head. "Not that far off," he said, glad of the distance.

The gentleman took a small telescope from the pocket of his coaching coat and focused it on the stern of the boat. "I can just make out the letters," he said; and he spelled them out — "S-U-R-E A-R-R-I-V-A-L."

"What's that?" asked Caleb.

"*Sure Arrival,*" said the gentleman.

"Thank ye, sir," said O'Mory.

DEATH OF RED PERIL

I

JOHN brought his off eye to bear on me: —

What do them old coots down to the store do? Why, one of 'em will think up a horse that's been dead forty year and then they'll set around remembering this and that about that horse until they've made a resurrection of him. You'd think he was a regular Grattan Bars, the way they talk, telling one thing and another, when a man knows if that horse had n't 've had a breeching to keep his tail end off the ground he could hardly have walked from here to Boonville.

A horse race is a handsome thing to watch if a man has his money on a sure proposition. My pa was always a great hand at a horse race. But when he took to a boat and my mother he did n't have no more time for it. So he got interested in another sport.

Did you ever hear of racing caterpillars? No? Well, it used to be a great thing on the canawl. My pa used to have a lot of them insects on hand every fall, and the way he could get them to run would make a man have his eyes examined.

The way we raced caterpillars was to set them in a napkin ring on a table, one facing one way and one the other. Outside the napkin ring was drawed a circle in chalk three feet acrost. Then a man lifted the ring and the handlers was allowed one jab with a darning needle to get their caterpillars started. The one that got outside the chalk circle the first was the one that won the race.

I remember my pa tried out a lot of breeds, and he got hold of some pretty fast steppers. But there was n't one of them could equal Red Peril. To see him you would n't believe he could run. He was all red and kind of stubby, and he had a sort of wart behind that you'd think would get in his way. There was n't anything fancy in his looks. He'd just set still studying the ground and make you think he was dreaming about last year's oats; but when you set him in the starting ring he'd hitch himself up behind like a man lifting on his galluses, and then he'd light out for glory.

Pa come acrost Red Peril down in Westernville. Ma's relatives resided there, and it being Sunday we'd all gone in to church. We was riding back in a hired rig with a dandy trotter, and Pa was pushing her right along and Ma was talking sermon and clothes, and me and my sister was setting on the back seat playing poke your nose, when all of a sudden Pa hollers, "Whoa!" and set the horse right down on the breeching. Ma let out a holler and come to rest on the dashboard with her head under the horse. "My gracious land!" she says. "What's happened?" Pa was out on the other side of the road right down in the mud in his Sunday pants, a-wropping up something in his yeller hankerchief. Ma begun to get riled. "What you doing, Pa?" she says. "What you got there?" Pa was putting his handkerchief back into his inside pocket. Then he come back over the wheel and got him a chew. "Leeza," he says, "I got the fastest caterpillar in seven counties. It's an act of Providence I seen him, the way he jumped the ruts." "It's an act of God I ain't laying dead under the back end of that horse," says Ma. "I've gone and spoilt my Sunday hat." "Never mind," says Pa; "Red Peril will earn you a new one." Just like that he named him. He was the fastest caterpillar in seven counties.

When we got back onto the boat, while Ma was turning up the supper, Pa set him down to the table under the lamp and pulled out the handkerchief. "You two devils stand there and there," he says to me and my sister, "and if you let him get by I'll leather the soap out of you."

So we stood there and he undid the handkerchief, and out walked one of them red, long-haired caterpillars. He walked right to the middle of the table, and then he took a short turn and put his nose in his tail and went to sleep.

"Who'd think that insect could make such a break for freedom as I seen him make?" says Pa, and he got out a empty Brandreth box and filled it up with some towel and put the caterpillar inside. "He needs a rest," says Pa. "He needs to get used to his stall. When he limbers up I'll commence training him. Now then," he says, putting the box on the shelf back of the stove, "don't none of you say a word about him."

He got out a pipe and set there smoking and figuring, and we could see he was studying out just how he'd make a world-beater out of that bug. "What you going to feed him?" asks Ma. "If I wasn't afraid of constipating him," Pa says, "I'd try him out with milkweed."

Next day we hauled up the Lansing Kill Gorge. Ned Kilbourne, Pa's driver, come abroad in the morning, and he took a look at that caterpillar. He took him out of the box and felt his legs and laid him down on the table and went clean over him. "Well," he says, "he don't look like a great lot, but I've knowed some of that red variety could chug along pretty smart." Then he touched him with a pin. It was a sudden sight.

It looked like the rear end of that caterpillar was racing the front end, but it couldn't never quite get by. Afore either Ned or Pa could get a move Red Peril had made a turn around the sugar bowl and run solid aground in the butter dish.

Pa let out a loud swear. "Look out he don't pull a tendon," he says. "Butter's a bad thing. A man has to be careful. Jeepers," he says, picking him up and taking him over to the stove to dry, "I'll handle him myself. I don't want no rum-soaked bezabors dishing my beans."

"I didn't mean harm, Will," says Ned. "I was just curious."

There was something extraordinary about that caterpillar. He was intelligent. It seemed he just couldn't abide the feel of sharp iron. It got so that if Pa reached for the lapel of his coat Red Peril would light out. It must have been he was tender. I said he had a sort of wart behind, and I guess he liked to find it a place of safety.

We was all terrible proud of that bird. Pa took to timing him on the track. He beat all known time holler. He got to know that as soon as he crossed the chalk he would get back safe in his quarters. Only when we tried sprinting him across the supper table, if he saw a piece of butter he'd pull up short and bolt back where he come from. He had a mortal fear of butter.

Well, Pa trained him three nights. It was a sight to see him there at the table, a big man with a needle in his hand, moving the lamp around and studying out the identical spot that caterpillar wanted most to get out of the needle's way. Pretty soon he found it, and then he says to Ned, "I'll race him agin all comers at all odds." "Well, Will," says Ned, "I guess it's a safe proposition."

2

We hauled up the feeder to Forestport and got us a load of potatoes. We raced him there against Charley Mack, the bank-walker's, Leopard Pillar, one of them tufted breeds with a row of black buttons down the back. The Leopard was well liked and had won several races that season, and there was quite a few boaters around that fancied him. Pa argued for favorable odds, saying he was racing a maiden caterpillar; and there was a lot of money laid out, and Pa and Ned managed to cover the most of it. As for the race, there wasn't anything to it. While we was putting him in the ring — one of them birchbark and sweet grass ones Indians make — Red Peril didn't act very good. I guess the smell and the crowd kind of upset him. He was nervous and kept fidgeting with his front feet; but they hadn't more'n lifted the ring than he lit out under the edge as tight as he could make it, and Pa touched him with the needle just as he lepped the line. Me and my sister was supposed to be in bed, but Ma had gone visiting in Forestport and we'd snuck in and was under the table, which had a red cloth onto it, and I can tell you there was some shouting. There was some couldn't believe that insect had been inside the ring at all; and there was some said he must be a cross with a dragon fly or a side-hill gouger; but old Charley Mack, that'd worked in the camps, said he guessed Red Peril must be descended from the caterpillars Paul Bunyan used to race. He said you could tell by the bump on his tail, which Paul used to put on all his caterpillars, seeing as how the smallest pointed object he could hold in his hand was a peavy.

Well, Pa raced him a couple of more times and he won just as easy, and Pa cleared up close to a hundred dollars in three races. That caterpillar was a mammoth wonder, and word of him got going and people commenced talking him up everywhere, so it was hard to race him around these parts.

But about that time the dock-keeper of Number One on the feeder come across a pretty swift article that the people round Rome thought high of. And as our boat was headed down the gorge, word got ahead about Red Peril, and people began to look out for the race.

We come into Number One about four o'clock, and Pa tied up right there and went on shore with his box in his pocket and Red Peril inside the box. There must have been ten men crowded into the shanty, and as many more again outside looking in the windows and door. The lock-tender was a skinny bezabor from Stittville, who thought he knew a lot about racing caterpillars; and, come to think of it, maybe he did. His name was Henry Buscerck, and he had a bad tooth in front he used to suck at a lot.

Well, him and Pa set their caterpillars on the table for the crowd to see, and I must say Buscerck's caterpillar was as handsome a brute as you could wish to look at, bright bay with black points and a short fine coat. He had a way of looking right and left, too, that made him handsome. But Pa did n't bother to look at him. Red Peril was a natural marvel, and he knew it.

Buscerck was a sly, twerpish man, and he must 've heard about Red Peril — right from the beginning, as it turned out; for he laid out the course in yeller chalk. They used Pa's ring, a big silver one he 'd bought secondhand just for Red Peril. They laid out a lot of money, and Dennison Smith lifted the ring. The way Red Peril histed himself out from under would raise a man's blood pressure twenty notches. I swear you could see the hair lay down on his back. Why, that black-pointed bay was left nowhere! It

did n't seem like he moved. But Red Peril was just gathering himself for a fast finish over the line when he seen it was yeller. He
reared right up; he must 've thought it was butter, by Jeepers, the
way he whirled on his hind legs and went the way he 'd come. Pa
begun to get scared, and he shook his needle behind Red Peril,
but that caterpillar was more scared of butter than he ever was of
cold steel. He passed the other insect afore he 'd got halfway to
the line. By Cripus, you 'd ought to 've heard the cheering from
the Forestport crews. The Rome men was green. But when he
got to the line, danged if that caterpillar did n't shy again and run
around the circle twicet, and then it seemed like his heart had
gone in on him, and he crept right back to the middle of the
circle and lay there hiding his head. It was the pitifulest sight a
man ever looked at. You could almost hear him moaning, and
he shook all over.

I 've never seen a man so riled as Pa was. The water was running right out of his eyes. He picked up Red Peril and he says,
"This here 's no race." He picked up his money and he says, "The
course was illegal, with that yeller chalk." Then he squashed the
other caterpillar, which was just getting ready to cross the line, and
he looks at Buscerck and says, "What 're you going to do about
that?"

Buscerck says, "I 'm going to collect my money. My caterpillar
would have beat."

"If you want to call that a finish you can," says Pa, pointing to the
squashed bay one, "but a baby could see he 's still got to reach the
line. Red Peril got to wire and come back and got to it again afore
your hayseed worm got half his feet on the ground. If it was any
other man owned him," Pa says, "I 'd feel sorry I squashed him."

He stepped out of the house, but Buscerck laid a-hold of his
pants and says, "You got to pay, Hemstreet. A man can't get
away with no such excuses in the city of Rome."

Pa did n't say nothing. He just hauled off and sunk his fist, and
Buscerck come to inside the lock, which was at low level right
then. He waded out the lower end and he says, "I 'll have you

arrested for this." Pa says, "All right; but if I ever catch you around this lock again I'll let you have a feel with your other eye."

Nobody else wanted to collect money from Pa, on account of his build, mostly, so we went back to the boat. Pa put Red Peril to bed for two days. It took him all of that to get over his fright at the yeller circle. Pa even made us go without butter for a spell, thinking Red Peril might know the smell of it. He was such an intelligent, thinking animal, a man couldn't tell nothing about him.

3

But next morning the sheriff comes aboard and arrests Pa with a warrant and takes him afore a justice of the peace. That was old Oscar Snipe. He'd heard all about the race, and I think he was feeling pleasant with Pa, because right off they commenced talking breeds. It would have gone off good only Pa'd been having a round with the sheriff. They come in arm in arm, singing a Hallelujah meeting song; but Pa was polite, and when Oscar says, "What's this?" he only says, "Well, well."

"I hear you've got a good caterpillar," says the judge.

"Well, well," says Pa. It was all he could think of to say.

"What breed is he?" says Oscar, taking a chew.

"Well," says Pa, "well, well."

Ned Kilbourne says he was a red one.

"That's a good breed," says Oscar, folding his hands on his stummick and spitting over his thumbs and between his knees and into the sandbox all in one spit. "I kind of fancy the yeller ones myself. You're a connesewer," he says to Pa, "and so'm I, and between connesewers I'd like to show you one. He's as neat a stepper as there is in this county."

"Well, well," says Pa, kind of cold around the eyes and looking at the lithograph of Mrs. Snipe done in a hair frame over the sink.

Oscar slews around and fetches a box out of his back pocket and shows us a sweet little yeller one.

"There she is," he says, and waits for praise.

"She was a good woman," Pa said after a while, looking at the picture, "if any woman that 's four times a widow can be called such."

"Not her," says Oscar. "It 's this yeller caterpillar."

Pa slung his eyes on the insect which Oscar was holding, and it seemed like he 'd just got an idee.

"Fast?" he says, deep down. "That thing run! Why, a snail with the stringhalt could spit in his eye."

Old Oscar come to a boil quick.

"Evidence. Bring me the evidence."

He spit, and he was that mad he let his whole chew get away from him without noticing. Buscerck says, "Here," and takes his hand off 'n his right eye.

Pa never took no notice of nothing after that but the eye. It was the shiniest black onion I ever see on a man. Oscar says, "Forty dollars!" And Pa pays and says, "It 's worth it."

But it don't never pay to make an enemy in horse racing or caterpillars, as you will see, after I 've got around to telling you.

Well, we raced Red Peril nine times after that, all along the Big Ditch, and you can hear to this day — yes, sir — that there never was a caterpillar alive could run like Red Peril. Pa got rich onto him. He allowed to buy a new team in the spring. If he could only 've started a breed from that bug, his fortune would 've been made and Henry Ford would 've looked like a bent nickel alongside me to-day. But caterpillars are n't built like Ford cars. We beat all the great caterpillars of the year, and it being a time for a late winter, there was some fast running. We raced the Buffalo Big Blue and Fenwick's Night Mail and Wilson's Joe of Barneveld. There was n't one could touch Red Peril. It was close into October when a crowd got together and brought up the Black Arrer of Ava to race us, but Red Peril beat him by an inch. And after that there was n't a caterpillar in the state would race Pa's.

He was mighty chesty them days and had come to be quite a figger down the canawl. People come aboard to talk with him and admire Red Peril; and Pa got the idea of charging five cents a sight, and that made for more money even if there was n't no more running for the animile. He commenced to get fat.

And then come the time that comes to all caterpillars. And it goes to show that a man ought to be as careful of his enemies as he is lending money to friends.

4

We was hauling down the Lansing Kill again and we'd just crossed the aqueduct over Stringer Brook when the lock-keeper, that minded it and the lock just below, come out and says there was quite a lot of money being put up on a caterpillar they'd collected down in Rome.

Well, Pa went in and he got out Red Peril and tried him out. He was fat and his stifles acted kind of stiff, but you could see with half an eye he was still fast. His start was a mite slower, but he made great speed once he got going.

"He's not in the best shape in the world," Pa says, "and if it was any other bug I wouldn't want to run him. But I'll trust the old brute," and he commenced brushing him up with a toothbrush he'd bought a-purpose.

"Yeanh," says Ned. "It may not be right, but we've got to consider the public."

By what happened after, we might have known that we'd meet up with that caterpillar at Number One Lock; but there wasn't no sign of Buscerck, and Pa was so excited at racing Red Peril again that I doubt if he noticed where he was at all. He was all rigged out for the occasion. He had on a black hat and a new red boating waistcoat, and when he busted loose with his horn for the lock you'd have thought he wanted to wake up all the deef-and-dumbers in seven counties. We tied by the upper gates and left the team to graze; and there was quite a crowd on hand. About nine morning boats was tied along the towpath, and all the afternoon boats waited. People was hanging around, and when they heard Pa whanging his horn they let out a great cheer. He took off his hat to some of the ladies, and then he took Red Peril out of his pocket and everybody cheered some more.

"Who owns this-here caterpillar I've been hearing about?" Pa asks. "Where is he? Why don't he bring out his pore contraption?"

A feller says he's in the shanty.

"What's his name?" says Pa.

"Martin Henry's running him. He's called the Horned Demon of Rome."

"Dinged if I ever thought to see him at my time of life," says Pa. And he goes in. Inside there was a lot of men talking and smoking and drinking and laying money faster than Leghorns can lay eggs, and when Pa comes in they let out a great howdy, and when Pa put down the Brandreth box on the table they crowded round; and you'd ought to've heard the mammoth shout they give when Red Peril climbed out of his box. And well they might. Yes, sir!

You can tell that caterpillar's a thoroughbred. He's shining right down to the root of each hair. He's round, but he ain't too fat. He don't look as supple as he used to, but the folks can't tell that. He's got the winner's look, and he prances into the centre of the ring with a kind of delicate canter that was as near single-footing as I ever see a caterpillar get to. By Jeepers Cripus! I felt proud to be in the same family as him, and I wasn't only a little lad.

Pa waits for the admiration to die down, and he lays out his money, and he says to Martin Henry, "Let's see your ring-boned swivel-hocked imitation of a bug."

Martin answers, "Well, he ain't much to look at, maybe, but you'll be surprised to see how he can push along."

And he lays down the dangedest lump of worm you ever set your eyes on. It's the kind of insect a man might expect to see in France or one of them furrin lands. It's about two and a half inches long and stands only half a thumbnail at the shoulder. It's green and as hairless as a newborn egg, and it crouches down squinting around at Red Peril like a man with sweat in his eye. It ain't natural nor refined to look at such a bug, let alone race it.

When Pa seen it, he let out a shout and laughed. He could n't talk from laughing.

But the crowd did n't say a lot, having more money on the race than ever was before or since on a similar occasion. It was so much that even Pa commenced to be serious. Well, they put 'em in the ring together and Red Peril kept over on his side with a sort of intelligent dislike. He was the brainiest article in the caterpillar line I ever knowed. The other one just hunkered down with a mean look in his eye.

Millard Thompson held the ring. He counted, "One — two — three — and off." Some folks said it was the highest he knew how to count, but he always got that far anyhow, even if it took quite a while for him to remember what figger to commence with.

The ring come off and Pa and Martin Henry sunk their needles — at least they almost sunk them, for just then them standing close to the course seen that Horned Demon sink his horns into the back end of Red Peril. He was always a sensitive animal, Red Peril was, and if a needle made him start you can think for yourself what them two horns did for him. He cleared twelve inches in one jump — but then he sot right down on his belly, trembling.

"Foul!" bellers Pa. "My 'pillar 's fouled."

"It ain't in the rule book," Millard says.

"It 's a foul!" yells Pa; and all the Forestport men yell, "Foul! Foul!"

But it was n't allowed. The Horned Demon commenced walking to the circle — he could n't move much faster than a barrel can roll uphill, but he was getting there. We all seen two things, then. Red Peril was dying, and we was losing the race. Pa stood there kind of foamy in his beard, and the water running right out of both eyes. It 's an awful thing to see a big man cry in public. But Ned saved us. He seen Red Peril was dying, the way he wiggled, and he figgered, with the money he had on him, he 'd make him win if he could.

He leans over and puts his nose into Red Peril's ear, and he shouts, "My Cripus, you 've gone and dropped the butter!"

Something got into that caterpillar's brain, dying as he was, and he let out the smallest squeak of a hollering fright I ever listened to a caterpillar make. There was a convulsion got into him. He looked like a three-dollar mule with the wind colic, and then he gave a bound. My holy! How that caterpillar did rise up. When he come down again, he was stone dead, but he lay with his chin across the line. He'd won the race. The Horned Demon was blowing bad and only halfway to the line. . . .

Well, we won. But I think Pa's heart was busted by the squeal he heard Red Peril make when he died. He couldn't abide Ned's face after that, though he knowed Ned had saved the day for him. But he put Red Peril's carcase in his pocket with the money and walks out.

And there he seen Buscerck standing at the sluices. Pa stood looking at him. The sheriff was alongside Buscerck and Oscar Snipe on the other side, and Buscerck guessed he had the law behind him.

"Who owns that Horned Demon?" said Pa.

"Me," says Buscerck with a sneer. "He may have lost, but he done a good job doing it."

Pa walks right up to him.

"I've got another forty dollars in my pocket," he says, and he connected sizeably.

Buscerck's boots showed a minute. Pretty soon they let down the water and pulled him out. They had to roll a couple of gallons out of him afore they got a grunt. It served him right. He'd played foul. But the sheriff was worried, and he says to Oscar, "Had I ought to arrest Will?" (Meaning Pa.)

Oscar was a sporting man. He couldn't abide low dealing. He looks at Buscerck there, shaping his belly over the barrel, and he says, "Water never hurt a man. It keeps his hide from cracking." So they let Pa alone. I guess they didn't think it was safe to have a man in jail that would cry about a caterpillar. But then they hadn't lived alongside of Red Peril like us.

CITIZENS FOR OHIO

I

THE rain was following a northeast slant; it was cold, stinging when it found the skin, as if the drops were tipped with steel.

The road was nearly empty. Early April travel was apt to be wet and even the pikes made slow going for wagons; but the six great horses of the west-bound freight had never faltered in their three-mile stride. The wheels of the huge wagon were wide enough to spread the ruts, eight inches across the tires. They rolled steadily to the slow beat of bells.

The teamster eyed the horses, then called to them. They stopped together, and the two leaders turned back their heads. It was getting dark, and bells did not carry far against the rain. He moved to his tool box, fished out his lantern, and worked for a moment with flint and steel in the lee of the high hood. The flame caught against the wick and the whale oil burned palely. When he hung it on its hook on the nigh side of the front bow, the light made a small spot on the road.

He went round his horses, speaking to them, punching the leaders. Their sweaty hides made pungent steam against the rain. They were chunky horses, with muscled withers, deep chests, and tremendous quarters. Back by the wheel team again, he said, "Gee-up!"

With effortless precision they leaned up into their collars. The reach of the wagon groaned, the wheels sucked through the mud, the hood shivered as if the cold were in it, the bells on the arches over the wheeler's hames jangled, shook out their notes, and caught their rhythm again from the long stride. The teamster matched it with his own.

He walked along the footpath, hunched against the rain, his hands in his pockets, his whip coiled round his right wrist. The rain had streaked his horsehide jacket; it was blotting out the valley with the growing darkness; it was bringing mist out of the warmed earth. The mist hid the lower slopes of the hills, and the drooping clouds dragged across their tops, so that the road alone seemed actual.

He had seen little travel all that afternoon. Even the east-bound wheat wagons had camped early. Since leaving Little Falls he had passed by half a dozen of them drawn up beside the roads, the teams under their oilcloth blankets standing nose to nose.

Three afternoons ago he had hauled out of Schenectady, and all the way he had made heavy going. All the way his brain had been heavy with the news David Hearsay had given him at the gate of the great bridge. The Senate had passed Clinton's canal bill.

A great thing for the state of New York, but five years from now, in the spring of 1817, a teamster would n't be able to find a wagon-load to haul five miles. A man might take to hauling boats. But a boat was n't a wagon. A boat had no life. Canal boats would be blunt-ended, square-shaped things, less boatlike in actuality than the box of a Conestoga. They would kill horses with their dead slow weight.

His eyes probed the rain for the next milepost. If the number was right he would keep on in spite of the closing darkness till he came to the teamsters' tavern kept by Sterling half a mile beyond Fort Herkimer. On a night like this the shed was certain to be jam-full of horses, but, as it ran east and west, he should be able to find a spot for his team behind it where they would rest out of the wind. For himself there would be a hot supper, a drink, and sleep in his wagon.

The lantern light began to assert itself, putting a shine on the rumps of the horses. Drops flashed from the iron tires of the wheels and a continual run of muddy water ran back from the rims into the ruts.

He slogged mechanically along, his eyes straining for the mile-post. He did not see the woman step out from an angle of the roadside fence. He did not even notice the raised heads and pricked ears of his lead team, until her voice called, "Whoa!"

It startled him. Even then he could not see her. But it made him grin. His horses kept right on. They would stop for no voice but his own, once they had set the wheels rolling. But another breather would not hurt them.

"Whoa!" he echoed her voice.

The bells fell silent, the mud folded over the fellies of the wheels between the spokes, the top shuddered, and the drumming of rain upon it came to their ears. She was on the nigh side of the wagon, so he stepped round, and found her standing on the edge of lantern light.

She stood stiffly erect, the rain shaping her shawl tight to her head, her arms straight, holding her sodden bundle against her skirt. Her voice was taut.

"Mister?"

He could see nothing of her face except that it was white.

"I won't do for you, sister."

She did not answer for a moment, but searched him with tired eyes.

"I won't do for you," he repeated, as if sure of her purpose. "I'm a teamster on a short haul — Utica."

"Where's that?"

"About eighteen miles west," he said. "It's no place for you."

"I turned a man down beyond East Creek," she said with a catch. "I turned him down for his split lip."

Her voice became bitter with self-mockery. She began searching his face again. It was hard, dark brown as his horsehide jacket. Under the lantern light she could see the bones etched with shadow. A thin, long jaw, close lips, and a curved nose. Like a queer picture of an Indian. His eyes were almost opaque. But as she spoke they became sympathetic. "Never mind, there's bound to be more."

"Where are you going, after Utica?"

"West. Home. Rochester."

"I'm going west, mister."

"There's no place for you with a teamster."

She seemed to reckon him up; then she flung her glance eastward against the darkness.

"You didn't see nobody on horseback?"

"No."

She looked relieved.

"I'd take smallpox for a ride."

He could see the tiredness in her shoulders, her back. It was in his own, a little.

"Have you got any money?"

"Not a cent."

The horses were looking round at them, their eyes dull coals. The steam from their hides drifted west over their heads.

"I didn't stay long enough to pay off. I couldn't bear it in the city. I come from a dairy country over back. I'm useful and strong."

"Here," said the teamster. "Here's a shilling. Somebody will give you supper."

She ignored his hand. She kept her eyes on his face.

"I don't want money, mister. But thank you, too. I want to get free of it. I'll work for any man, I will. To the bare bone."

"You'll find him."

He started to turn away.

"Mister, what will they do to me if they catch me?"

"I don't know."

"What's the law?"

"They can brand you. An R, in the palm of the hand. Or on the face."

She seemed to shiver.

"He'd put it on my face."

Suddenly she stepped up to him, close to the front wheel, under the lantern. She tilted her face so that the light fell full on it and, bringing up one hand, drew the shawl from her hair.

"How would it look there, mister?"

For an instant her eyes seemed to catch fire from the lantern. He studied her curiously. She had light hair, but her eyes were dark, nearly black, with black lashes and thick straight black brows. Her nose, short and broad, had wide-curving nostrils. She was not beautiful, he thought, but as he made his estimates she colored suddently, and her full lips drooped.

"All right, get in. I've lost time enough."

He caught her elbow savagely and thrust her up to the wheel. She perched for an instant on the broad tire, then swung herself to the foot rest and the high seat. As her legs flashed through the light he saw that they were bare.

"Here, catch!"

He flung her bundle hard after her, striking her breast as she caught it. She put it in her lap and folded her hands across it. She looked straight down at the bell arches of the wheel team, almost within reach of her toes.

"There's a sheepskin hanging from the bow, if you're cold," he said. "Or you can get down under the seat. There's straw and blankets there."

He walked round the wagon to the off side of the wheelers. The horses were getting restive under the rain. He uncoiled his whip, tossed the lash vertically in the air to limber it, and cracked it out along the off horses.

Mud covered the horses' pasterns as they stirred the wagon. The bells took up their chime against the rain.

2

He was sludging along the path again, beside his horses, their shadows pointing the light. The milepost had been passed.

"There's a fine for aiding runaway redemptioners. In these east counties it can be collected."

Redemptioners had no more standing under the law than slaves. They sold one, two, or three years to the shipmaster for the price of their passage to America, and whoever paid for their passage when they landed had unrestricted title to their services.

"You damned fool," he thought.

A teamster wanted no woman along on his wagon. She kept him too busy watching out for her. A teamster should have his women along the road, where he could leave them and not be bothered by them.

He'd turn her out when the rain stopped and let her take her chance.

"Are you going to haul all night, mister?"

She had climbed back over the seat and now she was leaning her elbows over the back of it. The lantern edged her profile, showing the comb she held in her hands. She had taken down her hair and brought it round over her shoulder.

"Three miles."

"Where are you going to stop?"

"Sterling's."

"Have they got beds?"

"Yes. But they'll be full."

"Where'll you sleep, then?"

She had been smiling. It softened her face for her to smile.

"In the wagon," he said coldly.

She continued to look down at his dark face, smiling as if she did not see him, and he turned from her.

"Mister," she said, after a moment, "you ain't asked me my name."

"No."

"Maybe you don't want to know it."

"I know it."

"How?"

"It's in printed bills. Ruth Havens, isn't it?"

"Yes."

Her voice was smaller and her smile was gone. "Where'd you see them, mister?"

"Little Falls, when I came through."

"Then they're ahead of me."

"Yes. What did you think?"

Poor fool. She ought to have cut across to the Great Western

and made it down through Cooperstown to the Pennsylvania border. He looked up at her again. She was staring out on the six
broad backs of his horses, her hands still foolishly holding the comb,
her body swaying numbly to the rocking motion of the wagon box.
If she went on alone, they would get her sure as fire, and take her
back. She said he would put it on her face. He thought of the
name at the foot of the handbill. Jacob Vandertromp. He dis-
liked the sound of it.

After a while her voice came again. It sounded more tired, now.

"What 'll you do when we meet the sheriff, mister?"

"I don't know."

She was looking at him again, and suddenly he grinned at her.
His teeth were white against the lantern light, flashing as if the rain
wetted them. She could see the cords in his thin neck, the jutting
Adam's apple and the hard jaw. She flushed a little and lowered
her eyes to the comb.

"What 's your name, mister?"

"George Martin."

She did not answer, but when he looked again she had disappeared into the shelter of the wagon.

3

At a bend the team halted unexpectedly. He did not try to start
them. The bald white nose of the nigh leader showed over his
mate's withers as he looked back for Martin. Without a word to
them he went round the wagon to get the lantern.

The girl was leaning over the seat again.

"What 's the matter, mister?"

"I don't know; Edward 's seen something. Get down inside."

He jumped up on the wheel and reached for the lantern. For a
moment he lingered, looking down into the cavernous dark box.
She had spread out her shawl and coat and opened her bundle
to dry, and she had made herself a nest under the seat among his
blankets. He could not see her face, but the light caught a wave
in her hair, like a pale metal.

"You keep down in there," he said. "Don't say anything, no matter what goes on."

"Is it the sheriff, do you think?"

"How in God's name would I know? Lay down and keep still."

He dropped back into the mud and ploughed his way forward. He stopped for a moment beside the leader to slap his wet withers. The chestnut dropped his white nose, rabbiting the man's shoulder gently with his lips. Then, as Martin started ahead, the horse gathered the team behind him.

A woman was standing in the middle of the road. His light swam up to her, touching her man's boots, her sopping gray wool stockings, her skirts, and rose to her face. She was middle-aged, small, tired, and frightened.

"What's the matter, ma'am?"

She answered, "Our wagon's slid over the shoulder of the road. It's stuck. We couldn't find no place to camp, and, being half in the road, my man didn't want us to stay there the whole night. He's gone ahead to find help. He allows there's a teamster's house a small piece on."

Martin swung his lantern round his head.

"Your man's right, ma'am." He ought to have recognized the turn with the riven hemlock stub. Sterling's was half a mile on.

"He's been gone quite a time," the woman said nervously. "I heard your wagon coming and went back to tell you. But I reckon he'll be back pretty quick now."

"It's a teamster's house," Martin said slowly. "A teamster hates to heat up a team when they're cooled, especially if he's on a long haul." He looked at her sharply. "What kind of a man is he? Take care of himself?"

Her eyes were bright and frightened in the light.

"I don't know, mister. We ain't traveling people. We had a farm in Montgomery County and we sold it last week. We're heading for west."

He stood still with her in the rain. Then Edward stamped.

"Come on," he said. "Let's look at your wagon."

The bells followed them slowly through the rain, the reach laboring noisily as the wheels found potholes.

Martin unexpectedly came upon the wagon.

"Ain't you a lantern?"

"Roy took it with him. That's why I went back when I heard your bells, mister."

She pushed back a wet wisp of hair and stared at the wagon with him, helplessness flooding her faded eyes.

It stood on the edge of the road, lodged precariously, the off wheels hub-deep in silt that was gathered at a culvert mouth. Huddled uneasily in their traces, one high above the other, the mover's small team lifted their heads at the lantern. In the lee of the half hood that covered the perishable part of their belongings an old half-bred Shorthorn dozed uncomfortably.

"I'm afraid we're stuck hard," said the woman. "Our team couldn't seem to do no more than make it settle deeper. Roy feared they'd dip it over afore they'd get it out."

Martin examined the wagon silently. The rear half was piled high under a loose piece of drill. In the lantern light he could make out under the cloth familiar household bulges, the head of a bed, a spinning wheel, a dasher churn. Strapped to the rear was an iron plough.

"She's kind of top-heavy," he said. A farmer had no notion of loading a wagon properly for a long haul. "The weight's too heavy over the rear axle."

"Maybe it is; I don't know. Maybe if you went on and told Roy?" She pushed at her hair again.

Martin walked down into the ditch. The axle had gouged into the road shoulder. But there was thirty feet clear to the wood shield of the culvert.

"I don't know," he said. "Wait a minute, ma'am."

He walked round the wagon to see if he could pass, then started back for his own wagon, leaving the light with the woman. Just beyond the light's edge, he found Ruth standing.

He caught her by the arm without speaking and marched her back out of earshot. Then he cursed her.

He could just make her out standing close before him in the rain. She was quite silent till he was through. Then she asked calmly, "Can you get her out?"

"Haven't I been telling you? We can get by and send back help. Do you want the whole country to know where you are?"

"I heard you telling her teamsters wouldn't like heating up a team and coming back," she answered.

"Maybe not."

"She's frightened."

"Nobody's going to hurt her."

"That don't matter, does it?"

He could feel her looking at him.

"All right," he said. "But you've got to hold her team."

"All right."

They went forward together.

"Got a shovel?" he asked the woman.

She laboriously found him one. With it he beveled off the shoulder of the road ahead of the rear axle.

"All she needs is a little extra power."

He tossed the shovel back into the wagon, carelessly. The woman cried out. In a moment she was in the wagon fishing among her bundles. She got down again carrying a small glass-filled window sash. She explained timidly, for fear of offending him, "I couldn't bear to have my sash broke, mister. It's such a comfort in a new house."

The teamster grunted.

"All right, get back along the road in case somebody's coming."

He unhooked the mover's light team and led them a little way up the road. They were still trembling from their struggle with the bogged wagon, tossing their heads and snorting.

"They're primed to run off," he said to the girl. "If you let them get away you might just as well go after them. I won't chase them."

She did not answer. But she caught the headstalls and whispered softly to the horses.

The teamster, swearing to himself, unhitched his leaders, and with a piece of rope hung the pole yoke to their open collars. Edward regarded him anxiously.

"Easy, now, easy. Gee-up, easy, boy."

He let them take their own time; they could handle the wagon alone. They dropped their heads to settle the damp collars. They started slowly. As they felt the weight, their haunches squatted, their shoulders raised, and the wagon creaked through every stick.

"Up, now!"

Their hoofs slithered in the mud. The off leader, in the ditch, scrambled heavily, went down on his knees. "Haw!" shouted the teamster, and Edward, with a strong heave left, swung his mate up. They gathered themselves again. The wagon groaned, then nigh wheels lifted. But the off leader got his forefeet on the crown of the road. He and Edward lifted together against the traces. With a long sigh the mud loosened its grip, and the wagon, reeling dizzily, came up on the road.

"Good boys," said the teamster.

He started unhitching his horses and returning them to the Pennsylvania hitch. Ruth came up beside him with the small team, placid enough now, and eyed Edward.

"That's a good horse, mister."

Martin grinned suddenly sidewise at her and nodded.

She went back for the other woman and she and Martin hitched in the small team for her, as she restored her glass window to its proper place.

"Can you drive?" he asked her.

"Not very good. Roy don't think so."

She looked up at him in the rain. Her lips trembled with gratitude as she tried to thank him. The girl turned to the teamster with shining eyes.

"I'll drive them," she said.

He did not look at her.

"All right, stick close."

He went back to his wagon. The horses were eager to go. They started on the word, swinging the big wagon past the other, and caught their long stride. The sound of the bells came back to the girl clearly as she swung up on the narrow seat of the mover's wagon, helped up the older woman, and shook out the reins.

4

Sterling's teamster's house, like all the rest of the valley, was walled in with rain. Only one window showed a yellow light against the panes, with the rain striking the glass and running down in small erratic rivers. A lantern, hung on a post before the door, shed a faint gleam on the creaking house sign.

The near side of the sign showed a teamster preceding his hitch along a snow-beaten road, and under his feet the words: —

Teamster's Travel

As the wagon passed the door, Ruth saw the window filled with men. Some were drinking, some were laughing, some lifting their hands to shout; but all were looking toward the centre of the room.

The Pennsylvania team swung on by and turned the corner for the shed. Ruth had thought the teamster might have stopped to look into the window for the woman's husband, but he was thinking that unless a man could take care of himself pretty actively he had no business in entering this house.

He was surprised to find several empty places in the long shed. He unhitched his team, stripped them of harness, and blanketed them. Then he led the mover's team into the end space, but left them harnessed. He said to the mover's wife, "You may be wanting to clear out fast. So just stay handy. . . . I'll go in after your man now."

"Thank you, mister," she answered.

"No thanks to me," he said. "What's his full name? Maybe I'd better know it."

"Ledyard. Roy Ledyard, mister."

"What's he look like?"

"Medium tall. He's got a beard, gray. He's allowed to be a handsome man." Her small face looked down at her nervously clasped hands. "He's wearing a brown linsey coat and black pants, mister."

The teamster thought a moment.

"Who'd you sell your farm to?"

"Mr. Gregson."

"All right. You stay right here."

He was halfway across the yard before he noticed the girl. "Get on back to the shed," he said harshly.

"I'm coming with you, Mr. Martin."

"Listen," he said. "You get back to the old lady. Those boys in the window looked kind of gay."

"What do you mean?"

"Don't you know you're a pretty girl?" he asked patiently.

Her eyes dropped. He could make out so much; but he could not see her flush. Then she looked up.

"You've taken me up with you, mister. I'll stay by you."

"Will you?" He lost patience. "You'll do what I tell you if you want to stay by me. Get on back to that shed."

"I won't."

"Now?" His voice was quiet.

"Let go of me."

"You going back quiet?"

"You're hurting my arm."

"I'm trying to."

He walked her back to the shed. After her first futile struggle she went quietly, letting him propel her through the mud.

"You'll stay with Mrs. Ledyard."

"I wish you would, ma'am," said the mover's wife from her dark perch.

The girl stood in the wagon light, silently rubbing her bruised arm.

"Listen," he said. "If one of those bezabors comes out, there's a muskit by the wagon seat."

She nodded sulkily.

He recrossed the yard swiftly. The latchstring hung out through the door. He pulled it, stepped in, and crossed the kitchen, lighted only by the banked fire in the chimney. The tap showed a small light through the open panel of the door.

He opened the door softly. The passage gave directly on the tap, and from the shadow he had a view the length of the bar to the front door. A couple of teamsters, grinning broadly, leaned their backs against the door while they watched someone in the centre of the room. Another man stood at the corner of the passage.

Martin walked up to the last man and glanced round his shoulder. The man started, recognized him, and grinned.

At a long table eight or ten teamsters were seated with their drinks in their hands. Their coiled whips and broad hats hung on pegs in the wall behind them. Two plump girls, in rumpled dresses of bright gingham, stood together in one corner. A cobbler, his last between his knees, sat with hammer poised, his tongue working the tacks in his mouth. At the bar, a stout woman with gray straggling hair leaned her elbows in a puddle and rested her cheek against a dry bar rag that she held in her hands. Mother Sterling was absorbed. Her breath came and went steadily, audibly.

They were all studying the man in the centre of the floor. He stood directly under the hanging lamp, his hat in his hand. His thin face was bearded, but the tanned skin was darker than the hair. His eyes were a pale cold gray, clear and dry, small over the high cheekbones.

"What's up, Garland?" Martin asked the man beside him.

Garland took his chin in his fingers and said judiciously, "He says his wagon's stuck half a mile back. He's been after one of us to pull him out."

"Why not?" Martin asked.

"Well, he bought himself a strap and tried to pay for it with that shillin'."

"What's the matter with it?"

Mother Sterling turned her eyes to Martin without moving the comfortable position of her head.

"It's counterfeit," she said hoarsely. Her tongue ran over her lips and her eyes slid back to the stranger.

He confronted them sullenly. "It's honest money."

Ma Sterling's voice rose. "Don't you think I can tell honest money? This here's a risk. I'll take it for the strap, but I won't give you change."

"Why don't you leave it?" Martin asked the man.

He turned his gray eyes and said, as if he had repeated it a dozen times already, "A strap ain't worth but six cents."

The men grinned delightedly. They were looking for trouble. They looked to Martin like a band of boys badgering a stranded snapping turtle.

"Listen," he said. "This man's all right. I know him. His name's Ledyard. He's moving for Ohio."

Ledyard's eyes brightened and for an instant the blood came into his face. Then he looked doubtful. His voice was strained. "I never saw you before."

"That's right, too," Martin said heartily. "I'm Gregson's nephew, that bought your farm in Montgomery County." He looked the man straight in the eye. "Mrs. Ledyard knows me. I've pulled her out and brought her along."

Ledyard swallowed with a dry crackling noise.

"That's right, I guess. Gregson said he had a teamster for a nephew."

"Listen," said Martin. "I'll put my shillin' down for his. How about it, Ma?"

"All right."

But the man Garland moved over quickly to block the passage.

"It's a funny thing, but I don't ever remember your telling me you had an uncle, Martin."

One of the girls giggled. Martin's face became frozen. "I guess there *is* one or two things I have n't told you, Garland."

He was standing quite still, his hands at his waist, his eyes measuring distances. He balanced on the toes of his boots. He saw that they had set their minds on roughing the stranger up and having a look at his purse. He grinned a little at himself for having developed this concern. It was a new thing for him.

Garland was saying with a kind of apology in his voice, "We don't want no argument with you, Martin. We 're feeling peaceable. Only we was going to give this counterfeiter a lesson. We said he could have his honest change if he could lick any one of us. Himself making choice. And he was just a-going to do that when you horned in." He laughed a little. "We got to protect Ma, here."

Ma Sterling snorted.

"I can look after myself. If it was n't for all you dumb bezabors I 'd have cracked his head by this time."

Martin said, "Pick up your shillin', Ledyard."

The man obeyed, and Ma was too surprised to stop him.

Martin had made up his mind. He could n't talk the man out. He would have to give him an opening, and then stand off the rush. Once the Ledyards got their wagon rolling, they would be all right. If he did n't take his chance, God help him.

He gave one last glance round the room, and he saw seated on the corner bench two men who were strange to him. One was a fat man with small piggish eyes and a simple mouth. But the other held his attention. He was the shortest man Martin had ever seen, scarcely five feet, with enormous broad hands. One eye was looking straight at Martin, but the other pointed aimlessly to the right. He had a flat nose, and as he crouched on the bench his flat mouth was grinning lewdly, like a frog's. His off eye winked deliberately as his good eye met Martin's. He understood what Martin wanted — to shift the attention of the room from himself. Unexpectedly he did it.

"My God, Plute! The cobbler 's swallowing his nails."

At the suggestion the cobbler jumped and gulped and choked. The fat man sprang up and rushed over to him and began thumping him prodigious whacks so that the cobbler had to lean over. His mouth opened and he began coughing tacks all over the floor. But in the moment that the others turned, Martin's hands wrenched at the coils of his whip. They slid in a circle round his feet and he leaped out of them.

"Get over, Garland!"

The tall man was caught off guard. He looked and then backed along the bar.

"Get out of here, you blasted fool!" Martin shouted at Ledyard; and Ledyard, with one look, bolted past him.

Martin jumped into the passage. It was close quarters, but the empty passage gave him lash room behind. Ledyard's feet were pounding through the kitchen; the outer door slammed. The men roared. It did not matter whom they went after — they wanted a brawl, and they had an excuse now. Martin braced himself.

But, before the men could get moving, the squat little frog-faced man had jumped beside him and his fat companion had left the stuttering cobbler. Mother Sterling opened her mouth to screech.

"He's left without paying. The water-livered punk."

"Now, now, lady," said the little man. "Don't give other folks your own diseases." He stamped his feet. "If there's going to be a mix-up," he said, "I like to mix in on the interesting side." He looked at Martin, his loose eye conveniently aimed. "I calculate I can stir pretty good, don't you, boy?"

Martin grinned back.

And then, as the others gathered behind Garland, the kitchen door opened behind Martin, and Ruth Havens stepped quietly into the room, holding his musket in her hands.

In the silence, Martin swore furiously.

"Didn't I tell you to stay out?"

She met his eyes imperturbably.

But the fat man snatched the musket.

"Give me that gun, girl. We don't want no actual murder."

He tossed up the musket and pointed it down the bar. Mother Sterling screeched piercingly.

"You be good boys," he said. "Go back and set down."

As they backed off, the little man said, "Plute'll watch them. Don't let 'em bust the lantern on you, Plute. We'll all hitch and move to-night."

"That's best," Martin nodded. "Can Plute hold them?"

"He can hold everything but three-X Ohio white-eye. And he can hold a man's share of that, too."

Plute said, "Any man that wants to feel this popper go off can just lay hold of its mouth end."

The girl and the two men filed out to the shed.

"The movers have cleared out," Martin said.

The little man chuckled.

"I reckon he'll beat the sun into Pittsburgh."

He turned to Ruth.

"You're quite a card, missy, butting in. But you sure meant good."

Martin was busy slinging harness on his horses. "Ruth," he said, "pick up the blankets."

"Yes, George." But she asked the little man over her shoulder as she bent, "What's your name, mister?"

From the other end of the shed, the little man answered, "Me, I'm Cosmo Turbe."

Martin led his team out and hooked up. In five minutes they were ready. Cosmo Turbe was running back and forth along his team, linking the traces.

"Good Lord," said Martin. "He's a mule driver!"

"Yes," said Cosmo Turbe's hoarse voice, "I skin mules. If a mule acts up, a little man like I am has got a chancet to bite his ear. Now you get going, boy, and then I'll holler for Plute."

Martin lifted the girl onto his wagon. The bells took up their slow march in the rain, the kingbolt squeaked as the wagon turned, and the wheels rolled heavily out of the muddy yard.

Behind them Cosmo yelled like a trapped panther. A moment later a dull report beat against the rain. Turmoil broke loose in the tavern; but after a space they heard Plute's laughing voice behind them.

Ruth said softly, "They're a funny pair."

Again, after a while, she called down to him, "George."

He did not answer. The rain was cold on him again.

"Mister Martin," she said timidly.

"Yes."

"You ain't mad with me?"

Behind them a roaring voice began to sing: —

> "The bachelor's a hobnail,
>   He rusts for want of use, sir;
>   The misers, they're no nails at all,
>   They're just a pack of screws, sir.
>   The Britishers will get some clouts
>   If here they chance to roam, sir,
>   For Yankee lads like hammers will
>   Be sure to drive them home, sir."

"You're a nice girl, Ruth."

"Thank you." Her voice was light. She watched his shape striding on in the rain.

It was beginning to slacken. There was a bite preceding morning in the air. The wind was turning to the northwest — clearing weather. They crossed a small stream and the bridge timbers rumbled hollowly. After a moment they heard Cosmo's wheels passing it in their wake.

Martin cocked his head.

"Those mules move smart."

"What are you thinking now?"

"Didn't I say?"

She smiled at his irascibility.

"Before."

"I was wondering if that canal would be actual fact. It'll kill freight wagoning. What'll I do?"

She looked out along the six broad backs. The bells were ringing clearer every minute as the rain died. Her feet seemed billowed in a sound of silver.

"Those horses could break prairie sod," she said suggestively.

"If it's actual." He seemed to be talking to himself.

She let him walk in his own thoughts for a way, but her lips still smiled. Behind the wagon the clouds were breaking and there was a sense of light upon the earth. She had one of his blankets wrapped round her, but her head was bare to the northwest wind, and color was coming into her hair as the light grew.

He surprised himself by saying: —

"I've got money saved up in the Canandaigua bank. Five hundred dollars. It's funny for a teamster to save money. But I'm thinking if I knew that canal was going through I'd haul my money out and roll for the Ohio River. There's hauling out there."

She said, "A man could buy him a quarter section with that and get himself a cow and raise a cabin and buy tools."

"A prairie plough costs money."

"A team like that could earn the money breaking sod for men with feeble horses."

"They're used to roading."

"They'd have their own barn. The way the man would have his house. A dry place to cool in. The way the man would come home for his dinner and find him a fire, and his glass ready, and his bread fresh in the oven."

The bells rang to the long stride of the six horses. A dog barked.

"We'll be into Deerfield Corners by sunup," Martin said.

He halted his team beside a water trough and went back for his leather bucket. While he was watering the horses, the mule team drew alongside. Plute came over to the girl and handed up the musket.

"How'd you make out, back there?" asked Martin.

The fat man chuckled.

"Easy. But say, young lady, what did you load that gun with?"

"I was n't sure whether it was loaded," she said, "so I loaded it anyway."

Plute laughed.

Martin looked at the panting mule team.

"What are you boys hauling?" he asked.

"Nails," said Cosmo Turbe. "Nails from Troy works for Utica. An order for Caleb Hammil, for canal work."

The teamster glanced up to meet the girl's eyes.

"What have you got?" asked Plute.

"Oddments for Utica," said Martin.

"Where are you hauling after?"

"Nowhere," he said. "I'm on my own for the Ohio. I think I'll take up farming."

Cosmo stared.

"A teamster in a farmer's breeching?"

"It don't come easy." Plute rubbed the back of his head. It was a new idea to him.

The girl laughed at the two of them.

"It would take gentle handling, I guess."

Cosmo wrinkled his nose.

"Do I smell a wedding, Plute?"

The fat man sniffed.

Martin said, "We'll want two witnesses."

"I can write Cosmo's name for him all right," said Plute.

"But there's a question of a sheriff. We would n't want to get you boys in trouble."

The two men looked from Martin to the girl. They caught the situation.

Then Plute rubbed his shoulder and burst out laughing.

"We ought to be able to handle most any sheriff, seems to me — the four of us."

BEWITCHED

I

FROM the moment of her arrival in the dairy she was a constant source of worry. Sanders's boy brought her over from Kruscome's; and he said that he had never known a cow drive handier along an open road. Old Sanders, who had come to take his boy home and collect the half dollar, remarked that any cow would drive easily so long as she was coming away from Kruscome.

Milking was done when she came up the road. Nelson was emptying the pails into the great cans for the cheese factory; and the herd were standing quietly in their stanchions. Nelson was a quiet man, nearly sixty years old, with mild blue eyes and tremendously broad shoulders.

He could outlast any of the young hands in a July hayfield and milk the whole herd after by himself, if it was Saturday and he had given the help permission to go to the dance. He was talking to the owner's little boy, who was sitting on a milk stool with his heels caught under him, so that his feet might not be wet when Nelson went through the exciting process of flushing the floor of the milk house.

The owner's boy was only eight years old, and he spent as much of every day as his mother allowed in tagging the old man about. He knew as much about the private life of the farm animals as a small boy could, and he was aware of his knowledge. It was fortunate that he had the serene old man for a guide.

It was he who first lifted his head to listen.

"Why are the cows so still, Nelson?"

Nelson set down the last pail gently and eased the straps of his overalls on his shoulders.

Outside the door of the milk house, in the dusk of the barn, the cattle were preternaturally still. There are two kinds of silence in a herd: the silence of rest, when each cow, eased of her milk, is weighing her own problems; and the silence they hold when, as a social organization, they are considering something that concerns them all.

Usually in a quiet barn you can hear the whisper they make over their cuds and an occasional light rasp of horn on cement as they change their feet.

The owner's boy said, "They're holding their breaths."

"They're listening," said Nelson. He took off his glasses and wiped them with a red cotton handkerchief and put them back on his nose. "I wonder what it is."

Then they both heard the light steps in the barnyard.

"I'll bet it's that cow your father bought last Monday, before he went back to New York."

He held out his hand for the owner's boy to take, and they went down the runway together, and the cows stared after them, unblinking.

Sanders's boy was looking in the door, and close beside him was the new cow. She was perfectly composed. She stood with her hoofs neatly placed. Her dark eyes were taking in her new surroundings as if she understood that she had changed her habitation.

"You stay by the door," Nelson said to the owner's boy.

He let go the boy's fingers and walked up to the cow. He looked at her in front for a moment, then stepped round to her right side and took a moment's stand there. Then he examined her from behind. His calm eyes shifted from point to point without haste, but marking every hair. He completed his circle in a minute or two, and finally stepped close to the cow to examine her with his hands.

"Know anything about her, Georgie?" he asked Sanders's boy. Georgie let his eyes wander coolly from the owner's boy, and he took a straw from his mouth, glanced at the mangled end, and said, "No."

Nelson then laid a hand smoothly along the cow's back.

"Know her name?"

"Old Kruscome called her Trixy."

Old Nelson put his hand down on her neck behind the ear and gave her a light pat.

"Looks as though that was a good name."

The cow's tail twitched.

Nelson's hand went down along her side, under her belly, felt the small bag.

"Not much of a milker."

"Here comes Pa," observed Georgie.

Sanders drove into the yard behind his flea-bitten milk horse. He was a saturnine, lantern-jawed man who got a chip off one shoulder only to find a new one on the other. He dropped the reins on the dashboard and shouted "Whoa" after the horse had stopped, and got out a chew of tobacco.

"Don't look much of a cow, that there."

Nelson said mildly, "I doubt if she's ever had a proper feed."

"Narrow-hipped," said Sanders.

"Kind of," Nelson admitted.

"I've always considered a cow that stands up on her toes that way was a rotten feeder."

"Well, that don't need to bother you, Sanders."

"Gosh, no."

"Know anything about her?"

"Not me. Why should I know anything about her?"

"How'd she come, Georgie?"

"Real handy," Georgie said, imitating his father's tone. "I had to wipe her off a couple of times with a piece of birch, but after that she come real handy."

"You get on this wagon, boy, or I'll wipe you with a piece of horsehide. Any cow coming from Kruscome's ought to come handy."

Nelson said nothing.

"How about that money for the boy?"

Nelson fished out his old leather sack and took a couple of quarters from it. Sanders pocketed them.

"Did W. D. have any notion why he bought her?"

Nelson came near to smiling.

"He said he did n't know. He was up at Kruscome's buying some broilers and he said he saw this cow and she looked so nice alongside of Kruscome he did n't want to leave her there."

Sanders gave a short bark.

"It takes money to make a whole fool of a man."

The owner's boy raised indignant eyes.

"I think she is pretty."

Sanders looked down at him with hard eyes.

"I allow it, boy. It 's nice to have pretty things, too."

He laughed again, yanked round his horse, and gave it the whip. The owner's boy watched him with hot eyes.

"She *is* pretty, Nelson, is n't she?"

"Yes," said Nelson, "she is pretty."

He muttered to himself, "She 's the prettiest cow."

"Come along," he said aloud again. "We 'll put her in the barn to-night, till she gets used to the place."

The cow turned her face to him as if she understood. They had no trouble in putting her in her stanchion.

It was only then that the owner's boy noticed that the herd were still preserving their extraordinary silence. They were all looking at the newcomer, but, among those that could not see, something like whispering began to pass. The boy could hear nothing, but he was quite aware of it.

Nelson said, "They feel chancy when a new cow comes. They 'll be all right to-morrow."

But just then the bull in the box stall at the far end let out a shuddering blast, and the owner's boy scurried round to see him pushing his curled forehead against the bars and staring with hot eyes.

"Come on," said Nelson, "we 'll get the rest out."

From nowhere his little black collie materialized. It seemed to take more barking than usual to get the cattle out. They rattled the stanchions needlessly; but, once in the yard, they did not make their usual file for the night pasture. The bells fell quiet, and they stood against the closed door, listening.

"I'd better put Rustum out," said Nelson, and he took a pitchfork and entered the stall. He had to prick the bull twice before he could get him to move, and when the bull was outside in his private yard he too turned and pressed against his door, grumbling to himself.

Nelson's wife came from the farmhouse.

"It's time you two was in to supper. Your ma is going to be hollering for you," she said to the boy, "and you're old enough to know better, Nelson."

"We had to put in the new cow," said Nelson softly, coming along with a box of bran and corn meal. He dumped it down before the cow, who licked it eagerly. They could hear her tongue slither over the cement.

Mrs. Nelson folded her hands under her apron and looked the cow over.

"Her name is Trixy," Nelson said.

As she stared, the old woman's wrinkled, fine face changed mysteriously.

"I don't like her."

"What's the matter with her, Melia?"

"I don't like her at all."

"She's pretty, ain't she?"

"Yes, she's pretty, all right."

"She handles kind."

"I don't like her. Look at that mark on her forehead."

"I saw it," Nelson said.

The cow was nearly black, except for white stockings from her knees down and three white hoofs and the mark on her forehead. The owner's boy had seen it first thing. He thought it lovely. It was a triangle of white; not solid white, but merely the outline of a triangle, as if a finger had drawn it there. Only the upper left corner had a gap, half an inch wide, where the dye had given out.

"I never saw a cow marked that way," said Mrs. Nelson.

"Me neither," said Nelson. "But I don't see anything wrong with it."

"Me neither," said the owner's boy.

With a sense of defiance he stepped up to the cow's side and put his hand on her flank. She had a beautiful, smooth coat; she was lightly and beautifully made; her horns were white and curved more like an Ayrshire's than a Holstein's; her eyes had long lashes, and her face was finely chiseled; above all things, she was feminine.

"Dainty," said Mrs. Nelson with a little sniff.

"She is."

"Get rid of her, then."

"She's not my cow."

"You can make W. D. do anything you want."

Nelson smiled reassuringly to the owner's boy, who was still stroking the cow, but looking from one to the other of the old people with harassed eyes.

The smile comforted him, and he said, "When Father comes back I'm going to ask him to let me have it for my own cow."

"No," said Mrs. Nelson.

"Why not?" Nelson asked.

"I don't like her. Look at that black hoof."

Her right hind hoof, surprisingly, was black, though the stocking was white.

"I never saw such a chancy old woman as you, Melia."

"Nor I," said the owner's boy.

The old woman took her hands from under her apron and said, "Well, come to supper, anyways."

"We'll leave her to-night," Nelson said. "By to-morrow the rest will be used to her."

They went to the door, the cow looking after them with softly lambent eyes.

The door closed with a thunder of trolleys.

It was dusk outside now. The boy ran out of the barnyard and across the bridge of the brook to the big house. His feet thumped dully on the dewy lawn, and he banged up on the verandah. His mother, in a white dress, came to the screen door.

"It's past supper time," she said quietly.

"I know, Mother. I'm sorry. Nelson and I were fixing the new cow. Did you see her, Mother?"

His mother smiled.

"Yes, I saw her go by."

"Didn't you think she was a beautiful cow?"

"I didn't see her very well, but she looked pretty."

"She was beautiful, Mother."

His mother smiled quietly.

2

Nelson was mistaken.

The herd would not accept Kruscome's Trixy. Nelson said that he had seen it happen before, but that generally there was some apparent reason for the policy. In Trixy's case he could discover no legitimate cause. But the cows would have none of her. They did not actively persecute her, but if she came too close to a group of them they would turn her off with a sharp butt or two.

At first old Sibyl, who had read the leaves for the herd for four generations, followed her round with pink-nosed, obvious sarcasm. Her big bag shook as she imitated mincingly the other's walk. She would stand side by side with Trixy, her blunt muzzle stretched out in reverie, and all the cows would look on and chortle.

On the third day, as they drank side by side at the edge of the brook, Trixy whirled, and her pointed horn laid open one side of the red cow's neck. It was enough. The old cow never bothered her after that; but a kind of shudder passed through the herd, and Nelson said they would never allow her to join them now, and Mrs. Nelson said she did not blame them.

In a way it made no difference to the new cow. She had a natural aloofness. By nature she was solitary, not given to the gossiping that delights the heart of an ordinary cow. One of the men said that she acted as if there were something on her mind.

One of the Irish maids from the big house, who was carrying on a flirtation with the man, said that she acted like a woman in love. A guffaw passed along the milkers, until old Nelson, even-eyed, came walking by with the owner's boy.

The owner's boy picked up these pieces of opinion and tried to fit them to the cow. She was friendly with him, and, though Nelson had warned him against it, he sneaked away from time to time to the day pasture to visit her.

He went in the three o'clock heat, the drowsing time of day, when the herd retired to the woods and a passer-by might hear only one bell clink in half an hour. He would find the herd easily enough, but it took him three afternoons to find the new cow.

She was standing in a tiny glade beside a spring. The hillock that surrounded it on three sides was semicircular, clustered thick with hemlocks which darkened the water of the spring, and though the rise of ground was only eight or ten feet high, it screened the cow perfectly.

Trixy was standing quite still, knee-deep in the soft woods grass, and her ears were pointed and her eyes filmed. She heard the feet of the owner's boy squelching through the mud, and she turned her head deliberately. But when he was close beside her she was once more mooning.

He sat down beside her front hoofs, and she lowered her head and covered his face with a sweet, grassy breathing. He wanted to say something. He felt like crying. But there were no words for him to give her. His throat closed. He wanted to take her head in his arms. He wanted to stroke the satiny throat. But he could say nothing.

Yet when the words urged their way into his throat the cow dropped her head still lower, and he saw her eyes luminous and pained. He did not understand, neither himself nor her. But somehow he managed to become aware of her understanding. In a minute she was rubbing his shoulder gently with her horn.

At the touch all the strength went out of him. There was no sound in all the woods, no breath of wind. The beech leaves that showed over the tops of the hemlocks hung relaxed and pendulous from their twigs. The hemlock needles glistened like burnished metal.

Dim beyond them they heard the drowse of bees in a tree. Only the water made a gurgling note over a red hemlock root as it issued from the grass, and a great pileated woodpecker passed over them and lit on a dead birch downstream.

They did not stir all afternoon, not till they heard the dog barking round the herd, counting out their names. In a moment they heard him snuffling Trixy's track, and then he had slid up to them, and Trixy laid her head down to his and they talked.

His tongue stopped lolling and he turned to the owner's boy. In a moment they all three drank from the spring: Trixy touched the boy's neck with her wet muzzle, and the touch set him shivering; and then she drifted away, and the dog with gently waving tail went after her.

After a while the boy heard the man whistling in the woods close by, and the dog's bark far down the spring and the crash Trixy made in the underbrush, and he heard the man swear to himself and say, "So that's where she hides out. We'll have to put a bell on her." And his lumbering feet went away.

The boy came home when the milking was done.

He stole into the dark runway between the empty stanchions. There is no place in the world more still and lonely than a cattle barn without its herd. As the boy stood there he was aware of the small stirrings of the outliers: the rustle of ducking mice; the distant mew of kittens high up in the hay overhead; the patter of a rat's feet; a cricket, taken in with the last hay, chirping to himself upon a beam.

The bull was outside in his pen staring at the moon, and the moon lacked a day of being full. It was the red moon of October, that rises before the leaves turn, large and hot and slow until the first frost plates it with silver. The dew was falling outside and it was cool.

The boy went down the runway slowly on tiptoe. In the horse stable at the far end he heard Nelson's voice, talking with the teamster. Through the closed door the words sounded soft but distinct. The boy stopped to hear. The drowsy smell of hay lay upon the stillness.

"I wish W. D. was back."

"He's coming back day after to-morrow," said the teamster, Eugene.

"I know. But Trixy's found her time, and she's nearly dry."

"Might as well serve her," said Eugene with something like a snicker. "Rustum's got his eye on her anyway."

"She won't be much of a milker, I doubt," Nelson went on, ignoring the remark. "But he had such a notion for that cow he may want her coming in in spring."

"Well, she ought to hold over all right for two days."

"She ought," said Nelson. "But I'd like to know now."

"Ask the Mrs., then."

"She's a lady," Nelson said. "I can't talk breeding to her."

The owner's boy heard the swish of his fork gathering up hay and the tap of the measure in Eugene's hand as they finished feeding the horses. He slipped out of the barn.

He was excited. Dark had come with the moon, and the yard was mysterious. Up the hill toward the night pasture the notes of bells sounded silvery and clear. Moon shadows were being born; and the moon streaked the ash posts and maple poles of the bull pen, and the shadows of them striped the spotted hide of Rustum.

The bull was standing quite still, muzzle raised to drink the night air and pointed to the sound of bells. He was making a kind of restless moan to himself, half defiant, half fearful. His curled forehead was a white patch in the darkness, his burning eyes red coals. His massive bulk loomed above the boy peering through the bars; he stood on crooked knees, straight-backed, broad-shouldered, lowering. The boy understood these things.

He heard Nelson coming into the cattle barn.

"I guess to-morrow I'll keep that cow inside at night. She's a wild thing, pretty as she is."

The two men came out to lean over the edge of the pen on the far side from the boy.

"He's hankering for her," Eugene said.

"Yes. He's got an unease to-night. He ain't set hard the way he ought. He looks half scared. Once before I seen a bull act that way. It's queer."

"He is a handsome animal, Nelson."

"He is." Nelson's voice was quietly proud. "He'll build the herd up. Let's see. We've had five calves dropped from his serve. Four of them was heifers."

The owner's boy slipped away.

He, too, felt the unease.

He ate supper with his mother and brother and sister.

"Where were you this afternoon?" his mother asked him.

"Out in the woods," he mumbled.

His brother, two years older than he, said, "I thought you were scared of the woods."

"I'm not," he said indignantly. "I never was."

"Father's coming up day after to-morrow."

"I'm glad. Nelson wants to ask him about Trixy."

"What are you thinking about that cow all the time for?" asked his brother.

"I'm not. I just heard Nelson say so."

But his face looked flushed and secret, and he turned his eyes from his mother's.

3

That night the moon was caught by the frost. The boy woke up hours later and listened. The brook was running with a small, brittle sound. A bar of the moonlight, like a tooth, was eating the blackness of the room. It silvered the underspread and cast a shadow in the fork his legs made under the blankets. He was hot and tense. But the night was still.

Then he heard the bull moaning very softly in his pen beside the barn wall; and he slipped out of bed and stepped across the moon-light to the window on the other side of the room and knelt there. His small face was white in the darkness, his eyes black and big.

Then he heard it.

Far away beyond the hill a cow lowed, not the low of a cow for her calf, but the almost human call a cow gives when her time is found. The sound of it came across the frost-white stubble below the hills, and the night about the buildings was made vibrant. It was not loud, but it was clear, and it carried far. The bull had heard it also, for he had fallen silent.

For a long time the boy knelt there; and then at last, so far away that for an instant he was uncertain, he heard the call of a bull. It came from high up, from above the hills northward, as if the cry had been loosed on a mountain beyond the darkness. The boy caught his breath.

Beside the barn the bull, Rustum, roared. Blast after blast echoed against the barn wall, and they went roaring off above the valley, harsh, blatant, terrible.

The farm awoke.

The boy saw a light bloom in Nelson's window in the farm-house, and a moment later the old man, carrying a lantern, walked across to the bull pen. After him came the two hands. The boy heard them crying to the bull, finally driving him into the barn, where his bellows were shut in. The men went in with him to leave him a lantern until his noise was hushed. The boy listened awhile, but could hear nothing more.

Slipper taps came down the hall to his room, and he slid back to bed and lay still when his mother entered carrying a candle, her eyes uneasy in the soft light.

She looked down on him awhile, drew up another blanket part way, and went on with her round to his brother's room, his sister's, and finally back to her own bed.

Before breakfast the boy ran out to the barn. Eugene was feeding the horses, Nelson caring for the milk, the third hand treading behind the music of the cowbells for the pasture. But the cows were walking with lowered heads, and the dog trotted listlessly behind them.

It was a hot morning for October; and the early sun was drinking mist from the brook, and on the hill a maple showed the first flush of crimson.

He slipped into the barn and saw Trixy in her stanchion. She was quite placid. She stood easily, her tail barely twitching as she chewed her cud rhythmically, slowly; but now and then her jaw stopped, and she appeared to listen.

The boy watched her awhile; then he noticed that when she listened Rustum, the bull, raised his nose from his manger and listened also, with his hide twitching at the spot where his neck was wedged into his thick shoulders.

He went over to the cow and laid his hand against her side. She turned her head and regarded him out of dark eyes, and all at once the owner's boy thought she was trying to tell him something, and he pressed himself against her and waited. When his body touched her she seemed to stiffen and hold her breath, and the bull blew suddenly through his nostrils.

Nelson came down the runway carrying a cluster of pails.

"Good morning, Nelson. What's the matter with Trixy?"

"I'm keeping her in to-day and to-night. I want to have your pa see her."

The boy did not answer, but he found the cow looking at him again.

That day he hung around the barns pretending to look for the kittens that anyone could hear from time to time in their hiding place in the hay. But he knew already where they were. It was a secret he had shared with the old tortoise-shell cat for several days. He was not interested in the kittens. Whenever he went into the cattle barn Trixy regarded him sombrely. He could see the white triangle on her forehead gleaming.

The day was still and hot. The men were digging potatoes. At four o'clock the gray team came down the hill dragging the lumber wagon piled high with sacks, and the men handed them down the steps to the farmhouse cellar.

The hand came in with the herd, and each one, as she entered, stopped to stare at the stanchioned cow. Now and then they paused by the bull pen. The hand had to thump old Sibyl several times before she would move on.

Nelson complained that the cows would not let down their milk. The heifer who had freshened a month ago wanted to see her calf. After milking they went out tentatively, and the dog was sharp to them, harrying their heels, but he made no barking.

The moon rose again at the full, a broad orange disk above the brook valley. Again the night was still.

The boy at his window saw it when it had turned white. A fleece of cloud came up to drape it.

Then he heard it, the distant crying beyond the hills. It was closer than before, but still far off. It did not have the blatancy of Rustum's roar; it was musical, and it roused no echoes. The boy shivered when he heard it, and for an instant the night seemed white before his eyes. Then he heard from the barn a low call from Trixy, and then all was still.

He was shaking all over. He could not get her eyes from his mind. She was pleading, and all at once he knew that she was calling him to help her. It seemed that he could scarcely stand when he got to his feet. He knew what she was after.

But he stole from the room in his bare feet, past his mother's open door, down the stairs close to the wall, slowly out the front door, and then he ran, with the dew cold on his feet.

He let himself into the barn and closed the door. He pressed the catch of the stanchion, and the cow was free. He was glad that she had not been belled.

He put his hand on her neck, and side by side they stole down the runway, the cow making hardly a sound. When they came to the bull pen Rustum reared up against the bars, but he was quiet.

He made no sound beyond a painful, moaning breathing, and then he dropped back and stood with hung head. The boy could not even see his eyes. But the cow never even glanced at him.

The boy lifted the hook in the cattle door and slowly pushed it aside. The cow stood still by him for a moment, her face to the night. Then without a sound she slipped through, and for a little way the boy could see her trotting in the moonlight.

He heard the cry ringing above the hills, but the cow made no answer. He left the door open and ran back to the house. Still shivering, he crept up to his room. There he stopped an instant, then stole into the bathroom, and quietly washed his feet.

Before he went to bed he stopped at his window. From time to time he still heard the soft ringing calls of the unknown bull, but now in answer he heard, each time fainter, the cow's voice answering. Stiff in his bed, he listened till the cries faded to nothing, and the moon had passed beyond his window, and the brook made the only sound in the darkness.

Nelson was worried. He asked to see the boy's mother after breakfast. He could not understand how the cow had got loose. His wife, beside him, with her hands clasped under her apron, said that she was not surprised. That cow was clever. She knew things. Nelson nodded doubtfully. It might be so.

When the boy's father arrived from the city Nelson told him the story. The boy's father said that the cow might have freed herself from the stanchion, but that someone had unlocked the door. The hand swore he had left it hooked. There was nothing to do. It was one of those things that happen on a farm.

The boy's father had a short vacation. He had the carriage horses hitched to the light buckboard and went up beyond the back pastures. He took the boy with him. They stopped at Kruscome's.

The father had a long talk with the ragged gypsyish man, who leaned against the wheel chewing an alder twig.

"I never heard no bull. Mine's been locked up two weeks. He's still there." He pointed to his calf pasture, where a small red bull grazed peaceably. "Ain't been able to find Trixy? She's got out. You got a fence down, maybe."

"I'll drive the back line before we go back."

They did a bit of crop and game gossip, while the boy watched the Leghorn rooster pursuing a fat old Spanish black.

"No, I don't know where she came from. I picked her off a lousy old feller way back on the White Lake Road. She was a dainty piece then. I liked her then. You made a good buy off me, I can tell you."

He slouched back from the wheel. The boy and the father drove behind the bays along the back line. Down by the creek, where the ground was soft, they discovered a new cedar post knocked over.

There were long horn scars in the new wood, and through the breach came a small cow's tracks, almost as pointed as a deer's.

"Those are Trixy's," said the boy.

"Probably. Look there."

All round the post stump, deep in the soft ground, were the broad, blunt hoof prints of a bull.

"He was a big one," said the father. "They look bigger than Rustum's, and he's the biggest bull around here."

They drove home in silence.

Nelson met them.

"She's off with a strange bull, Nelson. He's broken down the back-line fence. He's a monster big one."

"He must be to break that fence. We did it over last spring. I'll send Eugene up this afternoon."

"The cows don't get back that far this time of year. Leave it for a day. She might come back."

"I doubt if we'll ever see that cow again."

"I hope not," said his wife.

"Don't look so miserable," the father said to the boy.

"She was so pretty," mumbled the boy.

"Too pretty for me," Mrs. Nelson muttered.

On the morning of the second day Trixy returned. She came

walking equably into the barnyard, her sides shining with dew. The other cows looked at her and turned away. They offered no comment, but during the winter Nelson wrote to the owner in the city not one would have anything to do with her.

She had also a bad effect upon Rustum. Whenever she was near he would drop his head and stop eating. They even had difficulty at first in getting him into the barn at night. Nelson advised getting rid of the cow.

The owner wrote back that he wanted to see if she dropped a calf and what it would look like.

But Nelson continued to be worried.

4

By spring when the family returned no change had taken place in the mysterious attitude of the herd.

But the very first evening the boy went out to see Trixy. She seemed to remember him and laid down her head to be stroked. She appeared quite placid, ignoring the other cows, and going her own way. The hand said he thought she dreamed. She was always staring off somewhere.

By midsummer it was obvious that she was going to drop a calf. Her bag was forming slowly. The men agreed with Nelson that she would not be much of a milker.

During the first two months of summer, with the fishing in the brooks to occupy him, the boy saw very little of the cow. When, from time to time, he met her in the pasture, he noticed her belly was filling like the belly of any other cow.

She walked more heavily, she had lost her maidenliness; and if he thought of it at all, he wondered at the spell she had cast over him. She was still particularly gentle with him, allowing him to pet her; but even he could see that her mind was elsewhere.

Who can tell what animals see?

Trixy kept herself to herself. Even in the barn an aura seemed to play about her which no other cow dared enter. They hated her, but they left her alone. Civilization had laid its hand-print on them — the print of a man's hand. In reassuming the right of making her own choice, the new cow had lost caste. That was how the owner explained it.

Nelson shook his head. His wife openly scoffed. It went deeper than that.

The Irish maid, who had returned from the city to continue her flirtation with the farm hand, said that the cow was fey, and one night took her accordion out under the pine by the brook and made the boy a song in Gaelic about the gods; and when the boy asked what it meant she told him that she did not understand it herself.

But she still held that the fairies lived in the brook, and every night she took a spoon of cream surreptitiously and threw it into the running water. It was one of the fairies, she maintained, who had released the cow in the autumn to make her trip to the feet of the gods.

When she heard it Nelson's wife was shocked, and refused to let the maid into her house. The maid merely tossed her head and continued the flirtation with the farm hand under the kitchen windows of the farmhouse.

The story got round the river valley. People wondered. They dropped in casually at milking time to see the cow. She was showing the calf, all right; it looked like a big one. Even Kruscome came down, and, while the cow shuddered, went over her with his hands and said the calf would be a bull.

Through the hot weather of July, when the haycocks steamed with dew, Trixy came in at the end of the herd, walking carefully under her great weight, and the little black collie silently following her heels. He was easy with her, no matter how the young stock worried him.

Three weeks before her day, Nelson belled her with an old brass bell that had a low ringing note; and from the time he put it on a sense of unease stole once more over the boy. He could hear the bell at night, moving over the night pasture when the other bells were still. It had a queer quality of far-carrying. One of the men had found it near the back line, lying in a cow track, green with verdigris.

The boy went to see the cow more often, but she now ignored him.

One hot afternoon he went fishing up the brook by himself. It was a still day, and in the dry woods small sounds became great. Locusts whined unceasingly.

He was lying quite quiet, peering over a bank at a trout that scorned his bait. Sunlight dappled the gravel and he had to look hard to see the fish.

Behind him a little swamp of balsams made the air drowsy. Across the brook a bunch of sunflowers were pointing their heads westward. Far off in the dusk of the woods a thrush gave an early call. And up on a hill a partridge drummed.

The boy heard all these noises subconsciously. He was aware of the squirrel in the birch tree over him, who examined his attempts to strike the trout with a bare hook.

He was aware of the cowbells in the day pasture gathering together at the dog's barking, and he heard the long-drawn "Boss! Co', boss!" of the hand. He had three larger trout in his basket, but this particular fish had put him on his mettle, and he had been after it for half an hour. The sun was warm along his back, the earth cool under him.

He never heard the cow until she stopped and her bell gave out one note so gentle that it hummed like a bee's drowse in a columbine.

He drew back from the bank and squatted on his heels.

Trixy was standing under the sweep of a spruce branch, half in sun, half in shadow, so that her great belly did not show, and he saw only the delicate head with the shining horns and the curiously limned triangle of white upon the brow, and the dark eyes begging.

He knew she was asking him something again, and he had a vague understanding that he should do it, for it was the last thing she would demand. He shivered in the warm sun.

And then she came forward, swaying slightly, until she stood almost over him, and her eyes were feverish.

Slowly she lowered her head until the bell strap rubbed against his hand; and then she was still.

"What is it?"

But she did not move.

Even he could tell that her time was very close. He wondered what she wanted. Her eyes were filled with a secret gleam.

Finally he undid the bell strap.

The bell fell on the ground with one dead clank. Her nose touched his hand, and she wheeled and disappeared.

Still shivering, he gathered up the basket and rod. The dog came out of the woods and stopped to drink beside the stream. He looked at the boy, his muzzle dribbling water, snuffed once at the cow's tracks, and slid off, a black shadow, after the sound of the herd's bells.

Nelson said in the barn, when the hand told him Trixy had not shown up, "She 's stole off."

In the evening the three men and the owner, who was up from the city, went off to hunt her. They came back after dark, the owner out of temper with Nelson for not having been more heedful, the men grumbling that the cow was n't worth a tobacco squirt anyway.

The next day it rained, and the men took up the search in earnest. The boy went with them. He had an idea that he might find the cow. He took his place on the outside of the line, and the men went calling through the woods.

The rain sifted down through the leaves like mist; there was a persistent dripping. The woods smelled warm.

The boy struck off by himself and heard the searchers going on. He followed up the spring to the little glade, and when he came to the dead birch the pileated woodpecker was sitting still on a branch and staring. He heard the searchers calling his name, but he did not answer.

Ahead of him, knee-deep in the bright, green grass, was Trixy.

Her eyes were dull and she was moaning softly as she raised her head to look at him. The wet made drops on her horns, and the hair under them was curled tight. Her bag looked big and hard to bursting. She recognized him and dropped her head again to the grass at her feet. Then she got down on her knees and slowly lay down.

The boy stole forward.

Wet and glistening beside her lay two calves. They were great-kneed creatures, and, newborn as they were, they showed their high, broad shoulders and their sloping quarters and arched loins. And their coats were close, and on neither of them anywhere was so much as a single black hair. Even their hoofs were white as polished ivory.

Staring down at them, the boy was reminded of the picture of a bull he had seen in his mythology book at school, and he saw another thing, that these two calves were dead. He knelt there shuddering. The cow looked at him once and laid her neck along the ground and closed her eyes.

The dog slid out of the hemlocks and stopped. Then he pointed his nose at the rain and howled. Then all the woods were still but for the drip of spent drops, until the men all came and gathered round the boy, looking down. And when at last Nelson leaned over the cow she too was dead.

The hand, who was a Catholic, crossed himself.

BLIND EVE

I

At the blast of a horn, Perry Joslin came out of his house and looked away down the canal. That way was south. The evening sun still showed over the western lip of the gorge, sending the shadows of the hills to his very feet; but he himself stood in the light of the sun.

Canallers said that Perry was the craziest lock-tender in the Kill Gorge. All lock-tenders were crazy. A man had to be crazy or religious to stand the winds that went down the valley in the early spring or the late fall. And where Perry's lock was, the canal was turning the shoulder of a hill, halfway up from the Lansing Kill; and Perry's shanty stood outside the lock on a spot that made it seem to overhang the valley, and he could see from his window the whole curve of the canal to the next hill, and hear the top leaves of the big elms in the valley rustling underneath the sill. It was a wild, lonely place in the late sixties, when only the mules and the boats and the boaters went up and down the ever-lasting locks — with the shadows of the clouds.

The plank road followed the canal, but in this place it was high above, hidden by trees, and when a wagon did go past, Perry could not see it. It came with a rumble of wheels like thunder; and on a still day even the sound was swallowed by the echoes. In his first years there Perry had been used to look up for a sight of the wagon; but by this time his ears seemed to have lost the trick of hearing.

He did look crazy, standing there, tall and gawky as a heron, with his red undershirt flashing in the sunlight and his floppy hat shading the white hair that blew upon his shoulders.

His hands were chapped with the cold winds of March, and his thin face was red. The wind brought water to his pale eyes. He had fine small features; but they were weak, as if good blood somewhere in his forbears dared show itself only in a surreptitious fashion.

But the sound of the horn from southward had wakened gladness in his small face. He shaded his eyes and peered for the boat. He could just make it out in the shadow of the far end of the curve. It was the first boat coming upstream.

The canal had been opened for three days; but so far trade was slack, and the only traffic had been down. Perry used to say that for him the spring did not really come until he saw the first boat rising from the south.

The feeling of spring had not yet entered the gorge. What wind it had still came from the north; and the snow showed under the hemlocks on the upper part of the hills and along the Lansing Kill in the valley bottom. The Kill had not yet reached high-water mark; nor had it shown the thick brown turbulence of meadows laid bare at the head of the gorge. It flowed sullenly, its roar still hushed by snow banks, a yellow untossed stream.

The boat was coming on at a crawl, the horses bent low over crooked knees. The towpath was slushy underfoot; there had not been teams enough yet to churn through the frozen mud. The driver leaned into the wind, his heavy boots slipping, his hands in his pockets, and the long whip under his arm trailing its lash behind him.

Perry moved leisurely to the upper gates and closed them. The lock was at high level — he had filled it again, against regulations, hoping that at last a boat might come up from the south and put him in the wrong. If he took a chance of wasting a lockful the boat might come, he thought, and he had been right. But he had time enough to bring the level down before the laboring team could reach the gates.

He heaved up the sluice lever in the nearest gate and watched the water boiling out with a yellow froth. Then he went across the plank and opened the other. The water went down quickly, revealing inch by inch the blocks of which the walls were built. Wet moss and green slime grew in the cracks between and trailed water down with sleepy echoes in the pit of the lock.

The sound of the overflow stopped. Gazing over, Perry watched his reflection sinking until at last it was broken into bits in the nearest whirlpool and sucked out through the sluice. He often wondered where it went to, away down south to the Erie perhaps, to Utica, to Albany; from what he had heard it might ride all the way to New York City and the ocean. People bathing in June, on the beaches canallers had told him of, might see it rocking on the ocean waves. It never went north.

He threw his weight on the balance beam and marched it round to open the gate, and closed the sluice. He recrossed the lock to the other gate and opened it. When he looked up then, he saw the team close upon him, stretched against the boat's weight by the taut line. He could hear them panting as they scrabbled up the slope to the head of the lock.

The driver cried, "Hello, Perry! How be you this year?"

Perry smiled. "Good, good. How be you?"

"Are we the first boat up?"

"Yes."

"I thought we was."

He held out his hand and shook.

"You'd ought to wear mittens," he said.

Perry looked down at the cracks over his knuckles.

"Maybe I'd ought to," he admitted.

The team seemed to hang on their legs, racked by their panting. Their heads dropped. One showed a new sore coming under his collar.

"They're soft yet," said the driver, as Perry stroked them. "It's hard hauling. How's your lock? We had to drag it over mud on Five, below here."

"I guess it's all right. I been stirring it up and the mud's about gone."

The driver spat. He was a tough-built Irishman who thought Perry was soft-hearted as well as soft-headed.

"Well," he said, "the brutes ought to be grateful to you."

The boat came sliding in on its own slow momentum. The boater steered it through without lifting a splinter. Esau Brown was a rank hand at steering a boat. If there were any scars on the *Young Lion,* they were put on by other boaters shaving it. He was a little man with a sheepskin jacket on and skin breeches, and he wore a cap with the ear muffles down. You could see only his red nose till he tilted his head back and showed you two burning black eyes under the visor. He and his driver, John, made the toughest boat to fight with on the Black River Canal.

"Tie her by," he said to John, and jumped on the edge of the lock the minute the boat's deck reached the level. "How are you, Perry?" He shook hands. "Come aboard," he invited. "The Missus wants for you to have a cup of tea."

Perry looked up the canal doubtfully and then down. "No one's in back of me," said Esau; "and if anybody comes along, why me and John will swill them through. Come in."

"I'm glad to see you," said Perry slowly, in reply to the greeting; "real glad. Thanks."

2

The *Young Lion* was an old bullhead boat painted a yellow green. The very color of it suggested the first turn of the leaves into green. It made Perry's thin nose almost snuff for grass. John had put the gang out and tied-by to the snubbing posts above the lock. He was throwing blankets over the horses — they were glad of a rest.

Perry had to bend his long body nearly double going down the cramped steps through the door into the bright warmth of the cabin. Missus Brown was sitting on a rocker in front of the stove, of which she had opened all four leaves of the oven door. Perry looked round him appreciatively. He wished his house had pretty yellow curtains.

Missus Brown was a big woman, fat and blowzy, with stringy dust-colored hair and a broad red face.

" 'Ullo, Perry!" She held out a hand which had a mammoth emerald ring on it; the peddler had said it was emerald.

Perry took his hat off.

"Hello, Missus Brown!"

" 'Ow are you vis spring?"

"Fine," he said.

Missus Brown had come over from London, England, as a lady's maid. There was a charitable lady in Utica who went abroad every few years and brought back servants with her. When they got to Utica they decided six dollars a month and an unheated attic room were not so comfortable as joining on with Lucy Cashdollar, who ran the Agency for Bachellor Boaters in Bentley's Bar. Celia had struck on with Esau and now she was married.

"I 'm reel sorry, Perry, to 'ear 'ow your muvver is dead."

Perry pressed his hat between his hands and looked round and round above the heads of the three boaters.

"It makes me sad," he said.

"Well," said the lady, "there 's the pot boiling. Esau, 'and it to me. Drink some tea, Perry?"

"No, thanks."

"Just a little warm wet," she coaxed him. He consented. They all had it and a cruller apiece, the men drinking gulpily and Missus Brown sipping from her saucer in the proper way. She took plenty of brown sugar, keeping a little supply on the edge of the saucer and washing the tea up against it. She smacked her lips gently.

"Well," said Missus Brown, " 'ere we are again. Every week, abaht, I says to Esau, won't it be good, I says, to get back up the Kill Gorge and 'ave a wet of tea wiv Perry? 'E 's such a nice man. It always seems we 're boating again when we 'ave a wet of tea wiv Perry. Ain't it a fact, Esau?"

She poured a second cup.

"How many years have you been here, Perry?" Esau asked.

"Ten years, odd. I come here five years after the canal was open." He looked round him again with his restless vague gaze.

"It's lonely. The old lady must've been a trile to you, Perry. But you must miss 'er."

He did. He could think once how glad he would be to have her go away. She had adopted him. She had been trailing gypsies and had come down off the plank road one day and called herself his mother and adopted him, house and lock and wages. She took the last for monthly trips to Westernville to drink it up. She used to beat Perry sometimes. Now he missed her. She had died in the middle of February. He still owed eighty-five cents for the headstone.

"You ought to get married, Perry," said Missus Brown. "That's what you ought."

Married — he ought to get married, that's what he ought. Perry did not know how to go about it; but he wondered if it was true as he watched the *Young Lion* hauling north into the dusk. He did not care about it very much.

He was a queer fellow; everyone said so. "There's Perry," a boater would say. "He's the queerest coot on the whole canawl." And Perry would nod his head and say, "That's right, I guess." And lock them through. He did not know what it would be like to be in love. People talked about it. Would it be like Missus Brown? He had seen a shanty-boat once hauled by a rusty mule, and an old man on the deck kissing a young girl. The man had a beard as white as Perry's hair, and the girl had loose brown eyes.

He did not know what it was to be loved. He had just come upon himself in the world. He voted the ticket of the party in at Albany each fall and drew his pay from the pay wagon every month but one, which went for the party's war chest. At least no lock-tender ever saw the pay wagon in October. They did not ask.

Perry's neighbor, a wild Irishman, had asked and lost his job. He had licked the tar out of the pay wagon the next time it came. He had drunk for a day waiting for it, and he had jumped on and taken off the guns and thrown them in the lock, and thrown the men in too when he had done some things to them, and taken the harness off the horses and thrown rocks at them till they ran away clean crazy, and then he had spent an hour with an axe taking the wagon to pieces. Perry lived alone and did as he was told. He always had. He had no mother, no father. He was just in the world, appearing with his white hair out of nowhere, like a thistle seed in August. He could not even say that he had been born. He did not know. He was queer.

The queerest thing about him was that he could read. He did not understand that either. He liked reading. A minister had given him a Bible and he had *The Old Curiosity Shop*. He read that book over and over.

3

He got him his supper alone. No more boats had passed, but he did not feel lonely any more. When the Browns went up it meant that spring had come, for him.

He baked himself some beans and sat by the window eating them off a plate he held in his hand close under his chin. The stove purred and ticked with the dry wood. The lantern hung from the ceiling put the shadows in the corners. Now and then he would glance up at a picture, on the wall, of a lady in long gloves. It was in bright colors — purple, pink, and green. He had seen it in the leaf of a lady's book and cut it out. It was the most beautiful woman he had ever looked at. She was young, with a clean, hard, cold face.

That was all the decoration he had. And he had put that up only after the woman who had called herself his mother had died. She would have torn it off.

He had three chairs and a table and a bunk in the corner which the state had built in for him. He used to sleep in the loft room. But now his blankets were there on the straw he begged from boaters. . . .

Perry looked out of the window. The sun was gone. All the cup of the valley was full of darkness. It was still. So still that he got up at last and went outdoors.

The wind had died with the sun. It was warm. Warm, moist stars had appeared in the black sky. It would not freeze to-night. Even as he stood there he heard the tinkle of water running into the rain barrel. A cloud was coming out of the south and drops were falling. The note of the overflow round the lock, falling down the wooden stairs, was thick and soft.

He stood breathing great breaths until he felt the wet seeping through on his shoulders. Then he went inside again. He stretched himself on his bunk and took the Bible in his hand. He could not read. He could only think of Missus Brown; she had said he ought to get married.

The rain drove harder and harder against the shanty walls. It was washing the cold out of the air. Rolling and rolling. Spring was coming for a fact, even up the gorge.

4

Perry had the weather warm through the opening two weeks in April. He went about his work with a kind of joyousness, swinging back and forth across his lock and throwing off talk like any happy man. But odd moments by himself found him moody. It was nicer without the old woman round the shanty; but it was lonely, too. He kept thinking of Missus Brown's advice, that he ought to get married, that was what he ought.

Perry would sit by himself in the afternoon before the lock, with the clouds drifting overhead in the wet gray April skies, and watch the silent muster of the spring. The gorge was a small route for birds.

Squirrels and rabbits were tracking the last snow with crazy dancing patterns; the branches on the spruce trees lifted with the oozing out of frost; if a man got away from the roar of the Kill, he could hear a ticking in the woods, like a small clock marking time out of sight.

Perry had planted a lilac in front of his shanty when he first came there. A boater had given him a little plant out of a shipment for Carthage. It was a French lilac tree, and it bloomed a vivid purple red. Perry used to watch the buds every morning in the spring; but now he could see no change.

April closed that year with cold weather. The birds disappeared — no more were going north.

The men on the pay wagon the last day of the month had themselves wrapped up. They stopped in on Perry for a cup of tea; and they told him the canal would shut down for three days in the next two weeks while a culvert below the Five Combines was patched and new planking was put into the aqueduct at Stringer Brook.

"You might as well take the time off for your sparking," said the bigger one, which made the little one laugh.

Two weeks — that would make it fall on Monday. There would not be heavy traffic Sunday.

Sparking. So he would. Perry's face flushed and he went inside out of the cold and combed his long white hair. He had often wondered how it was a man could have such long white hair and no beard on his face. He darned his socks that night before the stove and thought about it.

Perry rose that Monday morning with a sparkle of excitement in his pale eyes. He had pressed his pants with the old iron the night before and greased his shoes. He had heard the water dying out of the waste weir, and this morning when he stepped outside it had the barest trickle tinkling down.

But Perry did not stop to look. The sky was deep blue and filled with golden sunlight; the clouds floating so still were warm and soft. Trees at last showed color. The maples were pink and violet and the birches and the poplars yellow-green.

Perry stood still on the end of his long morning shadow. He had a little leather-back satchel full of food, bread, cheese, tea, and a tart a boater's cook had given him the day before. His pants looked clean and his boots were soft with grease. He wore a blue flannel shirt under his old black coat with the swallow-fork lapels. With a deep breath he set out upon his sparking.

He had not thought of where he was to go; but he took the path down into the Kill. There was a footbridge there and a trail that led up onto Potato Hill. Before he looked round he would get up on Potato Hill and get a good look at all the world. That was the idea.

He walked with long easy strides.

All the spring had come at once. Pin-point blades of grass had pierced the old sod with green. Wild onion was flung in banners through the woods. There were pools still at the boles of trees, full cups in the root fingers, that showed blue at one's feet, and a man could search the limits of the sky by looking down. Perry went down to the Kill and stepped out on the bridge. The muddy water came within an inch of his feet and slopped little driblets against his boot soles. He looked down the straight wild-tossing stretch, while the roar sang in his head, and he found that he could hear the wind — the winter wind, and the sough of summer breathings, and the blasts of fall, all in the water's passage from the land.

Then he went on. The trail toiled up a slope so steep he had to use his hands to climb. The mud in the track had come up brown and thick. Ferns were unfurling, dogtooth violet leaves were stealing out. A little stream coming down gushed out suddenly from under a rock. He listened, and inside the hill face he could hear it falling.

He climbed swiftly until he was tired, and he thought he must rest when he came suddenly over the edge, and there he found the stream again falling into a hole in the ground, and a blue jay drinking at the edge of it.

It was warmer in the woods at the top of the slope, and Perry sweated with his walking. There were old trees there, and the ground was level, and far ahead he saw a color on the leaves, like snow with shadows of blue and rose, that had just fallen; and in a minute he came among the anemones. To walk over them made him feel dizzy. It was the first color of the year, and it was the purest and the sweetest.

Perry ceased to feel tired. His long legs swung him steadily on when the ground rose again, his hair swayed with his stride.

He was quite blinded when he stepped suddenly onto the shoulder of a hillock where the grass was short and showing green, and the sun came down full upon his shoulders. Over the edge of the hill he saw a house roof with a barn roof to keep it company. They rose up to his strides until he came to the barnyard and saw the road. It was a muddy track, stopping at the farm.

There was no paint on the buildings; they looked poor and ill cared for. Hens were scratching and picking in a garden patch. A black and white dog barked and fell silent. Some ducks marched round and round among the puddles slandering one another. Only a lone gray goose seemed really disturbed at his arrival. She screamed and screamed, and ran into the barn, and then looked out of the door at him and hissed. A cat was sleeping on the porch. A woman was hanging wash out. Two children in short pants played with sticks at being Indians. One was being scalped.

Perry stopped before the woman, panting slightly. She had a worn face and dull brown hair and tired eyes. Her age was what the world had made it. She said her husband was trading in Boonville, but that she had no objection to Perry's stopping in the barn to eat his luncheon.

Perry entered the barn doors and walked along the board run between the wooden stanchions to a pile of hay. It was a poor farm. He could see in the gutters the broken brakes the farmer had been using for bedding instead of straw. But the cattle were out and only the herd smell was left.

5

Perry sat on the hay and took out his lunch before he heard the girl. She was sitting in the shadow just beside him.

"Hello," said Perry.

"Hello, mister."

She spoke oddly, blurring the words in her throat so that they were hard to hear.

Perry offered her a bit of his cheese. She came out of the shadow slowly then, walking straight for him until he thought she was going to walk over him. She stopped, though, and held her hands out.

"What's your name?"

"Perry Joslin."

He put the cheese in her hands and she hunkered down like an animal in front of him. She had the most beautiful dark brown eyes Perry had ever seen and long black hair that came below her hips. She wore only a dress of faded gingham. Her bare legs were round and hard and her brown fingers quick and supple as she broke the cheese. Her mouth had red lips, moist, with a kind of wild look, but her eyes were very steady.

"What do you look like, mister?"

Perry drew back.

"Why?"

He saw then that her eyes were looking a little past him; but whenever he spoke they would turn to his lips.

She said, "I'm blind."

"Oh!"

"Can I feel you over, mister?" she asked timidly.

"Surely."

She moved forward onto her knees and he felt the balls of her fingers on his face. She was like a curious young animal — almost as if she used her nose; but when he looked for it he could not be sure. She was the most beautiful thing his eyes had ever noticed; her hair was so black, dull black, with blue shadows that moved. Her fingers were like light, quick-hovering moths. They had a faint sweet smell of earth and woods. As they touched him he could feel the coolness of the wind, the peace of grass, the tender swaying of the barley; he could smell violets by springs, the Mayflowers in the swamps; he could see the golden spots of marigolds, and old red trilliums all alone.

"What color are your eyes?"

"Blue."

"You've no beard. How old are you, mister?"

"I don't know."

"I'm seventeen."

"You're a tall, big girl for seventeen."

"Pa says I am. You're tall, too."

Her hands were shy, but had no bashfulness. Perry sat still under their touch. His heart was cool and peaceful. He felt gladness deep down almost out of touch.

"My, you've got long hair."

"Yes. But not like yours."

"No. Mine is long. Ma tells me so."

"It's beautiful hair."

He wanted to touch it.

"Is it? What color's yours? It's so fine to feel."

"Gold," said Perry.

"Pure gold?"

Perry stiffened. He had not meant to say so. But he had seen the admiration in her face. She was looking at him hard with her sightless eyes. He saw shadows there, like stirring depths. He would not unsay himself.

She was making a little pucker between her brows. "I can't remember gold."

"It's like yellow."

"Is it like buttercups?"

"A little."

"Blue eyes."

He felt so sorry for her.

"I'm glad you don't cut your hair, mister."

"Were you born blind?"

"No. I can remember seeing. I was sick."

"Oh! What do you do here?"

"I can't help ma so good, so I get the cows. I can milk. I take care of the ducks and hens. I can talk to animals and call them."

"Don't you get lost ever, going for the cows?"

"I call them."

"How do you call them?"

She made a noise through her lips. The old goose came with hurrying, web feet patting the floor.

"Like that, only that's goose talk."

The old goose came up to her and rubbed its head against her arm and looked wisely at Perry.

"What's your name?"

"Eve. Eve Winslow. They call me Blind Eve."

She looked up at him and her hand came out to touch his hair.

"Are you happy, Eve?"

"Sometimes." And her lips said to herself, though Perry could read, "Gold."

"Where are you going to, mister?" she asked after a time.

He said uneasily, "I'm sparking."

"What's that?"

"Looking for a girl to live with me."

"Oh! Where do you live?"

"I live by the canal and mind a lock. I have a house with two rooms, one above and one below."

"Have you found the girl?"

"No. I ain't yet."

"Can you hear the wind?"

"Yes. There's wind. The house stands high on the edge of the valley."

"Down there?" She pointed.

"Down there. Then up the other side."

"What's the canal?"

"It's water people go on in their boats."

"Can you hear them?"

"Yes. They blow a horn for the lock and they can't get through until I come out to let them. I let the water out below and the boat goes down and you can hear the water running."

"Oh, mister!"

Her eyes were shining.

"I'd like to live there."

"Would you?"

He told her all about the shanty; and then, as they sat in the moted air of the barn, she told him how she had always stayed on the farm. No one ever came to visit except when a child was born; it was the end of the road, with the forest just beyond. She could not talk with wild animals. It was hard sometimes talking with people. Some could not understand what she said.

From time to time in silences she touched his hair.

They shared the tart.

"Would you come and live with me?"

"Oh, yes," she said.

Perry was not conscious that the house he offered her was splendid — that he had found a poorer being than he. She was the most beautiful thing he had ever seen. He forgot that he had not gone up Potato Hill at first to take a look at all the world as he had planned.

"I 'll ask your pa."

"He 'll soon be back."

"We 'll get married."

"Like ma and pa?"

"Yes, like them."

"Ma 's told me how she got wedded in a city, with a gown and dresses. I have n't any dresses."

"I 'll bring one. Stand up."

She rose easily.

Her legs were straight, her back just curved to the proper hollow. She looked, as she stood, what Perry had never been — free. He saw then that her chin was strong and her neck round. It was like the wind to see her. He measured himself against her to know her height. She was as tall as he was, but broader in the shoulders, with hips and breast like a full-grown woman's.

He thought suddenly he ought to kiss her, and he put his arms about her shoulders. He had never kissed a girl. She was stiff at his touch. He felt her lips moist and cool and tight, and then they loosened, and suddenly she was shivering and shivering. He let go stiffly and felt cold; but the blood leaped up and sang in his ears. His voice shook; he took her hand; and they walked out like children and told her mother.

The woman was bent over her ironing board.

"Yeah. I didn't think it would happen, mister. You'll have to ask my husband. But I guess he'll be real glad."

They went out and sat on the porch.

Winslow was a short-spoken bearded fellow who was glad to see his daughter off his hands. She was no real help. But he spoke kindly of her and said she would learn to make a good wife, he made no doubt. They set the wedding time for two weeks. The mother wanted it at the house, but the father said it would cost too much to bring a preacher all the way from Boonville. It had been a bad year. And he was proud. Perry said he could come for Eve and take her to Boonville to be married.

6

He kissed her again and left her shining-eyed at the pasture bars in the dusk. As he went back to the gorge he heard the cows coming out of pasture. He did not look back. When he was in the woods he ran. He laughed to see an old buck rabbit jump and scurry ahead of him. He could hear in his ears Eve's low voice saying, "Oh, yes." His lips still felt her awkward kiss. He shouted out aloud.

He slept that night unconscious of the roaring of the Kill; he had done his sparking, done it proud; the blood sang.

He counted up his money the next morning. He saw that he must keep so much for food. He would have to buy some new blankets. Missus Brown would get them for him, he thought. He must get a license, as he had heard tell. He would have five dollars left.

Boaters coming by when the canal opened again two days later asked him where he had been.

"Sparking," he said, and they burst into laughter.

"What's she look like, Perry?"

"She's seventeen, but as tall as me."

"Cripus! A big girl! Is she pretty?"

"She's got black hair to her hips. She's the most beautiful girl you ever see."

They laughed and laughed.

"How'd you come to find her?"

"I went sparking."

"How'd she come to have you?"

"I don't know that. She said she liked my hair maybe."

They laughed again.

It made him uneasy. He gave up telling how she liked his hair. They made such a joke of it. They might tell her his hair was white, he was afraid.

But when the *Young Lion* came Missus Brown only smiled, and Esau swore he would show up, haul or no haul, to mind the lock for Perry for two days when the wedding day came round. John grinned and shook his hand, and said if he had trouble with the boaters just to let him know.

He gave Missus Brown the money for the blankets and they went in and looked at the shanty. It was bright enough outside where the state painted it salmon pink and white, but for the first time the inside disturbed his comfort. "No matter, Perry," said the woman. "She won't see. Even if she had sight she wouldn't see."

"She's the most beautifulest thing there is," he said huskily.

And standing in the door, his bow-legged shadow sprawled across the floor, Esau nodded. "Sure."

Perry saw he wasn't smiling, and looked at Missus Brown. It puzzled him to see her flushed and nervous, and her eyes shining.

Perry made time to get the license as Esau told him he should do. May slept drowsily along. The hot days of June were just coming into the gorge, and the trees and grass were rank with green. The Kill was a blue-green thread in the bottom of the valley. Horses went slowly with the boats. Men chaffed Perry for his wedding day. One brought an umbrella for a wedding gift to shield his golden hair, and it made a joke, canallers say, that went all the way to New York City.

Then at last the *Young Lion* hauled up with cement on the way to Boonville and tied by. Next morning Perry had his breakfast in the cabin and Missus Brown kissed him good-bye. Another crew, seeing him start off, began to cheer until John hopped aboard and offered to disconnect their heads.

Perry did not hear them. His thin face was bent seriously toward the ground. He felt afraid and glad. His knees did not seem to belong to him.

A hawk cut circles in the sunlight over his head and red-winged blackbirds jarred the air with song. It was warm, dusty; the land was ripe and ready for the harvests soon to come.

He came to Boonville in the afternoon and bought a suit for three dollars secondhand. He got a ring for fifty cents and strung it on a red ribbon round his neck. He took all his nerves in his dry hands and went into a dry-goods store and got a dress for two more dollars because it had a tear which a pitying saleswoman mended while he waited. He had fifty cents for the minister. He went to speak to him. The minister was a tall man, too, thin and sad. But Perry seemed to make him smile.

When it was all done Perry started out for Potato Hill. It was dark by now. The birds beside the road were twittering sleepily. Only the whippoorwills called clear and loud. He would walk onto the singing, and the bird would hush, and when he had gone a way it would break out again behind him, but he never saw the bird.

He came to the farm in the dark and stole into the barn. The goose remembered him and barely hissed from her nest under the stairs. He lay down close to it in his new clothes and slept.

When he awoke, Eve was stroking his hair. The cows had come in for milking and a row of their bony heads looked on him quietly as they switched tails and breathed softly over their cuds.

He undid his package and gave Eve her dress. She felt it all over; then ran into the house to put it on. He followed in a while. The two small boys gazed at him wonderingly and went round the house. The mother had dressed Eve. She had bound her hair with a piece of ribbon. She had no hat; and her shoes were a pair her mother had worn years before. But these she was to carry in her hand until she reached Boonville.

The mother was tearful now; but the farmer joked as they ate breakfast.

They walked away quite peacefully before the dew had risen.

7

"Forever and ever, amen."

Perry could hear the words as he and Eve walked down the tow-path with the afterglow still on the hills.

Here and there they passed a boat tied by, its lantern a firefly spot in the dusk. But the people did not see them. Only a child or two watched them pass, with big eyes. They walked hand in hand, Perry telling the road for her bare feet.

Eve said nothing. From time to time she raised the hand that had the ring to her mouth and touched it with her tongue. Her black hair swayed as she walked.

They had eaten supper out of Perry's leather-back satchel in a corner of a pasture lot, sharing the grass with an old cow and some hornets drowsy-winged with dew.

Now they were coming home.

Once she asked the color of the ring, and when he said "Gold" she put her fingers on his hair.

He saw the bow-lantern of the *Young Lion* at last.

He saw a bright light in the shanty window.

As they stood hand in hand in the door, he could smell the lilac tree in bloom.

Missus Brown was inside. There was a rocking-chair, a supper set of crockery upon the table, curtains at the window in bright blue, and a real oil lamp, wedding presents from the three.

Missus Brown said no word, but took Eve's hand and kissed her. But she looked round Eve's shoulder, and, seeing her eyes shine, Perry was made proud.

Esau and John came in laughing and took off their caps.

Perry saw then that they, too, thought that Eve was the beautifulest thing in the world, as he had said.

He wanted to thank them, but Missus Brown said to Eve, "Perry is a good man, dearie. And your house is the pleasantest one in the world. I know. I've been 'ere two days now."

They went out. Eve sat down, shading her eyes against the light. Perry stood still after he had closed the door. The bunk was made up; the room was clean and sweet. His heart came high.

He could hear the Kill muttering. He could hear the peepers singing. Outside the door he heard the lock sluices running as Esau and John locked the *Young Lion* through. They went north with the word of Blind Eve. Later they would go south; but they would find that the word of Blind Eve had gone before them, as had the joke of Perry's golden hair, all the way to New York City, till men talked about her all the way along the whole canal.

They lived together many years. Boaters tried to tell her that Perry's hair was not gold, but to such she showed the ring for an answer. He had said they were the same. Others tried to make love to her, but she had a fine indignation and was strong, and neither she nor Perry ever called on Esau or John.

Horses came to know her. No matter how worn they were she got them through the lock without a lash. She learned the house by touch. She learned to cook. Her feet on the plank across the lock were as sure as Perry's. Children loved to look at her and listen to her husky singing in the evening as Perry locked their boats through. Some of those children are men in middle life to-day, but they remember her story, and some will tell it to you.

For she never changed from Perry, and when he died she cut off a lock of his golden hair to remember him by.

THE VOICE OF THE ARCHANGEL

I

In the old days, Mrs. Lucy Cashdollar used to run a cooks' agency for bachelor boaters over Bentley's Oyster Booth and Bar in Utica. Her office was a large room, very colorfully got up, with wall-paper patchings, mostly of red and blue; a white china set in the corner cupboard, with broad red stripes round the bulge of the cups; a high walnut bed with a blue quilt folded triangle-wise at the foot; a green rag rug with a yellow border; yellow curtains at the window; and a Franklin stove. When she was n't on duty in the barroom, Mrs. Cashdollar held office hours. At such times she might have been considered the chief ornament of the room.

She generally sat in a Boston rocker, wearing a scarlet Mother Hubbard, her stocking feet — red or yellow, according to her humor — stretched out to the wood fire, the big toes curled back — through a hole, as likely as not. There she sat, very comfortable and quiet, her meerschaum pipe trailing smoke toward the flames; and, if no one came in for half an hour, her broad nostrils sang a song in very close harmony with the copper kettle on the stove.

Her face was remarkable for exceedingly blue eyes and a rubicund good humor which led one to suspect that she considered it her duty to sample the offerings of the bar before they were put on sale. Her face was plump, but not so plump as her bosom; and her bosom found ample support in the comfortable dimensions of her middle; and the whole of her was held up, in the occasional moments in which she was forced to make use of her feet, by a pair of ankles of proportions superior, if anything, to the rest of her.

In her capacity as cooks' agent for canal-boaters on the Erie, she picked up all the news; her room was a clearing house for gossip. Once a month or so the *Gospel Messenger* would send an editor down to interview her; and she always had on hand five or six stories from which the paper might take its choice, and which it wrote up with great literary taste, but — being a religious periodical — with considerable reversed English on the morals. Mrs. Cashdollar enjoyed these interviews hugely; and she kept a file of the papers containing "her articles" in a cedar chest under her bed.

It was in one of these dusty numbers that the present writer discovered the facts of the following story — disguised though they were with the religious principles of the *Gospel Messenger*. Had Mrs. Cashdollar been endowed with the ability to read, she would unhesitatingly have denounced the editor as a liar; but secretly she would have considered his point of view very beautiful and touching.

2

They had bought a boat to run together, and they came to her in search of a cook. Because they had the same name, most people spoke of them as brothers; but they were not kin. They did not resemble each other in any way. Stephen Glenn was about twenty-two or -three, dark, slender, and wiry, quick, high-colored. There was a dusky bloom on his cheeks and a sensitive mobility in his full lips suggestive of Southern blood. His smile was eager. Andrew Herkimer Glenn, behind him as they stood in the doorway of Lucy Cashdollar's room, towered a head above him. His blue eyes stared at a height from the ground equal to his own, and completely over Mrs. Cashdollar's head. The two of them, with the light of the fire playing on their dark shirts and ruddy faces, made quite a picture.

Mrs. Cashdollar removed her pipe from her mouth and sent a smoke ring over one of her big toes.

"What can I do for you two gentlemen?" she asked.

Stephen, who had removed his hat, made a lithe bow, and smiled.

"We come for business," said Andrew, heavily, and he took off his hat with both hands and spat over it into the fire and cocked his head to hear the hiss. Mrs. Cashdollar frowned. Then she saw Stephen smiling at her half apologetically, as if to say, "It's just his way — he don't mean nothing by it"; and she grunted and grinned, and thereafter confined her attention to him, without observing the effect of the firelight on the shaggy yellow hair of Andrew.

"Set down," she said to Stephen, motioning toward the Windsor chair with her right foot. "Excuse me having no slippers on — it's the gout troubles me." She smiled back at him; she was almost prettily plump in those early days.

The big man sat down on the bed, because there were no other chairs, and cleared his throat.

"It's nothing," he said. "I take off my own shoes, once in a while."

Lucy laid one finger to her right nostril and made a sort of snort through the other. Stephen raised his soft eyes from the toes of his boots and looked at her.

"We've a boat," he said. "We've just got her, and she's very nice; but we thought we'd need a cook, mam. Joe, downstairs, said you might help us getting one."

"I suppose the pay's all right."

"Fifteen dollars — doomed high, too," growled Andrew, shaking the yellow hair from his eyes and hawking his throat clear.

"Don't you spit again in my room!" cried Lucy, and a shudder ran up her back that made her quiver in front like a mould of jelly.

Andrew went over to the window, raised it, and put his head outside.

"That's better," said Lucy, when he had lowered the sash. "Of course it's over the front door — but that ain't my lookout."

"His'n," said Andrew.

Lucy took stock of the bigness of him for the first time. With his yellow hair bushy about his ears, his thick beard, and his great shoulders and hands, he looked monstrous. Stephen, somehow, in his fancy waistcoat and light-colored pants, suited his immediate surroundings. She liked to look at him across the embers of her own fire. Any woman might, she said to herself. But the old gray clothes of Andrew, the calluses on his hands, his long square-ended feet — they made the fixings in her room look contemptuously small and out of place, like a bed of zinnias planted in the prairie. And the bright, farsighted blue of his eyes, staring at the opposite wall, had a chilling vacancy.

"The wood basket's by your cheer," she said to Stephen. "Would you mind sticking a piece onto the fire?"

As she watched him laying it on, her ridiculous shiver passed up over her again. But the oily sputter of the birchbark soon sent a yellow warmth along her legs, and she pulled at her pipe and settled herself to business.

"Well," she said, "you boys want a cook? I've got one or two on hand looking for places. I guess you'd like one young and pretty?"

"I guess I would," replied Stephen, giving her his quick smile, so that even she felt a little fire stir under her side.

"Well, I got one might do — seeing your price is agreeable and regular."

"How old is she?" asked Stephen.

"Nineteen. She's new on the canal; but she's been cooking for me this week, and she's no slouch at it."

"What's her name?"

"May Friendly."

"Clean?"

"Yes, she is. She's a nice-looking gal, too; nice-complected; dark hair. Sort of pretty little chitter."

Andrew swallowed audibly, lowered his eyes to the back of Mrs. Cashdollar's head, and took over the conversation.

"Be her hands good strong ones?"

"What do you mean?" Mrs. Cashdollar was amazed.

"I want to see her."

"Oh, all right. She's in the next room. I'll call her."

Mrs. Cashdollar heaved herself out of her chair and went over to the door behind the stove.

"May!" she called. "May Friend-ly!"

Receiving no audible answer, she disappeared from view of the two Glenns. They caught her voice faintly from what must have been the head of a staircase and heard a subterranean mutter in answer. Then both voices faded into silence.

Stephen laughed softly.

"I wonder what the old gal will bring us."

Andrew grunted, stared round the walls until his eye fell upon a voluminous and lacy garment behind the door through which they had entered. To his eyes it bore a suggestive and embarrassing intimacy, and he shifted his feet and fixed his gaze on the lazy ribbon of steam that the kettle was spouting.

Stephen laughed again.

"If that bothers you, Andy, what 're you going to do with a cook on the boat?"

Andrew's gaze wandered back to the door.

"No funny business — not on my boat."

"Cripus!" said Stephen. "It 's as much mine 's 't is your'n."

"No funny business," repeated Andrew, gnarling his fist into a lump and laying it down very gently on his knee.

Stephen snorted.

"Shut up."

The slipperless steps of Mrs. Cashdollar could be heard painfully mounting the stairs beyond the door. They reached the top and paused while she let out a whistling sigh. Then the Glenns heard lighter steps coming up after Mrs. Cashdollar.

"Well," said that lady as she came into the room, "here we be at last."

She sank into her chair in slow bulgings, like a quilt tossed on the foot of a bed; and her breast rose and fell deeply. Stephen jumped to his feet.

"This here 's May Friendly, gents. Mr. Glenn and Mr. Glenn."

Her hand made a flourish and she went on wrestling with her breath.

"Pleased," said Stephen, looking the girl over boldly.

She glanced down and made pleats in her skirts. As Mrs. Cash-dollar had said, she was a nice-looking girl. Her hands were small and well made, though already the skin was roughened from her work. She wore a simple suit of dark gray, the short jacket drawn snug about her waist, its tails flaring piquantly in contrast to her smooth-drawn hair and demure face.

Andrew's gaze hovered between the suggestive garment on the back of the door and the girl's feet. For a moment intense silence hung over them, through which the wheeze of Mrs. Cashdollar's pipe became audible.

"Well," she said, by way of breaking the ice, "May says the pay's agreeable, and if you gents thinks she's ditto, you and me might settle my commission. That is, if she don't want to back out."

"There ain't only us two to cook for," said Stephen. "The boat's in good shape, new painted. It ain't hard working for us and we ought to get along good."

He gave her his smile. She nodded slowly and dropped her lids. Stephen noticed that they had uncommonly long lashes.

The silence was resumed for another awkward moment. Then Andrew's voice rumbled out of the bed corner.

"Where you come from?"

She glanced at him.

"Port Leyden."

"I come from Boonville," he said slowly. "I had a farm there. You've got better farming land down the river."

"Yes," she said, dubiously.

Mrs. Cashdollar wiggled her pudgy shoulders with impatience and drew in her breath in preparation for further conversation. But Andrew went on.

"Know anything about dairying?"

"Some," she said.

"I like cows," he said. "Only there ain't pasture for more'n dinkeys where my farm was."

"There isn't much good stock down my way," said the girl.

Mrs. Cashdollar sniffed.

"Durnedest things to ask a cook I ever see!" she exclaimed. "It's getting late. If you like her and she likes you, why n't you make a deal? You ain't asked how she cooks, but I'll tell you she's all right."

Stephen laughed.

"You ain't getting a wife, Andy." He turned to the girl. "We ain't hard," he said. "Ever been to the theatre?"

She looked up quickly.

"No."

"I'll take you to-morrow night, if you want," he promised.

"I'd like to."

"A woman like me's got to get sleep," Mrs. Cashdollar complained. "Are you suited, gents?"

"Yes," said Stephen.

"You, May?"

"Yes."

"My commission's two dollars," said Mrs. Cashdollar. "Cash."

Andrew slowly pulled a wallet from his hip pocket and paid her.

"Our boat's at the Butterfield dock," said Stephen. "It's the *Eastern Belle.*"

"Got a red stripe," said Andrew. "End boat."

"She'll be down in the morning," said Mrs. Cashdollar. "Excuse me not getting up, gents. It's the gout troubles me. Good night."

They went out, Andrew leading.

"What're you looking at *him* for?" Mrs. Cashdollar asked. "He ain't nothing but a lump of mud. Now that young feller's got looks — see him smile. He'll give you a good time, May — if you want it."

She had seen the girl's eyes fixed on Andrew's yellow hair as the lamplight picked it out through the darkness in the doorway.

"You get down and get 'em a good breakfast, and you'll start right. Give a man a good breakfast and you won't have to think about him till the next morning. Now go on out. A woman like me's got to get sleep."

She closed the door after the girl, knocked out her pipe, and took a yellow-ribboned nightcap from behind the door. In front of her mirror she let down her hair and skewered it up again and adjusted the nightcap with care.

"Yes, sir, he'll give her a good time if she wants it — or not. Them quiet ones like her's generally got a devil into them if a man can fetch a-hold of its tail."

"I wonder who they be," she said to herself as she began to undress. "I never seen them afore."

Mrs. Cashdollar never saw them again, but she heard about all three of them from time to time.

3

The two Glenns first ran across each other at an auction in Whitestown. Though they had come into competition over some smaller articles, they had taken no stock in each other until they found themselves and a third man bidding for a heavy work team. The horses were blacks, about eighteen hundred at sixteen hands, and handsome to look at. Andrew, whose passion was cows and horses, hung grimly to the bidding until he had reached one hundred and fifty dollars. Now and then he would turn his eyes from the team and scowl at the other two.

"One twenty-five," Stephen had said; and Andrew had called out, "One fifty," which was twenty dollars more than he could pay. Stephen had made a grimace and turned his back; but just then the third bidder had said, "One sixty."

This was a thin man with a pointed chin and sloping forehead who had been walking about with a heavy driving whip in his hand, much bored until the team was put up.

The auctioneer rubbed his hands together and echoed, "One sixty," in an ecstatic, whispering voice. "One sixty," he repeated. "Ain't anybody going to raise this gent's bid? Such a team, so cheap; four and five; own brothers! Look at 'em!"

Andrew swallowed hard and muttered, "One sixty-five," in his beard, but not loud enough for the auctioneer to hear him.

"Throw in with me," said a voice at his shoulder, "and we'll get him yet."

He looked down with a sudden gleam in his eye at the little dark man who had been bidding against him a moment before. Stephen smiled eagerly; and all at once a slow grin overspread Andrew's face, showing his big square teeth; a chuckle rose in him; and he threw back his head and opened his mouth and laughed to himself, a deep laugh, which shook him down in his bowels.

"How much?" he asked.

"I bid one twenty-five," said Stephen, grinning over the other's laugh.

The auctioneer was leaning beseechingly in Andrew's direction, his pudgy hands moving unctuously, his face sweating as he stretched his remarks to give Andrew time.

"Own brothers," he was saying. "Bred in this town. Equal to any weight. Up to any haul. Kind. Gentle. There ain't a kick into them. Set on their hocks," he invited. "Look at them quarters. There's power. Short backs. Look at them legs — run your hand down them. What do you feel?" he said to the hostler, who had complied with his request. "Nothing!" he answered himself. "Clean and sweet . . ."

The man with the pointed chin cracked his whip savagely.

"They're mine," he said. "No stretching! They was mine two minutes ago, damn you!"

"Going . . ." cried the auctioneer. "Look at them shoulders! Going . . . There ain't a sweeter set of legs in this state! You've see how they match as a pair, gents?"

"One seventy-five," said Andrew solemnly, his big hands quivering with delight.

The hot noon sun shone straight down on the group in the space the crowd had cleared for them, and touched the coats of the blacks with a gun-metal sheen.

"Ninety!" There was a snap in the voice of the man with the pointed chin, and he cracked his whip so that the pair threw up their heads and gathered their haunches under them.

"You shut up with that whip!" cried the hostler, running his hand over the withers of the nearest horse.

"Two hundred," said Andrew, and he took off his hat.

The crowd shifted round them in great amusement, and men eased the sweat out of their suspenders with their thumbs.

"Five," said the man with the pointed chin.

"Ten," said Andrew.

"Twelve."

"Fifteen."

"Sixteen."

The auctioneer rubbed his hands together. "Two sixteen," he whimpered. "Dollars. Cash."

"You'll get him now," Stephen whispered. "Twenty-five and he'll run."

"Not all to once," rumbled Andrew. "I want to make him wiggle."

It was his first experience in handling what seemed to him unlimited capital.

"Seventeen," he said.

"Eighteen."

"Nineteen."

"Twenty."

"Twenty-one."

The other drew a long sobbing breath, tried to swear, choked, and pushed his way through the crowd, the long lash of his whip trailing along the ground after him.

"Two twenty-one!" cried the auctioneer. "Going . . . What a team for the money! Ain't nobody going to say twenty-two?"

"You shut up!" Andrew growled.

"Going . . . Gone!" His mallet came down with a smack on the rail of his booth. "This team is sold for two hundred and twenty-one dollars to the big gent with the yellow hair."

Mixed laughter and applause rose from the crowd.

Andrew went over to the team and laid a soothing hand along their backs and grinned and grinned.

Stephen came after him. "Well," he said with his quick smile, "they're ours. I calculated sure he wouldn't go over twenty."

Andrew still grinned.

"Saved four dollars making him wiggle."

He ran his hand caressingly all over the horse, which twitched its skin with enjoyment.

"They're worth the price," the hostler vouchsafed. "I've see 'em when they was foaled and watched them this six year. They're a pretty team to haul with and used to handling boats."

"I thought they was four and five!" exclaimed Stephen.

Andrew gave him a pitying smile. The hostler spat.

"Was there ever a team auctioned which wasn't four and five if they was under ten and eleven?" he asked aggrievedly.

He thrust the lead ropes into Andrew's hand and shambled off with a friendly slap on the rump of the near horse as he passed. The team looked after him.

"Well, now they're ours, what're we going to do with 'em?"

"I got a boat this morning," said Andrew, running his hand down his nose and over his beard, "and I come up here to buy a team. I was aiming to boat it a season. There's no pay to my farm; it ain't no land for growth. So I sold it. I reckon I'll have to take you on to come with me as a partner."

"Suits me," said Stephen.

Andrew looked down at him, and, Stephen being so much younger and having that soft smiling look in his eyes, he felt a paternal kindliness overwhelming him. He had felt much the same way toward a heifer he had once had. She was the best blood he had on his farm, and she had gentle eyes.

"Suits me," he said.

They settled down to life on Andrew's boat, the *Eastern Belle* — one of the old bullhead Erie boats of eighty feet, with a well-built cabin aft and four stalls under the lift hatch forward. Most of their hauling took them westward, for they got pretty steady work from the Butterfield chain of feed mills; and they got to know Syracuse and Rochester and even Buffalo, and the points in between.

Andrew managed the culinary end. In his life alone on his farm he had learned to cook potatoes, and flapjacks, eggs, and coffee — good enough cooking for a man alone, for whom eating becomes part of the day's chores; but with someone to talk to over the food, there is more need for variety. It irked them both — Stephen especially, who was useless in such matters, and, consequently, particular.

He was city bred, born in New York, where he had acquired a grace which amazed Andrew but left him full of admiration. Beyond a certain gift and liking for horses, Stephen was of no value to the running of the boat. He went off as soon as they tied up at a town or city dock and moved about scraping intimate acquaintances with what women attracted his notice. He was eminently successful; he had a gift for clothes as well as his soft eyes and eager smile to help him. Andrew stayed aboard and growled to himself, for he had the heavy moral sense of inexperience. But his feeling of fatherliness grew deeper; and other men learned that to quarrel with Stephen meant quarreling with Andrew.

Stephen returned his ponderous affection with a bantering good nature, verging at times upon contempt. He listened attentively to Andrew's slow lectures on thrift and laughed them off with spending his share of the earnings of the *Eastern Belle*. It became a weekly ritual between them. In his way, each derived a certain pleasure from it.

But the cooking was another matter; the food palled. Stephen suggested a cook. Andrew scoffed at the extravagance until Stephen, appreciating his hold over his partner, began taking his meals in stores along the towpath when he could, and eating ashore altogether while they stayed in the larger ports.

A few weeks of this became unbearable for Andrew. One evening in Utica, as Stephen was leaving the boat, he suggested hiring a cook.

"It'll cost a lot," said Stephen with lugubrious hesitation.

"It'll save you buying your meals. She'll know better where to save than I do," said Andrew.

"I guess that's so. Still, you got to pay her a salary."

"I'll ask the 'keep over to Bentley's what's right. Joe would do right by me there."

Stephen shook his head and mumbled to himself in Andrew's sourest manner, and grinned to see Andrew's heedlessness.

"Joe'll know what's right," said Andrew.

Joe did, but it amused him to mention a top wage for Andrew's benefit. Being accustomed to all business involving womenfolk, Stephen scented a discrepancy.

"If you say fifteen dollars to Lucy up above," Joe whispered to him, "you'll get a danged good cook. She come in yesterday, and she's green to the canal"; and he gave an attractive description of a young girl, while Andrew down the bar ruminated over his backstrap. Fifteen dollars a month was more than he had planned to spend.

But he followed Stephen upstairs, and, between them and Mrs. Cashdollar, they secured the services of May Friendly.

4

She came aboard early, and from his bunk Stephen heard her chucking wood in the stove. Andrew, whose job it had been to build the fire and put on the coffee, still snored softly.

They slept in a small cubicle behind the cabin, directly under the steersman's place. What light and air there was came in through small ventilating slits just under the deck. It was a dim little hole, with the planks two feet over your head, so that you had to sit up carefully.

Stephen got up quietly and went out into the cabin with his shirt unbuttoned and his shoes in his hand. He got a drink of water from the barrel under the short steps and looked over the dipper at May while he drank. She was dressed in a red gingham work dress, and the sunlight coming through the small high windows at the side slanted across her back and made a small shadow between her shoulders.

"Good morning," Stephen said.

She gave him a cool glance out of her black eyes, which were pointed finely at the outer corners.

"Good morning," she said. "When do you mostly eat?"

"Seven," he said. "But there ain't no rush. Andy's sleeping."

He went out on deck with a bucket to wash. She listened to him sloshing round busily and then went on with her inspection of the cabin. On the whole, it was fairly clean. It was tiny — with little more than room enough for the stove and three chairs and a small cupboard in the corner. It was the first boat May Friendly had been on, and the disposition of pans and dishes in out-of-the-way lockers fascinated her. With all the sunlight streaming into its windows, it seemed more spacious than she had imagined a boat cabin could be. The walls were papered in a nasturtium pattern, the spruce floor was oiled. When curtains had been put at the windows and the shaving mug and razors had been relegated to properly remote corners, the room would have possibilities. She had resigned herself already to the apathetic satisfaction of a woman who has lived a life of conscientious routine.

At the back of the cabin was a curtain of faded green stuff through which she had seen Stephen appear. He had said that Andrew was sleeping, but she hesitated before lifting it. She could hear Stephen rubbing himself down with short gasps on deck. As her fingertips met the curtain, she blushed suddenly and vividly. Then she pulled it open. She could just see the bunks side by side, with their heads toward the stern, and she drew in her breath on observing that there was no partition. It was very dark and the air was none too good; but, above the even breathing, she could hear a pleasant sound of ripples along the stern of the boat. A finger of sunlight from a knothole had enabled her barely to see; and now she noticed that it moved slowly, as though the boat had swung a trifle on its moorings. Suddenly it caught up an answering gleam in Andrew's yellow hair, moved upward along his cheek.

When she heard Stephen walking back to the cabin steps, she slipped over to the stove and lifted the lid of the coffee kettle. The finger of sunlight had left a green spot on her vision, but in the sleeping cuddy it continued its slow creeping along Andrew's cheek. As Stephen entered Andrew sneezed violently and rolled over on his bunk.

Stephen came over to where she stood and got hot water for shaving. His beard was light and he shaved quickly; he was done by the time Andrew emerged from the sleeping cuddy, grumbling to himself. While he was on deck, Stephen showed May how to let down the table. It had two drop legs which unfolded to support the outer corners. In a recess behind it stood salt and pepper and vinegar and sugar, ready for the meal.

"Well, now!" exclaimed May. "That's real clever."

Wishing she had crockery, she laid out the tin dishes.

"Now you're here," Stephen observed, "and we're putting on shine like this, I guess we ought to have chineyware."

"I seen a nasturtium set over to Banton's, marked down reasonable and missing a cup. It would look real good here," she said eagerly, glancing at the wall paper.

"It would, at that."

He sat down, while the smell of frying eggs wove its way into the coffee perfume.

"Would you like to go out to-night, May?"

Her head came up jerkily, like a bird's, at the name; but she smiled and nodded. Her smile was slightly square, showing pretty teeth for a countrywoman, and gave one pleasantly the impression that she was startled.

Stephen pulled a handbill out of his shirt pocket.

Mr. WINFIELD (Professor of *Canagogy*) wishes to inform the CITIZENS of UTICA that he will give an EXHIBITION of his *Dog-School,* on Saturday Evening, July 12th (1856) at the *Mechanics' Hall.* Doors open at SEVEN, and *Performances* at HALF-PAST SEVEN. Admittance 25 cents.

He read it to her.

"Want to see it?" he asked. "The dogs is kind of cute."

"Yes."

Andrew came in wet and glistening, a damp towel in his hand. He had not bothered much in his dressing, as had Stephen. You were conscious of his undershirt. "Got to load up to-day. Pull out to-morrow morning. You be on hand, Steve?"

"This morning," said Stephen. "Got an errand this afternoon; and me and May's going to Winfield's dog show after supper. Come with us?"

"No."

"I'll pay," said Stephen with a grin.

Andrew growled and filled his mouth with coffee. Stephen looked at May with a smile, as if he had given her the reason for Andrew's reluctance. She smiled back. She did not know that Stephen had borrowed from Andrew the night before.

5

She made quite a picture as she walked down the gang to the dock. She and Stephen matched well. If it were n't for the old boat, you would have taken them for man and wife, gentleman and lady. And the boat did n't look so badly after all, Andrew told himself. He had chosen the red for the striping. Stephen had not cared; he kept up himself, where Andrew kept up his property.

Andrew watched them off from the cabin window. Not man and wife — he corrected himself — they did not look like man and wife: rather they might be lovers, girl and boy going together. The curtain over the window obstructed his view of them and he brushed it aside angrily. While he and Stephen had loaded in the morning, she had gone off on her own hook and bought this checked gingham, a sort of orange-brown, — too bright, Andrew thought, — but he had to admit to himself that it made the cabin look better. The cabin itself wore an appearance of unaccustomed neatness and smelt clean, and faintly of soap.

Over dinner he had watched Stephen making up to her. He wondered how she could be so cool about it. Toward the end of the meal Stephen had become almost awkward in his eagerness for her approval. Andrew had never seen him like that. He began to think that she must have been on the canal more than Mrs. Cashdollar had admitted.

In the afternoon Stephen had disappeared into the town; and he had not got back until supper. But Andrew had managed to finish loading the boat; he had not had to give time to getting the meals.

While he loaded, May sat in her rocker on the cabin deck and hemmed the curtains. The sun shone on her back and cast her shadow into the pit, where it fell upon Andrew as he moved from one side to the other. Now and then she looked down at him. He handled the bags easily. It was pleasant to see her shadow in the pit beside him — not that he put any stock in such notions. But afterward he went up and sat down on the deck beside her chair and smoked. She had smiled — a small smile that showed mostly in her eyes.

A breeze drew down the Mohawk Valley from the west and plucked up a ripple on the canal. There were not many boats along the canal front; most of the warehouses, with their yellow and brown windowless fronts, seemed deserted. A clerk, a little shambling man with a puzzled expression on his face, came along the planks and stopped beside the *Eastern Belle*.

"All right, Andrew?"

Andrew grunted.

"I've arranged with McCormick at the weighlock to pass you through to-morrow morning. Mr. Butterfield wanted you to get through to Boonville by Monday night if you could. McCormick knows your boat, so he'll let you right through, so it's all right. It's quite all right."

He shoved his hat back on his head and peered up at the two.

"It's quite all right," he said again. "He knows your capacity — so it's quite all right."

"Eanh," said Andrew.

The little man shuffled on. May glanced up from her sewing as he passed from sight round a corner of the Butterfield granaries.

"Poor old man," she said, half to herself.

Andrew grunted.

The city rose behind them up the gentle slope of the valley hills, the smoke pulling away to the east, and the church steeples piercing it like needles. On the other bank, the open meadows could be seen between the buildings.

He smoked on quietly to May's sewing. There was no sound but the wash of the ripples.

Then a faint bell ringing came to them down the canal, and away to the west they saw a line of boats drawing in. All at once Andrew drew his pipe from his mouth.

"What 'd you get them for?" he demanded, pointing at the gingham lying on her knee.

She looked down at him with her half smile, and he growled something about needless waste and frowned.

Deliberately she held the stuff up at arm's length, and the motion freed the line of her throat.

"Don't you think they would look pretty, now?" she asked, putting her head a little to one side, as though to appraise the curtains herself. She ruffled them slightly and held them out again. But he was not looking at the curtains; he was thinking how smooth her throat would be to kiss. The blood came to his cheeks, and he felt it there. It angered him.

"Don't you go wasting my money after this without asking me."

"I did n't," she said. "I got them myself."

He grunted — and she, seeing the look on his face, got up after a moment and went down into the cabin.

Andrew sat on by himself for a time. He heard the halters of the team in the bows rattling, and he realized that it would soon be time to feed them. But he stayed where he was. Perhaps he was expecting May to come out again.

About five-thirty, Stephen came aboard and went below. When Andrew had finished feeding the horses and came down to the cabin, he found the supper ready, and Stephen and May dressed up to go out. He sat between them glowering. The sunset slanting through the windows touched the faces of both and found nests in May's hair. Andrew frowned at the curtains, which were hanging over the windows with a sober sort of defiance, and ate stolidly. He scarcely returned their "Good night" when the meal was over; but he watched them go down the gang to the dock.

6

After a while he lit the lamp, bracketed to the wall, with a little vent in the ceiling above it to let out the smoke and heat. It became very still; the ripple alongside died away to a whisper. He heard one of the horses forward lie down in its stall. Then he got his Bible from the shelf, on which stood also a small black clock surmounted by the gilded figure of an angel with a horn. The angel was drawn up to his full height, and the arm carrying the trumpet was slightly flexed, as though the impulse to blow had just possessed his mind.

At times at night, when he heard the clock striking through his sleep, Andrew would jump up suddenly in his bunk, knocking his head against the beams above it, with a cold sweat on him, and a dream of the Last Judgment ringing out of his brain.

Now, as he sat down with his Bible, he let it fall open on his knees, and dropped the index finger of his right hand haphazard on the page after the manner of the superstitiously religious. The passage he thus chanced upon was new to his reading.

15. For this we say unto you by the word of the Lord, that we which are alive and remain unto the coming of the Lord shall not prevent them which are asleep.

16. For the Lord himself shall descend from heaven with a shout, with the voice of the archangel . . .

And at the word the clock behind Andrew rang the half hour. He turned swiftly on his chair — but the angel still stood in his accustomed attitude, with the impulse to blow written in the curve of his arm, still waiting the word.

When he dropped his eyes to the page again, he saw that in his start he had lost the place; but he was vaguely thrilled by the

words of the last verse he had read — of the shout, of the voice of
the archangel. Somewhere he felt in them the presence of a personal truth, too indefinable to be detected by one of his slow mind.
He sat brooding, the Bible closed upon his knees, his hands, half
clenched, hanging by the seat of the chair.

He was brought to himself by a knock on the door. It opened
to admit a man carrying a package.

"Banton's," said the man, mouthing a cigar. "Package collect
for Glenn. You him?"

"Eanh," said Andrew. "What is it?"

"How should I know! I've got trouble enough looking up this
sty so late a Saturday."

"You don't want to sniff at any sty you're into," said Andrew,
slowly. "You're kind of likely to get butchered."

"All right," said the man, with a tentative approach toward jocu-
larity in his tone.

"How much?"

The man named eight dollars, which Andrew paid.

"Give me a receipt," said Andrew.

The man pulled a notebook from his pocket and tore off a page.
"Glenn. . . . Glenn?"

"Andrew."

"All right."

He went out on deck and down the gang.

"Here, pig! pig! pig!" he called from the dock; and the next
instant his heels thumped rapidly away on the boards.

Hardly had the sound died out than Andrew heard a high unmusical whistle coming down the street. It reminded him of the
squeak of a knife-grinder's barrow. Methodically he folded the
receipt and placed it between the pages of the Bible, which he returned to its proper position on the shelf. He went out on deck
and sat down facing his shadow outside of the cabin door. Black
driven clouds scuttled across a half-moon high over the valley from
north to south; but on the canal there was no wind.

The whistle approached tortuously in tone and volume, and be-

tween the notes halting footsteps became audible. At length a
small figure of a man, surmounted by a large pack which gave
him the appearance of an immense humpback, rose out of the darkness by the boat side.

"Hullo, Andrew," said a high voice.

"That you, Harvey?"

"Eanh."

"Come aboard a spell."

The little man toiled up the gang and plunked his pack down
at Andrew's feet.

"Just packed up," he said. "Aiming to work through the Watertown road."

Harvey Cannywhacker was one of the cigar peddlers who used
to haunt the canal and the surrounding country. They moved
from town to town, rolling cigars according to demand; they were
met on back roads and the trails leading into the lumber camps;
they toiled along miles of towpath, sleeping in lock-tenders' shanties
or appearing out of the dark beside boats tied up for the night.
They went everywhere, knew everyone, saw everything, the bag
upon their backs a badge of privilege.

"Been up to Lucy Cashdollar's. She said you'd got a cook."

"Eanh."

"Any good?"

"I don't know," said Andrew.

"I seen Steve and her going into Mechanics' Hall," said Harvey.
"He looked like he was making a set at her. She's a good-looker."

Harvey slipped the palms of his hands outward along his knees,
as though he were rolling a cigar, and he murmured under his
breath his selling chant, "One for a penny, a penny for one; built
right and rolled tight; and warranted to drawr."

"Ah," he said aloud after a moment. "I knowed her back Port
Leyden way. Her family was a great one with cows. She's a
good hand for dairyin'."

"Is that right?" said Andrew. "Lucy Cashdollar said she was
new on the canal. I had n't thought so."

"Where're you a-hauling to?"

"Boonville," said Andrew.

"One for a penny," Harvey muttered; then aloud, "It's been a hard winter, last winter."

"Eanh."

"You like boating?"

Andrew grunted.

"Boonville ain't no land for heavy farming."

"No," said Andrew.

"You and Steve get along good?"

"Pretty good," Andrew said. It did not occur to him to be ruffled by this personal questioning. One expected it of a cigar peddler; besides, he knew Harvey.

"He's a good boy," he said, with an air of comfortable pride, as if he had been responsible for Stephen's character.

"Lazy," said Harvey. "Tags after women. . . . One for a penny . . ."

The dew was beginning to glisten on the deck, and the clouds under the moon grew thin.

"You don't like boating, Andrew," Harvey said suddenly. "You wasn't cut for it. You ought to go back to farming!"

"Where?"

"You ought to go west; go out to Ohio; go further."

"That's too fur."

"No, it ain't. Good land costs too much here. You was built for that land, Andrew."

"How do you know?"

Harvey hunched himself over his thin knees, and as he fronted the moon his eyes gleamed under his brows.

"I been there, Andrew. It's all flat country. It's a long, flat country. The earth's heavy on a plough. You can raise heavy cattle there."

"Eanh."

"I been there. But it ain't no land for a little man like me."

"I got money saved up," Andrew said after a while. "But I hadn't ought to leave Steve. He wouldn't come."

"He'd leave you if he wanted," said Harvey.

"I had n't ought to leave him."

They listened awhile to the water wash.

"You ought to marry," said Harvey. "A man ought to marry."

"Who? Who'd I marry?"

"Marry your cook — take her out to Ohio with you. . . . She's good for dairyin'. I knew her Port Leyden way. I knew her folks."

"Steve wants her," said Andrew.

"What's he done for you?"

Harvey got up from the deck and swung his pack on to his shoulders.

"Maybe I'll see you on the feeder. I aim to cut across Potato Hill and come down Delta way."

His pack bowing him down, he shuffled off the boat.

In the cabin behind Andrew the clock struck the hour, and he started again — the words of the verses he had read coming back to him.

"Go west," Harvey had said. "It's a long, flat country. You was built for that land."

The earth was heavy against a plough out there — his big hands itched for the helves. He had always wanted to go where he could raise heavy cattle.

But there was the question of Stephen. He had spent a life alone until he had come across Stephen; he could not leave him now.

Hunched forward, with his hands hanging over his knees, Andrew muddled over his problem. His years of loneliness had unsuited him for discerning his own wishes; his mind was dozing; he ruminated moodily, but he seldom thought — rather he accepted two sides of a question and drifted between them until circumstances reared one of them to actuality. All his life he had hungered after a fat land; and all his life he had hung on to the bare living of his little farm by Boonville. Now that he had sold it, he had only a vague idea of how the sale had come about. Someone had offered him more than the farm was really worth. He had been unable to refuse the opportunity of laying by a little money; his mother had left him a little money which he had refused to touch; his neighbors called him miserly. The boat had come as part payment for the farm; so now he was boating. That was all there was to it.

He got up and went back into the cabin and took off his shoes. His glance fell upon the package that had come earlier in the evening, but he did not open it.

May had fashioned a sort of partition between her bunk and the others, so that the sleeping cuddy was sufficiently divided into two rooms.

Andrew stretched out, with his arms under his head, scowling at the chink of light the lowered lamp cast over the curtains. The clock struck eleven in the cabin. May and Stephen were later than he had expected; or, seeing that it was Stephen, he might have expected it after all. . . . A man ought to marry, Harvey had said. . . . He heard the clock strike the half hour again, and he dozed.

He did not hear them when they came in a little later. They did not speak for a moment; but he saw their shadows make a single silhouette against the curtains. Then May's voice broke out, and Stephen warned her not to wake Andrew. They both laughed, quietly, a little awkwardly.

For a while each turned on the bunk on either side of Andrew; but his even breathing was undisturbed. The wind rose and riffled the water against the stern of the *Eastern Belle,* and the clock struck midnight, and finally the three slept.

7

They pulled out from the weighlock at six o'clock. Behind them the keeper of the lock stared sleepily at their wake and held the shuddering tails of his nightshirt down about his legs. A heavy mist lay on the water, which looked black along the quays and reflected the lower parts of boats, the decks of which remained invisible. Shadows in the whiteness marked the entrances to streets.

A delicious stillness hovered round them, imparting ghostliness to the smooth glide of the boat. It seemed to May upon the cabin deck that the world slipped by beneath them while they hung quiet as a cloud in a noonday sky. Only the plodding heave of the black team ahead and Andrew's long stride connected them with earth.

As the horses moved out on to the open towpath, a breeze from the hills brought them the smell of meadows; trees rose up beside them now and then with a whispering of leaves and restless shapes. Looking behind her, May saw the lower houses appearing here and there, and a dull gold gleam on the water; but the mist still clung to the crest of the city. While she watched, she heard a stir upon the air; and the high crown of mist was filled with the sound of church bells ringing early Mass. A cow floundered out of a swale alongside the towpath, her big head glistening, a pocket of denser mist loitering about her horns. Cowbells echoed faintly from the hills; a dog barked; and a rooster crowed away off on her left. And all at once the glow on the water shot swiftly after the *Eastern Belle* and fell about May's face; and as the mist lifted suddenly she saw that the sun was risen.

A little below her, on the small deck left for the steersman, Stephen stood, his brown shirt open over his chest, showing the smooth brown skin. He gave her his quick smile suddenly and cast a half-humorous glance ahead of them to where Andrew walked beside the black horses, hat in hand, with the new sunlight on his yellow hair.

"He says he's been telling you you been extravagant with them curtains and all."

"Eanh," said May with a slow smile.

"He'll probably give you some more talk every week. He was born kind of miserly; he can't help it."

He spoke with the consciousness of his own liberality strong upon him; he forgot that the preceding night's entertainment had been borrowed.

"He's a kind of a sod," Stephen said. "He likes to set quiet and let his roots grow down close. I'll bet he set here on the boat all last night."

May also glanced amusedly at Andrew and then looked back at Stephen, and they both laughed. Andrew heard them, for his head lifted quickly, but he walked on without turning.

"There's a package downstairs from Banton's," said Stephen. "I got it yesterday; it's for you. You'd better go and open it."

She opened her eyes wide.

"For me?"

He laughed again.

"You better go see."

She went into the cabin and sat down opposite the package. Her previous evening with Stephen had been a new experience to her. The crowded hall, the brilliance of the lanterns on the stage, the subdued murmuring of the crowd, at first had frightened her by their newness. But as she glanced round she perceived that Stephen was as handsome as any escort in the assemblage; when he leaned close to her to whisper some remark, he looked almost beautiful; the reflection of the stage lighting just lit his soft eyes. Then she saw that men watched her as she moved, and it came upon her that she suited his looks; that the pair of them could match with any pair about them. Contrary to Stephen's expectation, instead of making her dependent on him, the experience gave her native hardiness a sudden perspective and she found a reliance in her own judgment. She was fond of him already, he could see that; but she was not carried away. She had let him kiss her on their return, several times; and she had responded with a warmth she had never divined in herself; but at that point she had stopped him. Though she appreciated his beauty, it did not dominate her. Instead of her fearing him, her feeling was one of almost contemptuous friendliness. He might take liberties with her, but he could not claim her.

It was in this mood that she opened the package and unwrapped the nasturtium china set she coveted. A wave of pleasure swept her as the sun picked out the bright red and greens and yellows against the white. She ranged the pieces on the table to admire their lines. There was a commodiousness about the belly of the teapot which transmitted through her hand, as she wiped away the shop dust, a comforting sense of establishment. She held it up in both hands and then poured herself imaginary tea into one of the cups. Her knowledge of china was limited to the ancestral assortment of odds and ends common to farmers' houses. An entire set dazed her. She raised the empty cup to her lips.

Then she ran out on deck to thank Stephen. He held her with one arm, and in her delight she almost granted him the efficacy of his bribe, for she read it as such in his eyes.

"There's hardly room for all of it," she said.

"It ought to go into the cupboard."

"The teapot won't."

"Set it out by the clock."

"But there's only room for Andrew's Bible there."

"Set it somewheres else," he said.

She had longed for permission. She wanted the pot where she could see it continually. But as she turned to go down her eyes fell upon Andrew walking beside the team with his deliberate tread. The sight sobered her.

Andrew frightened her. Her instinct made her aware of a possible upheaval of his phlegmatic nature which would overwhelm her woman's nice sense of balance. Stephen was more easily understood, his purpose being readable and reducing all consideration of him in a woman's mind to the power of his beauty. Beyond his size and yellow hair, Andrew possessed no striking features; beside Stephen he resembled a somnolent great forest tree, unaffected by the surface breezes shivering the sapling, but terrible in the high winds. His blue eyes were not cold, but cool from lack of decision. His heavy face remained immobile, even in a fight, and was lighted only by a petty astuteness in money matters. She had had evidence of that already; he would give her no freedom. But at least she had a china set.

She placed the dishes in the cupboard, after hiding the former tin ones on a small shelf behind the stove, until she came to the teapot. This, as she had foreseen, would not fit in the cupboard, so she turned to the clock shelf. Andrew's Bible was one of the large leather varieties, blooming with many-colored prints; there was no chance of wedging the teapot between it and the clock. She took it down, and her shoulder sagged as she felt the weight. The pages opened slightly to let a slip of paper flutter to the floor. Hastily she stooped to pick it up.

It was inevitable that her eye should fall upon the writing, and as inevitable that she should read it. The penciled hand was sprawly, but sufficiently legible. It was the receipt for a package from Banton's, collect on delivery, made out to Andrew Glenn, signed by W. Ad. Joynt, agent. The date was of the preceding day. She went back to the wrappings of the parcel and turned them over until she found the letters C. O. D. It became evident to her then that, whoever had ordered the dishes, Andrew had paid for them.

8

They tied up for the night outside of Delta on the Boonville feeder. The town itself was a mile and a half back from the canal; but Denslow's Delta House took the town's place pretty well. It was a long rambling structure with odd wings growing out of the sides of a big square house of three stories, like whelps out of Scylla's belly. At times they could give forth as much noise, and almost as unlovely. But in the off season the house stood very quiet, with lights only in the ground-floor centre windows, and a white whisper of smoke coming out of one corner of the great chimney.

They had come down from Boonville empty, and ahead of them when they tied up at the wharf was another boat as empty as their own. It was a late hour for supper, for the sun was set, and a cloudy sky made it seem later. But Andrew ate deliberately across the table from May. Stephen had gone up to the Delta House as soon as they landed.

Andrew glowered. Although an air of established comfort and neatness now pervaded the cabin of the *Eastern Belle,* it was evident that he and May were ill at ease. Harvey Cannywhacker's advice had taken root in him, obsessed him, until he had approached May. He had asked her above Boonville, in the midst of the bleak hills in which he had been born, to go west with him. Slim and self-contained, as she walked beside him on the towpath, she had told him no. She had had more than a taste of his parsimony, which, as a farmer's child, she was born to understand, but which, in his present way of living, she found it hard to forgive. She had felt an unresistible impulse to hurt him, and she had given way to it. If she had expected an outward sign of pain, she was disappointed; and instantly she had regretted her weakness, remembering his unclaimed gift. He spoke nothing about himself, so that it was impossible for her to read any purpose in him.

Andrew had walked on beside the team and repeated her answer to himself. For his slow mind there had not been time for pain to sink in. He had asked her because a man, according to Harvey, ought to be married. He would not be hurt until he woke to the realization of being in love. At the moment it was another deal closed, as it happened, in his disfavor.

But the sight of her about his boat, and the feeling of her presence, made the idea of going to Ohio seem empty. That idea had run so supremely in his head that he had not realized his omission of a proposal of marriage. The two were synonymous ideas; and she had understood them so. But he had taken it for granted that her negative implied her attachment to Stephen. He could not know that a few hours afterward she had denied Stephen. Had he been informed of it, he would have refused to believe it. It was not in Stephen's character to be denied.

He finished his tea from the new nasturtium cup and rose from the table. May glanced up at him with a peculiar veiled expression in her eyes.

"They're real pretty," she said, giving him an opening. "I like them a lot."

He snorted.

"All puddery snick-snacks. It's land counts in this land — land and stock. Building on the land and growing on to it's what counts. You can't make no progress in a chiney set."

He reached for his hat.

"Where's you going?"

"I got to find Stephen."

He paused for a minute in the doorway and cast a long look over the cabin. It was this he would leave to go west — all of it pretty puddery, but he was growing to like it. But it was all puddery — he would go west. The horses forward stamped all at once. A big team — they ought to be pulling on a plough, not taking a square-ended boat back and forth between little nowheres. He looked at May — and she seemed to him very desirable there, sitting with her hands among the crockery dishes. She ought to be raising children. While he watched her, the color mounted to her face. His eyes fell on a small mirror across the cabin; and in it he saw the yellow of his hair, and his eyes clear blue, filling the small glass. He stooped to go out of the door, and he awoke to his own size; the boat had grown too small to hold him. As he came out on deck he heard the clock strike eight — clear notes, suddenly resonant on the night air.

There was a smell of frost in the night; the stars were beginning to show among the clouds; here and there they found reflections in the black water of the canal.

Andrew went over to the other boat and knocked on the cabin door; but no one answered him. He walked forward to the stable to look at the horses. It was inky dark there, and the horses shifted in their stalls at his unfamiliar smell. But he stepped in beside them and felt them over. They were heavy horses, as heavy as the black team, hard and in good condition — a trifle poor, perhaps. He knew the owner, Reuben Philmy, a little dazed man who wanted enough money to set up a little garden — a little garden! Andrew felt a quiver in the legs of the horse by which he stood, as if he, too, snorted at the thought.

When he came out on deck again, Andrew heard Philmy coming aboard.

"Hello," said Andrew. "It's me, Andrew Glenn."

"I thought that was your boat," said the other in a small, weak voice. "Hello, Andrew."

"I want to buy your boat," said Andrew.

They talked for a while in the starlight, and then Andrew reached into his pocket, and a little later he walked away toward the Delta House.

As he paused before the door, the moon, a full white moon, came out from the clouds, bringing a bright wind with it. He could see the white gleam of the plank road running straight away to Westernville, on the far side of the canal. Close at hand, it spanned the water over a bridge, the white rails of which arched from shore to shore like a web of silver mist. On this he heard now the thump of heels sounding with a tight, frosty ring; and presently a high unmusical whistle proceeded from the lips of the walker. In a few moments his humped shadow became visible, black against the gray-washed stillness of the roadside fields. Andrew went out to meet him.

"I guessed I might run into you here, Andrew."

"We just stopped for the night, Harvey."

The peddler dumped his pack down and leaned back against the snake fence where the protruding crossed ends of the rails made a rest for his back.

"Going on in the morning?" he asked.

"Eanh — as far as Rome."

"Where're you heading?"

"West," said Andrew.

The peddler pushed his hat forward over his eyes and drew in his breath with a low whistle.

"I bought Philmy's boat and team," said Andrew.

"Going alone?"

"Eanh."

The cold breeze rustled the roadside grass.

"A man ought to get married," said the peddler.

"I reckon," Andrew said.

"Did you ask her?"

"Eanh."

"She said no?"

"Eanh."

"Why?" Harvey asked.

"I reckon she wants Stephen."

"She's said no to him, too," said Harvey.

"How'd you know that?"

"He's setting up the road a spell by himself."

"He's tired of her," Andrew said.

"He wouldn't leave her with nobody else round to tag after. I'll bet she's turned him off."

With his forefinger Andrew outlined the toe of his boot in the road where he squatted.

"She'd make a good wife," said Harvey.

"I guess that's so."

"What I think is," said Harvey, "that she wants a bit of both of you."

Andrew was silent.

"Either you take her or you don't. One of you alone could take her in a minute."

"I can't leave Steve by himself," said Andrew. "It ain't right."

"You'll have to if you're going west. You'd better settle it between you right off if you're going to start west."

"How?"

"You could do it a lot of ways — you could fight it out."

"Cripus! He wouldn't stand no show."

The peddler chuckled.

"Well, you might draw lots."

Andrew deliberated.

"That'd be too sudden," he said after a while.

"I got some cards," said the peddler. "I allus carry them."

"Eanh."

"Well, you could mix 'em good and then draw off the top for the first queen."

This protracted method appealed to Andrew.

"That's all right," he said.

In the act of pulling the cards out of his pocket, the peddler cocked his head.

At the same instant Stephen's face appeared over the snake fence behind them.

"What do you want to win for?" he asked Andrew. "What good would that do you?"

Andrew hunched lower under the remark; he had not thought of that. For the first time he felt the pang at her refusal which had lain dormant in him.

Harvey cursed beneath his breath; then glanced up at Stephen. The moon shone in his small black eyes. He looked all at once like a crouched, inquisitive rat.

"I don't see as it'll help you an awful lot to win, either," he observed.

Stephen drew back, and his cheek darkened.

"If it wasn't for Andrew being round all the while, I'd have learned her already. Where are your damn cards?"

The peddler held them up.

"I'll mix," he said, and he did so, slipping the cards dexterously from one hand to the other with his nimble fingers, until, in the moonlight, they became a running thread, with a faint gleam now and then against their backs. Suddenly he offered them to Andrew, backs up, upon his palm.

"Let him draw first," said Andrew.

Stephen laughed.

"Andy's scared."

He took off the top card and held it slantwise against the moon. "Pip," he said.

Andrew drew and struck a match where he squatted and laid the card down by his feet. Stephen drew again; then Andrew. And again they laid down the cards.

Stephen took another card, quickly, and laughed as he turned it down. He seemed quite at ease and asked for one of Harvey's cigars and borrowed Andrew's last match to light it. Andrew drew and examined his card by the glow of the cigar end, the faint light just touching his nose and brows and the outer hairs of his beard. Stephen looked at the next card, and laughed again.

"There! The damn black hussy. Tough luck, Andy."

Andrew grunted.

He held his card close to the cigar — the two of clubs. Then he picked up the cards he had put down and handed them to Harvey.

Stephen vaulted over the fence.

"It's too bad, Andy," he said again. There was a note of genuine disappointment in his voice, and he added quite honestly, "We'll miss you."

Andrew got slowly to his feet until he faced him.

"Good-bye," he said. "You can have the boat."

Then he hit him with his full strength on the side of the face. Stephen crumpled backward on his heels and stretched out, his fingers plucking at the dust.

"Jeepers!" Harvey whispered. "Jeepers Cripus!"

And his hand went unconsciously to his own jaw.

"Jeepers!" he said once more.

Andrew stared from his fist to Stephen and back again. He shook his head.

After a moment he reached over and picked Stephen up and flung him across his shoulders.

"I'd better take him back," he said.

Harvey swung up his pack and they set off for the boats. As they went side by side their shadows looked like the shadows of twins.

9

"Come on in," May said.

Harvey opened the door and Andrew bunted his way in and

dropped Stephen in the rocking-chair. Then, as if to survey his work, he stood back and looked him over in the lamplight. Stephen's skin was waxy, with an unpleasant yellow tinge beginning to show. The long lashes folded on his high cheeks might have been a woman's, as might his slim-fingered hands. He lay back with a grotesque crumpledness in his arms and legs. On his waistcoat there was still a white spot made by his cigar ash.

May looked from him to Andrew with a wondering horror.

"What 've you been doing?" she cried suddenly. "What 've you done to him?"

Though she did not mind picking a flower herself, she could not bear to see one wilt under another's hand.

Andrew gazed at his fist before answering her.

"Why, I guess I hit him one."

"Jeepers!" exclaimed Harvey. "I 'll bet your neck!"

"Eanh."

May got some water from the butt and began daubing Stephen's face and neck. Andrew watched her for a moment. Then he turned heavily to Harvey.

"I reckon I better start now. Will you steer me 's fur ' Rome?"

"Why, yes," Harvey said. "I reckon I might as well."

May glanced up quickly.

"Where 're you going?"

"West," said Andrew. He banged the cabin door after him.

Harvey started to pick up his pack; but before he could swing it up May caught his arm.

"Tell me," she said breathlessly.

He looked at her with relish.

"Why, you could n't pick neither one of 'em, and Andrew would n't let him have you while he was round, so they played for you with these-here cards," — he produced them as evidence, — "and Steve won, and Andrew busted him for it. He did it real handy."

"You know," he went on, reading her expression, "he 's liable to do that."

He swung up his pack and opened the door. They heard the

tump-tump of the horses coming down the gang of the boat ahead and a jangle of traces.

"It's a good boat, but I'll bet it's dirty," Harvey said.

"You stay here," said May. She ran out after Andrew and went aboard the other boat while he hitched the team to the eveners.

"All right, Harvey," Andrew said, as he came back and pushed the gang back on deck.

"All right," replied Harvey, from the bow of the *Eastern Belle.* He grinned as the boat swung away from the wharf. In the pale light he saw May Friendly raise her arm to him. He waved back. The moon traced the wash from the stern as the boat went round a bend. He waited a few minutes longer.

"Low bridge!" he heard Andrew's deep voice calling.

"Lo-ow bridge!" May's voice faintly gave the steersman's answer.

Harvey chuckled as he returned to the cabin. He sat down at the table and opened his pack and began rolling cigars.

"One for a penny, a penny for one," he chanted. "Built right and rolled tight, and warranted to drawr."

Behind him, Stephen moaned.

"That you, Harvey?" he asked weakly. "Where's Andy?"

"I guess he woke up," said Harvey. "Them sleepy ones wake up once in a while."

He sifted the filling onto a leaf.

"It's like something inside of them said, 'Jeepers!'" he went on, "and they didn't hear it for a while."

"Where's May?"

Harvey chuckled.

"She don't seem to believe in cards," he replied. "By grab!" he added. "Durned if she didn't wake up, too!"

He licked his thumbs with relish and rolled the wrapping on tight.

WATER NEVER HURT A MAN

HE trudged with his hands tight fists in his pockets, his head bowed to the wind and rain. Ahead of him in the darkness, so that he could hear the squudge of their hoofs, the towing team bowed their necks against the collars. He could not see them in the darkness. When he lifted his face, the rain cut at his eyes; and when lightning split the darkness he shut his eyes tight and pulled his head closer into his coat collar, waiting blindly for the thunder. Once in a lull he looked back. He could barely make out the bow-lantern and the arrows of gray rain slanting against it. Between him and the light he caught glimpses of the towrope, dipped slightly between the team's heaves, and the roughened water in the canal. Somewhere behind the light his father stood by the rudder-sweep, his beard curled and wet, his eyes slits, sighting for the bank. John wanted to go back, wanted to tie-by for the night, wanted to be in the bunk with his head buried in the friendly, musty smell of the blanket, where the storm could not reach him. He had gone back once, but his father had reached for his belt, saying, "Go on back. Watter never hurt a man. It keeps his hide from cracking."

John had gone back to the team. They did not need his guidance. But it was his place to keep the rope from fouling if a packet boat coming their way signaled to pass. He was afraid of his father at night, afraid of the big belt and strong hands with hair on the fingers over the knuckles. He caught up with the plodding horses and let the rain have its way. At each stroke of lightning his small back stiffened. It was his first year on the canal and he was afraid of storms at night.

He had been proud that spring when his father said, "John's old enough to be a driver-boy; he's coming along with me and the

Bacconola." He had showed his dollar to his brothers and sisters, first pay in advance, and his father had bought him a pair of cowhide boots from the cobbler when he came to the village. Later, when the frost was out of the mud, John would go barefoot.

He was proud of his father. In Westernville, with other small boys, he had heard the dock loafers talking about his father, George Brace, bully of the Black River Canal. In some strange way they had news of every fight his father fought a day after it happened. "George licked the Amsterdam Bully Wednesday mornin'. Lock fifty-nine. It tuk nineteen minits only." "George is a great hand. Them big ditch bezabors is learning about George." A stranger had said, "Wait till Buffalo Joe meets up with him." There was silence then. Buffalo Joe Buller, he was bully of the western end of the Erie. A pea-souper, a Canadian, he fought the Erie bullies down one by one, and when he licked them he marked them with his boot in the Canadian style. It had a cross of nails to mark the beaten man's face. "You wait," said the stranger.

Little John, listening, felt shivers down his back. But now, with the wind and rain, and the lightning tumbling the clouds apart, he forgot. They were on the long haul westward, to Buffalo, with ploughs aboard, full-drafted in Rome. They had had to leave three hundredweight on the dock.

He felt his muddy boots slip in the towpath. He heard the squelching of the horses. Squelch-squelch, a steady rhythm as they kept step. Once the lightning caught his eyes; and he had a clear view of trees beyond the canalside meadow, their budded twigs bent down like old women with their backs to the storm, and the flat, sharp wall of a canal house sixty yards behind him. He had not even seen it as he passed. The rain was finding a channel down his neck. It crept farther, bit by bit, with a cold touch. He could feel his fists white in his pockets from clenching them. His legs ached with the slippery going. They had had supper at six, tied up by the bank, and John had eaten his plate of beans. He had felt sleepy afterward, barely noticing his father's big body bent over the dishpan. It was warm in the cabin, with the little stove roaring red-hot, and his small hat hanging beside his father's cap on the door.

He had been almost asleep when his father's hand shook him roughly, then tumbled him from his chair. "Get out, John. Them ploughs we 've got has to get west for spring ploughing. We 'll pick up Bob in Syracuse, then we 'll have a better chance to rest. Get out now," and he had reached for his belt.

What did John care for the old ploughs anyway? But it had n't then begun to storm, and he had gone, with a tired sense of importance. One had to keep freight moving on the old Erie. The old *Bacconola* always made fast hauls. He had been proud and shouted in a high voice to the tired horses and kicked one with his new boots.

But now he did not care about the ploughs. He wished the crazy old *Bacconola* would spring a leak in her flat bottom, so they would have to stop till the hurry-up boat came along and patched her up. He thought of her now, bitterly, with her scabs of orange paint. "Crummy old blister," he called her to himself and made names for her, which he said aloud to the horses in a shrill voice. He was only twelve, with all the bitterness of twelve, and the world was a hateful thing.

"God-damned old crummy bitch of a tub . . ." But the lightning caught him, and his throat tightened and he wanted to cry out under the thunder.

A water rat went off the towpath with a splash, and a frog squeaked.

He glanced up to see a team on the opposite towpath heading east. "Hey, there!" yelled the driver in a hoarse voice; but John was too tired to answer. He liked to yell back in the daytime and crack his whip. But he had dropped his whip a while back. He would get a licking for that in the morning. But he did n't care. To hell with the whip and the driver and Pa!

"Hey, there!" shouted the other driver, a voice in the rain. "All right, all right, you dirty pup. Eat rain, if you want to, and go drownd." The rain took the voice, and the boat came by, silently, noiseless as oil, with its bow light a yellow touch against the rain. The steersman gave a toot upon the horn, but the sound bubbled through the water in it, and the steersman swore.

They were still on the long level, alone once more. It must be midnight. If only the lock would show. In Syracuse, Bob would come. He took turns driving and steering and cooking — a little man with a bent shoulder who had dizzy spells once in a while.

At the lock John could sit down and rest and listen to the tender snarling at his sluices while the boat went down, and heaving at his gate-beam, while John's father heaved against the other. He was crazy, the lock-keeper was; all lock-keepers were crazy. John's father always said so. John had seen a lot of them in their week of hauling, but he did not see why they were crazy. They looked no different even if they were. He hoped the lock-keeper would be asleep, so it would take a while to wake him.

Squelch, squelch-squelch, squelch. The horses kept plodding. Suddenly John caught a break in the rhythm. One foot sounded light. He pushed his way up beside them against the wind and laid a wet hand against a side. He could not see, but the side felt hot and wet, and he got a smell of sweat. Yes, he could feel the off horse limping. Hope filled him. He waited till the boat came up where he was, a small figure, shrunk with cold. The boat's bow, round and sullen, slipped along, the bow light hanging over and showing an old mullein stalk in silhouette against the water.

"Pa!"

His voice was thin against the wind.

He saw his father's figure, rain dripping from the visor of his cap, straight and big, almighty almost, breast to the wind.

"Pa!"

The head turned.

"Hey, there! What you doin'? Get on back, or I'll soap you proper!"

"Pa! Prince has got a limp in his front foot. Pa!"

The voice turned hoarse with passion. "Get on back, you little pup! Fifty-nine's just round the next bend. Take your whip and tar him, or I'll tar you proper."

John sobbed aloud. For a bare moment he thought of staying still and letting the boat pass on. He would run away and join the railroad. He would get run over by an engine there, just when things went well, and they would be sorry. He started to draw himself a picture of his body coming home in a black box, and his mother crying, and his father looking ashamed and sorry, and then the lightning made a blue flare and he saw the straight figure of his father ahead, on the *Bacconola,* which seemed struck still, a pill box in the flat country, and he was afraid and went running desperately, hoping he could get back to the team before he was missed.

He caught the horses on the bend and, lifting his face to the storm, saw the lock lanterns dimly ahead. And even then his ears caught, coming up behind him, the harsh blast of a tin horn.

He looked back and saw a light, two rope lengths behind the *Bacconola.* Even while he watched over his shoulder, he saw that it was creeping up.

"John!" His father's voice beat down the sound of rain. "Lay into them brutes and beat into the lock!"

He could imagine his father glaring back. If only he had not dropped his whip. He would have liked to ask his father for the big bull whip that cracked like forty guns, but he knew what would happen if he did. He shrieked at the horses and fumbled for a stone to throw. But they had heard and recognized the note in his father's voice, and they were bending earnestly against the collars. A sudden excitement filled John as his father's horn rang out for the lock. The wind took the sound and carried it back, and the other boat's horn sounded a double toot for passing. John yelled shrilly. The horses seemed to stand still, and there was an odd effect in the rain of the canal sliding under them inch by inch laboriously, as if with his own feet he turned the world backward.

Minutes crept at them out of the rain, and the lights of the lock did not seem to stir. Then John heard the squelching of the team behind his back. Little by little they were coming up, past the *Bacconola,* until he could hear them panting through the rain, and saw them close behind, behind dim puffs of steamy breath. He watched them frantically. Then the lightning came once more, a triple bolt, and the thunder shook him, and when he opened his eyes once more he saw the lock lanterns a hundred yards ahead.

At that instant the driver of the boat behind yelled, "Haw!" and the following team swung across his towrope and they were snarled.

The horses stopped of themselves, shuddering. They were old hands, and knew enough not to move, for fear of being thrown from the towpath. The boats came drifting on, placidly as water-logged sticks. The light of the following boat showed a dark bow coming up. John heard his father roaring oaths, and saw by the bow light of the other boat a tall, clean-shaven man as big as his father, crouched to jump ashore. Then both boats came in by the towpath, and both men jumped. They made no sound except for the thump of their shoes, but John saw them dim against the lantern light, their fists coming at each other in slow, heavy swings.

The strange team was panting close beside him, and he did not hear the blows landing. There was a pushing upward in his chest, which hurt, and his fists made small balls in the pockets of his trousers. The other boater and his father were standing breast to breast, their faces still, cut, stonelike things in the yellow light, and the rain walling them in. He saw his father lift his hand, and the other man slip, and he would have yelled, for all his cold, if the lightning had not come again, so blue that his eyes smarted. He doubled up, hiding his face, and wept. . . .

A hand caught him by the shoulder.

"A little puny girly boy," said a voice. "I would n't lick you proper! Not a little girly baby like you. But I 'll spank you just to learn you to let us come by!"

John opened his eyes to see a boy, about his own height, but broader built, squinting at him through the rain.

"Take off your pants, dearie," said the boy in a mock voice, digging in his fingers till John winced. "Joe Buller can handle your captain smart enough. Me, I'll just paddle you to learn you."

John, looking up, was afraid. He did not know what to do, but without warning his hands acted for him, and he struck at the square face with all his might. A pain shot up his arm, making his elbow tingle, and the boy fell back. John could feel the surprise in that body stock-still in the rain, and had an instant of astonished pride.

Then panic laid hold of him and he tried to run. But the other boy jumped on his back. They went down flat in the mud, the older boy on John's shoulders, pummeling him till his head sang, and forcing his face into the track, and crying, "Eat it, you lousy little skunk! Eat it, eat it, eat it, eat it!"

John could taste the mud in his mouth, with a salty taste, and he began to squirm, twisting his head to escape the brown suffocation. He heaved himself behind, throwing the boy unexpectedly forward, twisted round, and kicked with all his might. The boy yelled and jumped back on him. And again they went down; this time the boy bent seriously to business. And this time John realized how it was to be hurt. At the third blow something burst loose in his inside and he screamed. He was crying madly. The other boy was heavier, but John squirmed over on his back, and as the brown hand came down on his face he caught it in both his own and bit with all the strength of his jaws. The hand had a slippery, muddy taste, but in a second it was warm in his mouth, and there was a sick, salt wetness on his tongue. The boy struck him once in the eyes and once on the nose, but John held on and bit. Then the boy howled and tore loose and ran back. There was another stroke of lightning, and John saw him doubled up, holding his hand to his mouth; and he got stiffly up, turned his back to the thunder, and saw his father bent over the other boater, taking off his shoe.

John walked up to them. His father's face was bleeding a trickle of blood from the right eye into his beard, but he was grinning.

"I'll take his boot for a souvenir," he said. "How'd you come out, Johnny?"

"Oh, pretty good. I guess that other feller won't bother us no more," said John, examining the fallen man. He lay half-stunned, by the water's edge, a smooth, big man, with frightened, pale eyes. And one crumpled arm was in the water. John's father looked at the man and then at the boot he had in his hand.

"I'd ought to mark him by the rights of it; but he ain't worth the work, the way he laid down. Who'd ever know his name was Buller?"

Buller. . . . John gazed up admiringly at his big father and studied how the blood ran from the outer corner of the eye and lost its way in the black beard, which the rain had curled. His father had licked the western bully proper.

"Hey, there!"

The hail came in a thin, cracking voice. Turning, they saw the lock-keeper, white-bearded, peering at them from under the battered umbrella he held with both hands against the wind. The tails of his nightshirt whipped round the tops of his boots.

"Hey, there, you. There'll be some down boats by pretty quick, so you want to hurry along now, while the level's right."

John was aware of his father standing looking down at him.

"Shall we tie-by where we be?" asked his father.

John felt pains coming into the back of his neck where he had been pummeled, and his knuckles ached.

"We can stay here a spell," said his father. "The storm's comin' on again. There'll be bad lightnin', I make no doubt."

As he spoke there came a flash, and John whirled to see if the other driver-boy was still visible. He was proud to see him sitting by the towpath, nursing his hurt hand. John did not notice the thunder. He was elaborating a sentence in his mind.

He made a hole in the mud with the toe of his boot, spat into it, and covered it, the way he had seen his father do at home on a Sunday.

"Why," he said, in his high voice, eying the old *Bacconola*, "I guess them poor bezabor farmers will be wantin' them ploughs for the spring ploughing, I guess."

"Me, I'm kind of tuckered," said his father, raising his shoulders to loose the wet shirt off his back. "And the rain's commencing, too."

John said importantly, "Watter never hurt a man; it keeps his hide from cracking."

His father jumped aboard. He took his horn and tooted it for the lock. John ran ahead and put back the other boat's team and cried to their own horses to go on. They took up the slack wearily, and presently little ripples showed on the *Bacconola's* bow, and the lantern showed the shore slipping back. On the stern, George Brace blew a blast for the lock. The old lock-keeper was standing by the sluices, drops of water from his beard falling between his feet.

The boat went down, and the horses took it out. Ahead, the team and the boy left the lantern light and entered once more the darkness. The rope followed. And once more the *Bacconola* was alone with its own lantern.

Presently, though, in a stroke of light, George saw his son beside the boat.

"What's the matter? Hey, there!" he asked.

"Say, Pa! Will you chuck me your bull whip here ashore? Them horses is getting kind of dozy. They need soaping proper."

"Where's your whip?"

"I guess I left it a while back. I guess it was in that kind of scrummage we had. I guess it needs a heavier whip anyhow. I guess a man couldn't spare the time going back for it."

"Sure," said George.

He reached down and took it from its peg, recoiled it, and tossed it ashore. The boat went ahead, slowly, with a sound of water, and of rain falling, and of wind.

DINTY'S DEAD

I

IT was slow hauling up the Lansing Kill Gorge. The rain had turned to snow, hiding the tops of the hills. The dead grass and goldenrod were whitened as the broad flakes piled up, and the canal water and the water in the Lansing Kill way down in the valley looked black.

Floundering along in the wake of the team, John hunched himself against the snow and fingered his whip. He would like to dose the horses, but they were doing their best. The towpath was fetlock-deep in greasy mud, and the old *Bacconola* at the end of the towrope hung back. She was about as easy to keep moving as a sulky cow.

John looked back at her. Her brown blunt bows loomed up in the snow dimly. He could just make out his father on the steersman's deck, a great hulk of a man in his red shirt, with the snowflakes snarled in his black beard.

John was coming home. For five months he had been driving for his father on the old *Bacconola,* and not once had they turned into the Black River Canal. It was his first year's driving, and the whole time he had been on long hauls. Even his father admitted that was rare for a young lad.

"Git there, Pete!" he shouted to the off horse. But he shouted just to let his father know his mind was on his business. Actually he was thinking that to-morrow they would be unloading in Boonville — fertilizer from Spuyten Duyvil; and then they would haul back empty to Westernville and tie-by for the winter. He and his father would go home. There would n't be any more tramping for him. He could take things easy. He 'd have his summer's pay in his pockets — thirty dollars, he'd have, and his pa had promised him five of those dollars for spending money. Five dollars was a lot of money. They'd take notice of him when he went to school. He thought about what he'd say. He'd say, "Yeanh. I seen Joe Buller one afternoon. It was in Bentley's Oyster Booth and Bar. I was having me a beer with Pa and we was waiting for a load of iron stoves for Buffalo." That sounded pretty good, if you said it in an easy voice. He'd have to work in the way his pa had licked Buller at number fifty-nine. "I had a kind of a wrassle with Joe's driver, but he handled easy." Pea-souper. He'd have to remember Joe was a pea-souper. Maybe he'd say, "Yeanh, I seen Pea-souper Joe. . . ." Then they'd want to know about his wrassle with Joe's driver; but he wouldn't tell them much. "It was dark," was all he'd say. "We had a kind of a scrummage in the dark. He wouldn't fight fair, so I had to use my teeth."

The snow was in his eyes and he felt cold, but he didn't let on when he looked back again and saw his father raise his arm. He raised his in reply.

"How're you coming, Pa?" he yelled.

"Wake up them crummy brutes!" his father roared. "This ain't no funeral."

John unlimbered the whip and cracked it a couple of times. He was getting to be a masterful hand at cracking a whip. It sounded like a cannon in his hands. You could see the horses were scared of a whip when a man handled it. But he wouldn't bite them. That was the only thing wrong with his pa. He'd drive the lights right out of his teams. But it made for fast hauling. Everybody knew the *Bacconola* for a fast boat. It made John proud.

The snow blinded him as he slopped along. He lowered his face against it and squinted his eyes. They'd passed Sucker Brook aqueduct a long while back, and they were well into the gorge. The hills came close, hemming the wind in, so that it carried the snow like birdshot against John's chest. He shivered and flogged himself with his arms. Pretty soon they'd get into the Five

Combines and he would have a chance to rest while they locked upward. He'd get close under the horses' rumps.

As they came out of the balsam stretch, John saw the valley floor close under him. A soughing in the wind made him look up at the two spruces that marked the bend. The boat swung round slowly and the Five Combines came into view. They looked like great steps rising up against the hillside, the timbers dark brown and the lock walls gray. Up at the head of them a light burned in the lock-tender's house.

John stood still on the towpath to let the old boat draw up to him. He watched the towrope sliding past, tight under the heavy hauling, so that the snow stuck to the top side. John shivered inside and counted with his eyes shut. He counted ten slowly and opened his eyes to see the bluff brown bows cuddling up a ripple in the black water.

"Pa!"

His father had been leaning against the rudder-stick. His hands looked red on it in the cold. He jumped when he heard John, and swung his eyes to the towpath. Then he looked forward again, so that the wind bent his beard back against his throat. He had to watch the bank on the curve.

"Get back, you!" he roared. "What in hell do you think you're doing?"

"The Five Combines," shrilled John. He had to walk now to keep abreast.

His father cursed him.

"What did you think it was?"

"I thought I'd tell you," John cried.

"I'll tell you something," his father bellowed. "You get back there and get those horses walking!"

"It's awful cold, Pa."

He saw his father's face get purple over the beard. His voice was hoarse with anger. John couldn't hear what he was saying, but he guessed. He began to run to overtake the team, and when finally he came up with the straining eveners, he was sobbing.

"God damn you lousy brutes," he shrieked, "can't you walk? All the time getting me in trouble with Pa." He swung blindly on them with the whip. But the horses scarcely flinched. Their quarters trembled under the hauling, their hoofs slithered and brought up balls of mud. They were bowed down in the unceasing agony of hauling up the Lansing Kill current. John wept.

And suddenly he felt sick. He was n't yet thirteen, and the cold was in his bowels. He wished he could die. He forgot about his money and the tales he had to tell when he got home. All he wanted was to get warm. And he knew he would n't get warm until it got too dark to see, and even then his father would light the lantern and they 'd have to keep moving until eight o'clock. Because it was said his father could steer the Black River Canal without a light. He was the only man on the canal that knew it well enough. It used to make John proud, but now it made him wish he were dead.

The tears on his cheeks traced icy patterns, his sobs were gulped from his mouth by the wind, and the flakes melted on his lips with a salt taste. He did not hear the overflow coming down the tumble-bay. He did n't know where he was in the world, except for the towpath coming back endlessly against his feet. He did n't know anything until his toe stubbed itself upon the eveners and he lost his balance and buried his nose in Pete's tail. He caught hold of it for support, his hands aware of the tremor of the exhausted beast. The team had stopped.

He glanced back in terror to see the rope lying slack and the boat beginning to overtake it. He stooped desperately for the evener, grasped the rope by the hook, and screamed at the team. They wearily mounted the steep ramp round the lock, barely in time to keep the rope from fouling.

Back in the snow, George Brace sounded his horn. The harsh flat note was muffled by the big flakes. It echoed dully from the wall of the tender's house.

Automatically, John scurried back to lift the rope over the balance beam, and then ran out on the coping to look down on the long shape of the *Bacconola* as his father steered it into the low level.

His father looked up at him and grinned. John saw his teeth white through his black beard. And he hated the sight.

George Brace grinned wider when he saw his son's angry face.

"Never mind, Johnny. We'll quit soon and I'll give you part of my noggin."

"I don't want no noggin," John said. "I want to get warm."

"You're a man," said his pa. "I thought you was, anyways. I'm pretty cold myself, and I have to stand still. You ain't going to give out on me, are you? I hadn't thought to have to take Pearly next year."

"Hell no," said John, suddenly. Pearly was his younger brother. "It's just the cold shivers a man."

He tried to grin.

They looked up and down at each other for a moment. Then George Brace's face darkened.

"Where's Mike?" he bellowed. "Mike, Mike!" He put his horn to his mouth and blew on it as if he would gut it with his breath. The clamor in the well of the lock rose hideously. "God damn that dumb bezabor!"

"God damn him!" yelled John.

He looked up at the tender's house and saw the door opening.

Mike's wife stood in the light, her head shawled. Then she dragged shut the door and came down to the lock. She leaned over on the far wall and peered down at John's pa.

"What's all the racket for?"

"Where's Mike?" John saw his father mouthing under his beard.

"Mike's gone up to the fourth lock."

"What's he doing up there?"

"He's been up all day."

"What's he doing?" roared George.

"He's up to Dinty's."

"What's wrong with Dinty?"

"Dinty's dead."

2

She helped them lock through and they made the short winding stretch to the Three Combines, where the other lock-tender's wife came down to them.

She was a stout woman with a choleric, perpetual flush. Her eyes blazed.

"He never was worth a cent. He was always borrowing money off Alec. 'If you go up there,' I says to him, 'you need n't expect to say howdy to me to-night,' I says to him." She sniffed largely and wiped her nose against the wind and swore.

John watched his father's face. George took no notice of the woman, but worked the locks in silence. He looked sad.

The woman leaned on a balance beam and went on: "Mike come by close after noon and took off Alec. They walked up together. 'You ain't brought in my wood,' I says to Alec. But he would n't hear me."

She turned the sluice lever and looked down at the rising water in the upper lock. The old *Bacconola* ground heavily against one wall as she rose with it. John pressed himself against Pete's quarters, the smell of lather hot about him, and watched his father.

"When did he die?"

The woman became shrill.

"Last night. The new bank watch told Alec. Found him dead in his bed. A Roman Catholic he was, and not quite decent, either. Were n't no woman would live with him I ever heard about. His house was like a dirty barn. *I* never spoke to him. I would n't speak to the Devil, would I?"

George grinned sourly.

"Maybe the Devil would n't speak to you."

The woman tossed her head. She sniffed. She looked as if she had a cold in her head.

"I hope not! I've been an honest woman all my life."

She gave them a look, damning them all — George, John, the

horses, and the boat. The *Bacconola* rose up above the walls, cabin roof and stable roof and rudder-stick and cat-walk. The wind laid its hand on the tarpaulin cover to the pit, drumming on it. The sound awed John.

His father was gruff with him. "Well," he said, "you'll have a chance to get warm now, John."

The top gates to the Three Combines gaped wide and the level lay open before the *Bacconola's* bows. John started the team ahead and stopped them when the towrope had tightened.

Alec's wife stood back by the lock, laughing raucously. Her laughter sounded indecent to John. Dinty was dead, and by his father's face that was no laughing matter. It made John think that the woman must be a brute kind of a beast to laugh at death; he felt himself awed, and it seemed to him that as he looked back she was standing low down in the world. His narrow body wriggled itself inside his clothes.

"All right, John."

George's voice sounded full of solemnity. It had a deep, tragic significance, coming through the whirling snow. It carried sorrow.

John spoke softly to the horses: "Giddap, you." The horses bowed down. It seemed to John that they bowed down like worshipers in camp meeting. The stamp of their hoofs in the mud was like the slow clapping of hands. He bowed his own head to the snow and heard the voice in the wind.

The canal crept in against a hollow hillside. There were dried shivering cat-tails along the far bank. On the right the land sloped steeply for the Lansing Kill. It had become too dark to see the creek, but now and then in the lulls John heard the frothing water. He thought it was like a voice in the middle of the dark earth, and his eyes began to trace shapes in the whirling snow. Like ghosts, the shapes were — Dinty's ghost, flying wildly, like a scared pup.

The team made slow progress, but John's father was silent. When John looked back he could not see him. He could just make out the towrope, tightening to the horses' heaving. He wished his father might have lighted the lantern for him to look at. For comfort he put his hand on the rope and walked with it that way.

They came into the lee of the next bluff, and then the canal swung out above the Lansing Kill so that John seemed to look straight down on the snowstorm. The wind took hold again, with voice and cold. The breath was snatched from John's lips. He put his elbow up over his face and breathed against his coat sleeve. He thought they would never get to Dinty's.

3

But the team stopped at the foot of the lock.

There were no farms here. There was nothing but the snow, and the push of the wind and the voice of it in the darkness, and one lighted window like one eye in the black wall of Dinty's shanty.

John went back to the boat.

He found posts set into the towpath.

"We 'll tie-by here," George said solemnly.

He tossed the stern tie-rope off to John and the end struck his shins a stinging wallop. John hitched it round the post the way his father had taught him to and then lent his small weight to the horse gang, setting it on the towpath. His father tied up the bow. John went for the team and brought them back, dragging the heavy eveners. The whiffletrees clattered dully over the mud.

They unhitched the horses and took them on board and fed and watered them. Snow swirled in through the open trap, but the horses were already making the tiny stable warm with their sweat scent. John gathered armfuls of hay. It felt warm against his chest. He was dreadfully tired. He felt that he would like to lie down beside Pete with the hay in his arms. He did not know why he wanted to do that.

"Hurry up, John."

He put the hay in front of Pete and followed his father out on deck. The snow and wind seemed doubly cold after the brief warmth of the stable. His father let the trap fall with a thud, shutting the team in, and John felt that the closing of the trap had shut him out from the world. He pressed close against his father as they went back to the cabin. They went down the narrow stairs, and in the darkness John saw the red eyes of the stove drafts. It was warm here, too, but the warmth was dead with the smell of his father's clothes and his, of the potatoes they had fried for lunch, and his father's pipe.

His father scratched a match along his pants, and there was a blue fizzing in the darkness before the flame grabbed hold of the stick and was transferred to the lamp wick. It crept round the wick, joining on the far side, and his father blew the match out with a rasping breath. John saw the cabin, small and familiar, with the dishes on the sink-board, the kettle steaming on the stove, the blankets piled up on the foot of the bunk, and his best coat hanging beside his father's on the door.

John's father put the basin on the washboard and got a dipperful of water from the barrel under the stairs; then he warmed it with water from the kettle, stirring slowly with his thumb. He washed his hands and neck and threw the dirty water out through the door. Then he repeated the operation for John.

John had taken off his shirt and undershirt. As he stood before the washboard, the ribs stuck out in his skinny body; his back looked white and frail over his baggy trousers. He washed his hands and face and rubbed himself with a dry spot of the towel. He put on his dry undershirt and shirt, as his father was doing, and they stood face to face.

They had the same hooked nose and broad mouth, but John's eyes lacked the man's bold impudence. Whenever he saw his father stripped he was awed by the sight of the deep-sprung ribs, and the thin mane of black hair on the breastbone, making the white skin look tender. It looked like a woman's skin till you saw it blending with the coarse red just over the swelling biceps of his arms.

His father had a smell, too, that he did n't have. It was strong, stinging, and full of life. Whenever he smelled it, John began to want to grow up like his father. Sometimes when he undressed that way, close to his father, he had the awful thought that some day he might himself get strong enough to knock his father down.

The dry wool next his skin made him feel better. He followed his father to the door, and when George put on his good coat John yanked his own down. They swung into them together.

George hesitated at the door.

"I don't know if your ma would think it was right."

"What, Pa?"

"You coming along to Dinty's."

"I don't want to stay here on the boat."

"There wouldn't nothing happen to you."

"I'd be afraid." John did not dare look at his father when he said that.

"What would you be scared of?"

"I'd be scared of Dinty coming here."

"You ain't never seen him."

"That's why."

John's father looked at him for a while down his nose. He seemed to be grinning inside his beard, but his voice was serious.

"Dinty never hurt a louse, but there wasn't anybody liked him, only a few of us. He was a peculiar kind of old dingus for a man. He just liked his drink and a game of cards, once in a while."

"Can't we have supper now?" John asked.

"You can get it for yourself."

"If you and me had supper, maybe I'd like staying better."

"I got to get along, John." But he spoke kindly.

"What you going for?" John asked.

"He was a Catholic, Dinty was. Catholics like people setting with them till they're buried. That's why."

"What's a Catholic, Pa?"

George Brace had a thwarted look. Finally he said, "Your Aunt Minnie's one."

John thought that over. It seemed to him that Dinty must be something well worth seeing.

"I want to go with you, Pa."

"All right," George said impatiently. "You can come along. Only don't tell your ma I took you. And keep out 'n the way."

4

When they came up on the level of the lock, they saw another boat tied by. The night lantern was swinging in the windy snow, but there were no lights in the cabin windows.

George pointed to them and said, "Maybe there 's a cook on board and you could sleep with her."

"I 'm a man," John said stoutly. "I don't sleep with no women."

He thought he heard his father chuckling, and he checked over his statement to see if he had said anything silly. But as he thought it over he decided that his father must be proud of him. He felt proud himself. He let go his father's hand, and, instead of walking down the horse gang, he vaulted off onto the towpath the way a man would. He had seen cooks on boats, and he never liked them. There was n't any cook on the *Bacconola*. His father cooked, or else old Bob, who took turns with John at driving on hauls. John was glad old Bob was n't with them now. He liked being alone with his father. It put them on an equal footing. So he turned his face to the wind and let his knees spring as he tried to match his father's long stride.

There was a wail in the wind. It found voices in the eaves of Dinty's shanty. The snow whirled round all four corners of it, and tongues of blown snow kept licking over the shingles. There was a light in the kitchen, which was the only room, and the light showed in both the windows John saw. Inside he could see men sitting round on boxes and chairs. It looked warm in the room. The stove had a spot of red in the firebox. And some of the men had taken off their coats, as if they were hot.

The house stood by itself on the outside edge of the towpath a piece above the lock, for Dinty minded that lock and the one next above toward Boonville. Its outside wall was right on the edge of the bank, and underneath, sixty feet down, the Lansing

Kill made a curve, so that the roar of water uprose in spite of the wind, almost as if there were falls in the shanty cellar.

John stared at the men through the windows, trying to make out which one Dinty was. He looked for a sharp-faced man, with a thin pale nose and a hooked chin with a wart at the right-hand corner of the mouth, — like his Aunt Minnie, — but there wasn't any man like that sitting there.

Then his father marched up on the porch and knocked on the door with his fist, so that there was a booming against the noise of the wind. And it seemed to John, hanging back, that his father if he had knocked any harder would have knocked the whole house backward into the Lansing Kill, upsetting the liquor in the glasses the men had in their hands, and maybe drowning Dinty, even if he was dead.

The door opened and a steam of hot air, smelling of men and tobacco and noggin, billowed out against John's face.

A black-haired man with a crooked shoulder stood in the door.

"Hello, there," he said, peering out against the darkness. "Say, boys, it's George Brace."

"Hello, Mike," George said. "I just heard from your wife Dinty was dead, and I stopped to sit in with him."

Mike opened the door wide and stood to one side rocking a little tipsily on his heels.

"Come in," cried a hoarse voice, so hoarse that John shivered, thinking it might be Dinty's. "You're freezing the whole of us."

But Mike had caught sight of John.

"Hello, George, who're you fetching with you?"

"It's my boy," George said, striding in.

"I live and declare," said Mike. And he grinned at John and gave him a wink. "Come in, Handsome. Dinty will be glad to see you. He was always partial to your pa."

There were three men sitting round the stove. One of them, a thin, morose-looking individual in a yellow shirt, had a chew of tobacco going that he pushed into a cheek when he was ready to drink. The other two were furry fellows who sat close together, obviously the crew of the other boat. Mike and John's father seemed much younger, and John noticed that his father was far and away the biggest man there.

He greeted them by name — "Hello, Alec," to the morose man, " 'Lo, Mart, 'Lo, Jerry," to the other two.

They said, "Hello, George." And Alec asked, "How is it outside?"

"Damned cold," George said, and walked over to the fire.

The three old men were looking all the time at John, and he stood a little way off from his father, afraid to come too close, and not liking to be by himself. He wondered why they stared at him that way. It did n't seem proper to look round for Dinty while they were looking at him. Then he realized that he had n't taken his hat off, so he took it off as stealthily as possible, and when·they saw him do that all three old men switched their eyes to the corner of the room behind the door.

John looked too. And he felt keen disappointment. All there was to see was a plain pine coffin set up on a couple of heavy chunks of wood. The lid was off, naturally, but from where John was standing the high edge cut off his view of the inside.

Alec looked awhile at the coffin, and then he said, "Well, by all accounts Dinty ought to be hot enough."

Mart, who had a straggly reddish beard shot with white, snickered in it. John looked at him and then looked back at the coffin. He thought it was warm in the room, but that corner on the windy side of the room way off from the fire could n't be. He looked back at Alec and became aware of something wrong with Alec's eyes. They were n't the same color to begin with, and the one that looked toward Dinty was black, and kept looking that way, but the other was gray and moved all over the room.

But his father was saying solemnly, "Dinty was all right." John had never seen his father look so solemn. It made even Mart look ashamed. He poured himself another glass.

Alec said to George, "What did you fetch the boy for?"

"He did n't want to stay alone on the boat."

"Why not?"

"He was afraid of Dinty's ghost."

"Ghosts!" snorted Alec, and his light eye came round to John again with an orbital swoop. John felt ashamed. But Jerry said, "I'll bet his ghost is out there working with the lock right now. He was always scared a boat would go by with somebody owing him money. Thank God I don't owe him nothing."

"Me neither," said John's father. He had sat himself on a box, very upright, and now he took the glass in his fist and held down his beard and set the rim against his lips and tilted his head and poured the whole glass down. When he let go of his beard, John thought his face looked redder.

"How old was Dinty?" asked John's father.

"Older 'n me, I guess," said Alec.

"Older 'n me too," said Jerry.

"Does anybody know how old he was, anyway?"

"He'd come here when they opened up the canal in fifty, I know that," said Mike, hunching his crooked shoulder against his cheek and peering round. "He towld me so himself. He was old as old."

"Older 'n sin," said Mart, and he giggled.

"You're drunk, Mart," John's father said and turned his back. John looked away from Mart and then looked back surreptitiously. None of the others were looking at him, and Mart's face was redly embarrassed.

"He was a good old bezabor," said John's father. "Who's paying for his funeral?"

"He is," said Mike. "I found forty dollars in his sock under the board behind the stove."

"He had funny notions about money," said Jerry.

"He said he could always darn his sock, but nobody could keep a bank solid."

"He could n't read nor write."

"What's the funeral costing, Mike?"

"I argued Troutbeck down to thirty-one dollars, allowing used gloves. I thought that would please Dinty."

"Yes," said John's father. "He did n't like undertakers."

"What did you do with the rest of it?" asked Alec.

"It's in his coffin with him."

"He used to like cards an awful lot. He used to be lucky."

"Nine dollars!"

"It's a lot of money to put underground."

John listened dimly to their talking. He had backed into the corner behind the stove and leaned himself against the wall with his hands behind him. The heat and the smell of liquor were making him drowsy. Once in a while his eyes would start to close. Then he would snap them open, and stare hard at Dinty's coffin.

He would have liked to go over and look at Dinty. They had put out two tall candles, one by the head and one by the foot of the coffin, standing them up in a saucepan and a whiskey bottle. The candle flames burned feebly and rather red against the smoke.

There was a table in the middle of the room, two chairs, and some old boxes. Over the sink was a shelf with a teacup or two and some tin plates and a knife and fork and an old long loaf of bread, cut open. On the wall over the coffin was a calendar with a big bright picture of a girl putting her foot on a stool and pulling up her stocking. Her stockings were red and her dress golden yellow. She had her side to the room, but her head was turned so that her downcast eyes looked straight into the coffin. And she was smiling.

John considered her a beautiful woman, but he only looked at her when the others were not noticing him; for it did not seem decent for a girl to monkey with her garter in the same room with a dead man. It seemed unholy, but maybe it gave Dinty pleasure. He would like to see Dinty. He wanted to know what he was really like. He felt a queer kind of desperation about it, because, if Dinty were to appear to him some night, and he did not know who he was, he would not be able to speak his name. It was very important to know a ghost's name. If you called them by name and were reasonable with them, they would go away.

John felt a hand on his shoulder. It made him start. He looked up to see Mike McCarty grinning at him over his hunched shoulder and offering him a glass half full of noggin.

"Have a drink, Johnny," he said. "You must be tired with tramping all day."

John flushed with pleasure as he accepted the glass. All along he had felt that the men were uneasy with him there, and that made him uneasy.

Mike hovered over him as he sipped the warm drink. It warmed him all through; he could feel it in his arms and fingers. It swam in his head, and he did not notice the smell of liquor in the room.

"Would you like to take a look at Dinty?" Mike asked.

John nodded.

Mike walked across the room toward the coffin and John followed him with sure steps. They stopped beside the coffin together and John got a good look at the girl doing up her garter. She had a fresh red mouth and arched eyebrows, and the eyes, just showing through the black lashes, were dark brown. Her leg was n't the way John had thought it was; it was n't like a girl's leg at all. It was much fuller and softer. The stocking fitted it so closely that he realized she was just a picture after all.

Then he felt Mike's hand on his shoulder and remembered they had come to look at Dinty. He drew his breath in and took a tighter hold of the glass, feeling the warmth of the rum against the palm of his hand.

Dinty did n't look at all the way he had imagined.

He lay all dressed in his best clothes straight on his back, and he fitted the coffin with perfect economy. His eyes were closed, and his skin was a strange ivory color and it had a very soft shine all over it. The nose was thin and straight and looked as if it had been very beautifully whittled with a small-bladed pocketknife; the forehead was high and round; the hair and the long full beard were white, and they looked alive and thriving.

John thought that was the most peculiar part. They hid the tightened lips and the flat ears, but they looked more alive than his father's black beard when he washed himself on deck and the planks were white with hoarfrost. John thought it was a strange thing Dinty should be lying in the same room with these ugly-looking men, and he understood why his pa and Dinty had been friends, even though Dinty was so much older.

Mike chuckled as they looked down together. His voice was warm with friendliness for Dinty.

"He'd never look at a woman, Dinty would n't, and the women would n't ever forgive him that. They said he was crazy." He chuckled a little. "He always carried an umbrella, but he was the luckiest hand at cards I ever saw."

When they were through looking at Dinty, John backed away three steps because it was the proper thing not to turn your back on the dead, and he went back to his corner and sat down. He was n't afraid of Dinty any more, and as he sipped at his noggin he wished he might have known Dinty before he died. Just from looking at his face he knew that Dinty would have liked him, too.

The noggin took hold of his empty stomach, and he began to feel drowsy. His head nodded. He had to brace himself to finish the glass. He sat down in the corner and leaned back. He could hear Alec saying, "Nine dollars is a lot to put underground."

A little later his ears picked up the words of Jerry: "Why don't we have a game of cards?"

It seemed to him that he saw their feet moving round and he heard the table being dragged to the middle of the room. Mart was hunching himself up to it on his stool. Mike had produced a pack of greasy cards. They were all having another drink.

5

A sharp sound waked him. He opened his eyes without raising his head. His father was standing up like a giant in the middle of the room with his hand over his head to turn up the wick in the lamp. The rest of them were sitting round holding their cards against their shirt fronts. But the sound came again, like the slap of leather.

John's head cleared of drowsiness and for a minute he was sick with fright. Dinty was sitting at the table, and Alec was slapping his face.

"Why don't he bet?" asked Alec. "Hugging his money that way!"

They had propped Dinty up in a chair. He didn't sit in it. He leaned back at an angle with his hands at his sides. His back was toward John, but John could just see the five cards on the table in front of him and his money beside them. There weren't just the nine bills that had been in the coffin on Dinty's waistcoat. There were some bills and a small heap of silver.

"He ain't even anteed," Mart said sorrowfully.

Jerry leaned forwards and took out the ante from the silver.

"All he does is ante. He don't bet. It's going to take forever to get his money out of him."

John's father sat down and said, "Stop the blather. I want two cards."

Mike, who was dealing, gave him two. He went round the table. When he came to Dinty, he asked, "How many?"

But Dinty did not answer.

"Give him a drink," suggested Mart.

"He won't," Alec said with a still fury in his voice.

They all looked at Dinty, and suddenly John met his father's eye. For a minute he and his father looked at each other. Then John saw an extraordinary thing. His father looked ashamed.

But Mike repeated his question, "How many, Dinty?" His voice was still friendly.

Suddenly John felt a tremendous sense of righteousness in himself. He realized that only his father, of all these men, really liked Dinty, but his father was too weak to go against the crowd. Dinty and his father were the only decent people in the room, but his father was either drunk or afraid.

"I don't want anny," John said suddenly in a strong voice.

The other men started. They all looked at Dinty. Their eyes were like owls' eyes surprised by crows in daylight. They looked a long while and then picked up their cards.

And John felt an awful power in his insides. He felt that he and Dinty had joined hands, that Dinty's death had given them a dignity.

He had heard his father play poker; he did not know anything about the cards, but he remembered what to say.

Alec asked in a thinnish voice, "Do you bet anything, Dinty?"

"Five dollars," said John, in the same strong voice.

Mart's jaw opened, showing his uneven teeth.

But the sweat came out on Mike's forehead, and Alec looked afraid.

"Five dollars to come in," breathed Jerry.

They waited a moment, and then Mike said, "Wan of us has got to win it off him or we'll never see it again."

But John's father said, "I'm out."

"All right," Alec said acidly. "But stay out. I'm in, myself," and he pushed five dollars into the middle of the table.

Mart giggled.

"I'll raise the old bezabor a dollar."

The others pushed in their money.

Little trickles of excitement went down John's back.

"I'll raise two dollars."

His father came over beside Dinty and counted the money out.

"It's all he has, barring ten cents."

"Put in the dime," John said in his loud voice.

He was shivering all over, now. The lamplight was in Dinty's beard, making it glow.

Alec laughed.

"All right, Dinty. I'll follow and I'll raise you a dollar. What are you going to do about that?"

Mart giggled again.

But John's father said, "That ain't decent, Alec. He hasn't got the money."

"I know it," said Alec. "It's his tough luck."

John's father swore at him.

"No, you won't, Alec. I'll lend him money myself."

John saw Alec's face grow even whiter under his father's elbow.

"That's a dirty trick, George."

But his father did not answer. He took a dollar from his money, covered Alec's bet, and raised him another dollar.

Then, with a sudden thought, he took all of his money out of his pocket and said, "Meet that, you crummy pup."

The rest counted it.

"My God!" said Alec. "Thirty dollars!"

The others added up the money they had left. They mustered twenty-five between them.

"It ain't fair," Alec said, sweating.

"It's fair enough," roared George. "If ye don't think so, ye can talk to me about it."

John began to feel proud of his father. It would be a heavy wrassle, but his father could handle the lot. You only had to look at his fist to see that.

But he was too excited to keep quiet.

"Take out the five dollars, George," he said. He had never been able to talk deep like that before. The voice startled even his father.

For a long while they hesitated, then Alec said, "Lend it to me, boys."

They put the money on the table against Dinty's.

There was considerable silence in the room. Then Alec turned up his cards.

Mart leaned over. "Three jacks," he said.

"Tough luck," said John.

His body felt hot, but his brain was light and excited, and he knew without looking that Dinty had won.

His father turned over Dinty's cards. There was a moment's silence. Then his father laughed.

"Four aces."

His big hands reached out for the money.

The others said nothing.

Then Alec asked, "What are you going to do with it?"

"I'm going to put it with Dinty," John's father said. "And anybody that don't like that can speak to us both."

"It's a dirty trick," said Alec.

"Get out of here!" roared John's father. "Get out of here, the whole lot of ye. We're sick of ye. Go on."

6

For a moment John cowered down, shivering and shivering. Then he felt ashamed. He got up behind Dinty and put his hand on the dead man's shoulder. He looked at the lot of them, and he saw that his face made them afraid.

"It's damned cold," Mike said. "We've got to walk."

But they went.

His father looked at him.

Then without a word he picked up the old man and laid him back in the coffin. He put the money back on his waistcoat, but it made a large pile now.

"Do ye want to count it, Johnny?" His voice was sorrowful and humble.

John looked at his father.

"No," he said.

His father sighed and sat down, putting his forehead on his hands. John stood still by the coffin and looked down on Dinty's face. It hadn't changed at all.

He looked up at the picture. And the girl was still monkeying with her garter.

Then he noticed the candles burning low.

"Pa, had we ought to keep candles burning?"

His father looked up.

"I don't know, John."

"Are there any more?"

His father got up and looked all around the room.

"No," he said, "there ain't any more candles."

"These are going out pretty quick," John said.

"I've got some candles on the *Bacconola*," his father said. "Do you think they'd do? Maybe they'd ought to be blessed."

"I don't know," John said. "I guess maybe Dinty would like them all right."

"I'll fetch them — if you ain't scared to be here alone for a while."

"No, I ain't scared, Pa."

"They might come back for the money."

"No, they won't."

"Ain't you scared?"

"No," said John, stoutly, "not with Dinty here."

BIG-FOOT SAL

I

THE twilight behind the old boat had faded from the water and the sky with a last shimmer of green on the heart of the clouds. Ahead, except for the dim shapes of the mules and the driver, the country was deserted. Twice lights in farmhouses were passed, but they showed only as dim slits under window curtains; and the houses and barns were no more than blurred bulks against the darkness of night and approaching snow. In all the long flat stretch of farm land, the bow-lantern was the only discernible moving object.

The *clop* of the mules' hoofs in the half-frozen mud made a close sound that only the driver heard. He walked hunched over, with his hat on the back of his head, the broad brim protecting his neck. A gleam of white forelock showed over his eyes. He plodded heavily, step for step with the mules. He did not bother to look at them, but their reek came hot in his face when the wind eddied. His hands were in his pockets, and the lash of the long whip, which he clasped under one arm, trailed behind him through the mud. The hock-deep prints of the mules' hoofs were all that he was aware of — an endless procession coming back to his own feet.

The towline dipped in the interval between the heaves of the mules, and the bullhead bow of the old boat cuddled a ripple. It made no sound, but the ripple slanting to the bank set the dry grass stirring and whispering. Thick curtains were drawn over the cabin windows. The smoke, snatched from the stove-pipe by the wind, was evidence of at least one warm spot on the Long Level.

The steersman was standing beside the sweep, one shoulder hunched against the wind, his gaze fixed on the water's edge, along which the bow-lantern cast a running yellow gleam. Occasionally, though, his eyes wandered to the cabin door at the foot of the steps just to his left, and he appeared to be listening for something in the rush of the wind. Then he turned his attention again to steering.. He could make out nothing of the land beyond the towpath except when a tree or shrub floated into the lantern light. He could see the towline pointing toward the team, and he could just follow the moving shape of Alice, the gray mule. The black one was quite invisible.

Once the gray shape vanished into even deeper shadow, and the driver's voice came floating back hoarsely, "Bridge!" The steersman answered him, "Bridge," and swung his boat three feet into the canal to clear the abutment. As the boat passed under, the lantern lighted the stringers overhead, and he heard the water lapping against the wood sides of the towpath. The captured light gave a brief glimpse of him also. He was a big fellow, with a young brown beard; his eyes were bright and restless, and his face looked white.

As the bridge cut off the wind for an instant he heard plainly a low moan under his feet, and he swallowed hard.

Once more in the open, he glanced right and left, seeking a light. But there was none. Snow began to fall, a flake at a time, passing through the zone of lantern light. He had no hope now of seeing a darkened house even if it stood beside the towpath. He would have to listen for the echo of a footfall against the wooden walls, to be alert for a slackening of wind if they hauled through the lee of a barn.

He yelled ahead to the driver.

"Ben!"

There was no answer.

He cupped his hands and roared, "Ben!"

The mules went on, dragging the boat. But in an instant the light passed over the knees of the driver, showing his pants stuffed into muddy boots.

"Hey, George!"

"Ben, keep watching and listening for a house."

"Getting bad?" asked the hoarse voice.

"A bit worse, I think." There was a hectic note in the steersman's answer.

"All right. You holler if you want to stop. I can hear, all right, but I can't holler back against this wind."

The steersman watched the muddy boots clumping hurriedly back through the light, leaving him alone again in the wind. They were hauling on the Long Level from Salina to Rome. Thank God, he did n't have to haul any farther. If he 'd had any idea that Opal was going to have it so soon, he 'd have tied by in Syracuse and never have accepted this load. There was work there on the railroad for a man and team. But the canal was holding open for another week; they had time, Opal thought, for this haul; and after Rome they could move light into Utica, and Opal could stay with Lucy Cashdollar till the business was over. Lucy took care of her girls that way. She 'd told him when he hired Opal that she would. But neither he nor Opal had had any idea it would come so soon. It was queer how little a girl could know about her works. He wished now they had got married in the first place — they liked each other well enough. If she should die . . . He felt a cold sweat between his shoulders where the wind reached him.

It seemed to him that they had been hauling through a week of darkness since they cleared fifty-four. He 'd asked the lock-tender's wife in, and she said they 'd better wait. But they had thought better. Now he could n't see a light anywhere. And the old *Ohio* seemed to be the last boat hauling the Long Level.

2

The wind was easing perceptibly, but the snow was falling more heavily every minute. It made a close pattern of large flakes that swam in and out of the lantern light, feathering the deck and making dapples in the dark mud of the towpath. As it gained weight upon the earth, the night became quieter. There came spots in the wind when the steersman could not hear it at all.

In one of these lulls he heard plainly from the cabin under him his own name called. "George, oh George!" For a few breaths he was a great hulk bending over with parted lips to listen, refusing to believe. He had teased himself into believing that they would make Rome. "George! Please, George!" He straightened up. He would have to face it. He could n't just go on, leaving her down below.

"Ben!"

His voice cracked. The driver, catching the urgency, scrabbled back.

"Eh, George?"

"We got to tie up."

"Coming bad, are they?"

"Sounds so."

"Put her in right here, then. The mules just got to a pair of posts."

The steersman swung the boat in, straightened her out, and she drifted slantingly against the bank. The light of the bow-lantern picked out two posts rising a foot above the towpath about ninety feet apart.

"Whoa!" screamed the driver. The towline dipped, fell dead. The old *Ohio* slipped up against the bank, eased on the mud, shivered, and lay still. The steersman, coming to life suddenly, tossed ashore a rope and ran to the bow. There he found another which he flung to the driver. He ran back along the gangway, his pounding feet leaving black tracks in the snow.

He jumped down on the narrow stairs and flung open the cabin door. Watching from the bank, the driver saw a burst of light, of warm air that turned to steam, a deep view of falling snow extending skyward, and then he was left in the darkness. His mittened fingers were clumsy in throwing the hitches. When he was through he went ahead for the mules, unhooked them from the towline, and led them into the lee of a slight rise of ground. On top of the rise were some small spruces, so he climbed among them and squatted down. Feeling stiffly through his pockets, he found a plug, cut off a chew, and wedged it into his jaws.

"The young squirt might've let us know how long he aims to stay here. If it's all night, we might as well get aboard." He addressed the mules. One of them sighed and coughed. The other was shaking its withers to loose the sticky collar. The driver shivered. It was blasted cold.

"He don't know nothing," he said aloud contemptuously, and spat down at the mules. "Now if I was running this rigging, I'd have a woman with me, or I wouldn't come at all. Anyway I wouldn't leave a driver die of cold."

This made him feel better. He decided to go back to the boat and find out how matters stood. He climbed down stiffly and once more approached the boat. There was no sign of George. He jumped, caught the four-inch rail and climbed the bolts. The snow hit his face sharply, and he turned his head to shield it and went stumbling for the cabin steps.

He opened the door quietly and slipped into the cabin. There was no one in it. He looked round as he luxuriously absorbed the warmth. It wasn't much of a boat. He ought to have known better than to hire onto a young pair like this. The girl just knew how to cook, and there were enough blankets; but beyond that it was pretty simple. Two chairs and a box, and the same old hinged table that had been put into the boat at the beginning of time. Two sides of the cabin had had two coats of yellow paint, but the other side was only one-coated, and the green showed through. There hadn't been money enough for more paint. Well, they were just starting in; it was a good thing there was one experienced head on the boat. He blew upon his fingers. Then his head bobbed out of his hands to look at the curtains. She was making a fuss all right — first one. Imagine having a baby before you'd learned to read and write. Just imagine. His ratty face looked slyly at the curtains, then switched to the windows. They had one geranium slip in the boat, and they'd left it right beside the

pane. He took it down and set it behind the stove. It was lucky
there was one person could keep his head all right, or that plant
would n't have looked like much by morning. He sat down before
the stove and opened the double oven doors and put his feet inside.
He was pretty comfortable like this; but his shiny black eyes kept
jumping to the curtains of the sleeping cuddy.

3

When the steersman had entered the cabin, he paused to turn up
the lamp, throw a couple of sticks into the stove, and glance at the
clock. Eight past eight. That was a funny time to read. He had
never read it before. He stood looking gawkily at the clock. He
was over six feet tall, and with his hat on, except in the middle
of the cabin, he had to stoop. His soft dark beard was mussed with
the wind, and melting snowflakes gave it drops of water that shone
in the lamplight.

Then his worried eyes swung on the curtains of the sleeping cuddy
at the back as the voice cried, "George!"

He threw his hat into the corner, pulled the curtains, and bent
down low over the double bunk. It was dark in there, with no
light but what came from the cabin; but she had wanted it dark.
She was a little thing. When she stood on the deck beside him she
did n't come to his shoulder. The wind always mussed her hair,
— it was the fine kind of dust-colored hair that never looked neat,
— and if she managed to get it in place, he enjoyed nothing better
than mussing it with one sweep of his hand. It always made her
blush near to bursting. He could hardly recognize her now, lying
there, getting up her nerve to open her eyes, and then turning
her head. She 'd been crying. She did not know her own age,
but Lucy Cashdollar that ran the agency guessed she could n't be
over nineteen. It was n't fair.

He put out his big hand tentatively toward her forehead, but she
seemed to feel it coming.

"Don't touch me!"

His hand jerked as if it had been struck.

She lay quite still, drawing a deep breath. Suddenly she heaved under the blankets, her breath caught.

He tried shutting her cry out of his ears, but it did n't work. The sweat broke out on his face. He reached up and opened the ventilator over the bunk. She caught his other hand.

"George! I wish you 'd get me someone to stay with me. Could n't you?"

His voice shook.

"I 've been looking for a farm all along. There ain't a one." He looked down. "I 'd ought to have stopped by the lock."

"It 's all right, George. It was my fault."

"I 'd ought to have known. Is it too bad?"

She managed a little square grin. "It 's bad enough, George."

They were silent. He listened to her breathing. Outside the wall of the boat he heard a rat working the mud of the bank.

"George!" she cried. "Get me a woman to stay with me. Don't be mean, George. Please."

She was squeezing his hand again.

He tried praying to himself. He could n't think of anything to do.

"Oh, please, George."

"I 'll find someone," he said desperately.

"Don't go way. You won't leave me, George?"

"But I 've got to find someone."

"No. No. You can fix the sheets now."

They had bought a pair of sheets in Syracuse. It was a luxury, but they had felt nice about it. He got them from the shelf and, under her directions, began putting them on one side of the bed. It was a cramped place to work in, and she was irritable at his clumsiness. But when he was done with them, wrinkled though they were, she smiled. "They feel so nice, George."

Then in the same breath she was crying for him to find some-one, anyone.

"Honey, honey," he said. "I will."

He burst out of the cuddy into the cabin and stood there, swing-

ing his hands and staring round desperately. The sharp face of
the little driver was staring up at him over one shoulder.

"Well, George, it's kind of tough. How about them mules?
If we ain't going on, we might as well bring them in. It's pretty
cold."

"Damn the mules."

"Sure," said Ben with a dollar-a-week wise look. "The first one's
always tough."

"What had I ought to do for her?"

Ben jumped.

"Cripus! How do I know? I've never been bothered that
way."

George stared at him wildly, hopelessly inefficient in his strength.

"I can't get anyone. I can't leave her. You get out and find a
woman. You get out. Go on! Quick! And if you come back
without anybody, I'll harrow you proper."

"What?" whined Ben. "Make me go out in that cold? Me
an old man!"

George stepped toward him. He was ugly.

"Get out."

"There ain't no farm."

He saw the great fist close.

"All right, all right. I'm going, George."

He caught his hat and scurried out.

Left alone, the steersman looked round him hopelessly. He had
been brought up on a farm. He racked his brains, trying to find
some expedient he could apply to the girl's case. She was quiet for
the moment, and he moved softly to the stove, from the stove to the
china cupboard, from the cupboard to the table, from the table
to the water butt, and back again to the stove, seeking without seeing an inspiration. And all the time his slow mind kept running
back — to the time he had run from home and hired on as driver —
to the time when he had saved enough money to buy the old *Ohio*
and this team of mules — to the stop he had made in Utica when
he had dropped in on Bentley's Bar and gone upstairs to Mrs. Cash-

dollar's Cooks' Agency for Bachellor Boaters. He could see the old woman as plainly as if she were in front of him, sitting before her Franklin stove, warming her stocking feet, sipping her rum noggin, smoking her pipe, pulling her red wig back into place, and regarding him shrewdly out of a pair of fine blue eyes.

"Want a cook, eh?" her very words. "Kind and gentle? No, no, I mean you. I fix things. Well, you look so. Young, ain't you? Well, when you get in trouble bring her back to me. She's a nice sweet girl, and she don't know much; but if you're patient to her she'll make you the best kind of a woman."

And she had called in Opal. Little timid figure in the door of the back room, sweet mouth, big eyes looking him over, and him blushing and squeezing his hat. Right then he had seen the change creeping up all over her. First he had seen it in her waist and then her eyes; and then there was the devil in her very actions, and then her eyes lowered, and she was just what she had been.

But he had learned all about her during the long spring and summer, hauling back and forth, while she half-ruined his insides practising on them new ideas in food. But she was pretty good now. Some day he would have saved enough money to fix her up the way he wanted, so anybody could see what a dandy she was. And yet it had been a comfortable feeling to be aware that he was the only one who knew.

He had taken the news of the baby pretty easily, — it hadn't meant much to a farmer, — but it hadn't any business being like this. He jammed another stick in the stove. Please God, send them a woman!

And then he heard Ben pounding down along the gang; a shout: "Here's a boat coming west, George!" He rushed into the cuddy, stooped and kissed Opal, and she managed him a smile. Then he was out on the deck, bareheaded, with the snow drifting into the curls in his hair, Ben grabbing him by the arm and pointing a mitten to the east. "Must be a bridge it's back of now. It's a-coming, all right. Don't you be scared, George."

All at once George realized that the driver must have been scared, too.

Then he saw it, several hundred yards away, the bow-lantern of a boat, coming toward them, very slowly.

"Will they stop, do you guess?"

"Yes," said George.

"How'll you get 'em acrosst?"

"Easy."

He was in no mood for talk.

4

The light came forward with the deliberation of a drifting leaf. It was still over a hundred feet away when the two canallers made out the team.

"Horses," whispered Ben. He could tell by the tread.

"Hey!"

The team passed them.

"Hey, there!" roared George. "Stop!"

Ben, with more presence of mind, suddenly shrieked, "Whoa!"

The team stopped dead; and their driver, totally numbed by the cold, bumped into the horse's rump, started, and looked up.

"Hello?"

George shouted across the canal, "Is there a woman on board?"

"What say?"

"Got a woman?"

The man came back. They could just make him out, cupping an ear.

"What say?"

"Got a lady on your boat?"

"No."

George's heart sank.

But then the other boat came drifting in, and a tremendous voice demanded, "What's the trouble?"

George answered, "I just stopped you to see if you had a woman with you."

"Well, I have."

"Can she come over? My girl's in trouble."

"What is it?"

"Baby."

"Damn my luck!" bellowed the voice.

As he spoke, the cabin door opened in front of him, sending out a blaze of light, and George and Ben saw that he was a little man, bent and old as a gnome. Before he could say anything further, a gin-soaked voice that seemed to come from the bottom of the world asked shrilly, "Cooney? Did he say a baby?"

"Yeanh."

"I'm coming!"

"Thank God!" cried George.

The little man threw a rope ashore.

"Tie up, Pete," he directed. "Sal's gone and got it again, and we got to stay." He turned enraged eyes to George. "How are you going to get her acrosst?"

"I'll carry her over."

"Cold work." He seemed resigned.

George did not hesitate. He jumped into the water and started wading. The bottom was muddy, but he did not sink deep. The water came to his armpits. By the time he reached the other towpath his breath came fast with the cold. But his heart was lifting. He would have someone for the girl after all, someone who would carry the horror and responsibility.

A broad, squat figure was stumping along the towpath. As she came into the zone of light, George saw a middle-aged woman with hair of indeterminate color straggling from under her shawl, and the biggest feet he had ever seen. Her eyes were bleary and her breath whistled; but she looked like an angel, and she asked kindly, "How is the dearie? First one?"

George nodded.

"You're a fine strong boy. Cheer up. I'll do the whole thing."

"Thank you, mam."

He stooped down while she scrambled up his back. She got

straddle of his neck and grabbed his hair. "All right, Boy. Am I too heavy?"

He shook his head.

"Don't do that again. I can't abide cold water, Boy."

It took all his nerve to keep from hurrying, but he got her safely over at last and followed her into the *Ohio's* cabin. There he had a good look at her, a sodden old wreck. But her loose mouth smiled kindly. "Take a drink of something, quick, Boy. Where is it?"

He pointed to the cuddy.

"Not her. You first. She'll keep."

She made him take some whiskey and took some herself.

"Now," she said, her lips trembling, "you get back to Cooney. It's wet, but he'll fix you. I'll tend everything here. I won't be bothered by no boys. Get along."

She waddled after him to the stairs. He went up reluctantly. Behind him he heard her shuffling back to the cuddy and her voice saying, "All right, dearie."

He felt better. He and Ben put the team aboard, and then he carried Ben over to the other boat. There they already had their horses fixed for a stay. The little man was waiting for them on the deck.

"Come down," he shouted.

He led them down into a comfortable cabin with many shelves for bottles and a great stove. It smelled strongly of cheese and ham.

"Take your clothes off," he roared. "Have a snort. Sal don't look so good, but she's the best damned cook on the Erie Canal. When you get as old as me, you don't care how they look so long as they keep you comfortable. Bar her taste for gin, she's all right."

He brought a towel for George and saw him rub down. The young man's body, straight, white, and steaming, towered over the three old men.

He smiled through his beard.

"You give me a scare," he said to the driver.

Cooney said, "He didn't mean to do it. He's deef and goes to sleep walking."

"Yeanh," said the driver, pulling his boots off.

Ben said to him, "Do you like horses?"

"I do."

"Me, I like mules."

"That's all right," said the other patronizingly.

Cooney was shaking his white head at George.

"I don't blame you for being worried, Boy. I've never been troubled that way. Sal's never had one."

A little clock behind them struck eleven.

5

The little clock struck two. George got up from his chair and looked through the window. The three older men were playing cards. Cooney said, "Mine again, boys." George turned round. The deaf driver wore his habitual expression of disgust; Ben looked dismayed. Only old Cooney was chuckling as he counted up a score.

"My God," said Ben, "does it always happen this way on this lousy boat?"

Cooney grinned, showing misshapen teeth.

"Boy, Boy. You need to learn the game. But don't begrudge me any fun. I'm going to have a bad time soon."

He gathered up his winnings and offered drinks all round.

"When the old girl gets back she's going to have a spell. Always does when she sees a baby borned. Expects me to fix it for her." He sighed. "A week of rotten eats for us, and the old girl shedding tears. She's always wanted a baby. Funny thing — here she is forty-four years old and every year she wants it worse. There wouldn't nobody else hire her on. Takes too much to keep her in likker, for one thing, and there's her feet for another — Big-Foot Sal." He named her with a certain pride. "Except she's sleeping the last one off, it's all we can do to get her by a bar, ain't it, Henry?" he turned to the driver.

The driver nodded.

"Well, well." He called to George, "See anything doing?"

George could see only the bow-lantern of the old *Ohio*, a glint from one window which the old woman must have opened, the falling snow, and the dim white shore. For an instant the stillness of the whole night came in upon the boat, bringing out the smells.

"Carrying potatoes," observed Ben.

Cooney nodded. "Syracuse."

From the window George said, "No."

Cooney nodded again. "It takes a time, the first one, generally. Never mind, Boy. You'll have plenty more. You'll get used to it. How'd you come to get caught this way?"

George did not answer, and Ben explained dramatically, particularly emphasizing his own cold waiting on the bank, and taking credit for spotting the light.

"They ain't never worth the bother," said the other driver cynically.

"You wasn't," said Cooney.

The driver ignored him. He began pulling on his boots. Ben got into an argument with him about the best kind of hobs. Cooney got up and felt George's clothes. "They're about dry, son. Put 'em on and we'll go on deck."

George dropped his blanket and obeyed swiftly. They went out together, leaving the drivers in an altercation about the shape of the earth. Ben said it was flat and that the canal's Long Level proved it. Henry had a volume of geography. But the canal wasn't in the pictures.

Outside it was clearing. The stars were big and cold, the wind had died, and all the world seemed sleeping under the snow. They could see smoke and steam coming from the *Ohio's* stovepipe. The ripple had died on the canal. George had an odd feeling of music far off. Cooney chuckled at the notion.

"Listen," he said, reaching up for the other's elbow.

George concentrated and heard it. A thin little stifled squeaky cry. He realized all at once that it wasn't Opal, that he had not heard Opal.

"What is it?"

"Listen," said Cooney once more.

This time the cry was hushed by a woman singing. Her wheezy voice went up and down on three notes monotonously. George understood. He sprang to the side of the boat. But Cooney was before him.

"I got to get right back," cried George.

The little man put up a hand against his chest. George suddenly saw his eyes glaring.

"That's all right, mister. Just a minute. We stopped here to help you out. It's going to play billy-bubs with Sal's works. Let her alone for a few minutes. It ain't much to listen to, but it's her idea of a tune. Let her finish it."

George pushed forward.

"Have a heart," said Cooney, earnestly. "She's drunk away everything else in her, but she's got that. Give her a chance."

And George waited. The tune went on and on, over and over, until at last it was done. Then Cooney called for Henry, and the drivers emerged. He shook hands with George. "Luck, Boy."

"Thanks."

"It's all right."

"You can see by the stars it's so," Henry said to Ben.

"Look at that watter," Ben replied.

George grabbed him and carried him over. "Get the mules out," he ordered.

Ben grunted something about a loon and education, and went forward.

6

When George entered the cabin of the *Ohio,* the old woman was just carrying the baby into the cuddy. She came out in a minute and said, "It was one of the easiest I ever see. It's a nice pretty boy."

She stood quite still, her lips trembling. He hardly saw her. In a moment he was in the cuddy, bending over Opal. She was all right. She looked tired, half gone, but she was all right. And she

gave him a smile and opened the blankets. He saw it and bent
over, dripping as he was, and kissed both of them. He looked
round. Everything was to rights. He lingered.

When he reëntered the cabin the old woman had finished fixing
things.

This time he saw her — dumpy body, shawl-wrapped, square face
and loose cheeks and trembling mouth and big feet, and something
shy in her eyes. Then the red lids seemed to swell and tears came.
She put out her arms and kissed him.

"Quick," she said. "Fetch me home to Cooney."

He said nothing. But all the way over he felt her crying.

Cooney took her without a word. The horses were ready. Before George was back on the *Ohio* the other boat had slipped off.
It was just a light at the corner of the bend. And it was gone.

He went below for dry clothes, still tasting the gin.

It was all still and peaceful there. He went into the cuddy and
looked down as he stripped. It was all still and peaceful — like a
gift that Big-Foot Sal had left. He felt his throat closing.

Outside the mules were tramping over the gang.

He had to get on deck.

THE CRUISE OF THE CASHALOT

We sawed the last cut on the last tree and sat down side by side on the log. John got out a wad of Happy Days, when he saw that I was lighting my pipe, and stowed it away in his right cheek. His eye was taking in the river valley, with the canal beyond. Some plover were calling down the river, but he did not hear them. And then just as I was getting back my wind, he swung his eye round at me.

"Say," said he, "did I ever tell you about my Uncle Ben?"

I

My Uncle Ben Meekum was kind of a dingy old coot. They say in his early days he was a pretty fat kind of a spark; but when I first remember him he 'd married Aunt Em, and the two of them made just about the most respectable kind of home life a woman could want. Uncle Ben would load his boat, and him and Henry Plat, who done his driving, would get the old boat along with the aid of Ben's mules; but inside the boat the old lady ruled the roost.

It was kind of hard on a man, after he 'd run a boat to suit his own notions for forty years, to have the bad luck to get married to Aunt Em. You could n't spit out of the window or knock out your pipe on top of the stove or have a drink in your own cabin (or anywhere else, for that matter), and she used to make him and Henry, who was bothered with soft feet, wash 'em every night before they come to supper. It was a pitiful sight to see them two old coots setting and easing their toes into a basin. Every time he felt the touch of water, Henry 'd say he was going to get loose and leave, but Uncle Ben 'd beg him to stay.

"You can go ashore and get drunk, Henry," he 'd say; "but I can't hardly swaller without the old girl's looking to see what I got in my teeth. Watter," he'd say, "has so saturated my inwards that another drop will just about make me sick."

But Henry'd never have gone off and left him. Them two had been boating it together ever since Uncle Ben'd got his boat, and Henry was just as scared of Aunt Em as Uncle Ben was. If he'd have left, he'd have been scared clean crazy of her coming after him.

I don't say Aunt Em was a bad woman; but she was too big to live in a boat. She'd always been in heavy flesh and her blood pressure generally kept going up on her. Quick-tempered. And she could have taken on both of them old men at once, if she'd been a-mind to; and she probably did when she got restive.

You see she belonged to my family, and Uncle Ben only got in by marrying her. His name was Meekum, and he had to take about everything that was coming to him.

He used to talk to Pa about it and ask what a man had ought to do, and Pa'd tell him: "Strop her up and if that don't work use the hone." But Uncle Ben'd shake his head and say Pa was a young man, and then give Pa some of his own early history until he'd start off home with active ideas. But the minute the old lady'd get her eye on him, he'd lose his nerve.

It went on that way till the time Uncle Ben busted loose in New York and made a deal. He'd often thought before that of sneaking out on her; but she'd put all the money he used to keep on the boat in a bank in Boonville in her own name, because Uncle Ben couldn't read nor write, and she took the money the boat earned off of him as quick as it come in.

Well, sir, Uncle Ben did bust loose, and this is the way it happened.

2

The spring of the year him and Henry had loaded up their boat with ice at Forestport and picked the old girl up at Boonville, where they spent the winter in her mother's house, and started off for New York.

They made a regulation haul to Albany and left their mules in the round barn and got into a tow on the Swiftsure and had the

ride down the Hudson. All the way Uncle Ben kept considering
what he'd get to haul back. Fertilizer would have made him a
good haul, and he thought the trip to New Jersey after it might
be pleasant. But Aunt Em would n't consider it. She said it
would make the boat smell too strong.

She took a lot of pride in that boat even if it was Uncle Ben's.
She'd had it painted up a good bright yellow with a white trim,
and she had the cabin fixed up dainty with curtains at the windows
and the best geraniums on the Erie. She was a good hand to cook
and keep house, and the best meals I ever ate I ate right there. She
could make a pie to bring the watter to a man's eyes. And it did
look nice. It was all painted blue inside, with the cupboards white
and the stove black and the pans always hanging in the same place.
She had a little brass clock, too, that struck the hours with a bell.
It did n't keep very good time, always being slow; but the way
she polished it you would have thought it had come from the
factory in the morning mail.

The boat's name was *Louisa* and you can see it laying in that
set-back below Hawkinsville to-day, what's left of it.

So the old lady'd said there'd be no fertilizer, and Uncle Ben
had to agree. Him and Henry had had it all figured out, but
Henry was riding on one of the other boats most of the time and
so Uncle Ben got to New York without knowing what he was going
to haul back.

Well, they tied up in the East River docks the same as usual waiting for a calmer day to get the boat across the harbor and they
had n't more than got to the Swiftsure office to pay off before the
clerk handed Uncle Ben a letter for Aunt Em. Uncle Ben was an
ignorant old bezabor when it come to civilized ideas. Pa used to
say he'd been born with just as much sense as anybody else, but
that he'd lost progress since then. When the clerk explained who
the letter was for, Uncle Ben paid off, and him and Henry went
back to the boat.

Uncle Ben walked right up the gang and down into the cabin.
Getting a letter that way made him feel important.

"Wipe your feet," says Aunt Em.

"To hell with my feet," says Uncle Ben. "Here's a letter, Em."

"For me?" she asked, and Uncle Ben says, "Yes, sir."

She dropped the potato she had commenced peeling into the wrong pan and grabbed that paper. It took her just a minute to figure it all out and she turned kind of pale.

"Ma's sick," she says. "I got to get right home. It says that she's real sick again with sugar diabetes."

"I don't wonder," says Henry from the door, "the way she eats it with her coffee."

But Aunt Em didn't notice it. She was all dithery.

"I got to start right out," she says.

"And me unload this ice into the river?" asks Uncle Ben.

"You danged fool," she says. "Do you think your cheap mules can get me home in time? Poor Ma, with such a son-in-law. It's a lucky thing she's got a daughter."

"Well," says Uncle Ben, "if you want to beat out the *Louisa* you'll have to take a train of cars."

And that's what she done. She got out her old satchel and her hat and she put off with them for the station as tight as she could make it.

"You come right home the minute you've got rid of that ice," she says.

"Yes, Em," says Uncle Ben.

"And you make Henry mop out the floor every other day and don't you set down after eating till you've done the dishes. And don't you dasst to use that new china set."

"No, Em," says Uncle Ben.

"And you put the money in the box when you get paid, and don't you touch a penny."

And then the train took her off.

3

There ain't anybody to tell to-day how Uncle Ben commenced getting drunk, except only Henry Plat, and he wasn't very reliable that afternoon, and he's dead now. But he kept setting a pretty good pace right along till they got back to the boat. Anyhow, they got back, Uncle Ben hugging up a great big demijohn under each arm, and saying what an awful thing the sugar diabetes was for an old lady to have, and they took the ice across the harbor, and it was the first time in ten year Uncle Ben had n't got sick making the voyage. He stood on the cabin set-back holding the sweep, with his shirt unbuttoned and the spray slopping against his wishbone; and every time a gull hollered he 'd look up against the sun. And Henry Plat, he lay on his stummick looking at Uncle Ben's nose and whiskers, full of admiration at the way watter in a man's in-wards can dilute his drinks.

Well, sir, they unloaded that ice and they took a tow back to the East River dock, and halfway across they seen a lot of boats rowing to beat the nation and right ahead of them the scaredest whale that ever got mixed in the traffic of New York. There was a lot in the papers after, how that whale got into the city anyhow, and they had pictures of it, and a picture of Uncle Ben a-standing on the *Louisa,* holding a cap in his hand and looking modest. After it was all over Uncle Ben had bought him a secondhand skipper's hat in a slopshop and let on how he 'd been around the Horn in his early manhood.

But what happened was that that whale seen the old *Louisa* butting her stummick on the waves and I guess he thought she was another whale.

Uncle Ben seen her coming and yelled at Henry to look and tell him what in Crimus was coming and Henry looked and just hollered. Uncle Ben was always quick in a tight situation and he grabbed his horn and let out a good one on it, but the whale run up alongside of him and squirted the boat with watter and blood and Uncle Ben lost his temper and grabbed his boat hook and jammed it against the whale to keep her off and stuck her right in the eye. I guess the old brute was pretty near exhausted because it just raised a fin and died right there.

Well, the other boats come up, and the men in them claimed the whale was theirs; but Uncle Ben had his boat hook well set

in the brute's eye and he would n't listen. Seems as if the whiskey
he drank was just about striking home, because he made a great
impression and they laughed and asked one another what they
would do with a whale anyhow, and pretty soon they asked Uncle
Ben would he buy out their share. And he smacked his hand
on his wallet and fishes out the money, and what with counting
and the motion of the waves and Henry Plat he had only just
enough left to pay for a tow up the river and get his mules out of
the barn in Albany.

4

When they got back to the dock again and the watter got calm
Henry Plat got up and commenced taking notice.

"What," he says, "are you going to do with that whale, Ben?"
And then he remarks, "How Em 's going to make you squeak
when she finds out what you 've spent your money on!"

But Uncle Ben was too likkered up for solid thought.

"Shut up, you poor bezabor," he says. "Em has n't got nothing
to say about this whale."

"No," says Henry, "I guess not."

Well, right then a lot of reporters come aboard and they begun
asking questions. Uncle Ben got him his hat with gold braid and
a shiny visor and had his picture took. And just after the whole
of them had left, along comes a boat with a chesty bung in uniform
that comes aboard and wants to know how long Uncle Ben aims
to keep his property in New York harbor. Well, Uncle Ben gives
him some drinks and says he 'll get it out of the way pretty quick
and salivates him handsome, and that was that.

But he still had Henry Plat to talk to before he could get any
rest.

"What am I going to do with it? What am I going to *do?*"
And right there he got his idea. "Why," he says, "I 'm going to
load that whale aboard the *Louisa,* and take her up the Erie."

"Be you, Ben? What are you going to do that for?"

"I 'm going to show her for a nickel."

Henry sneered. "How much money will that make, when anybody can look at her from the towpath for nothing?"

"You shut up," said Uncle Ben.

He'd got more up-and-coming every minute since Aunt Em had gone back to Boonville, and he wasn't going to let no bum bezabor like Henry Plat gum his fun. He just walks up the dock and goes off to the public library. Now he'd got a whale he wanted to know all about it. So he walks in and says to the lady, "Please show me your whales, Miss." Well, that caught her attention and she was a pretty girl and in two minutes had got the whole business out of Uncle Ben. "I want to find out what kind of a whale it is, and all about it."

Well, she took him through a lot of books, and they discovered about fourteen different kinds of whale.

"What does he look like?" asks the lady.

"Well, ma'am, she's round, in good flesh, and kind of dark, and she's got a pleasant eye."

"Oh," says the lady, and commenced educating Uncle Ben. . . .

When he come back about supper time, Henry asked him again what he aimed to do with his fish.

"Fish? That ain't no fish. My God, Henry, you're a ignorant bird all right. Why, that's a mammal!"

"What," asks Henry, "is a mammal?"

Uncle Ben just looks him up and down.

"Henry," he says, "your mother was one."

"Do you want to fight?" asks Henry.

"No," says Uncle Ben. "You've been upset by this business, Henry. Of course, it's been different with me. I've been around the Horn in my young days. In my day I've speared more'n a hundred of this identical variety. I've got sperms, and speared narwhales, and blowed the very guts out of a killer oncet, at three hundred yards with my old thirty-eight."

"What's the name of this variety?"

"It's a cash-a-lot."

Henry looks at him kind of wondering. "Honest?"

Uncle Ben nods to him. "Honest," he says.

"My God," says Henry; "maybe there is money in her, after all."

"Listen, Henry, did you ever hear about a feller named Jonah?"

"Sure, he got swallered by one of them animals."

"That's right, and then he got spit up. Well, look here, Henry. Anybody that wants to can look at the outside of this whale for nothing; but them that want the whole works is going to have to pay me fifty cents."

"How're you going to show them the whole works, Ben?"

"I'm going to dig 'em out and make room in his inside!"

Uncle Ben looks proud.

"But Ben," asks Henry, "if you dig them out, where in Sarah are you going to put them for people to see?"

"My God, Henry, can't you think of nothing but inwards? I'm just going to have a room there and a bar and a — I guess I'll just have a kind of refreshment parlor — then I'd ought to get the ladies and children, too."

"That's an idea," says Henry, and it was.

They got the whale hoisted onto the *Louisa* next morning, with her nose on the cabin roof and the rest of her laying along the pit beams and the stable, and her tail hanging over the front end. Then they joined their tow and started back for Albany.

Well, the old *Louisa* was the first boat in that line; but along about Spuyten Duyvil the wind changed to the north and the rest of the boats made the tug change the line to put her on the back end. They'd thought at first a whale was a pretty handsome thing to examine; but about there Uncle Ben and Henry had got through the outside layer of fat. You could see them any time, burrowing in like a couple of beagles digging out a wood-chuck. They had little shovels, very sharp, and they certainly made progress.

At first Uncle Ben was real mad at being stuck onto the back end of the tow, but Henry pointed out it would be handier getting rid of the insides, so he didn't argue very hard. He was having too good a time. He hadn't had likker in that long that now he had it he could n't smell nothing but drink. Henry was n't so well fixed. And what with digging back of Uncle Ben and getting the throwout he was so danged greasy that he would n't dasst to scratch a match along his back end, no sir, not even without his pants. No sir, and what 's more he was n't fitted out for hard work and he could n't keep up with Uncle Ben. That old coot was just about possessed. He 'd got a dish towel tied around his beard and cotton in his ears, and even at that about every ten minutes he had to walk out and let himself dreen over the edge.

Well, about the second day they got pretty well into the core. They 'd mixed themselves a mess of beans down in the cabin and Henry wanted to lay down on his bed, but Uncle Ben had n't time. He kept explaining, "I got to get the outfit in afore we get to Watervliet." So up he went and walked in, and the first stroke he took he went through between two bones and the yell he let out come right out of the whale's mouth and Henry come a-running.

"Where 've you reached to, Ben?" he asks.

Uncle Ben did n't know. He was kind of puzzled, inside and looking out, and Henry looks around too, and says, "I don't see where that feller Jonah managed to get along. I don't believe he was a whole week down inside like us are here. The ventilation 's no damned good at all."

"You poor twerp," says Uncle Ben. "This ain't the same whale."

"I don't see what that 's got to do with it."

"No, you 've never been around the Horn. But I have and I 've seen whales blow out the bad air fifty feet high."

"If there was that much pressure of bad air, I don't see how Jonah lasted out a minute."

"Well, maybe he was that kind of a feller," says Uncle Ben.

Well, when they got the insides into the river, Uncle Ben begun to fashion out a room. "Right here," he says, "is going to be the refreshment tables for the ladies. I 'll get them in Albany. We won't need so many cheers, with what we got in the cabin. And then," he says, "seeing as how the lighting ain't very good, I 'll

arrange a winder on each side." He stood there looking around
kind of pleased and wondering. "Henry," he says, "what kind
of curtains do you think would go best with these walls?"

Right then some blubber went into the back of Henry's neck and
got the best of him.

"You're going to need something waterproof to wall this room,"
he says.

"Nonsense," says Uncle Ben, but it was a hot day and he discovered for himself there was a leak in the roof. But his ideas had
got pretty well formed. And by the time he'd showed the outside of his whale in Troy for fifteen cents he'd got the inside all
fitted out. And when he hauled out to number one, the whole
contraption did make a display.

First, the two mules, a couple of crummy old screws, had had
their harness blacked and tassels and rings hung out to hide the
bare spots in their hides till they sounded like a circus parade.
And then the towline had a twist of yeller cloth on it and a big
bow ribbon. And then come Henry Plat. Uncle Ben had rigged
out the poor bezabor in a secondhand coachman's outfit, and he
had a top hat with a ribbon bouquet on it and a coat with tails —
and Henry's back end wasn't the kind to carry tails, it stuck out
between — and white pants like knickers and a pink westcoat, and
then there was the boots with flesh tops. Henry had tried them
out in Albany, but they pinched him so that he hollered and
argued till Uncle Ben allowed him to go back to the old boots
he always wore and the red socks Aunt Em knitted him for
Christmas. But even then the poor twerp's whiskers and little
eyes looked kind of wistful as if the clothes had got him and
was taking him somewhere where he didn't want to go.

But then come the boat. They had kind of washed her outside
but she looked a little greasy; but as Uncle Ben said, everybody had
seen a bullhead boat anyway. It was the whale they'd look at.
And sure enough, there was the whale stretched out on the boat,
looking Uncle Ben right in the eye where he stood steering. She
had a door in her side opposite the gang, and a flag stuck into her

nose hole saying CASHALOT in green letters. And over the door was a sign saying, "Be a Jonah for fifty cents." And underneath it said, "Complete equipment."

And that was n't all. Getting familiar with the whale the way he had had made Uncle Ben kind of affectionate, and he wanted her to look her best; so he 'd got a pair of glass eyes off an oculist in Albany which was as big as apples and he 'd arranged them in her, which gave her a real active appearance. He himself got a sailor's coat and his hat and a new tie and done the steering. Every time he come to a village he blew on his horn and put into the dock. And the whole town come down. And danged near everyone would go inside the whale. It certainly was rigged out.

Uncle Ben 'd built a regular room out of matched lumber and he had a winder on the far side opposite the door, and a chair and table in the front end, and a bunk and a stove running through a double pipe, which he did n't never get up his nerve to light. And on the shelf in the back end he had a cupboard with all Aunt Em's best china set out. And as he told the people, it was all real shipshape and very actively arranged, all but the plumbing.

And a lot of those farmers thought all whales was rigged out like that, and commenced to take the Bible seriously after.

Well, the first day Uncle Ben paid all his expenses, and every day he went along he made more money, because the word got into the papers and there was the picture took of him in New York and a picture of the complete whale, and even of the mules and Henry Plat. Farmers come from fifty miles away to intercept the creature and get a look at his insides.

But what was more important, Uncle Ben began to get more owdacious every day. By now he had killed whales in his early days with his bare hands; this one he 'd fixed with his boat hook — you could read it in the papers — but of course he was getting old, and the number he had shot with his old thirty-eight was financially extraordinary. He showed you the thirty-eight to prove it and the notches he had cut in it for woodchucks became whales. He could look any man in the eye, and spit on a dime. You 'd

never have guessed he'd ever have been married to Aunt Em.
And I don't suppose he ever remembered her at all. When he
wasn't talking whale or serving tea to the ladies, he was having
a snort on his own.

You won't believe it, maybe, but that old coot had made over
a thousand dollars before he got to Rome. And by now the
Utica papers had the whole story and described the boat and the
china and remarked on the pattern, which was in forget-me-nots
and roses, and Henry Plat begun to wonder if it wasn't about time
they heered from Aunt Em.

But by the time they got to Rome there had been a week of hot
weather and the whale had swollen some, and on the last day
Uncle Ben had to do some trimming to get her under the bridges.
And when he done that, even though he'd been living in that whale
for two weeks, he had to admit that she was getting higher. And
every day after that, the more he trimmed her the higher she got;
and at Rome, for the first time, the price of admission went down
a quarter. But Uncle Ben had become a regular Wall Street
wizard, and he bought out two perfumery peddlers and did a handsome business in that line.

By this time, too, Henry Plat had become used to his uniform
and was beginning to regret that the smell was getting so bad
it threatened to stop the show. He hadn't ever had so many free
drinks in his life before, nor had he ever had such light hauling
to do. His breathing system had got used to blubber; and he felt
real apprehensive when, sure enough, there was Aunt Em on the
dock, in front of the crowd, with her bag in her hand and her hat
over her eyes, looking half as big as the whale and more than
twice as powerful.

She'd been reading the papers. She didn't even look at the
mules or Henry Plat or the yeller bow on the towline, and if her
nose was working she didn't even show it.

She waited till the boat had tied up and the gang come out and
then she marched right aboard.

Uncle Ben come down the gang walk.

"Hullo, Emmy," he says, and Henry was real startled to hear him so cool.

She stopped right still and kind of shivered.

"You runty little spider," — she was always naming him by an insect, — "is this the way you spend our money? Is this the way you hurry home to the bedside of your blessed mother-in-law?"

Uncle Ben sounded patient.

"I was detained on business," he says.

"Business?"

Henry Plat kept feeling little cold winds climbing up the inside of them white pants. But then he seen Uncle Ben wink.

"Well, old girl," he says out loud, "welcome home. I'm surprised you was so long gone; but, now you're back, you're welcome."

He must have had that speech all figured out, I guess.

The crowd let out a cheer. Here was the whale killer being met by his loving wife. Crowds like that kind of thing. If there'd only been a baby on hand for Uncle Ben to use he could have collected a dollar, instead of twenty-five cents.

Well, Aunt Em took a look at the crowd and went below without talking.

In a minute up she come hollering mad. "Where's my chiney?" she hollers. And outside of the condition of the blankets, the fat had come through onto her Bible and the brass clock was running about forty-two hours a day with the oil that had got into it and striking faster than a man could wind it. Her curtains was streaked and the geraniums looked kind of sickly, and there hadn't been a dish washed in two weeks.

But she couldn't make no headway into that whale; it was jam full of humans; and when she finally did get in she slipped on the floor and set down.

Uncle Ben helped her onto her feet and begun to explain the inside workings of that cashalot. And when he come to the money in it, Aunt Em was impressed. Even she could see that Uncle

Ben was the killer of a whale, and was n't scared of a woman any more, and so she commenced to cry.

"Look at my chiney, look at what you have done to my pretty boat," she says. "How can I expect to live in a cabin full of a smell like that?"

"If you don't like it, Emmy, you can go home," says Uncle Ben.

But there was too much money involved. She stayed, and when she complained again, Uncle Ben told her to try whiskey; and danged if she did n't do it. She got mellower and mellower, and when the price of admission had to drop to two for a nickel, she did n't even open the winders; and when they had to sell the whale for fertilizer in Rochester, for eighty cents, and Uncle Ben said to her, "This smell of fish is kind of strong. You'd better give the boat a good clean up," she did n't say a word, but got right to work. Even when Henry Plat come in with his boots on, she did n't say a word.

And Uncle Ben just set in the cabin looking on, having his evening snort, and looking at them two glass eyes hung up where the geraniums used to set. He'd put his money in a bank himself, and his heart had gone with that whale, and Aunt Em wanted to keep what was left. Once she'd been unloosed by whiskey, she turned out a fond woman.

They worked the *Louisa* back through hogs and potatoes to grain, until she was as nice as ever. But Uncle Ben had become a kind of old mariner, and Aunt Em continued a changed woman till she died; and if you want to see them glass eyes, my Pa has got them in his house.

THE THREE WISE MEN

I

As the west-bound freight slowed for the grade, the body of a man, who had been riding the rods, jumped from under a car, lost its footing, and rolled down the embankment. For an instant it whirled over the snow, a jumble of short, fat arms and legs; then, with a grotesque flurry, it vanished into a deep drift.

When the tramp had floundered out, the empties at the end of the train were clanking by above him, gathering momentum as the engine passed over the height of ground. The cars faded away in the falling snow with a last flash of light from the windows of the caboose and a single gray wisp of smoke from its stovepipe. The tramp blew on his fingers and shook the loose snow from his collar. He had a round, red face; and his twinkling black eyes, like polished buttons, looked out over his pudgy nose. There was something elfish about him, as he stood alone, breathing white steam into his hands, with the flakes drifting down upon his head and shoulders.

Suddenly he cocked his head on one side and his little black eyes glanced right and left. Over the collars of his three coats his ears had caught the sound of voices. Then his eyes, glancing up the tracks, saw a tongue of blue wood smoke curl out of the side of the embankment and drift away into the snow. Treading cautiously, his round belly quivering under his clothes, he approached the spot from which the smoke had appeared, inexplicably, like a wraith. The buttress of a culvert rose out of the drifted snow, and, running along its base, he found the footprints of two men. He followed these to the opening of the tunnel and peered stealthily round it with one eye.

" 'Oo 's there?" asked a sharp, nasal voice. "I sye, there, w'y don't you show us 'oo you be?"

Partially reassured, the tramp thrust his head completely round the corner. The barest trickle of a spring ran along one wall of the culvert, leaving plenty of room for two hoboes, who were sitting before a small fire. The smaller of the two renewed his invitation.

"Come in," he said. "Come in out o' that 'eathen cold. This are n't no bloomin' clink for you to 'old back out of."

The fat man stepped into the light, his small eyes dancing, a grin on his plump lips.

"London!" he cried. "London Joey! What be you a-doin' out here?"

The cockney sprang to his feet.

"If it are n't me old frien' Tarfy! 'Ow are you? W'ere 'd you drop out of, Tarfy?"

"Number thirty-seven, fast freight out o' Utica. N' York, N' Haven, 'n Hartford box car. The trucks was so durned loose, I thought I 'd lose me teeth with the shakin'. And I dursn't put 'em in me pocket — they might 've dropped out."

"I thought you knowed better 'n to pick one o' these blymed buggies."

The cockney remembered that an introduction was due.

"Tarfy, this is me frien' Sudden 'Enry — Mr. Tarfy Jones — shyke 'ands."

As he surveyed the two, Taffy Jones's shoebutton eyes twinkled. Sudden Henry was obviously a Swede. He sat against the wall of the culvert, his great bony body hunched forward, and his shadow ran out above him with a strange tapering cock to its head. The firelight shone on his red heavy-knuckled hands clasping his knees; it cast deep shadows about his eyes, which stared over his hard high cheeks with a cold calm. They were blue and pale, with deep lines at the outer corners which made them look as though they always stared at the hills upon the sky line. As he sat there before the fire, Taffy Jones hunkered down beside him, using the man's body as a bulwark against the cold, and chuckled because the Swede looked so stupid beside the nervous little cockney.

"Well, Mr. Henry," he asked, "where be you plannin' to visit next?"

Sudden Henry turned his head to face the fat man. His long body shifted uneasily upon his hams, and his voice rumbled in his chest and up his throat before it broke from his lips.

". . . Arrh . . . arrh . . ." He hesitated, slowly pulled a block of tobacco from the pocket of an inner coat, and gnawed off a chew with his big, square teeth. ". . . Arrh . . . I be goin' . . . I be goin' . . ."

He shifted the quid between his molars and began to chew with a deliberate, ruminating pressure of his jaws. London Joey leaned over and put his lips to Taffy Jones's ear.

"Gawd bless 'im for a stoopid moke," he whispered. "Don't ask 'im w'ere 'e's goin'. 'E don't know."

Taffy Jones chuckled between his teeth, musically, like a robin. The Swede was staring at the opposite wall of the culvert. Now and then his lips moved as though he were still talking; but he said nothing.

The fat man searched through his innumerable pockets. After a minute he drew out a tin box, opened it, offered the cockney the longest of a collection of cigar butts, and chose one for himself. London Joey picked a glowing stick from the fire and they lighted up, their eyes tight shut against the wood smoke, their lips curling round the butts as they puffed. They leaned back again, smoking contentedly.

"W'ere 've you been, Tarfy, since I seen you last?"

"Ain't been so far," began the fat man, trimming the end of his cigar with a small knife. "Went out to Chiny. Nice trip. Stayed out there quite some time, too. Took a journey down to Java. Ain't been there, has you? Watch out for them Java girls if you goes there. They dances somethin' fancy, but they're black 'uns, they be; and they're cussed mean. I come back comfortable through th' canal and then up th' coast."

"Niggers ain't right," said the cockney. "I made a error, I did, bein' drunk, and got landed off in Africa. Fooled round up-country there, but it ain't no kind of a country. Took me a year to get back. 'Opped a 'ooker, I did, and went up th' coast. Ended up in Rio."

"Where's he been?" asked Taffy, nodding toward the Swede.

"Blymed if I know. 'E just comes and goes — nobody knows w'ere or 'ow. 'E'll take up with you, and then 'e'll 'op it w'en you ain't watchin'."

The cigars fizzled close to their faces, and the heavy smoke hung rank about their clothes and swayed over the fire.

It had grown dark at the end of the culvert. The small fire, burning with increasing brilliance, sent its beams into the night and picked out occasional drifting flakes against the black sky. The two smoked in silence, while, at their right, the Swede chewed steadily, pausing now and again to spit into the fire. Suddenly he raised his head.

"Wind's comin'," he said.

They listened.

It had become much colder. In the distance they heard a faint whining that grew swiftly in volume. All at once the flames of the fire bent to the lower end of the culvert and a long tongue of smoke licked away into the darkness.

"You might've knowed," said the cockney, "that if wind was goin' to blow, it'd blow into here."

Taffy breathed on his knuckles and held his palms to the fire. The rumble of a train swept upon them; the roaring of the engine and the grumble of the wheels passing above their heads filled the culvert with prodigious echoes that bounced from wall to wall long after the cars had passed. Then, in an instant, the first gust of the wind swept the passage clean of sound. It was bitter cold.

"We carn't stay 'ere," said the cockney.

"There used to be a barn up the tracks, about a mile from the top of the grade," said Taffy. "A hay barn — without any house close to it."

2

He scrambled to his feet and the others followed him to the end of the culvert. The snow had stopped falling with the rise of the wind, and the stars had come out clear and small. The air was piercing cold, and bitter in their nostrils. The frost had hardened the surface snow, so that the crust shone with a gray gleam. The trees had flattened to silhouettes that barely showed above the sky line. Against the snow, the thin trunks wavered. The wind made the two cigars flare up until they burnt the smokers' lips, and they tossed the butts away. The wind caught them up and rolled them along the surface of the snow with bursts of sparks which glowed behind them in long streamers.

The three tramps climbed the embankment to find easier walking on the ties. At the top, they bent into the full force of the wind, drew their collars close round their necks, and, with their hands thrust deep in their trousers pockets, they started off abreast.

After about a quarter of an hour's walking, Taffy raised his head, shielding his face with his hands, and looked away to the left. The roadbed ran almost level with a wide expanse of bottom land, and a hundred yards away the bulk of an old barn rose like a black shadow on the snow.

"There she be," he yelled in the cockney's ear. Seizing the Swede's arm, he led the way. They climbed a ridge of snow banked up by the ploughs and began to flounder through the soft going beyond, pausing, now and then, for one to look up and locate the barn.

In one of these pauses, when the three were close upon the building, Taffy pointed ahead and shouted, "There's somebody into it! There's a light there!"

" 'S trewth!" London yelled back at him. "But we carn't stay outside."

They tried the big door cautiously. Apparently it had been hooked on the inside, for even when the Swede laid hold of it and bent his shoulders till his arms cracked, it would not budge. So they tried knocking instead. Instantly someone stirred within and moved close to the door.

"Who be you, out there?"

" 'Ow should we care 'oo we be?" yelled the cockney, pounding the door till it shook. "We wants to get in."

"All right," said the voice. "But stew your noise, can't you?"

The three tramps could hear a fumbling inside, and presently the door rolled back a foot or two and they slipped through. The man who had admitted them closed the door quickly and dropped a heavy iron hook through a ring, locking it.

Then he turned to take stock of them. In his right hand he held a smoky barn lantern, the light of which shone upward along his body and cast queer, arched shadows about his shoulders and his face. They saw at once that he was one of their kind: his clothes were baggy, three coat cuffs showed on each wrist; his trousers fell straight from his waist to his ankles, where they gathered in loose puckers; his flat shoes were worn thin and moulded over his toes; his face was quiet, almost hard; but his eyes were feverish and kept shifting to a dark corner of the floor between the mows.

He gestured to a mound of hay.

"It's warm in here. Set down and put yourselves up comfortable."

As he moved ahead of them toward the rear of the barn, the shadows fled in troops before the advancing lantern and vanished under the hay in the corners with sudden whisking motions, like rats; while behind the four men new shadows crawled over the floor to the swinging of the light.

The three tramps sat down. The smell of hay lay upon the air with heavy mustiness. Outside, the wind blew gustily, whistled through knotholes, and caught up the chaff in whorls of golden specks that danced in the lantern light. The man who opened the door was stooping over a pile of hay in the far corner. After a minute he came back to them, his eyes bright and his face very red.

"Well," said the cockney, "w'at 've you got over there you 're so precious about, any'ow?"

The color in the man's cheeks deepened.

"It 's me skirt," he said, and fell silent.

"Oh," said Taffy Jones, "I had one myself, oncet. Young skirt, she were, too. Regular high-flinger."

He sighed, folded his hands over his belly, and looked down at them sadly.

"She was too high-flingin', I reckon; and she flung me."

" 'Ell," snarled London Joey. "W'at did you try to for? W'en they 're squidgy, don't let on you 're sorry — sock 'em. Then you leaves 'em flat before they can run off. An' then, if you wants to cut loose, there ain't anythin' to 'amper you. That 's w'at I 'm a-doin' of now. Cuttin' loose. Goin' to 'Frisco, I be. Maybe drop onto Chi on the way."

The fourth man gazed at him admiringly.

"Me and me skirt was plannin' to do that, too. Come all the way from N' Yawk — roadin' it mostly. Then she got sick, she did, two days ago — right here. 'Widgin,' she says, — that 's me name, — 'I figgers you and me is goin' to have a baby,' she says, 'right here.' 'An' spoil our journey?' I asks. She was bred up tender, and Baptist, so I talks to her gentle like that. She says she is, though. . . . And glory! If she ain't been an' done it!"

3

The Swede spat out his plug. He leaned over to Widgin, his eyes deep blue and staring, his face sad. Words rumbled in his chest and his lips moved.

". . . Arrh . . ." he said. ". . . Arrh . . ."

He pulled out his plug of tobacco and broke off another chew with his big teeth.

The black eyes of Taffy Jones twinkled like bits of a broken mirror, and his smooth cheeks shone in the yellow light.

"Me," he said, "I've never had no baby of my own, but I'd like to see yourn."

Widgin glanced nervously over his shoulder.

"Me skirt's young, and she ain't used to it, I reckon. Maybe she'd let you, though, if I asked her."

He went over to the corner. The three watched him bending over the pile of hay and heard him whispering.

"Yes," said a woman's voice.

Widgin beckoned to them. They got up slowly, London pushing Taffy Jones ahead of them while the Swede brought up the rear. Taffy shuffled forward, twisting his hat in his hands.

"I hope you does n't mind," he mumbled. "My frien' here, he's kind of curious."

While Widgin held the lamp for them to see, they looked down at the woman. She was thin and young, and her face was white with a relaxed weariness. There were traces of deeper lines about her mouth and nostrils, as if she had been hungry not long before. The lantern brought out the pallor of her cheeks with so ghastly a light against the gray dead color of the hay that Taffy's fingers went to his own plump cheeks and lingered there. Her hair, in a single rough braid, coiled over her shoulder and lay upon her breasts. Widgin's longest coat was spread over her like a blanket, the sleeves flung haphazard on the hay, like the arms of a drunken man. . . . Cradled in her arm was a bundle made of one of her skirts.

"I hope you does n't mind," repeated Taffy.

She looked up at him quietly, and smiled. Her free hand reached slowly across her body and gently drew open the skirt.

The three tramps leaned over, Taffy upon one knee, with the cockney glancing round his shoulder and the Swede looking down from above. The lantern cast their shadows upward against the wall of hay until they were lost in the darkness of the mow.

London caught his breath in a sharp whistle.

"Gawd's mercy strike me gentle, if it ain't pink!"

"It ain't got no hair," whispered Taffy.

Over their heads the voice of the Swede boomed suddenly.

"Look!" he said. "It be a boy!"

For a minute they stared in silence, breathless. Taffy swayed forward, and his coat swung open. As the woman raised the skirt to cover her child, it caught on something at his waist. He glanced down and saw that it was his cup, which he carried on his belt.

"Look," he said, turning to his companions, "it's like he wanted it. I'll give it to him."

His pudgy hands trembled as he undid the buckle.

"See," he said, holding the cup to the light. "A gypsy give it to me oncet."

It had been beaten out of copper, and in the smoky rays of the lantern it gleamed like pure gold. He put it down beside the baby.

London Joey felt through his pockets.

"The nipper," he muttered. "W'en he grows up like 'is pa, if he don't chew, 'e 'll smoke this."

From his coat pocket he produced a blackened clay pipe with a cracked bowl, which he placed beside the cup.

The two of them looked up at the Swede.

"Ain't you a-goin' to give him nothin'?" asked Taffy Jones.

The Swede stared down out of his blue, barbarian eyes. His big red hands strayed over his pockets and fell away with a hopeless gesture. He bent over the boy farther and farther, until he was forced to kneel to keep his balance. His breath came hard through his nostrils. He took off his hat and put it to one side, as though that were to be his gift, and his flaxen hair gleamed above the baby's head. He bent over farther yet, and, while the others looked on wonderingly, quite suddenly he kissed him. The woman gazed into his eyes and smiled; and he blushed, and climbed clumsily to his feet, and moved away to the door of the barn. In the utter silence, the others still heard his heavy breathing.

Taffy and the cockney looked down at their feet.

"Now we've got warm," said Taffy, "I reckon we ought to be moving on."

They joined the Swede at the door, Widgin following them with the lantern.

"What're you goin' for so quick?"

Away down the track a train whistled, three long notes and two short, and the sound in the thin, frosty air was elfin-clear, and musical.

"That," said the cockney, "is the west-bound freight. She'll be runnin' slow past 'ere, and we can 'op 'er easy."

He shook hands with Widgin, solemnly.

"Luck to you. Luck to your skirt, and the nipper."

The Swede pulled back the door, and the three stepped through. Taffy Jones shrugged his shoulders and pulled his collar about his ears.

"Glory!" exclaimed the cockney, letting his breath out long and shrill, as if he had been storing it up in his lungs for the past fifteen minutes.

"Glory!" he repeated. "We'll 'ave to 'urry if we're a-goin' to catch that freight."

Behind them the door closed with a soft thud and they heard the heavy iron hook clank as it dropped through the ring.

The Swede was staring away into the distance. His arm felt hard, like iron, under the cockney's fingers.

"Look at them stars," he said.

The wind had died away to nothing, and the stars had suddenly grown big. For a full minute the other two gazed along his pointing arm.

Then, with the Swede leading, they floundered toward the tracks.

SPRING SONG

I

HER day began at five when she came down to get her uncle's morning coffee. It was bitter cold then and the gray shadows that crossed the valley before dawn reached just to the window sills. The kitchen was full of the languid old smells that are born in a house between the end of night and the beginning of day.

She wore a white nightgown under one of her uncle's worn-out coats. The nightgown was thin and outgrown, and, with the largeness of the coat, it made her look timidly aware of herself. She slippered over to the stove in the half light, laid kindling and paper, bent over, struck a match.

After a moment a thin sputtering began in the firebox, and she removed the lid again and carefully placed the wood. Leaving the draft open, she filled the coffeepot from the bucket of water by the sink and measured the ground coffee in her hand. Then she set the pot on the stove, and, taking up the bucket, went out through the snow to the pump.

She placed the bucket under the spout and stood awhile, motionless and straight. Sixteen years old, in the house she seemed a frightened child; now all at once, as she gazed over the valley, she was older. For an instant her body had promise of stature and fine proportions. With her long braid of wheat-colored hair coming forward over the front of the coat and the rise of her breast as her lungs tasted the damp air, she was alien to the hand of man as it showed in the bleak brown house and the old red barn near her.

Of all her toil-burdened day, this hour was her own. She could see ahead of her the hills beyond the valley. Her eyes followed the downward curve, picking out here and there dim buildings of other farms. There was no life visible about them, and her gaze went to the bottom of the valley. Here under the snow she could trace the course of the empty canal and its attendant towpath. It was silent now with the bitter hush of winter, but in a little while, she knew, the water would come, bringing the boats and the faint sound of horns.

The bed of the canal led her eyes southward down the valley to a group of old beeches. When the canal emerged beyond them, it came to the first locks leading it down into the gorge to the Mohawk Valley, and the great cities, Rome and Syracuse and Utica. She had heard of them and they had been called places of sin. She was told that she had come from one of them, but she could not remember which one, for it had been too long ago. Only now in the hovering breathlessness of dawn she felt them stirring in her. A pale flush crept into her white cheeks, and the dim light, kind to her blue eyes, showed no fear. Slender, fair-colored, she suggested in that instant the moonlight in the beeches and the old things of earth, perpetually new.

The excitement went. Her thin shoulders slumped suddenly; she felt the cold. Heavy footfalls were thumping across the kitchen floor. The pump rattled and creaked as she worked it; the water came at last in lazy glittering gushes.

Her left arm stretched out shoulder-high, she carried the bucket indoors. The fire in the stove roared hollowly as she set down the bucket; she cast a covert glance at the man before the stove. He seemed aware of her glance, for he said without turning, "You're late again to-day."

She made no answer, and he said, "It's got to stop."

He was a man of slight build, but his gray eyes had the hardness of cut glass. When the coffee boiled, he poured himself a cup, drank it quickly, and went out to the barn.

The girl went over to the stove and took down her clothes from a peg. She dressed quickly without enjoying the warmth. Then she set about getting breakfast. As she turned the potatoes, she kept an eye on the bedroom door. Suddenly a woman called, "Is it warm yet?"

The girl replied, "Yes."

The woman yawned audibly and could be heard turning over. "Bring me some coffee," she said.

The girl obediently filled a cup and took it in. In the big double walnut bed, with its garnish of carved pears, lay a woman with reddish hair and a full red mouth. Her brown eyes had a chill on them which even the languor of the warm bed could not hide. She stretched out a plump white arm and her little finger curled tightly as she took the cup. "Hold the saucer," she commanded, and the girl, with skill of long practice, followed the cup back and forth from a comfortable position on the patched quilt to the red mouth.

When she had finished the woman let herself fall back against a pillow and sighed elaborately. She was one on whom false refinement sat too heavily. She resented her life on the farm, but, because she feared her husband, she let resentment fall upon the girl.

Lying under the covers, she gave the child her orders for the morning. "Scald the churn," she said. "And after breakfast you can kill and pick them hens in the coop. We'll want 'em for dinner. I'll have the cream ready then for churning."

She turned to the wall.

"How long's Jed been out?"

"Five minutes," said the girl.

"All right. Call me when he lets the horses out to the trough."

She would be ready when her husband came to breakfast.

The sun was rising now and the shadow of the brown house was walking into the valley beside the shadow of the barn. While the girl laid the breakfast for two (they did not allow her to eat with them) she watched the sunlight finding its way across the snow. The slight mist of morning was wavering over the bed of the canal and stealing away upstream with a faint jerky motion that could be seen only by eyes looking for this very thing. She had seen it waver so for two mornings. This was the third. In the winter the mist settled and went southward; but when spring came it would begin its run into the hills. Then the canal would open.

It was the sight of boats moving on the water that gave relief to the monotony of her drab days. She had been born outside the law to the woman's only sister; and when her mother died her aunt and uncle had adopted her. They did not actually abuse her; but they were wearing out her spirit.

2

They had only beaten her twice, when she tried to run away. The second time they had trailed her through the woods with the Kentucky coon dog kept chained throughout the year. She was ten then, and in the dark woods she could hear his baying and the weird echoing of it ahead of her in the dark branches. When he found her he had danced round her, barking happily, until her uncle came with his lantern to drive her home to weeks of bitter penance.

For five years she had gone to school up the valley; but the other children knew her story, and it was almost a relief each day to return to the bitter house.

On Sundays they took her to church. She rode by herself in the back seat of the surrey, holding the big Bible on her knees, keeping her eyes on the floor when they stopped for conversation.

But one day she had looked up as they crossed the canal bridge that led to their own road. It was in the autumn. A boat was going under, drawn by a chestnut team. Behind the horses walked a big man, black-bearded, with the shoulders of a bull. He swore when the wagon suddenly rattled the planks over his head, a hot oath of surprise, and from the far side returned her uncle's cold stare. Then he caught her eye and smiled — a wide smile that flashed in his black beard; and the kindness of it left her tremulous.

Her aunt turned around to see her watching him.

"Rose!" she said sharply.

The girl dropped her eyes again. And her aunt said to her

uncle, "We've got to be careful." It had come to her that the girl could look pretty. Thereafter she took pleasure in exacting menial service from the child about her person. She seldom let her leave the house alone; and when they went out in the evening to a meeting she locked the girl in.

But the girl rode home with the tremulousness still on her. When she stepped from the surrey she found a weakness in her knees, and she slipped and muddied her dress. She spent a long hour cleaning it under her aunt's eye; but for once she found the painful supervision pleasant.

She had always liked the boats, but since that Sunday morning she had had the big chestnut team to look for. And at times she saw them with the man walking at their heels. She could see his black beard way across the valley and she learned to know the note of the horn an old man blew from the deck. It was not the ordinary horn that boaters carried; it was a long curving silver thing and it blew in a lower scale, not loud, but with a slow suggestive note that carried to the heart of things.

Rose recognized it one night. Something insistent in it had penetrated her sleep, and when she slipped out of her attic bed she found moonlight on the valley, and a silver sheen on the twigs of the beech grove. While she watched, she saw the night lantern stealing from behind the trees, and the sound of the horn came to her then, low and insistent, and she felt afraid. She thought of him walking with long strides of his heavy legs, his great shoulders bent, and she saw in her mind's eye the black beard, and the black hair on his arms, and all the great bulk of him.

Suddenly the light had stopped, and she had heard the horn again as if it called. The fear went from her. She crossed to her door, but it was locked. She returned noiselessly to the window to see the distant light once more moving.

Thereafter, all through the autumn, her door was locked at night. Only when the winter came did they leave it unlocked. For with the canal frozen in and the boats still, there was no escape for her.

Escape. She had run away as a little child, twice. She had been caught. Now for four months the snow shut her in. Falling steadily, a little at a time by day. . . .

Her mother had called her Rose, a name of which her uncle disapproved. She had a vague memory of a small room, with noise beyond the garish curtains, and a tall woman gracefully lying in a bed and a man who came to see her. He must have been handsomely dressed, for the woman was very proud of him. . . .

Her uncle was late to supper; but when he came he told his wife that in the morning boats would clear from Rome. The lock-tenders had come back to their shanties. Down the gorge you could see supper smokes against the sky.

That night they had rain. She lay awake listening to the drumming on the roof and the steady chatter of drops from the eaves. She heard her uncle climb the stairs to lock her in and she lay still until he had gone down.

It rained all next day, a gray wall that seemed to shut the farm in upon itself, and the woman nagged the girl without rest.

"She 's sullen," she said to her husband at supper. "I thought she was going to answer back."

Her uncle stared at the girl's bent shoulders.

"She 's going to need a hiding," he said. But he set her to picking over the seed potatoes in the cellar.

She worked by the light of a candle beside the bins. The hound who had tracked her down years before, an old dog now, with silver on his muzzle, came down and sat beside her. He patted the floor with his tail once or twice; then stretched out with his chin resting on the toe of her slipper. It was dead still, and the hard earth floor had a nasty smell. Outside the rain had stopped, and the air was getting cold.

Only twice was she disturbed. Once when her uncle came to the head of the stairs and stood looking down on her small bent back. He went away without speaking.

The second time, it was a sound, the low insistent note of a horn. She recognized it, and her shoulders straightened as if the sound had physical touch. The hound heard it also, for he lifted his head and she saw his old nostrils working. It came again into the walls of the cellar, and the sound of it hung in the damp air all around her, until she seemed to hear it singing in her head.

3

There were hired help to cook for. The crops were going in. The long furrows were black in the meadows and the teams went slowly back and forth all day. Men sowed the grain, walking in long strides and giving the seed in wide swoops of their right hands. They did not notice her as she moved timidly about the kitchen at meal times. In her old print dress, with her childlike braid on her back, she gave nothing to interest them. Her eyes kept to the floor. Only when she was alone did she lift them to the window. . . . She saw him twice again, moving heavily behind his team, and her heart swelled.

The men talked after they had eaten. They sat around with their pipes, the smell of the fields still on them. While she washed the dishes she could listen to their speaking. Generally it was of crops or horse trades or stories out of the woods; but once they told about a fight between one of their friends and a boater.

"A great mammoth," they called him. He had beaten their man badly.

"The bearded son . . ." they said; and described him, hating him aloud. . . . But she knew who he was and treasured their ill-nature.

It was the first warm night of spring, with a few small stars a prelude to the moon. She watched them from the bed. Below her the house slept noisily. She could hear heavy snores from the rooms of the hired help. Her uncle had gone off to town after supper; he had not yet returned. And her aunt had forgotten to lock her in.

The girl got out of bed and dressed. Then she went down the stairs a step at a time, feeling patiently for the creaks in the treads, pressing close to the wall. There was no one to hear her in the hall, and she crept to the kitchen. The floor creaked at her first step; she stopped as if frozen.

The low light of the lamp showed her in her white Sunday dress, in stocking feet, her blue eyes filmed and her lower lip drawn in against her teeth. Her thin figure was straight and tense; for a time she gave no sign of breathing.

The latch clicked as she turned the knob, and she stood still again with the lamplight on her back and the kitchen all but behind her. But the house slept steadily, and she stepped outside. The old hound, chained to the stoop, whined faintly. She went over to him and stroked his ears. She remembered how he had found her once before, and she decided this time she would take him with her. She unfastened the snap and walked to the stoop edge. He went ahead of her, dancing stiffly on old legs.

The valley was quite still; but there was a movement in the shadows and the moon came over the trees. Slowly the light was born; the woods took shape, and far down the valley a wash of silver touched the beeches. She was shaking. It did not seem that she could take her feet from the last step. There was a loneliness in the dark worse than the sleeping clamor of the house. It was still.

Then far up the valley she heard the horn. The low clear sound of it brought her courage.

She stooped swiftly for her shoes, and remembered that they were lying by her bed. Then the horn sounded again, far away, plaintive, insistent, and she looked up to see a lantern coming swiftly along the road, touching a horse's flank and the shining wet ruts; and when it turned a corner she had a glimpse of its red eye in the dark.

Panic swept her. She ran downhill like a white shadow under the moon, and when she reached the fence the house looked far back and high above her. A cow, heavy with her calf, lifted her head and blew out a misty breath, thick with the new grass smell, and waited for her word. But she was watching the barn.

The wagon wheeled up to the door and the horse stopped. She

had a moment's view of her uncle's back and the dark quarters of the horse, and they were gone. And she ran again.

The rain upon the ground was cold, and the stones bruised her feet, but she felt neither. She splashed through a small brook with the water coming to her knees, icy cold, and she halted again.

The house was merely a dark square against the hillside, with the moon touching the chimney top. Then as she watched a high shrill whistling broke out for the hound. He pressed against her leg, glancing up in the shadows, and she felt him sway to his wagging tail.

She fled to the beech grove at her back. As soon as she was among the trees, the sound of the whistling was cut off.

In her sudden plunge into the grove she had lost her direction; and now she ran, blind with fear, and at her heels the old hound who years before had been so glad to catch her. She ran until her heart ached and a dry pain entered her throat.

She came to the edge of a small circular clearing, where the moon was bright and a gnarled tree stood, the mother of the grove. It was not slender and straight as the other trees, but heavy upon its roots, and its branches stretched over the ground. She fell down under it, lying flat on her breast, with her arms out before her, quivering. After a while she looked up to see the old hound gazing back into the woods.

His tail wagged excitedly and he lifted his chin and barked. Following his eyes, she saw a yellow lantern light swooping into the limbs overhead. Great shadows came to life; she heard the stamp of men. The hound barked again and one of the men shouted: "The dog's found her."

She would have cried out but for her hopelessness. She only lay silent before the tree, breathing as if she prayed. . . .

And then into the clearing an old buck rabbit hopped, bright-eyed, his ears high; and the hound greeted him like a friend.

"She's run again."

The man swore as he turned to cut across the angle made by the rabbit.

"Bear right!" he shouted.

In a moment they were gone. The lights flickered in the branches and went out. The shadows sank into the ground.

4

The stillness returned to the clearing with the white light of the moon, and with it came also the beginning of sound. Far away in the swamp a frog tried its pipe, very low and shy, a single note. And presently it tried again and then it was still.

The girl pulled her arms under her eyes where she lay and began to cry, and the strength she had had went out of her like water running. She could not have stirred then if the men had burst upon her with their lights and shouting. Even her sobs were slow dead things.

She was tired, so tired that her senses could tell her nothing. She could not tell at which point she had entered the clearing. There was only the moon, and the old tree casting its shadows on its roots, and far away the single note of a frog.

She must have lain beneath the tree for a long time, for when at last she heard it she was cold. It came low to the earth, with the smell of leaves and old things of the trees, slow and gentle, as if the man had breathed into the horn.

She got to her knees and faced the sound, for it was easy to find. It came again, and she rose to her feet and went toward it out of the clearing, through the woods. There were old things in her, but she did not care. Among the beeches it did not matter what had been right in the cold brown house where men lived righteously.

She walked as if she walked blindly, for twigs bent across her cheeks. She did not seem to feel the strokes. Her wet hair shone pale as the dress upon her shoulders. It too was wet with the dew and spotted brown where she had lain beneath the tree. It hung close to her, showing her thin child's body. Her feet fell into a path that deer might have made and it brought them straight to the canal.

The water flowed quietly with a black sheen round the curve. As she stood on the towpath she could hear the mutter of it in the bank-side grass, and she saw the water weeds weaving from side to side. Here and there the moonlight caught the arrow-headed ripples. It flowed out of the stillness of the grove with the trees thick along the towpath, giving darkness, and it went past her feet southward under the moon, a thread of silver. Far down she could see the sky upon the water where it entered the gorge.

Then above the curve her ears caught the tread of horses coming toward her. With them came once more the sound of the horn, and she knew it was he.

Till that moment it seemed simple to her. There would be no need of talking, she had thought. All through the winter it seemed to her that she belonged to him. She would be there, and he would take her and put her aboard with no word spoken.

But when the team appeared in the arm of the curve, their necks bent before the collars, and the towline a thread of silver behind them, drawing on something still out of sight, she was afraid. He came upon her in the shadow without seeing her. But the horses stopped and snorted at her gently, letting out steam from their nostrils. Then he stood before her looking down, his heavy legs wide apart, his broad hat back on his head, his long whip looped on his shoulder, and his black beard sweeping his shirt; and the bigness of him came over her like a blanket.

"Hullo," he said. "Who 're you?"

She said, "I 'm Rose."

His voice rumbled to himself deep in him. He said over his shoulder, "Put her in a minute, Pete, and look at this."

The old blunt bow of the boat came into sight with its own momentum, cuddling a ripple before it, and the lantern burning on the stern threw a light against the trees.

An old man jumped ashore with a rope in his hand and hitched it to a tree. Then he joined them. A horn hung in a silver circle over his arm and as he walked he blew gently in the mouthpiece, and a low note went ahead of him, like the sleepy murmur of bees. He was a little man with silver hair and a face smooth and alert as a squirrel's. He wore a red waistcoat to his thighs and he stood beside the driver's arm.

"Hullo," he said. "Who're you?"

She said once more, "I'm Rose."

She could not say any more; it was all she had to say; but she looked at them with a silent hopefulness.

"Jeepers!" he said after a while.

The old man echoed, "Cripus!"

They exchanged glances.

"What're you doing here?" he asked her.

"I've run away again," she said.

"They caught you before?"

"Two times."

"What did they do to you?" asked the old man.

She did not answer.

The boater rumbled in his black beard. It was like thunder on the earth at night.

"They would do that," said the old man, Pete.

"Why did you find me?" he asked, bending his black beard toward her.

A shiver passed up her, and she barely whispered, "I heard the horn."

He looked at the old man. Pete touched the horn with his mouth, and it seemed to her that the sound hung around them both.

A thought came to him; he asked, "Was it you they're after, them with lanterns and the hound?" He tilted his head back toward the grove.

"Yes," she said; "but it's a rabbit now."

Suddenly they heard the happy cry of the hound coming toward them.

He swore deep in his chest. "I've seen him. I'd run away, too. Get aboard with Pete, Rose."

She felt the blood flooding to her hair. Then his arm was about her and he had hoisted her to his shoulder. The old man went back and jumped nimbly to the deck.

He said, "We'll push on past the combines. Then we'll eat, and we'll haul all night. I'm working down below this summer."

He handed her up and the old man took her.

"Will you cook for us, Rose?"

"Yes."

"Keep inside the cabin, then. We'll look out for you."

"Sure," said Pete. "If he comes we'll give him a twister."

He touched his horn again and the team started of their own accord.

"Better get down," said the old man. "They'd see you here in the light."

As she went down the narrow stairs, she felt the old boat move under her.

"There's some supper on the stove you might keep your eye on," Pete called after her.

5

A glass-bowled lamp lighted the cabin from its bracket on the wall. The little cookstove to the right of the stairs had the air hot and filled the room with a comfortable smell of potatoes heating in a pan. There were old green curtains drawn across the windows.

She went forward softly as she had in the kitchen in the gaunt house above the valley. Her eyes explored the sleeping cuddy with its three bunks, two made up with soiled blankets; she observed the old dust and the old food smells of the wood; and her eye fell on the table, let down on its hinges from the wall, with the grimy salt and pepper shakers set back in the shelf behind it. It was dirty and full of the odor of men living alone; but it brought her a great comfort, and by degrees her back straightened and her eyes grew bright. It was comfortable and friendly for all the dirt, and its warmth went through her. . . . It was a place for her to live.

Her heart hurt with its gratitude. He had taken her in with nothing. She thought of the words of the hired man, "You're pretty, Rose." She looked at herself in the small mirror and her small face grew pink.

"We'll look out for you," he had said.

The old boat moved along, and as they went she heard beyond the window the same frog in the far swamp finding his song. While she listened, he found it; confidence crept into the clear notes, and suddenly other voices took it up, and the sound of their singing came closer until it went with them along the water, voice upon voice uplifted.

Overhead she heard Pete, the old man, sound his horn loud for the lock, and she knew that the grove was left behind, and the hunting men, and the bay of the running hound, and the old buck rabbit leaping.

The boat sank down between the walls and went on, and again the horn blew from the lock, and again they sank and went on, and the bitter farm lay far back in the high valley.

It came to her then in the cabin that she looked upon her house; and there was work for her to do. When she looked between the curtains, she could see him walking behind the heavy rumps of his horses, his great shoulders bent and his whip wound round his arm. Overhead she heard the shifting of the old man's feet, and from time to time the old insistence of the horn. In a while they would come down; they would look to her for food.

She stood there before the stove, minding the potatoes, and as her senses found root in the cabin she smelled cheese. A smile curved her child's mouth and she went to the cupboard and found there what she wanted.

So while they went on she worked, until her back ached from beating in the bowl and bending over the oven. But the ache pleased her, for she knew that she was working well. Beside herself, it was the only gift she had to bring him.

Outside, the team stopped and the boat went to the bank. She heard the horses come aboard and settle down in their stalls and

Pete go forward to help feed them. She did not hear them talking, only the deep mutter of his voice.

"I wisht he'd come after us," he said to Pete, "so I could've told him a few things, and hit him once."

"I'd've told him a few things," the old man echoed him. "He's as low as they come."

And he brought a sweet note from the horn.

"What'll you do with her?" the old man asked.

"We'll let her stay."

"She's pretty," said the old man.

"She ain't only a child," he growled.

She did not hear him, for she was bending before the oven. But when they sat down at the table, and she laid the eggs and potatoes before them, the old man hung up the horn with a fond glance at it, and said conversationally, tucking his handkerchief into his shirt collar, "I used to know your ma, Rose. She was a famous lady down there, and well liked." She looked up at the boater and he nodded his black beard.

"I knowed her, too," he said. "She was a beautiful woman."

She felt the blood rush into her face.

They waited with their eyes on hers. All at once a dark look came over his face.

"Set down and eat," he said. And the old man growled to himself and cast his eye to the horn.

Then shyly she went over to the stove and brought forth the pie to set it before him, and her heart sang because she saw that it was good.

The old man cleared his throat and cocked his eye, and he said, "I've allus held there'd be cows in Heaven, just for a cheese pie."

But he said nothing. Only when she ventured to lift her eyes to him, he gave her a wide white smile through his beard. . . .

So they went on after a while, refreshed, with a warm rain washing the deck; and she went to sleep in the bunk, with the sound of frogs singing, the soft voice of the water on the planks, and the low note of the horn.

BLACK WOLF

I

For two days they had not seen a bit of blue, in heaven or on earth. An endless succession of steel-gray clouds had been moving up from the southeast. They had moved without perceptible wind. But at noon they had halted. When Martin stepped through the door of the cabin, he could see their swollen bellies pressing down the upper twigs of the trees.

The forest was hushed. The air had a suffocating thickness when he breathed it in. The whole world had turned gray. Even the snow in the clearing had lost its whiteness. Sunlight was a memory.

His sister, Polly, opened the door again behind him and stood holding it with one hand, while with the other she put the end of her brown braid to her mouth. Her childish face and large gray eyes were unnaturally serious for a girl only nine years old.

His mother's voice came through the door from the old cord bed, where she lay propped up against the feather pillow. Her body made a great swelling under the blankets, and her thin hand with white transparent fingers held the almanac for 1809 face-down beside her.

"You had better try and bring in a big log, Martin — one that will last all night."

He glanced uneasily at the clouds.

"All right."

Outside the cabin the heavy air made his voice fall flat. His mother spoke again between deep breaths. She was reading by what light filtered through the greased-paper panes of the only window.

"Father Abraham says, 'Keep a good fire.' That's for the seventh. 'Expect snow,' it says for the ninth."

His voice had a manful note: "It looks like snow, all right. I'll cut off a piece of the old beech."

"Don't try to bring too heavy a piece, Martin."

"Oh, shucks!"

He shouldered his father's axe and started across the clearing, his free hand trailing the shovel. Behind him he heard the door squeak on its leather straps.

The snow came halfway to his knees. It was light and powdery. He looked about him as he walked. There was not a sign of life anywhere in the clearing — not even a stir under the bark shed. They had sold their horse after his father died to get money for flour during the winter. They hadn't had the money to move away. The wheat had been blighted that summer; they needed every penny for food; and his mother had no strength for walking.

The cabin stood at one end of the clearing. Ahead of him the wagon track toward Sangerfield made a black tunnel through the balsams. Ransome lived there five miles away. The Squire's double cabin was a mile and a half beyond that.

The old beech, the last tree in the clearing, had fallen in the autumn winds. It had a trunk like a rod, forty feet long, ten inches through. If he cut off five feet of it, he thought he could slide it over the snow as far as the cabin.

He was dressed in an old homespun coat, too large for him, a flannel shirt of dark brown, skin breeches. He had a worn fur cap on his head and on his feet Indian shoes stuffed full with coarse gray socks. His body had reached the long thin stage of thirteen, when the joints are loose and clumsy. His brown face was drawn and pinched from overwork, his dark eyes sullen with worry.

When he reached the fallen tree, the branches of which alone stuck over the snow, he laid down his axe and shoveled clear a section of the trunk. He would have to make two cuts this first time.

He made two notches ten inches apart below the branches, spit on his hands, and swung up the axe. The blade bit with a clean sound in the wood. He worked easily, his body arching and relaxing as the blows fell. He was handy with an axe and had a true eye, and the cut sank swiftly and cleanly. The bevels touched at the under-bark. He delivered an underslung cut and the trunk tapped gently on the snow.

He shifted his position. The blows fell again. They made dull sounds under the clouds like mallet strokes. His face reddened with the exercise. He tossed off his cap, baring his mop of long brown hair. Without the cap he looked like a half-tamed animal.

When the second cut broke through, he put on his coat and cap and slipped a leather thong round the butt of the log. He drove his axe into the trunk and leaned the shovel against it. Then he passed the strap over his shoulder and heaved. The log rolled over and swung into line. He paused a moment, staring at the sky, his eyes weather-wise.

The clouds seemed even lower. As he breathed he was subtly aware of movement above the woods. A change was beginning.

Suddenly he felt it: a cold biting breath — not wind, not storm, but a chill that sank into him as his axe had sunk into the beech tree.

He shifted his fingers on the strap and started tugging for the cabin. His shoulders bent heavily, but he kept his chin up. The log moved slowly behind him, leaving a furrow in the snow.

He stopped again after five minutes. Barely perceptible flakes were drifting down. They seemed incongruous under the swollen clouds, and they fell straight, without fluttering.

He tugged his way forward for another five minutes and stopped again. His thin chest was heaving now, and sweat was running down his cheeks, and the cold was biting at the drops. The snow was coming with greater swiftness; but still there was no wind.

He whirled suddenly in his tracks. Down the road a blue jay squawked twice in characteristic horror. He stared toward the sound, but he could see nothing. Then, with no warning, the clearing darkened. There had been no change in the clouds. A curtain seemed to have been drawn above them, shutting out the absent sun from all the world. But still there was no wind.

He bent his back sullenly to the strap.

At his next stop the cabin was fifty feet before him. Its bark roof and log walls made a dark blot against the forest wall, only relieved by the faint light of the hearth against the paper window. They had used their last candle at Christmas.

He took deep breaths for the last pull, but just as he bent his back his glance froze.

A black shape had slunk across his path. It made no sound. It moved with the ease of flowing water. But he had seen its outline plainly: the pointed ears, the sharp muzzle, the thick fur, the bushy tail, the tongue lolling in spite of the cold. A shiver caught his knees and mounted his back with a swift stabbing convulsion. The animal was bigger than a fox, bigger than any gray wolf he had seen. But it was gone.

He put down his head and heaved frenziedly. Wolves came here only before great cold, and already he could feel the ache in his hands.

He heaved his way to the door and banged heavily upon the adzed boards. It swung open. His sister looked out at him reproachfully.

"Mother can't bear knocking like that, Martin."

"Never mind," he said surlily. "You've got to help me get this log over the sill."

His mother's voice spoke out of the darkness, bravely: "I hope it's not too heavy."

He did not answer, but his eyes flashed to the rifle leaning by the hearth. He flushed with pleasure as Polly said, "Oh, Mother, it's an enormous log. It's beautiful." Her small hard hand patted the smooth bark.

"Take this strap and pull when I raise the log."

The sill was only an inch or so higher than the snow, but it took all their strength to get the end of the log over it. Once there, he fitted a roller under it, and in a minute more they had it halfway into the cabin. From that point he could pull it easily while Polly took the extra rollers from the rear and stuck them under the front end.

"I can feel the cold," said his mother.

Polly swung the door to.

The clay hearth was level with the floor. Clay backed the end wall, to keep the fire from the logs, and the chimney was a square funnel of clay and sticks resting on two split logs five feet overhead.

A good bed of coals was glowing in the ashes, and when they rolled the end of the beech log head on into them it immediately began to hiss and smoke.

Martin sat straddlewise of the beech log and patted it with his hands.

"It was quite a job to haul."

He glanced slyly at his mother. Little flames springing up over the end of the log dimly lighted her face. It made a white spot against the pallet, with the eyes unnaturally large and dark. The lips, too, looked large and loose; but when she caught his eyes she smiled.

"Hand me the measuring stick, Polly."

He took the little rod on which their father had calculated burning time for different thicknesses and different wood, and marked the hours in the bark of the log with notches. He could feel his mother's smile on his back. When he was done he let his breath out between his teeth and said, "There. That ought to do it, all right."

His sister watched him admiringly, and without comment set their corn meal mush to cooking in the iron pot.

"Hungry to-night, Mother?"

Their mother shook her head with sudden fret.

"No. I can't bear any more mush. I wish we had milk. I wish we had some white flour, for bread."

A shadow passed over the faces of the children. Then, with a sharp intake of breath, the mother said, "Had n't you better get the axe, before it gets quite dark?"

The boy said, "Oh, there's time enough." He had been dreading the question. The black shape kept trotting before his mind's eye, even when he put his mind on something else. He was afraid.

But he knew that he must take no chance of losing the axe. His mother knew that too — he could feel it in her eyes on his back. He got up.

"I guess I had might as well fetch it."

He drew the collar of his coat close about his neck.

"It's getting cold," he said importantly. "You've no idea, Polly."

He took up the gun nonchalantly.

"Kiss me, Martin."

He bent dutifully over the bed. She took his head in both arms and brought his ear to her lips.

"You're a brave boy," she whispered.

He flushed hot all over and wriggled away. He was not. He was afraid to death. He didn't dare hesitate.

2

The cold bit hard. When the door closed behind him, though, he realized that the clearing was not as dark as he had supposed. And there was a sound of wind high up, a shrill crying that his ears could barely catch.

He looked all around him. There was no sign of the wolf. Trailing the gun in his right hand, he set out.

The snow was feeling the drive of the wind. It sliced out of the northwest and stung his cheeks. The trough the log had made was feathered like a bed.

The axe helve struck through the snow like the head of a snake. When he took hold of it the sweat in his palm made his hand stick to it momentarily. He did not dare let go the rifle, and he had to wrestle with the shovel to get it to his left shoulder together with the axe. He turned home eagerly.

As he did so he heard, far off, a growing roar. There was a peculiar note in the sound to make him shiver, like finger nails drawn over silk. He hurried to get in before the wind snatched the clearing.

The snow had begun to whirl in eddies. Close to him he could see the flakes rioting; beyond, they made a gray solid wall in the darkness. And the wind came in silence, bending him down and drawing the breath out of his lungs. A gout of snow was whipped from the top of a stump and broken to mist. The tracks he had made coming for the axe were flattened out.

He stumbled, and his eyes turned to the snow at his feet. Instinctively he raised his feet to step over the track. He saw it fresh and plain. The wolf had crossed right before him. He looked wildly to his right — and saw it. It was sitting on the stump from which the snow had just been blown, its forefeet neatly placed, and its tail curled over them. It stared a minute at the boy, then raised its muzzle and opened its mouth. But there was no sound.

He did not dare shoot in the uncertain light. He had no extra charge, and if he should miss he would have no time to load again even had he had the powderhorn.

The wolf seemed to know it. For a long moment it stared at him, then, with a flourish of its tail, sprang off the stump and vanished.

The boy clattered into the cabin. He pushed the door frantically against the wind, and pulled in the latchstring.

3

The storm gripped the cabin with icy fingers. The night was full of voices. Sitting close to the hearth, the children picked them out.

There was above all the sound of the snow against the oiled-paper panes of the window — they could hear it, if they listened, even through the wildest moments of the wind's hullabaloo. There was the ticking the logs made as the frost bit into the walls, and the steady *shish-shish* of loose snow moving on the crust and creeping up in drifts against the cabin. The wind worked here and there through the clearing. They heard it skirling through the bare branches of the hardwood and shrieking in the evergreens in the swamp. It made hollow bottle-noises over the mouth of the chimney and whistled at the four corners of the eaves. Now and then it seemed to lift over the clearing, and then the full-throated roar of it was audible high up in the sky; and once, in what seemed a lull, they heard it blasting through the pines on the hill a quarter of a mile behind the cabin, and they formed a picture of the gaunt old trees bending down their backs.

The beech log burned steadily with an unctuous crackling. From time to time Martin would have to get up and set the pry-stick against the butt end and ram it in an inch farther among the coals. Then as he sat down again the bark would give them fresh light and they could see all round the cabin and draw a sense of comfort from familiar things.

But there was little enough to see. Their mother's bed in one corner; their own small bunk, in which they slept together in winter; the two rude stools on which they sat; the shelf with the old Bible, in which were written their own names, and their father's and mother's names, and the names of ancestors whom they knew nothing of; the iron skillet and the mush pot; the old Whitney rifle and powderhorn and shot pouch close to the hearth; the shallop of deer's fat; their father's hat and coat and boots and snowshoes; the axe and shovel and hoe; their mother's linsey dress hung over the door — they seemed pitifully few, but they seemed to crowd the twelve by fifteen feet of cabin space.

But the cabin was warm; the walls held out the wind; if they had only had a candle. . . .

4

He wondered what they would do in the spring: if he should try to work their three acres of cleared land or if he should hire out. By then his mother would be well enough to work out of doors, and his sister had shown that she was old enough to mind the house, and their new brother or sister, whichever it was. If only they had a little more money, they could move to some town where they could all find work.

He revolved the thought in his mind, slowly, luxuriously. He could just remember when they lived in Catskill, where his father earned a little money as a carter. He could remember the ships on the river moving up to Hudson under their great sails, and the nimble Albany sloops. They had been poor there, but not so poor as this attempt at farming had made them.

His eyes wandered to the bed.

His mother's eyes were closed, her lips parted, and her breaths were short and sharp. Her cheeks were red; but even while he watched, the blood left them and her mouth opened and her hand clenched the almanac beside her knees.

She was a small woman, with long brown hair, like Polly's, and deep-set eyes. As long as he could remember her face, he had seen it smiling. No matter how worried the eyes were, they could smile if he looked at her. And she always had a peculiar clean free smell that he had never found in anyone else.

Suddenly he scrambled to his feet. She did not seem to be breathing. Both hands at the ends of rigid arms were clenched. Her skin was glistening white.

He went over to the bed. The wind was hooting down the chimney and smoke coiled over him.

"What's the matter, Martin?"

His sister's voice quavered.

He gestured with his hand behind him.

"Be still, can't you?"

He put out his right hand tentatively.

His voice was high.

"Mother."

For a moment there was nothing but the roaring of the wind. Then a lull came. His mother's eyelids fluttered. Her breast heaved. Her back sank. Her nostrils opened.

"Oh, oh, oh . . ." he heard her faintly.

The dark eyes wandered over the poles that made the loft, over the sapling ladder, the door, the hearth. They were dismally frightened. He put his hand on her forehead and felt the hair wet and cold.

"Mother. What is it?"

Intelligence slowly returned, and as her eyes found his he felt sobs climbing his throat.

The corners of her mouth shook, and smiled, and a flood of comfort poured over him. He let out his own breath with a gasp.

"I didn't expect it yet awhile," she said as if it were a kind of joke, and he felt himself ready to laugh. Then her face hardened.

"Martin, do you think you could get down to Ransome's?"

"Yes, I guess I could."

But he was prickling. The wind beat the door as he spoke, and he thought of the black shape scudding through the clearing with its wind-blown tail.

"I guess so."

"It's awfully cold, I know." Her voice was tired. "But I think it would be better to go. Mrs. Ransome said she would come when my time came. But I didn't expect it so soon."

He looked down at his feet and took his hands back.

"I don't mind the wind or the snow."

"You're a stout boy now, Martin."

She smiled.

"You're the father of this family now, Martin."

He tried to smile back.

"It isn't the cold," he mumbled.

When he dared lift his eyes, he saw that hers were lost again.

"You've got to go. You've got to go now. Please, Martin."

Her breath gasped in her throat and her body arched on the bed.

He heard her saying "Please," over and over, as if to herself, without sense, and he saw her dreadful terror perfectly naked.

His sister was sniffling, hunched upon the stool, wet round eyes bewildered. The wind cried and cried. And the snow crept against the walls with its everlasting *shish-shish-shish*.

There was the long minute of breathlessness, and then his mother lay relaxed and spent and wet again, shivering ever so slightly. Her breathing came back to her.

"You'd better put on the snowshoes. The snow must have deepened."

"All right," he mumbled. He did not say he was afraid. But his hands made fists.

"All right, Mother."

He went over to the clothes pegs and took down his sheepskin waistcoat and put it on under his coat. He took his father's mittens off the shelf by the Bible and reached down the snowshoes. He put the shot pouch in his pocket and slung the powderhorn over his shoulder.

His mother said, "You'd better not take the rifle. It's unhandy to carry on snowshoes."

She was right. He couldn't tell her why he wanted it, though. He saw that he had to go, and that if he did tell her she might keep him. He took off the horn and put away the pouch, but when she wasn't watching he slid the skinning knife into his belt.

Polly's eyes widened.

"Martin, what's . . . ?"

"Shh!" He was important. But his hands felt cold, and when he bent down to tie the snowshoe thongs his fingers fumbled.

He said to Polly: "You won't be scared to stay alone with Mother, will you?"

She looked at him soberly.

"No, not much."

"You mustn't be," he said fiercely. "There's nothing to be scared of. You don't have to go out there . . ."

He nodded his head at the door.

"I wish you wouldn't go."

He felt a peculiar kindness for her; for he could see how much younger she was than he.

"Be a brave girl, Polly. Do what Mother asks."

He tied one shoe snug.

"I'll be back before very long."

"Is it coming so soon?" whispered Polly.

"Pretty soon."

He stood erect.

"Martin, come here."

He clattered over to the bed. She put out her arms for him and drew him convulsively against her.

"You're a brave boy," she said for the second time. He wished he were. She kissed him thrillingly. When he drew back to put his cap on and saw her still face, he felt more miserably afraid than ever.

He looked at Polly and mumbled, "Back pretty quick," and went to the door.

"Pull the latch in after me."

Then he saw that it was already in and he remembered why he had pulled it in himself.

5

He stepped out and felt the cold. Wind swooped into the cabin and set the walls in motion. The door banged shut. The dark had him.

He would not stop to think. It was pitch-black. He could see nothing. No tracks, no trees, no sky, no snowflakes. The world was even without smell. There was nothing to hear but the voice of the storm. Only feeling was left: the icy cold, and the sting of driven flakes, and the agony of breathing.

The snow had risen against the cabin walls halfway to the window, but out in the clearing it was scarcely deeper than it had been that afternoon. It made a dull steel-colored carpet in the dark.

He set out, bowed down to the wind, his snowshoes scrunching. The cold made them feel tight and light on his feet for all they were so oversized. But they bore his scant weight without any sinking whatever. He had only the wind to fight; it shook and racked him and bent him over; and the fiercest blast forced him off his track.

He went blindly, heading for the beginning of the wagon track that led to Ransome's. Even the wolf, he thought, would take cover now. He began to listen for the scrunch of the snowshoes, for a rhythm in his walking. At times he could not hear it for the wind; and in those moments he felt as if he stood still.

When he reached the trees he was not sure for a moment on which side of the wagon track he had entered them. Then he remembered the direction of the wind and struck to his left. He must not lose touch with the clearing until he had the road.

In five minutes he had found it, and with the balsams to give him shelter he set out for Ransome's. The wind scarcely touched him now, but the voice of the night was hideous. He could hear above him the clash of tossed branches and the whistling shriek through the balsam boughs; and once, when he blundered into a maple sapling, he could feel the tremor in the stem as the top thrashed.

The snow drove through the trees. The darkness was so black that he could not find the turns by sight. But he kept ahead. He kept his feet moving. He listened for the steady scrunch of his shoes. When he heard it he marked a point gained.

He did not once dare to stop, for his chest felt small and dry; and the ache in his hands and the bones of his face told him the cold.

After a while he began to wonder how far he had come. He thought he recognized a dip in the snow for a gully the road crossed on corduroy. That would make it half a mile to Ransome's burnt acre, three hundred yards to the wheat piece and the meadow and the barn and the cabin. He had to turn the lower end of the barn and come round the back side of the cabin. He would knock on the door and they would let him in and give him tea. Maybe they would even give him a bit of maple sugar in the tea.

He struggled ahead for an hour more. His legs ached. The snowshoes had gained twice their natural weight and more than twice their width. His crotch was stiff from walking spraddle-legged. Little shivers went up his back, and came down and loitered in the lower part of his abdomen. He would have to stop now. It was n't his fault. He could n't help a thing like that. It was the cold and the heat of walking and the fingers of the cold again. He turned himself around, backing the wind, and fumbled with his trousers and let himself go. The tears came to his eyes. He began to cry.

Presently he stopped. He could see better with the wind. He saw a leaning black shape. He peered and peered. It was the hemlock that leaned across the road still a hundred yards from the corduroy. He thought he had passed that long ago, and now he had still almost a mile to go.

He was turning himself round again when he saw it coming up the road toward him, trotting serenely in the snow. It saw him or smelled him at the same moment and whisked aside. He shivered and shivered. Then he saw it sitting on the sloping trunk of the hemlock, level with his eyes.

"Get out!"

It did not move. He felt for the knife and pulled it out.

"Get out!" he cried again. But he did not hear his own voice. He raised the knife; his mouth kept shouting. He stepped blindly forward. The shape was gone.

After a minute he turned round and began again the endless plod. But his eyes were trained now to the storm and he saw more clearly. He saw the dip in the snow, this time, as it really was, and after a while he came out into the clearing. He looked round again, but he did not see the wolf. He tried to run.

Once or twice the snow led him over hummocky stumps, and once he fell, biting snow as he screamed. He floundered desperately to his feet, feeling the shape almost on him. He still clenched the knife, and he whirled to meet the open jaws. But the wolf was scudding past with wind-blown tail.

He came out of the burnt acre and into the wheat field and saw the shadow of Ransome's log barn. He ran at last a few shuffling steps, and the wind seemed to lessen for him. He found the lee and a cup in the drift and stood still with laboring chest.

A wave of comfort came to him as he smelled the warm ox

smell through a chink. He began to shake. He could hardly walk now; but he fought past the corner, and round the back side of the house.

His snowshoes scraped against the doorsill. He hammered with the haft of his knife.

The cabin was dark and the wind was shrieking. He hammered with all his might and tried to shout. Nobody came. He was tired out. He hammered once more, feebly, and leaned against the door. He began to cry. . . .

He did not feel the door opening or himself falling. He did not hear Mrs. Ransome's voice saying, "Good land, it's Collins's boy! Marthy's found her time."

6

When he could see and hear again, he found himself lying on a blanket in front of a great blaze on Ransome's hearth. His body was burning all over. His eyes smarted to the bright light of the fire and the two candles on the old Welsh dresser that was Mrs. Ransome's greatest pride. He could hear voices all round him, but his eyes were occupied with little things — the comforts of this spacious cabin; the sleigh bed of shining wood, the spinning wheel, the copper pots; the trammel, with its row of hooks; the shotgun and Uncle Roger's Continental rifle. Ransome was doing well; he had come here to settle, and he had founded a home.

Martin smelled tea — right under his nose.

He heard Mrs. Ransome's shrill Welsh voice saying, "Give him the tea now, Jane. He's all right if we can get him to sweat."

"The little snipe," another voice said, which he recognized as Uncle Roger's. "That was a bleary way to come. We're going to have a job breaking through."

He heard Ransome himself saying approvingly, "He's a stout lad." He closed his eyes and felt luxurious.

"Here, Martin. Here's tea."

He opened his eyes to see Ransome's oldest daughter, Jane, bending over him. She was sixteen, and she had the spry Welsh figure and the fiery black eyes that must have been her mother's in a younger day. A witch's face — it was beautiful edged with firelight in the shadow of the black hair, with the red and white skin and the clean small mouth. He saw a glint of amusement, too, in the eyes, which made him aware of himself.

They had taken his clothes off. He was lying there on the hearth as naked as a young rat. The blood struck his cheeks.

Jane whispered, "Don't be a fool, Martin. Drink it."

He saw the faces of the five small children peering like mice through the loft opening. The light struck in their dark eyes. They made glints, some red, some green, some copper. He mustered his dignity and managed to sit up with the blanket round him. He took the teacup, but she wouldn't let go. He felt foolish drinking from a girl's hand.

The tea was scalding and very sweet. He felt it sinking down painfully in his inside, mounting, blossoming, and all his body was warmed. The heat moved outwards to the heat of the fire on his skin. His skin prickled tremendously, and he felt the sweat trickling out.

Jane said over her shoulder, "He's sweating active, now."

Mrs. Ransome stepped up to him and gave him a dark glance.

"Put on your clothes, Martin."

She waited till he was dressed.

Had the pains started? she wanted to know. When did they first begin? Would Polly have the knowledge to heat water? Was his mother breathing through her mouth? Were her lips white? Did they have a bit of cotton to put the baby in?

He mumbled what answers he could think of, feeling that these children considered him an awful block. These Ransome children knew everything there was to know.

Mrs. Ransome shook her head and got together a bundle: lard from a suckle pig, a bottle with rum, a brew of boneset, a swathe of cotton cloth, some sugar, a little turpentine, a loaf of bread and a small cut of cheese.

She scurried here and there like a ruffled old Canada-Jack, putting her nose in this corner and that, bringing out a bit of this, touching a bit of that; going with a kind of instinct to the very spot in her disorderly house. He had heard his father say that the Welsh had a craving to bury things.

She made a bundle of everything, and then the door opened and Ransome came in. The cold snatched at Jane's woolen nightgown, showing her flat, haired legs. He turned his eyes away. He had seen her barelegged often enough, but this was strange.

Ransome took up the bundle.

"I'll carry it myself," said Mrs. Ransome.

He let it fall and she gave a little screech and snapped it up. Martin heard her puffing out to the sled.

Ransome came straight up to Martin.

"You did fine. Feel like coming?"

He was a hearty man with gold-brown hair and a thick moustache. His face was very red, and always sweaty, as if he had a superabundance of blood. He could work all winter with no mittens to his hands.

"You know the road better than us. That's why."

Martin nodded, dumbly.

Now he was here, in these comforts, in this warmth, he was afraid to go back; and yet he was afraid not to go back.

Ransome said, "Uncle Roger wants his rifle."

He took it from its pegs, and Martin was relieved.

7

The wind was still howling, but the power of its thrust had risen over the clearing.

Mrs. Ransome was hunkered down in the straw in the bottom of the sled, only her nose and eyes showing above the bundle she hugged to her breast. Uncle Roger on snowshoes stood beside the oxen. He was a little withered man with a stringy Adam's apple and a hoarse voice. In the Revolution he had lost his left ear to an Indian tomahawk, which he claimed Brant himself had thrown. Once he swore he had had a bead on Guy Johnson. He would have drilled him, sure, if a bat had not fouled the sight at the trigger instant.

He took the rifle from Ransome, and set out walking.

Ransome put on his snowshoes. He said to Martin, "You ride."

He pricked the nigh ox with the goad and the beasts snorted and set out.

They were a heavy yoke of red and white steers — red all over, with white heads and white horns and a white line down their backs. They were slow, but they would go through anything up to their eyes. If they could not see they would not move though a man skinned them alive.

The sled slid crisply on its fat runners; the oxen walked with powerful deliberation. They kept their heads together, mistrusting Uncle Roger's erratic track. The spry old man shouted over his shoulder, "You can't lose a Ranger in hell or whiskey"; but the oxen found the road for themselves and he had to flounder in behind them.

In the woods the noise of the trees blotted out the creeping progress of the sled. The snow at times came over the briskets of the oxen; and they paused for consultations. In those halts Ransome would come up beside the yoke and give them a moment before touching them and sending them forward.

It was a slow march; but to Martin, in the safety of the sled, it seemed quick. His glance kept roving from side to side, ahead and back. But he could see nothing beyond the glimmer of the oil lantern in Ransome's hand. There was only the dizzy fall of snow, endless, everlasting, icy.

They reached the Collins clearing at last and made better time toward the cabin. It looked half-buried in its drifts; the snow reached nearly to the window. Martin stared numbly at it. He could not see any light. He was stiff with cold, once more, and into his fear a new dread was creeping. The oxen halted beside the door.

All four people for an instant kept still.

Then Mrs. Ransome was bustling over the tailboard, raucously shouting directions the rest of them could not hear. Martin kept close to her. She panted through the snow to the doorsill and knocked. She knocked again.

A long lull fell in the storm. But they heard no sound. Mrs. Ransome knocked again, taking off her mittens to bring her knuckles to bear. And at last they heard slow footsteps coming to the door.

Martin scarcely dared look in.

His eyes went back to the black night. Behind him Ransome was standing, the lantern held shoulder-high as he peered toward the cabin through stiff lids.

Under his arm Martin saw two hot red points. He saw them plainly, and so close he thought he could make out deep in them the motion of fire. He raised his arm to point; but in the instant he saw Uncle Roger kneeling, pointing the long rifle.

A flash, a roar, a shriek from Mrs. Ransome, and a long string of oaths from the old man's beard. He was standing now, his sharp eyes wandering from the night to the gun held limply in his hands.

"I saw it plain," he said shrilly, "I saw it just as if it were drawed in the lantern. I had a bead laid square against his chist."

He shook his head.

"What was it?" Ransome asked.

"A wolf," said the old man. "A great black wolf. Right there."

8

Martin felt a great load on his heart. The door was open. Polly was standing holding it. She did not answer them. Her childish eyes were staring past them. Her face was thin and drawn and dry. She could neither cry nor speak.

Mrs. Ransome took one look and walked past her to the bed. She stood over it, fussing with the covers. Her breath was sharp and short.

"Bring the light, Arthur."

He set the light down beside her.

"Shall I take the oxen back? There's no barn."

"No."

"I'll blanket them, then."

"No. You needn't. We'll all come back with you."

He bent over.

"They're both dead," Mrs. Ransome said. "She hasn't ate enough to feed a bird. Poor silly dearie — not to let a neighbor know."

Martin took hold of Polly's hand. They stood quite still, watching Ransome taking out their mother and the baby. They saw Mrs. Ransome gather up in one arm all their belongings, and pick up her useless bundle in the other.

They heard words drifting through the door.

"They've got an aunt in Cooperstown. We'll see the Squire."

"We can keep them the winter."

"The Squire'll send them."

"We'll bury them to-morrow morning. This snow's mounting now."

"Lay her straight. It's the cold I'm thinking of."

"No coffin."

Ransome came in to lead them out.

The oxen started.

The two children were still silent.

But behind them they heard Uncle Roger muttering: —

"I drawed a mortal bead on that wolf's chist."

WHO KILLED RUTHERFORD?

I

"What I would like to know," remarked Denslow, when discussion of the early frost had palled, "what I would like to know is who killed old Rutherford — if anybody."

The fat woman, who was Solomon Tinkle's cook on the *Maud Merrick*, raised her folded chin over her glass and nodded her head until the ribbons of her bonnet quivered and the leaden yellow cherries rattled like dice.

"Ah," she said, "that's it — who did?"

The three others lifted their lips from the rims of their glasses and stared at the two. All five of them drew slightly closer to the stove, as if to get their backs as far as possible from the black window-panes on which the frost was already marking gray lines. For the sake of economy, and because of the smallness of the company, only one lamp had been left upon the bar, and it sent its light horizontally over the wood, just touching the long rows of glasses with orange half-moons, and falling squarely on the face of the fat woman, who sat with her back to the wall. Bolt upright on her chair, she seemed to be enjoying her conspicuousness, for she smoothed her plaid woolen skirt over her knees and opened the red-centred Paisley shawl about her shoulders to let the light fall on the gold locket she wore at her breast. Her immense weight diminished the breadth of her shoulders and her height, and, had it not been for the bow-legged diminutiveness of Solomon Tinkle beside her, one might have thought her squat. She arched her bosom and patted her dyed red hair.

"Who did it?" she repeated.

Solomon Tinkle wound his legs intricately through the rungs

of his chair. He leaned forward impressively, his right hand on the door of the stove, which he held open.

"If Rutherford was murdered," — he turned from the Judd brothers and spat neatly into the coals, — "somebody must have done it."

And he closed the door of the stove with a clank.

"Eanh," said the younger Judd; "that's right."

His brother let his sombre eyes wander over the faces of the others and return to the spots of light in the bottles behind the bar. He pulled at the stem of his pipe with pursed lips.

"Eanh," he said slowly; "that's right."

The fat woman held out her glass, her little finger curled pudgily.

"Will I make it another of gin, Mrs. Gurget?" asked Denslow.

"Eanh. On the luke side of hot with a squirt of lemon to cultivate the air with."

Denslow returned with the glass, and the fat woman spread her nostrils over the tingling odor of lemon.

"Well," said Denslow, as he resumed his seat and crossed his legs, "here we be, real sociable, and the last time afore winter, probably. I didn't even expect your boats comin' down so late.". . . He sipped his gin leisurely. "It comes hard to think of old Rutherford lyin' by and cold, and him with such a taste in whiskeys. He was a good man, too, by his lights; easy on a loan, and friendly when in liquor, but not when drunk. He'd made a load of money with his line of bars 'tween Utica and Syracuse. Made more out of his posthouses. I wonder who got it."

"We was in Boonville the night it happened," said Mrs. Gurget. "But the will wasn't read yet when Solomon let on as how he'd got to get through with them potatoes before the frost got too heavy."

"I said we'd wait awhile," interposed the little man. . . .

"Eanh," said the fat woman, looking fixedly at him in a manner unobserved by the rest, "but you was so anxious about 'em, I thought we'd better come."

"You was very sweet, my dear," said Solomon, returning his nose to the rim of his tumbler.

"We stayed there," said the younger Judd. "Joe, here, was bar-keep at Bentley's Oyster Booth and Bar in Uticy when Rutherford had it on his line; and Joe'd done a lot of work for him, so we thought we'd ought to wait, maybe."

"What was into it, in the will?" asked Denslow.

"Nothin'."

"Nothin'?"

"There wasn't any — not as you could call a will, anyways."

"No?"

"Eanh. There was a paper by his bed, though, in the upstairs front bedroom."

"What of it?" asked Solomon Tinkle.

Sam Judd wriggled his shoulders and glanced at the fat woman.

"I let on we was cousins of Rutherford, and Williams (he was the old man's lawyer), he took us along that mornin' to cast last eyes at the corp'e. It was a very unpleasant thing to see."

He paused, but seeing Mrs. Gurget's snapping gray eyes fixed on his own watery ones, and being encouraged by Denslow with a tumbler on the house, he took up his narrative.

"Well," he said, after a close reference to the replenished glass; "well, Mr. Williams he took us along with him up to the front bedroom on the second floor, where the old man was laid out in his city clothes and a waistcoat red enough to keep any livin' man warm and his top hat set down orderly on the chair, which was nice enough as far as it went. 'Well,' says Mr. Williams, a-rubbin' his hands and lookin' round the room, which was swept out partic'lar, — it bein' Sunday, and a death in the house, — 'Well,' he says, 'what a pleasant sight Mr. Bilberry has made of the remains. They look very handsome.' 'Uncommon,' says Joe, 'not to mention this here.' He puts his hand on a knife handle, which was stickin' so close to the old man it might have been druv' in back-'ards from the other side of him. It was that dark in the room — bein' only one candle, and that on the dresser, and the mirror with a crape bow onto it — that I hadn't seen it."

Here Sam paused to refresh his depressed feelings with the

tumbler on the house, and to glance at Joe for corroboration, which was given with a lugubrious nod.

"Eanh," he went on. "It was uncommon dark there, and cold, too, so early in the mornin'. 'Very curious, that knife, Mr. Judd,' says Williams. 'We could n't pull it out at all, though Mr. Bilberry used his feet tryin'. It took a very strong man to put that knife where it is, Mr. Judd.'"

"Man?" cried Denslow. "Then it was a man — and he *was* murdered!"

"No doubt of it, and a strong man at that. 'It took weight skillful applied, Mr. Judd — power, I might say,' the lawyer says to me. 'He was lyin' like that when we found him. He had n't stirred, sir.' 'Well, Mr. Williams,' says I, 'though the sheriff don't know who done it, — nor never will, most likely, — you and me and Sam can see he's dead. That bein' so, there's property to be got rid of; and, such bein' the case, there must be a will.' 'There was n't,' says the lawyer, without a blink. 'What's more, there's no more money left than what's needed to bury him and pay my bill for clearin' the estate.' 'No!' says I. 'I am afraid so,' says the lawyer. 'The old man was takin' a long time to die, — if somebody had n't 've touched him off, he might still be dyin', — but he went willin', I might say; he went meek.' 'No doubt of it,' says Joe, lookin' at the old feller's legs, which was very stiff under the blankets. 'Yes,' said the lawyer, 'he invested his money in charity and told me he hoped the interest, which he'd heard was uncommon big in that line, would help him into Heaven. . . . "And anyways," he'd say, "there's somebody I don't want to get it.". . . So he invested it in charity, which is a mighty tight investment so far as gettin' your money back is concerned — whatever the interest.'"

"Jeepers!" exclaimed Denslow. "Who'd have thunk it? He was such a snortin' old boar-hog for hell and high-livin' when he was on the canal."

They all looked at the stove, the walls of which were gradually growing red.

"I've heard tell," said the fat woman, drawing a harsh breath, "he could be meaner than a Baptist."

"So he could," said Sam. "He was a mean man with a horse. . . . But he's dead, and givin' the worms what he took out of the horses."

"So he was stabbed, was he?" mused Denslow.

"Uncommon," said Joe Judd.

"Heart, liver, or lungs?" asked Solomon Tinkle, fogging his glass with a long breath.

"They'd shifted the third button on his waistcoat to let out the handle," said Sam.

2

The fat woman appeared to be growing nervous over the general interest in Judd's story. She bridled forward in her chair and leaned toward Sam, her hands folded loosely about the empty glass which lay in her lap. The mellow lamplight lent the movement a reminiscence of grace which Solomon Tinkle drank in with staring eyes. She smiled and arched her brows.

"You said there wasn't any will, Mr. Judd. But you did say there was a paper beside the bed, didn't you?"

"So I did, mam, and a queer paper it was, at that. Eh, Joe?"

Joe lifted his eyes to the fat woman's.

"Uncommon queer," he said, and looked away.

"It must have been," said Mrs. Gurget. "What was in it?"

"Why," said Sam, rubbing his hands a little diffidently, "I ain't much in the readin' line; but Lawyer Williams give us a copy, seein' as how we was relations like I told him — *he, he, he!* And here it is. Perhaps you'd like to read it, Mrs. Gurget."

"Eanh, Lucy," said Solomon, reclining himself against the back of his chair and looking on her proudly, "take a shot at it, do. You read real nice."

Mrs. Gurget fluttered the paper carelessly about in her lap, and her mouth made inaudible words in a hesitating manner. She laughed nervously and looked up.

"The light's so bad here, and the writin' ain't very good. Mr. Denslow, would you be so kind? You've a better light where you set."

Denslow leaned forward for the paper and leaned back with an air of importance. After a moment's close scrutiny, he cleared his throat and read slowly: —

"This is to say, not that I care particular, that Rutherford aint my real name. I aint tellin my real name. Theres only One person knows it anyhow and I have told her she wont get none of my money which is bound hard in charities for soul's rest (X) if it can help him which I dont think it will seein as how he was such a mortal mean man. for which and other things I done this to him so he could not collect interest, on his damned charities."

"It is queer," said Denslow, looking up and clearing his throat again.

"It doesn't make sense," said Solomon Tinkle. "It's all mixed up with 'I' and 'him.'"

"If it was any other man," said Mrs. Gurget, caressing her bosom with her left hand, "I would call it tragical."

She straightened up with a small sidewise shake of her back that set the cherries clicking on her bonnet.

"If you'd seen the paper it was copied from," said Sam Judd, taking the note back from Denslow, "you'd 've seen it was clear by the writin'. It changed after the word 'rest,' where I've marked a cross. It was quite different from there, wasn't it, Joe?"

"Changed radical," his brother agreed, sombrely.

"The writin' of both parts was uncommon bad, but the second was worse. Lawyer Williams said it would have looked like a woman's hand, only he didn't see as how a woman could have got there after the old feller was killed, him bein' still warm when the cook found him. She must've been spry and delicate-footed for the cook not to have heard her at that, for the stairs creaked real dismal and loud."

"Well," said Denslow, "it don't figger anyhow. You said it must've took a strong man to put the knife there."

"Eanh," said Sam, "that's right."

They sat silent for a time. The cupola top of the stove had been pushed aside on its pivot to make room for a kettle from which the company might add hot water to their chosen liquor; and, in the stillness, it began suddenly to spout a wisp of steam and to murmur with the boiling water. Now and then the lid lifted and fell back into position with a light clink. The red spots on the wall of the stove had spread and merged until they formed a glowing band; and, as the light of the lamp grew fainter, this glow began to touch the knees of the fat woman and reflect in the rings on her fingers.

Quite suddenly, she took up her opinion of the dead man.

"A mean man," she said.

"Well, I've seen worse," said Denslow.

"He was all right with men, perhaps, but you said he was mean with horses — he probably was with all animals."

"Dogs didn't like him," Solomon Tinkle broke in, "nor any animal I ever see on his place. Once he owned a horse or a dog, they didn't have a show."

"There's lots of men like that," said Sam.

"I wonder who killed him," mused Denslow. "He'd been off the canal so long, and he kept so quiet, you'd think nobody'd have thought of him up there. That old brick house of his'n stood outside of town and off the canal, quite a ways."

"Eanh," said Solomon, "about half a mile, but it wasn't so far from the Watertown branch. You could walk up to it from the first lock in ten minutes."

"Did the sheriff find anything round the house?" asked Denslow.

"Nothin' to point to murder," said Sam. "There was pictures of pretty nigh all his posthouses set into frames in his parlor. But they don't count. And there was calendar pictures which he got for his tradin'."

"Lots of 'em," said Joe. "There was one in his bedroom on the second floor."

"That's right," said Sam; "there was, at that. Picture of a

woman, taken off a lithograph, and real pretty. Queer thing for him to have."

"He'd an eye for a gal," said Denslow.

"What was it like?" asked Mrs. Gurget, over her glass.

"Real pretty girl, with a yellow skirt, kind of full, and a red shawl, drawed down tight in front of her, with a geranium into her hair. She looked like she was dancing. It was a perfumery calendar, with something about odors made individual to suit the taste, with a special bottle of Nancy Haskins Perfume for postage-received, as a tryer."

"Nancy Haskins!" exclaimed Denslow. "There was a girl! I wonder what happened to her."

"She was a good-looker by the picture," said Sam. "I wish I'd 've seen her."

"She was afore your time, young man," said Mrs. Gurget, folding her hands and smiling at him in a patronizing way.

"I've heard tell of her," said Sam. "She used to be at Bentley's Oyster Booth in Uticy, did n't she?"

"Yes, she was Bentley's niece afore Rutherford forced him to sell and took over the place. All the boaters knew her. She used to do a dance with red-heeled shoes on, which took 'em all in their Sunday throats and left 'em thirsty. She was good trade for Bentley."

"Dance!" cried Solomon Tinkle, rubbing his palms over the calves of his legs. "She could dance! She'd put a geranium into her mouth, and then she'd stomp her heels on the floor and swing round to every man partic'lar till they was nigh crazy, and they'd stomp to keep her time, and she'd laugh with her head way back and her neck naked in the light, and smile to a man, and whirl till her skirts came up and brushed his legs!"

The fat woman stroked her throat.

"That must 've been when you was workin' the roads, Sol, and afore you settled down respectable."

"So it was," exclaimed Solomon, stiffening up on his chair and planting his feet on the floor. "People knowed me then! Me and

Gentleman Jo worked the beat from Syracuse to Utica, and there was good pickin's from the stage and boats for our trade."

He brushed the thin hair from his forehead.

"But you ought to've seen Nancy dancin'," he said, turning to the Judd brothers. "I wonder what ever become of her."

"She wasn't ever seen no more after Bentley sold out," said Denslow.

"That was a thing to see, that last night, I've heard tell. They made a clock round of it, the strong drinkers; and they saw the second mornin' in."

"That they did," said the fat woman.

"Was you there?"

"Eanh. Old Bentley put his head under the spigot of his number one-eight-seven Jamaicy rum, which he kept partic'lar, at the second three o'clock, and the swamper found him there at nine."

"I've heard there was a row about Nancy," said Solomon. "They says she was real riled at Rutherford. And when old Bentley went out broke, she didn't have nobody to keep her."

"It wasn't that," said the fat woman, settling her bonnet a little more over her eyes. "There wasn't a man who wouldn't have turned out his cook with a month's pay ahead and taken on Nancy Haskins. They was all cryin' for her."

"Then what did she take on so for?" asked Sam Judd.

"Well," said the fat woman, "she was kind of young, I reckon, and gals has notions in their heads. She'd always set up above the boat cooks, and she must've thought she was about to make a come-down in society. Gals is notional — that's why men like 'em and lick 'em. She was ashamed, I guess, and she wanted to be ashamed right up to the notch. That's how I figure it."

"She auctioned herself," said Denslow.

"That's right," exclaimed Solomon, "and they says as how she was right smart about it; played the filly and the auctioneer to oncet. And she showed her paces with a dance she done (keepin' up her patter all the while), till the room was bellerin' and the smoke was shook clear to the ceilin'. Knocked herself down for three hundred dollars, owned and broke, to Jotham Klore, who said he was biddin' for somebody else."

"Eanh," said the fat woman, "and then he took her out — cold as a razor — with the money in her fist."

"Cold and straight," said Solomon. "Her skirt was hangin' quiet over her legs, she walked that stiff."

"And they said she did n't look back oncet," added Denslow.

"I wonder who it was bought her," said Sam.

"Klore never telled who."

"He said he never seen her after. She walked with him along in the rain, he says, and never pulled the shawl over her head at all; and the rain wetted her hair so the drops looked red and yeller when they passed a window; and the rain run down her chin and neck, but she did n't take no notice. She was such an uncommon good-looker he said he 'd take her for himself, if she 'd come, any wages and a free bill of ladin' for anything she wanted to take aboard. But she looked at him kind of queer — and she says she 's made a bargain and been bought square, and she 'll stick to the man as bought her. So Klore left her in a room at Bagg's Hotel after tellin' her the man that bought her 'd come for her there, and he left the number of the room at the desk; and nobody saw her again."

3

The pause that followed drew out to the ticking of a clock out of sight behind the bar until the sound of measured seconds fell upon their ears with the sharpness of axe strokes. Solomon Tinkle wiped his eyes with a blue handkerchief and blew his nose loudly.

"I suppose," said Sam Judd, "that Rutherford took hold of Bentley's then."

"Not personal," said Denslow. "But he put in Klore for a barkeep, and quite a come-down it was after seein' Nancy there. But they left the old sign. Bentley was n't seen afterwards, and Rutherford did n't come down from Boonville for a year or two, only for a trip he made once every six months to see how things was going on. He was real jokin' them days, a good man to take a drink with. But not long after he commenced to sour some, and he got nasty, they say, with men as well as animals."

"I guess," said the fat woman, "he was rich enough then to own some. He was a mean man to the animals he owned. — Mr. Denslow, would you make kind with another glass? With a squirt from the other half of that lemon?"

"Surely," said Denslow, getting up and going to the bar. He turned up the lamp and rummaged about.

"Jeepers!" said Solomon Tinkle, all at once. "Jeepers! Nancy was a pretty gal! Outside of you, Lucy, she was the only gal I ever wanted to live with."

Mrs. Gurget patted out her skirt and made eyes at him so brightly that he caught his breath. She tilted her chin to a laugh.

"Go along," she said.

"I wonder who it was bought Nancy Haskins," said Sam Judd. "Nor why she never come back."

Denslow called to them from behind the bar.

"Say," he cried excitedly, "I got one of them perfumery calendars right here."

He held up a thin cardboard and a glint of yellow flashed under the lamp.

"Let's see it," said Mrs. Gurget, rising from her chair and going over to the lamp. The others crowded behind her.

"She must have been right pretty," exclaimed Sam, looking over the heavy shoulder.

"No wonder they bid high for her," said Denslow.

"Three hundred dollars is a lot of cash," said Sam. "It seems strange that anybody'd 've had it there. . . . He must have been rich."

"Nobody, only me," said Solomon Tinkle, "could have showed that all to once; and me, I was up the Rome road gettin' it. Nancy'd said the day before she was goin' to auction herself. But the mail guard winged me as I was gettin' away," — he pressed his trouser leg tight over his knotted right knee, — "and I got back too

slow. There could n't have been no one else. . . . Only Rutherford."

"Jeepers!" said Denslow, half under his breath.

"He 's dead now," said Sam Judd.

"Uncommon," said Joe.

"You ought to have seen her," said Solomon Tinkle, with a
whine in his voice. "You ought to 've seen her dance. She was
the prettiest gal I ever see. . . ."

The fat woman whirled round on her heels, and her skirt fluttered slightly, flirting with her ankles. She held the picture of the
girl in red and yellow in front of her for him to see, and looked
down over the top at him.

"She was real pretty," she said, glancing at the dancer's face.
"Look at her hair, kind of soft and yeller. And the smile to
her mouth."

The little man leaned forward, one hand resting on the bar to
steady his bowed legs, his thin nose drooping in reminiscence, and
gazed for several seconds. The others watched him silently.

"She was a real pretty gal," said Mrs. Gurget, and her broad
mouth curved miraculously between her fat cheeks. Solomon
looked up at her.

"Prettiest gal I ever see," he said, the whine in his voice pronounced. "There won't none of us see the like of her again."

The fat woman laid the perfumery calendar face down upon
the bar. Denslow handed her her glass of gin with a touch of
water from the kettle, and she spread her nostrils over the sharp
odor of lemon.

"What I would like to know," he said, "is who killed old Rutherford, anyhow?"

"That 's it," said Mrs. Gurget, as they all sat down again —
"who did?"

MR. DENNIT'S GREAT ADVENTURE

I

On a bright Tuesday morning, late in May 1836, Atwater Dennit, the warehouse clerk for Jones and Trumbull, Feed and Provision Merchants in Utica, came hurriedly down the front steps of his small Bleecker Street house.

At half a glance it was evident that this was an unusual procedure for Mr. Dennit. In the first place, just as he set foot on the narrow boardwalk, the bell in the great white spire of the Presbyterian church on Washington Street bonged out the hour of eleven. In the second place, though he was dressed in his shiny everyday blue coat that showed green at shoulders and elbows and wore his gray high Lafayette hat (outmoded now some ten years), he was carrying a carpetbag in his right hand. In the third place, when he remembered at the end of the block that he had forgotten to shut the door, he did not have to hurry back at his wife's shrill summons. Cornelia was out at marketing. He had been able to slip in and pack his bag, to write a note for her explaining why the whitefish would not arrive and why he would not be able to wait for her. He was on particular business for Mr. Trumbull.

Mr. Dennit was very conscious of the particular business, for he carried it in a thin belt next his skin — five hundred dollars to be delivered to Mr. Jones in Syracuse by seven o'clock on Wednesday morning. Mr. Trumbull had intended to take it out himself, but a card party had turned up that he did n't care to miss, and he had offered the commission to Mr. Dennit. They had intended to send someone out to audit Waverly's accounts in Rochester anyway — Mr. Trumbull had put his beefy hands on Mr. Dennit's narrow shoulders and rocked up and down on his toes — why could n't Mr. Dennit combine the two, hey? And make it into a holiday for himself, hey? After all, he had been with Jones and Trumbull for fifteen years without a holiday.

Even now, two hours later, Mr. Dennit's heart flopped up and down as he thought of it — a holiday. He had never been out of Utica in his life. Mr. Trumbull had said there was no danger: "Nobody will suspect *you* of carrying that belt of money, Dennit, my lad! Just wear that hat of yours!" He had rocked up and down and roared with laughter. But it was a lot of money to be responsible for.

Mr. Dennit looked covertly right and left to see if any of his neighbors had observed him. But except for the water cart, with its drowsy yoke of red and white oxen, and Mr. Brierly's smart pair of chestnuts at the corner of Chancellor Square, the street was unnaturally quiet.

So Mr. Dennit set out. He lifted his thin face and breathed in the sun-filled air. Nesting sparrows were twittering in the branches of the Square elms. Overhead, in the bluest sky that Mr. Dennit had ever seen, great white fleecy clouds were floating. A flock of crows were winging their way over the city, but they were so high up he barely heard their cawing. His mild brown eyes were shining, his puckered forehead smoothed until it became almost bland; his inoffensive pursed lips twitched an instant, then his mouth opened with pure pleasure. He was on a holiday!

It was at that particular instant that the church bell bonged. Instinctively Mr. Dennit's hand strayed to his waistcoat. He yanked out the heavy silver watch. Eleven o'clock. Before he could breathe he heard the warning notes of the packet boat's bugle, floating over the drowsy city noises. Mr. Dennit sprang like a hare. His thin knees lifted into a run. With his right hand he grabbed the brim of his Lafayette hat, in his left the carpetbag swung wildly back and forth against his shanks. His old shoes, newly polished, flashed up and down under the strapped snuff-yellow trousers. His cravat worked free of his waistcoat, the black ends fluttering, and the narrow tails of his blue coat rose and sank at every stride.

2

His breath laboring shrilly, he clattered over the bridge and struggled across the packet landing. He had had to run every foot of the three blocks, but he had got there in time.

The passage agent of the Red Bird Line regarded Mr. Dennit with undisguised surprise.

"Atwater Dennit! Where are you going to?"

"Syracuse."

Mr. Dennit just managed to get out the word.

Aware of the amused glances the bystanders were casting in their direction, the clerk said nasally, "Want a passage, hey?"

Mr. Dennit nodded breathlessly and mopped his pink cheeks with his frayed handkerchief.

"Well," said the agent, "you get your dinner and supper on the boat, thirty cents apiece. Fare costs a cent and a half a mile. Sixty-one miles makes ninety-two cents. One-fifty-two does the trick. Always did and always will."

Mr. Dennit caught a titter from a bystanding couple. Even he knew the fare to Syracuse, but it happened to be Abel Whitely's notion to give him a turn-around. He did n't mind. He was fishing in his old black leather purse, getting out an Oneida bill and four York shilling pieces and a fip. Abel looked at the bill, turning it this way and that; then he bounced the shillings on the counter of his little office, dropped them on the stove lid.

"I don't trust a York shilling very good," he said. "Howandever, I might as well chance it. Here 's your change."

He handed out four cent pieces, while Mr. Dennit alternated his gaze between the waiting boat and Abel Whitely's grimy hand. There was a touch of whiskey smell about the agent, though he looked sober enough, and his small eyes twinkled over his swollen red nose.

"Don't rush yourself, Atwater. That brute can't start his boat until I give the word, for all he blows his horn so loud. I never knowed you was a traveling man. What are you doing in Syracuse?"

Mr. Dennit was putting the pennies into his purse. Now he reached down for the bag he had been holding between his legs, and tried to say in an offhand manner, "Just a business trip for Mr. Trumbull."

"Auditing?"

Mr. Dennit nodded casually. "Auditing Waverly's accounts."

"Waverly? He's in Rochester. What are you doing in Syracuse?"

"An errand. Our company's got houses in Syracuse and Rome and Manlius and Rochester and Buffalo, you know."

"Surely, surely — famous concern, Jones and Trumbull." The agent eyed Dennit's face. He noticed little prickles of sweat on the thin high forehead. "Well, Atwater, you know your business. But if anyone asked me I'd say you was making off with the company dollars."

He was surprised at the sudden blanching of Mr. Dennit's face. The clerk had pulled his high gray hat lower over his eyes — of all people to wear a Lafayette hat! — and stared right and left. Then he turned back to Abel Whitely and affected laughter.

"Don't tell on me," he muttered.

The agent guffawed. His eye met the captain's eye, and the captain's eye was angry.

"All right, Atwater. Hop on." He raised his voice. "Saunders!"

"Yeanh?"

"That gent's for Syracuse, paid down!" he bawled. "Haul out!"

To the loiterers he said, "I don't believe Dennit's ever been out of town in his life. Funny feller. Scared half to death half the time, and plain scared the other half. But who'd ever think he could act out a joke like that?"

3

Mr. Dennit ran to the boat and up the gang. As he did so the driver boy gave the dock-end a heave and the steersman caught it in and yanked it onto its rack.

The captain stared down his nose at Mr. Dennit and said to a man in a black top hat and a neat black coat, "Lost us all of two minutes."

"I 'm very sorry," said Mr. Dennit.

The captain grinned through his brown whiskers. He had the build of a barrel wrestler and snapping black eyes.

"All right, sir. It 's that scab Whitely held me up, for a fact."

He stuck his bugle through his whiskers and broke out an intricate call. In the warm morning air, Mr. Dennit could hear the notes floating off above the noises of the town. He took a deep breath, and looked along the boat. A couple of idlers were tossing in the tie-ropes and the steersman was coiling them round the cleats in the forward deck. The driver boy in his red coat climbed up on the rope-horse. He snapped his light five-foot whip over the leader's withers. The horses took up the towrope, the dip lifted between the whiffletree and the standard in the bow over which it had been passed to clear the boats along the docks, the boat gave a series of infinitesimal jerks under Mr. Dennit's feet, the horses scrambled, the captain leaned against the rudder-beam, and the packet swung away from the dock.

> *Towdy-owdy-dil-do-dum,*
> *Towdy-owdy-dil-do-day.*

The bugle notes lifted jubilantly as the boat gathered way. The team was struggling into a trot. Fresh horses; their collars and traces were shining black, the brass on their bridles glittered in the sun. A little whisper of water sounded alongside, a ripple forked away from the stern. Mr. Dennit heard it lapping along the dock planks. He could feel the breeze in his face. Ahead, the Genesee bridge made a dark tunnel. A freight-boat team swung out for them, letting their slack rope trail in the water while the boat nosed wide to the far side. They passed between. The faces of people looking down from the bridge were reflected whitely in the water. People who knew took the Red Bird packets — good food and speed; Syracuse in just under fifteen hours;

Schenectady to Buffalo in four days; regular as time. Mr. Dennit glanced along the shining red walls of the saloon and cabin, the white windows and the yellow blinds. The *Belle of Rochester* was one of the company's crack boats, and he was on it.

"Steward!" shouted the captain, taking his bugle from his wet lips.

The steward, in a red jacket, appeared at the foot of the saloon steps.

"Show this gent where to drop his bag. What's your name, sir?"

"Atwater Dennit."

"Pleased to know you. Hope you're comfortable. My name's Henry Saunders. See you later."

The saloon took half the length of the boat, thirty-five feet, three windows on each side. It was handsomely paneled in maple, with a maple floor. The deck boards that made the ceiling were painted white, but the arched rafters were maple. Down the middle were two long tables at which the passengers ate. Under the rear deck a small cubicle housed another table and four or five chairs beside two small bookshelves. Two passengers, obviously husband and wife, were glancing through the last Albany papers.

There were perhaps twenty other passengers scattered through the saloon, most of them men, traveling west on business, though one couple, with an English accent to their talk, were sitting under an open window watching the town.

The steward led Mr. Dennit to a forward corner and showed him his berth, an ingenious iron frame, like a stanchion, hinged against the wall. Laced to the frame was a piece of canvas.

"That's yours, sir," said the steward, and ducked through a door in the left front wall to the kitchen.

A couple of men in natty clothes eyed Mr. Dennit amusedly as he wondered where he could safely leave his bag. One of them got up in a leisurely fashion, glanced casually at a white-haired gentleman reading a pocket Bible, and swaggered across to Mr. Dennit.

"Name's Markus," he said, extending a slim soft hand.

Mr. Dennit turned round and smiled uncertainly.

"Dennit, Atwater Dennit," he said, "at your service."

Mr. Markus placed the toe of a polished boot on the seat of a chair and rested his chin on his hand. He smiled guilelessly at Mr. Dennit.

"Off on business?"

"Yes, sir."

"Long trip?"

"Not to speak of. Just to Syracuse."

"Well, it's a nice boat. Nicely run. Fast. I can't stand any other line. I've tried them all — Ohio and Erie, Michigan, Blue Lions, Ohio boats."

"Dear me," said Mr. Dennit. "You must have to do a great deal of traveling."

"Quite a bit," said Mr. Markus, flicking his soft hand. He smelled faintly of lilacs. "Traveling for a company?"

"Yes," said Mr. Dennit. "Jones and Trumbull."

"Big people," said Mr. Markus with admiration. Mr. Dennit felt himself important. "Now my business keeps me moving, but it's small. One-man stuff."

He peered through the window.

"Noisiest basin in the line, I've always thought. But it looks thriving." He glanced over his shoulder. "Hope I'll see more of you. — Look here, come over and let me introduce you to a friend."

He took Mr. Dennit delicately by the elbow and led him over to his companion.

"Mr. Dennit, let me make you acquainted with Mr. Burton — Joe Burton. First-rate fellow. Joe, Mr. Dennit's traveling for Jones and Trumbull."

A glance flashed between them as Mr. Burton got up and bowed.

"Very pleased."

Like his friend, Mr. Burton was immaculately dressed. Mr.

Dennit bowed. His thin face was beaming. He had had no idea that packet traveling could be so pleasant.

"Join us?" suggested Mr. Burton, motioning to a couple of glasses. "Just beer. Morning beer is a great thing for traveling."

Mr. Dennit was tempted. But the thought of the deck sights was too much for him.

"Thank you, sir. Not just now. I believe I'll run upstairs for a moment. Just for the air, you know. I've been in the office all morning."

"Absolutely. The best thing. Looks like rain, too," said Mr. Markus.

"Dear me, do you think so?" Mr. Dennit's face fell.

"Positive. Thunder showers. Sure as shooting."

"Then I think I'll get what sun there is. But I'm very much obliged."

"Sit with us at dinner," suggested Mr. Burton.

"I'd be delighted."

"We might kill some time afterwards with a touch of the cards," said Mr. Burton.

Mr. Dennit started. "I'm not a card player. I hardly know any games."

Mr. Markus laughed.

"We're nothing. Blackjack, sledge, euchre — that's our limit. It doesn't signify anyway. Just a suggestion."

"Well," Mr. Dennit said dubiously, "it sounds very pleasant."

He managed to get away. Behind his back Mr. Markus winked soberly at Mr. Burton.

"Steward!" called Mr. Burton. "More beer."

4

It was without doubt the most beautiful day Mr. Dennit had ever seen in his life. He came up the six steps to the steersman's deck and stood beside the man. It seemed to him that the sky had never been so blue, the clouds so white, the water so sparkling.

The spring sun shed a golden warmth over the long basin, bringing out the colors of boats that had been newly painted. Greens, blues, reds, magentas, yellows, and whites — their reflections, broken by the packet's passage, threw glittering spots of color against the docks. Boats were everywhere. Men swarmed in the pits while others rolled down barrels from the warehouses. Invisible men were lowering crates from the overhanging second stories. Mules stood about, their eveners idle at their heels, and they waggled their ears at the sparrows and pigeons which billed their droppings. Voices were lifted on boats and on shore — the curse of a man with a barrel, the shouts of men catching swinging crates; a driver hollering "Back, you!" to a team as he hooked on the towrope; a woman crying out at a child; back east, the blow of a horn for the weighlock. It was a babel. Mr. Dennit had heard it every weekday of his life. But he had never listened to it from the water.

His eyes found Jones and Trumbull's — a great red warehouse. A tackle swung from the second story. A brown boat was loading. He saw Candler, the watchman, sitting on his accustomed bucket inside the yawning door, as usual occupied in trying to slip a straw over the leg of a spider. He did not see Mr. Dennit.

Mr. Dennit's narrow chest arched. The easterly breeze was fresh and cool, and thick with the smell of the docks: of flour, of pork, and grain, of potatoes, of stove wood, and iron farm machinery; and in the midst of it, as a boat passed, a smell of sage.

He looked at the boat. The steersman leaned against the rudder. A woman was stretching clothes in a line over the pit. The driver lurched along behind the mules, dragging his whip like a tail. Mr. Dennit breathed deep. Their faces might seem hard, but they were free. Their very curses lacked care. They worked for their living, but their work took them to places. And, for the first time in his life, Mr. Dennit was traveling with them.

"Do you think we'll have rain?" he asked the packet steersman.

The steersman's red coat would have looked bright enough from the towpath; seen close to, it was wrinkled, worn, and stained.

The front edge of his varnished straw hat was broken. His face was plain tough. But he answered Mr. Dennit politely enough, "Surely will. Wind's drawing through the east. I'd say we'd get some showers in a couple of hours."

"That's too bad."

"Yes," said the steersman. "Specially if you got to stand out here and take the worst of it."

Mr. Dennit eyed him. It hadn't occurred to him that boaters were ever uncomfortable.

"Well," he said uneasily, "I think I'll just get up on top for a spell."

"You'll just have to come right down," said the steersman. "You couldn't even lie down under that bridge." He spat over-side. "Even me, standing here, I've got to take my hat off."

Mr. Dennit eyed the bridge: two stone abutments and sleepers laid over; eight feet above water; and the boat was seven. Even as he watched it drawing nearer he saw the team pass under it. At the bow end of the deck, the captain's head uprose. He gave his horn a toot.

"Bridge!" cried the driver's high voice.

"Low bridge!" bawled Captain Saunders.

"Low bridge!" the steersman echoed him gutturally.

The bridge glided toward them; to Mr. Dennit's romanticized eyes it seemed to swoop over them. There was an instant of cool shadow, of loud-lapping water. Looking back he saw the entrance to the long basin small in the distance, as if the bridge framed it in a picture. They were out of Utica. Faintly on the east wind he heard the bell in the high white spire of the church bong once.

"Why n't you go up forward?" said the steersman. "There's chairs to set on. There's only three ladies in the ladies' cabin and they're all down below in the saloon. You can see out at the country better until we get clear of these eternal bridges, and then you can get on top."

"That's a good idea," said Mr. Dennit.

There was a twelve-inch cat-walk past the saloon windows on either side of the boat. He chose the outside walk, manœuvring his feet carefully and keeping a hand on the top deck rail for support. He passed the saloon windows to the kitchen window. The pipe was right beside his head. It breathed heat into his face, and the acrid smell of a hot wood fire. Through the open window he smelled roasting beef, potatoes, and frying parsnips. It seemed to him that he had never smelled anything so delicious in his life, and he wondered how he could manage to wait till noon.

He avoided looking into the three forward windows of the ladies' cabin, and edged himself round the corner. The forward deck was a small place, low over the water, with room for half a dozen chairs. The captain was sitting there with the gentleman in black.

The captain greeted him respectfully.

"Sit down, Mr. Dennit." Mr. Dennit flushed and sat down. (To think that the captain remembered his name!)

"Enjoying your trip?"

The man in black addressed Mr. Dennit courteously. He was an obvious gentleman, with an educated voice.

"I certainly do enjoy it," said Mr. Dennit. In the flush of his happiness he could n't help confiding in them. "You see, it 's my first trip on a packet."

The captain's beard parted. But his eyes fell on the clerk's face, his flushed cheeks and his sparkling eye. He grunted. "Look here," he said. "Let me make you two gents acquainted. Mr. Dennit, Mr. Wallet. Mr. Wallet 's in business in Albany. One of my regular passengers."

Mr. Wallet bowed.

"I 've got to go down," said the captain. "Dinner 's in half an hour."

He left them together.

Mr. Wallet had a pleasant smile.

"I remember my first trip," he said kindly. "I was one of the first passengers on the *Montezuma,* from Rome to Montezuma,

when the canal was open only that far. I still think of it whenever I take a boat."

"I remember them digging the culverts through Utica. We
used to use the Pennsylvania wagons in our business," said Mr.
Dennit. "Then we went into boating. But I've never been on a
boat before."

"It's very restful. It's apt to be hot in summer. But now, I
think, it's the most beautiful way to pass a few days in spring."

"It is," said Mr. Dennit. "It certainly is."

His narrow chest heaved. His eyes sparkled.

"You've no idea how I'm enjoying myself." He leaned con-
fidingly over to Mr. Wallet and his face got very red. "I'll tell
you something. I thought I'd pretend I'd traveled a lot. But
I'm not going to. You see, I'd lose half the fun."

Mr. Wallet nodded sympathetically.

Mr. Dennit felt that there was nothing more to say. You didn't
have to talk to this gentleman; he understood. So he composed
himself to watch the clouds, the water, and the banks sliding by.
He was so near the water that he heard the ripple plainly in the
grasses alongside. He watched the tree tops, with their small new
leaves, drifting back beyond the banks. A couple of meadow
larks bombshelled out of a field. A hawk was soaring against
the sun. A house on a little knoll had lilacs blooming by its door.

But the loveliest thing of all was the clean touch of the wind.
Because he was so low under it, Mr. Dennit felt, as he looked into
the sky, that he could see the wind moving under the clouds. His
heart surged beneath his waistcoat. He thought of the dusty
office he had quitted, the noise of the city, the hurrying people,
and in this placidness he experienced a lifting gratitude even toward
Mr. Trumbull. He could not remember ever in his whole life
a moment so happy.

5

Mr. Wallet tapped his knee.

"Perhaps," he said, "I've no right. But I just thought I ought to warn you. I overheard those two gentlemen inviting you to a game of cards."

Mr. Dennit started.

"Yes."

"Well, I think, as one gentleman to another, I ought to warn you. Their names are Markus and Burton?"

"Yes." A shadow crossed Mr. Dennit's horizon.

"Then I ought to warn you," said Mr. Wallet earnestly, "that they're professional gamblers."

"No!" said Mr. Dennit in hushed tones.

Mr. Wallet nodded soberly.

"But they were so cordial!"

"Naturally. It's part of their lay — their business."

Mr. Dennit felt as though his world had dropped out from under him.

"What will I do?" he cried.

"Why, just keep clear of them."

"But I promised to play. I practically promised."

"Well, feel indisposed. Travel sickness. Something like that."

Mr. Wallet seemed genuinely anxious to help him.

"Do you think,". — Mr. Dennit hesitated; his face was quite pale now, and there was a kind of misery under his eyes, — "do you think they'd rob a person?"

Mr. Wallet laughed reassuringly.

"They hardly would dare on the boat. Anyway, I'll look out for you."

"Thank you, thank you very much. I — I haven't much experience, you see. It isn't that. You see, I'll have to get off at Syracuse. About three o'clock to-morrow morning."

"That's very fortunate," said Mr. Wallet. "I'm leaving the boat then too. We can keep together."

He gave Mr. Dennit a keen, friendly glance, then looked away. Mr. Dennit looked out over the banks. It seemed to him that the sunlight was gone from the world. Indeed, he could see clouds mustering behind them in the east. But then, he felt, perhaps

he was fortunate anyway. Yes, he was fortunate. If it had not
been for this gentleman, he would have fallen right into the
hands of those two robbers. But he was still troubled. He felt
uncomfortable; his belt chafed him now, though before he had
hardly been aware of it. Something induced him to be artful
in his question.

"Mr. Wallet. Supposing — supposing a clerk was carrying a
large sum of money."

"Yes," said Mr. Wallet, encouragingly.

"Do you think, supposing he was, that he would do better to
confide it to the captain's care? That is, supposing he was on a
packet?"

Mr. Wallet stared thoughtfully at his boots.

"Do you know, I think it would be better not. It would be dif-
ficult to do it inconspicuously. Of course, if your suppositious clerk
thought the rogues had particular knowledge of his charge, he might
pass it on to a trusted friend." Mr. Wallet paused for the frac-
tion of a second; then he shook his head. "But on a boat — no, I
think he had better keep it."

Mr. Dennit had been listening with a heart full of woe, his eyes
on the cleat that held the towrope. The rope jerked on it gently,
almost imperceptibly, and a tiny vibration was transmitted from
it to the deck under his shoes. As Mr. Wallet finished, Mr. Dennit
turned on him suddenly, and surprised an extraordinarily sharp
glance from the gentleman's eyes.

"By God," said Mr. Wallet, turning his eyes away, "it makes me
boil to think of those rogues allowed to travel in decent company!"

"Yes," cried Mr. Dennit, relieved by he knew not what. "It's
outrageous."

Mr. Wallet got up suddenly. "I must go down. I'll sit with
you at dinner, if you like."

"Oh, thank you. But I promised those men."

"Then I'll sit just across. They can't do anything. Cheer up.
Enjoy the trip. I promise you they won't take a cent." His hand

jerked suddenly inside the cuff of his coat. It reappeared holding a small four-barreled derringer. "I'm prepared. It's a habit. So don't worry."

He walked jauntily back.

Enjoy the trip! Mr. Dennit could have wept. What fearful luck! His only holiday disturbed by a couple of ruffians. Then his face brightened. He mustn't complain. He was really lucky to have scraped acquaintance with Mr. Wallet and found so true a friend. He thought of the derringer and smiled. Mr. Markus, indeed! Mr. Burton! As long as he was on the boat, he needn't worry for a thing.

6

He gave his attention to the canal. Behind him the steersman shouted, "You might as well get on top, mister. No more bridges till Oriskany."

Mr. Dennit took him at his word. There was nobody on the top deck. And though it seemed extraordinary to him, he was glad. From his new eminence he could see out over the fields, the riverside meadows, the Mohawk flowing sluggishly through its coiling channel. The brilliance was out of the air; there was a faint mistiness. And back where Utica lay, beyond Whitesboro, a dark shadow slanted to earth. It must be raining.

The horses had subsided into a walk. Through Whitesboro they had trotted, — a kind of advertisement for the line, — with the driver shrilling, and the captain playing a bar of "Anacreon" on his bugle. Mail was tossed on board from the dock and a bag thrown back in exchange. They had never stopped.

Now they were in the open country. Way ahead, Mr. Dennit saw a couple of boats approaching and a line boat going away. Twenty minutes to catch the line boat, said the steersman. They were doing a mile and a half an hour better time. Red Bird packets were surely fliers.

Mr. Dennit, facing forward, heard a cough, turned round, and beheld the white-haired old minister he had earlier observed in the saloon.

"Pardon me, sir. My name is Prentice. I'm a minister of the Gospel." He held out his pocket Bible. On the flyleaf Mr. Dennit read, "To the Reverend Josiah Prentice, from the admiring and respectful parishioners of Trinity." The date said Christmas, 1828. The place, Rochester.

Mr. Dennit doffed his hat to the old man's white hair and cloth.

"My name is Atwater Dennit," he said.

"Mr. Dennit," said the old man soberly. "Just a word. Listen to me — it's for your own good. I'm a minister and, I trust, an honest man. You may ask the captain or any Rochester passenger. There are five below. I've traveled the canal often. I saw you speak just now to a man named Markus and a man named Burton."

He paused.

"Yes," said Mr. Dennit, his eyes bewildered.

"They asked you to cards?"

"Yes."

"I make no comment on the practice. But I can see that you're not an experienced traveler. Those men were interested in you. When you bent down to put down your bag, your coat tails parted and an excrescence was visible at your waist. Then they spoke to you. Sir, they're gamblers and robbers. They are bad company — distinctly bad. I warn you."

"Thank you," said Mr. Dennit. "I have been already made — "

The Reverend Prentice held up a white hand.

"Listen, sir. Did your information come from the gentleman who calls himself Wallet?"

"Why, yes."

"Let me warn you. Those three often travel in company. I should beware of him above all others. I don't know what your mission is, but they have made up their minds to something. Just now Wallet came down and spoke to Markus — just a word as he passed. I was reading near by. Wallet said, 'Easy.' That was all. Do you understand?"

Mr. Dennit was staring at him with stricken eyes.

"I had better go down. You're safe on the boat. It is better that they should n't see us talking. I should not show my suspicions to Wallet. Good day."

"Stop," cried Mr. Dennit. "What shall I do?"

"Keep your head and trust in the Lord," suggested the Reverend. "And avoid cards."

He went below as if he had suggested the proper way through life, as if he had rescued a soul, and solved for it all earthly problems.

But poor Mr. Dennit's soul was shrunk by a spasm. For an instant he thought wildly of jumping onto the bank and hiding in the fields. But his best blue tail coat was in his bag. And just then the steward's bell rang for dinner, and the wind blew gustily and rain began spattering the deck. Mr. Dennit summoned his nerve and went down. As he passed, the steersman said, "Did n't I prophesy? And me out here like a rotten sponge!"

7

Mr. Dennit went hurriedly through the saloon to the little washroom off the kitchen. A tank held water to trickle into a basin from a spigot. He washed his hands and returned timidly.

Burton and Markus waved to an empty seat between them. The steward backed him with a steaming platter of red slices in thick brown gravy. Mechanically Mr. Dennit helped himself. He helped himself to potatoes and to parsnips and pickles. Whatever was passed he accepted. His plate was heaped before him. He sat looking down dismally on the mountain. His appetite had fled. A large glass of brandy was the only encouraging thing he could see. He gulped a stinging swallow of it and mustered nerve to look round.

Across the board he met Wallet's encouraging eye. He shrank under his coat as he thought of the derringer, and lowered his face. Down the table the clergyman was helping himself and eating with gusto. Beside him Mr. Markus suggested wine.

"A little Madeira? How about it, Mr. Dennit? First-rate. No Governor Kirby's old Original, but they carry a good bottle of

Graby's Red Seal. No? Sherry, perhaps? Lobo Pale or Town Amber. Holloway's Port, then? No? Brandy, like a true blue. I agree. Nothing like brandy. Touch of travel sickness? Phut! Gone in a couple of hours. Take a turn after lunch if the rain lets up. By George, listen to it!"

The saloon had grown shadowed. The pictures of Washington, of Lafayette, of Clinton in the garb of a Roman Emperor, were spectres against the walls. On the boards overhead, rain drummed louder and louder, until the sound of the fall was blotted out in a rising wind. Lightning flashed beyond the windows, showing the canal bank livid white, the grass like bending ghosts, and the black skeleton of a broken tree. The thunder rumbled down upon them, shutting them all in.

The steward entered with a long match to light the lamps swung from the rafters. The light crawled across the wicks and dropped down over the tables.

People talked little. A few words on the work of the Assembly in the present session, a mention of crops, talk of the weather again. At the second table, a traveler remembered a story and proceeded to tell it. The others listened, using the dull narrative as an excuse for silence. Mr. Dennit did not hear a word. He nibbled his food, saw the lightly touched plate give way to pie, drank some coffee. The belt round his waist seemed to communicate a chill to his insides. He was not even aware of the narrator's laughter as the story reached its pointless close.

He did not know whether to be glad that the meal was over or to apprehend the advances of the rogues on either side of him. As he feared, they suggested cards, but he pleaded a headache and Mr. Wallet sympathetically suggested that he be given a comfortable chair under the rear windows. A lady half-heartedly offered a bottle of spirits of ammonia. Markus and Burton started a card game. The minister retired to a far corner and read to himself.

Mr. Dennit was left alone.

Sitting there in the semi-darkness while the rain sloshed over the banks of the canal and the water outside murmured round the rudder, he considered what he should do. He thought he might escape at Rome and make for the company office, but when Rome came in sight, at three-fifteen, Mr. Wallet kindly left a game of euchre to sit down beside him with a newspaper, under cover of which he whispered, "Everything's going to be all right. They don't suspect us, I believe. You acted finely at lunch."

Mr. Dennit writhed. He did not dare to get up. There were no passengers; the captain was in a hurry. The new team was brought out. In five minutes they were on their way. The notes of the bugle overhead were watery.

8

The rain continued with a steady roar. The thunder had long since marched overland ahead of them, but the darkness remained. Little of the country was visible beyond the windows. Outside, the driver-boy was hunched like a wet red burr on the top of his bay wheel-horse, and both of the team strode savagely with bent heads. An east-bound packet from Montezuma slid past with a bare exchange of bugle notes. From time to time they passed freight boats, the drivers sludging through the mud, the steersmen hunched inside their coats, the rain spouting from their wide hat brims.

Three miles out of Rome they passed Wood Creek and entered the Blacksnake of the Long Level. The boaters had named it for the twisting course of the canal through an eternal swamp of pine and hemlock. Again and again setbacks like ponds branched off from the canal. In some places the towpath gave way to a floating bridge, and the horses' hoofs thumped heavily.

The travelers became more and more silent. The card game was given up. Some men stood glowering at the windows. Traveling, thought Mr. Dennit, was the most miserable thing in the world. There were still ten miles of the Blacksnake to traverse.

But at five o'clock a cold breath cut through the airless windows. Suddenly the rain stopped. And even as they watched the clouds breaking, there came a shrill cry from the towpath, a yell from the steersman, and the boat bumped against the bank. The captain's boots pounded forward overhead; and then in the bows his voice was profanely uplifted.

"We 've hit something."

"A boat sunk in the channel!"

"Tom!" A woman's voice.

The steersman bawled through the open door at them.

"Don't get flusterated. No harm to the boat. We 're just agin' the bank."

Mr. Dennit lifted his head.

Like a kind of promise of better things he saw the sun way westward at the end of a straight stretch of the canal. He picked up his hat and followed the minister on deck.

The captain had jumped ashore, dragging a tie-rope behind him. "You 'd better get off and hold in the stern!" he shouted to the steersman. He swung on the driver-boy. "Why in hell don't you watch where you 're going?"

The boy rose up out of the grass, a smear of mud across his face. Then Mr. Dennit saw the head of the rope horse upraised. The animal's eyes were wide, his nostrils red. He gave a lurch, and then a shudder ran down his neck and his eyes closed. The driver-boy caught hold of the bridle and yanked. The horse gave another horrible, helpless lurch and lay back.

The driver-boy began to blubber.

"What 's the matter with him?" bawled the captain. "Tar the ugly brute."

The boy pointed. "He 's broke his leg."

"Oh, Jesus!" said the captain.

He stamped ahead.

"How did it happen?"

The boy was casting round.

"There 't is." He pointed his hand. "That God-damned eternal muskrat hole got gouged out by the rain. There 's the mouth. There it runs under the road. The horse broke through. End over he went, and me on him. God, Mr. Saunders, it ain't my fault. There was n't nothing to show. God, Mr. Saunders!"

"You ought to be tarred and oiled!" shouted the captain. "You ought to be boiled down into salt."

He pulled open his tangled beard and got ride of a gigantic quid. Then he swore.

"Four miles to Oneida Creek Station. One horse can't drag us. We 've got to get a new team. What in thunder are you waiting for, you little bastard? Get up on that horse and ride the brute in and bring back a team. If you 're over an hour and a half I 'll mince you personal."

The boy unhooked the lead horse, which was standing with scared raised head, scrambled onto his back, and went off at a heavy gallop.

The captain turned round.

"Any of you gents mind killing a horse? Me, I can't do it."

Mr. Dennit blanched and backed behind the minister. There was a complete silence. After a moment Mr. Wallet said, "If you 've got a heavy pistol or a rifle, I 'll do it."

"Thank you, mister. Steward!"

The steward fetched a heavy horse pistol. Mr. Wallet took it, examined the cap, jumped onto the towpath, and walked over to the horse. His face was quite expressionless. One of the ladies gave a little shriek. Mr. Wallet heard her and asked the captain for a handkerchief. The captain took one from his neck and handed it over. Mr. Wallet expertly tied it over the horse's nose and mouth. "I don't usually miss," he said. He stepped back and leveled the pistol. There was a heavy report. A balsam, close by, shook down drops of rain. There was no movement from the horse. But Mr. Dennit felt his stomach small and cold like a little bag of cold water hung against his backbone. Mr. Wallet looked down at the thread of blue smoke trailing from the pistol mouth in his hand.

Then he came aboard. And as he did so the travelers, according to custom, began to bewail the delay.

"Can't be helped. Can't even blame the driver, though he 's

a lazy little brute," said Captain Saunders. "I 'm sorry, ladies and gents. But we 've got to make up our minds to a wait."

He stood looking at them over his black whiskers.

"I 'll suggest something to pass the time. There are some mighty good bass and catfish along here. Now I 've got hooks and some line aboard. What do you say? I 'll push the boat over on the other side and let you off and you can fish."

"By Jupiter!" exclaimed Mr. Markus. "That 's a suggestion! I 'm not much of a fisherman, but I 'll put up four dollars for the biggest fish. Let 's make a pool!"

"With you, 'Kus," said Mr. Burton, flashing a wallet. "Let 's make it two dollars, though, so everybody will feel they can come in. Let 's give it to the captain. He can hand over the award at supper."

The idea took. Except for the minister, every man put up some money, and even one of the ladies brought out a small purse.

"How about you, Mr. Dennit?" asked the captain.

Mr. Dennit flushed. He had n't fished since he was a small boy. He had almost forgotten what it was like. And his mind was confused with all the events that had confronted it during the day.

"Why — er — er . . ."

"It means thirty-eight dollars to you if you win," suggested the captain. "Everyone else is joining up."

"Why, yes. I 'd be glad."

He pulled out his shiny old black purse and fished out a couple of dollars. It was a lot of money, a fearful lot, but he could n't appear backward.

"Now then, Steward!"

While the steward got the hooks and line and cut the latter into equal lengths, the captain and the steersman poled the packet over to the far bank. They fastened it, bow and stern, to a couple of trees. The captain waved his arm. "Now, ladies and gents, we 'll put off supper till half-past six. I 'll give a toot on my old bugle fifteen minutes before we leave. Here 's the rules for this

contest. Any bait is fair. Any man can cut him a pole to suit
his own ideas. But he's got to bring in his fish — and me, I weigh
it. And I hold the right to examine the winner for shot or stone
in his guts — that is, I open up his fish if it suits, see? Now there's
lay-backs and there's the canal. Most anywhere you might catch
most anything."

<h2 style="text-align:center">9</h2>

Mr. Dennit was enjoying himself. He was sitting on a fallen
tree trunk that ran far out into a setback several hundred yards
up the canal. He had a pole he had broken off a birch tree and
trimmed nicely. And on the end of his line he had a prime fat
worm he had found under a log. Carefully wrapped in his handkerchief were two more. And, best of all, a minute ago he had
had a most encouraging nibble. So that already he was considering various ways of spending thirty-eight dollars.

He had had a bad moment or two before he left the boat. As
a matter of fact, he had intended not to leave it, but when he had
found that both Markus and Burton were going to fish from the
deck, he had jumped over the side. After all, once out of sight
in the woods, he could keep hidden until the bugle sounded. He
wouldn't be worried by those sinister faces, and he could fish.

When he was thirteen or fourteen he had sometimes gone fishing in the Sauquoit or the Mohawk, — once he had caught a handsome bass right off the back side of Bagg's Hotel; those were the
days when Durham boats plied the Mohawk, — but since then he
had always had to work, even Sundays.

This was really a treat. Something, he thought, would turn
up at Syracuse. "Trust in the Lord," said Mr. Prentice, and it was
really the best advice. If the Lord would only send him an especial bullhead, everything would be all right.

In five minutes he had another bite, a real bite this time, and he
struck carefully. He had him. He had him, all right. He pulled
up slowly, and the sluggishly revolving bullhead came up on the
hook.

It was not a very large bullhead, but Mr. Dennit took it as a lucky omen. He beat it carefully over the head for a long time and then cautiously extracted the hook. There was even a good piece of the worm left. So he baited up a super-hookful.

He was just going to lower it into the water when he heard footsteps on the far side of the setback. Instinctively he drew back into the bushes and crouched down. In another instant his heart was in his mouth. Carefully parting the bushes appeared a pair of white hands. And between them Mr. Dennit saw a pair of eyes. Then the bushes parted wide and Mr. Wallet stepped out on the shore. Mr. Dennit hardly breathed. The man was staring right across.

He looked toward Mr. Dennit for a long time before his eyes wandered first right and then left. And Mr. Dennit began to breathe again. The man had missed him. But little shivers chased each other up and down Mr. Dennit's back, and he felt the money belt round his middle like a zone of ice.

As soon as the man had disappeared, Mr. Dennit crawled back, tenaciously dragging his fish and pole, and in the shadow of a hemlock considered what he had better do. He knew perfectly well that he ought to get back into the company of other travelers. But there was in his nature a curious streak of stubbornness. He had made up his mind to win the pool. And the more he considered it the more possible it seemed. He told himself that by being careful he could elude the villains — he had just seen an instance. He would follow the setback farther into the swamp.

Making a little curve, he tramped over moss and wet rank bog holes. The branches kept loosening his hat and the water from dripping branches sprayed down his neck, but the exercise made him warm, and he did n't mind.

Quite unexpectedly the shore appeared again. As he stepped out on it he realized that the setback extended a long way round a bend. He thought that here he would be perfectly safe, as the bend had not been visible from his first station. And just then he heard a hoarse, "Hello, there!"

He fairly jumped.

Not far from shore on his left a boat was floating in the water. It was the strangest boat Mr. Dennit had ever seen. Forty feet long, it was perfectly flat, with a small house-like structure, six feet high, occupying its middle. At the end nearest Mr. Dennit, the house roof was extended in a kind of porch, and in the shadow of this sat the hairiest old man Mr. Dennit had ever seen. It was he who had hailed.

"Hello, mister!"

"Hello!" said Mr. Dennit.

"You off the *Rochester Belle?*"

"Yes."

"Had any luck in the pool?"

"Just a small one," said Mr. Dennit. He was no longer afraid. Nothing made him afraid but Mr. Wallet and his two satellites.

"How'd you like to win it?"

"I'd certainly like to."

"Would it be worth five dollars to you to win it?"

"It would," said Mr. Dennit. "Just as long as I caught the fish myself."

"I could manage that."

"Well?"

The old man grunted and got to his feet. His gray beard reached down to his belly-button. He had a thin gray mane over his chest and belly. He was dressed only in underdrawers of faded red and a wide green hat.

"Just you wait, mister. I'll fetch you out here. Off this boat is the deepest piece of watter anywhere on this canal. And inside the deepest watter you're going to catch a mammoth fish, mister. And an actual mammoth."

He went round to the other end. Mr. Dennit heard him grunting and wheezing. He had heard of shanty-boats that appeared and disappeared along the canal. This was the first he had seen. Most stayed west of Utica.

There was a clatter of oars and presently the boat appeared, the old man bending in powerful strokes.

The boat skidded round on its flat bottom and presented its stern. Without stopping to think, Mr. Dennit stepped in.

"All right," said the old man. "Now set."

He began to row back. He had powerful broad shoulders, but it was his face that interested Mr. Dennit's attention. Just now it was wreathed in a whiskery grin; but the eyes had a cold slant about them.

Mr. Dennit suddenly asked, on top of his amazed thought, "How do you know about the boat?"

The old shanty-boater chuckled.

"There's lots of shanties round here. We know what goes by. Anyway, I could hear Saunders a-cussing and a-swearing fit to eat a polecat. Noises carry over watter. Especial after rain."

Mr. Dennit felt relieved.

"Are there many boats like yours?"

"Well, now, 'pends on what you mean. Reckon, I do, there's one or two to a setback. This-here's mine. Nobody dasst take it off me. I found the fishing. Kind of I'm the boss shantier. You might say," he squinted round at his houseboat, "you might say, mister, there's a hundred boats in the 'Snake,' maybe three hundred people."

"No!"

"Yes."

"I had no idea."

"Not many does. We've got arrangements. Don't let more'n so many outside in a day."

"It's amazing. How do you live?"

"Fishing. We send round fortune-telling. Gypsies, kind of. We do a mite of hoss-trading."

He seemed perfectly willing to talk; but at this moment they slid under the bow, and with a huge hand he stopped the boat and steadied it for Mr. Dennit to get out. With a strangely active spring he jumped out beside the clerk. A twist of the painter fastened the boat.

"Come along, mister."

He led Mr. Dennit down the cat-walk to the porch. The windows near the bow were closed up with board shutters. The rest looked into the main room. Mr. Dennit had a glimpse of a stove and a couple of bunks and a big cupboard. The old man showed him a chair on the porch.

"Set," he invited. "You're right over deep watter. What's your bait?"

Mr. Dennit exhibited the worms with some pride.

"Wait till I get you a piece of pork.'

He slouched into the room and came forth with a small piece of whitish stuff in his broad fingers. Mr. Dennit smelled it easily. The man baited the hook for him.

"Heave over. It's a short line, but the pool goes for the same length. I reckon they'll nose up to you anyway."

He sat down on the boards and leaned against an upright. Mr. Dennit was mightily puzzled.

"I don't see how you learned about the pool."

"Gal, Lissa, was onshore when the horse went down. She listened. I said, 'Maybe one of 'em will come this way. Maybe I can get him the winner.' Lissa is going to be married to-morrow. Marries Tommy Fly. He's young. Been acting up to be my boss. Thought I'd best get him in family. Lissa was good bait. Living's like fishing, mister. Depends on the bait you use."

"Is she your daughter?"

"Kind of. Lived with me since she was fifteen. But I'm getting old."

"By the way," said Mr. Dennit, "how'll I get back to the boat?"

"There's the bugle. You don't need to worry about it, though. I'll fix you."

The old man's eyes lifted sardonically. He grinned at Mr. Dennit. And for a moment Mr. Dennit was troubled. But just then he had the king of nibbles; and then he was hauling with all his might.

The old man had rolled over on his naked chest, tucking his beard in not to wet it, and peering far overside.

"He's a mammoth!" he shouted. "A real Masterman fish. People call these fishes Masterman fishes after me. There ain't any like them in the state of New York."

Mr. Dennit's eyes were bright. His Lafayette hat was tilted far back on his head, showing the trace of baldness. His timid face glistened a bright beet red.

"If the line holds, if the line only holds," he prayed. "Oh, Lord!"

"Pull, mister! Pull hard! Set back against the mammother. Haul him!"

The shanty-boater had picked up a heavy brass bolt.

"Now then, up and over."

With a desperate effort Mr. Dennit hauled the fish onto the deck. For a second it lay there flapping its massive black length. Then the boater was on it. One blow of the bolt and the fish lay still. Its fat mouth opened pink, its feelers stiffened and went slack and stiffened. Convulsive shudders mastered it from nose to tail. The old man dropped the bolt and leaned back. He watched the fish die with complete calmness. But Mr. Dennit felt almost nauseated. The fish was over two feet long. It was more an animal than a fish. He looked away.

The sun was setting red and gold behind the hemlocks. Deep shadows were creeping over the water, purple and blue. A faint mist rose wraith-like here and there.

When he looked back at the fish it was dead.

The old man, with head braced by his hands, looked at Mr. Dennit with a broad grin. His teeth were stumpy and brown.

"Well, mister, do you think that's the winner?"

"I should think so."

"How about the five dollars?"

It was a sure thing, thought Mr. Dennit. He said, "Here you are," and passed over the bills. The thrill had been worth it, even if he lost.

The old man wadded the bills and stuck them in a crack.

"Maybe I ought to get back," said Mr. Dennit.

"No hurry, no hurry. I'll row you, mister. I reckon you want to get back without those others getting after you."

"What do you mean?" cried Mr. Dennit.

"The gent with the derringer, or the other two."

"What do you know about them?"

"Lissa heard them talking. Tom, he's trailed you."

Mr. Dennit froze, solid.

"You see," said Masterman, "I don't allow no such goings-on. We don't want the sheriff in after us. So you set here. It's quite a fish, ain't it?"

Mr. Dennit, for all his worry, could not help feeling gratified as he examined the fish. It really was a beauty, for a bullhead.

The shanty-boater said, "Now my idea is we have a snort. You come in."

He led the way into the cabin. It was a magpie sort of room. There were pots and pans laid every which way among fishing tackle, a gun across the table, a couple of boots of odd sizes under the bunk, extraordinary scraps of clothing. It had a queer musty smell, of old spirits, tobacco, snuff, and fried fish.

The old man pointed to a chair.

"Set, mister."

He lighted a candle set in a lump of clay. The wick shed a feeble smoky glimmer. Outside the window the sun went down behind the hemlocks. A strange stillness settled on the water. The only sound was the old man's step and his wheezy breathing as he gathered two glasses, stained and brown with fingermarks, and a stone bottle. He tilted the bottle over the glasses.

"Consarn!"

It was empty.

He paused irresolutely a moment, then his face cleared. He lifted his head and Mr. Dennit thought he could see the red ears stretch. Then he too heard the cautious oars.

"That's Tom," said the old man, suddenly. "He rows a funny way. Right and left. The one-over-one, I call it." His eyes fastened on Mr. Dennit's. "Tom's a bodacious kind of boy. Up and rising. He'd of had me soon if it wasn't I had Lissa. He's ambitious for money. Kind of unmoral. Mister," he stopped to whisper, "I calculate you'd better lay hid. You'd better step in here. Tom's keen. He's a knife-itchety. I'll send him for a snort and then I'll get you out."

Before Mr. Dennit could think, he was seized by the elbow and pushed into the forward room. The door was closed softly after him. He crouched down in almost complete darkness.

10

Mr. Dennit trembled. The oars came closer. Suddenly it occurred to him what a fool he had been — what an utter fool to be lured onto a boat by this outlandish creature of a man.

The old fellow spoke fair enough, but, if he chose, Mr. Dennit was at his mercy. He hadn't even a gun — nothing but a silly penknife. And he didn't know how he could use even that. He tried to pray there in the darkness, but his tongue was dry. He could not even think a prayer.

The boat came closer. The oars ceased to plash. There was a faint bump that he could feel against his hams, and then Masterman's voice.

"'Lo, Tom. Glad you came. How about you lending me a drink? I'm all out and dry as feathers."

Tom's voice was low and hoarse.

"All right, Benj. Have you . . ."

"Shussh! I'll come along with you and row myself back."

Mr. Dennit's heart rose. That sounded fair.

Then the hoarse voice asked, "Where's Lissa?"

"Outside in the woods somewheres," said the old man. "How should I know?"

The other grumbled.

"She needs a powerful taming. I'll have to train her down."

The old man chuckled.

"You've bit off a chaw, boy."

"I've got back teeth, Benj. She'll learn."

"All right, but we might as well get going."

Mr. Dennit heard a wash of water as the old man stepped into the boat. He crept to the side of the dark room. There was a knothole there, and through it he saw the light from the candle shining through the window directly into the boat. The young man's face was turned toward him. The young man was a giant in build, but his face was abnormally small and very dark, and the eyes were a light brown, so light that they looked almost white. And while Mr. Dennit looked, the face grinned, and the man said out loud, "How about him?"

"He's safe," said the old man, shoving off. "He'll keep. He couldn't swim. I seen it the way he watched the watter."

"How about Lissa?"

"I've got the key, Tom. There ain't no axe. She's queer, I know, but he's safe."

Safe! The boat stole away. Safe! Mr. Dennit began to weep. It was plain now. They were waiting till the *Rochester Belle* hauled out, and then they would murder him. Safe! As if in answer, he heard the notes of Saunders's bugle stealing over the water. The captain was playing an air, doing himself proud: —

> Row, brothers, row,
> The stream runs fast,
> The rapids are near,
> And the daylight's passed.

Desperately Mr. Dennit got to his feet and felt his way to the door. It was locked, as he knew, but he threw his weight against it. For all its crazy appearance it was soundly built, and his puny strength made scarcely a tremble. He felt his way to the window and battered against the boards with his fists. But they were heavily nailed. He crawled round the room, feeling the walls. There were shelves with jugs and boxes. There were a pair of shoes in a corner. He took them up in his hands. Women's shoes. Somehow they comforted him. But he passed them by. Nowhere in the room could he find a hopeful weakness.

He went back to the door and tried to examine the lock. A chink of light came through beside it. He wondered if he could whittle past it with his knife. He got the knife out of his pocket and opened the blade, but as he started to work it dropped through his damp fingers. Whimpering to himself, he hunted about the floor. It took him five minutes to find it, and when he tried whittling again he produced only pitiful scratches.

But he worked till his fingers ached.

And then he heard a sound, — oars coming toward the boat, — and he sat down weakly and gave up.

II

The boat came very quietly. He did not even hear it touch the shanty-boat. But after an instant bare feet patted past the window and entered the cabin. They were so stealthy that he knew that his end had come. He tried to think of his wife, Cornelia. He thought instead of Mr. Trumbull and the office. He would n't have to face Mr. Trumbull again, but the office — only now did he realize how he loved its familiar dustiness; the ink spots, the ledgers, the rows of red and black figures emerging from the neat point of his pen and always coming right. If he could only get back to his desk, mount his high solid stool once more before he died!

A hand tried the door; but there was no sound of the key. Then a voice, soft and musical, the most musical thing Mr. Dennit was ever to hear, said, "Mister?"

"Yes," he whispered.

"They 've got you, then?"

"Yes."

"I can't get in."

"Can't you break it down?" cried Mr. Dennit, springing up in a last desperate hope.

"No. Hush, mister."

There was an interminable silence.

"Mister, can you swim?"

"No."

There was a small oath; then more silence; then, "You 'll have to."

"Don't go away! Don't leave me!"

"Hush, will you?"

He heard her feet slipping out. The silence lasted longer and longer. Then there was a faint splash. Mr. Dennit slid down on his knees facing the door. His breast ached with misery.

Then he sprang to his feet.

12

Somebody was knocking on the floor, directly under him. Two little taps.

He stood still, sweating and trembling.

Two taps.

"Yes," he whispered.

"Do you hear me?"

The voice was oddly muffled.

"Yes."

"Listen, there's a board loose at the back. I'm knocking underneath it. You find it."

Then Mr. Dennit began the queerest game he had ever played. It was pitch-dark; and he had to crawl on his hands and knees. He kept bumping off his Lafayette hat against the rear wall, and he was getting cobwebs on his face. And all the time while he worked toward the tapping, his ears kept stretched for the sound of oars.

The taps continued their one-two signal all the time he approached. But when he made a false cast they came in a triple rap, that somehow sounded impatient and angry to Mr. Dennit. Lord knows, he was doing his best to please. His knees felt as if his trousers and drawers had worn away, he had splinters in his hands, and the blood was throbbing in his forehead. It seemed to him that hours had passed before he heard the voice say, "Right. Lift that one."

Mr. Dennit felt eagerly with the tips of his fingers down one crack, across the end, up the other crack. The board was a short length and a double width. He could not get his fingers in and was forced to look for his penknife. It was not in his pockets. He realized then that he must have dropped it at the door.

He explained to the voice apologetically.

"All right, mister. Go get it. Don't talk. It's cold in this water. But leave something on the board to mark it."

He scurried back on his hands and knees to the door and fumbled for the knife. For once luck was with him. At the second swoop of his right hand along the floor, his left hand rested on it. In a moment he was back, and the Lafayette hat was easy to find. He stuck in the blade. The board lifted easily enough. He flung it off.

In the well he could just see dimly the girl's white skin. The face was upturned and he could hear the ripples against her neck as she trod water.

"It's a bother you can't swim. Will you be scared to get in with me?"

"I'd drown rather than stay here."

The girl laughed softly.

"I don't exactly blame you. Now listen — you've got to promise to get in here and hang on round my middle. And you must n't try to swim. I'll get us out under the boat. Do you see?"

Mr. Dennit nodded, and then, remembering it was dark, he said. "Yes, miss."

"All right, climb in. We've got to hurry."

Mr. Dennit put on his hat and lowered himself into the water. He did n't wonder the girl was in a hurry. It was very cold. Inch by inch it crept up to his knees, his waist, and then he had to let himself go. He went down sickeningly. The girl caught him by the armpits.

"Don't be scared, mister." She faced him in the water. He could feel her knees chugging the water against his. "Round my waist. And then get in all the air you can into your lungs."

Mr. Dennit gasped. He put out his arms under the water and felt her waist come into them. His hands closed on her back. He gasped again. The girl was as naked as the day she was born. He would have let go had she not cried, "Now!" And he had just time enough to draw in his breath before she shoved them

under with her arms. He felt her legs trailing under his. She
was creeping along the bottom of the boat with her hands. The
water was over him, round him, in his ears, in his nose. His eyes
were tight shut, but the cool pressure made him think of a dream
he used to have as a boy. A light coppery glow pressed against
his closed eyes, and swimming in the copper were specks of every
color in the world. His lungs seemed to swell like balloons. But
he clenched his teeth and gave himself up to the water, and the
powerful thrusts forward of the girl's arms. And at last, when
he knew that he would have to breathe or die, he felt them shooting upward through the water, and they broke out into the light
from the cabin window, face to face.

The girl was looking directly at him. She was shivering. But
not half so hard as Mr. Dennit. He had to clench his jaws to keep
his teeth from chattering.

She did not speak, but turned over and, taking his hand, laid it
on her shoulder. Then she struck out from the rear of the boat.
There, where the shanty-man had landed Mr. Dennit, a skiff was
floating.

"Grab hold of the back," she said.

Mr. Dennit obeyed. In an instant she had left him, to swim
round to the side. She gave a strong kick and rose out of the water
like a silver fish. Mr. Dennit turned away his eyes while she slid
herself over the gunwale as lithely as an otter. The boat rocked
gently in his hands.

After a minute, she directed him to pull himself round to the
side. There she seized his wrists and told him to kick upward.
The boat rocked dangerously, but, with her strength added to his,
he managed to flop in.

"Lay still, mister."

She had taken up her oars and was skimming the boat into the
shadow of the shore.

Lying on his back, Mr. Dennit watched her row. She had
slipped on a shirt and a loose pair of trousers, and she stroked with
the ease and vigor of a boy.

"Miss," said Mr. Dennit, "it's hard to thank you enough."

"Don't," she said. "I did it because I wanted to."

"It was a noble thing for you to do. And I'd given up hoping."

"You was in a bad way, mister."

"I've never been so scared in my life."

"I don't blame you. Benj and Tom are pretty bad for people like you."

"Would they have murdered me?" asked Mr. Dennit. "Truly?"

"I don't know. I reckon they'd have just passed you through the way you got out, with something tied on your feet. That's what they've used it for."

"Miss?"

"Call me Lissa."

"Yes, miss. I ought to have known better than to bring the money. It's been awful. And now I've got to chance that boat again."

"The *Rochester Belle?* She pulled out an hour ago."

"What'll I do?"

"I'll put you on a freight boat."

"Will you really? I'm terribly grateful. I'm terribly indebted to you. I'd like to give you something."

"I don't want nothing, mister. Then Tom would find out. Now they'll find your hat floating in the well and figger you found it and drowned yourself."

All the time they whispered she was oaring the boat swiftly along the setback. The stars overhead were bright and large. Against them the fringe of tree tops with their May softness of leaves floated dreamily.

Suddenly the girl leaned on the oars.

"Shh!"

Mr. Dennit held his breath.

She slipped in her oars and pulled them against the bank. "Lie still."

Then he heard the dip of other oars coming closer, and a hoarse voice singing throatily: —

"A roguish youth asked me to woo —
    Heigho! The buds were blowing!
And I was puzzled what to do —
    Heigho! The buds were blowing!"

The drip of the oars passed close, the voice faded slowly. The boat rocked gently under Mr. Dennit as the wash came against it.

"There goes Benj and Tom."

The girl waited endless moments — too long, thought Mr. Dennit. Then she said, "Now we've got to push."

She bent swiftly to her oars. Mr. Dennit could feel the urgency in her strokes pulsing through the boards. He sat up, his bare head trickling little streams down his neck.

The girl said, "So long as I get you into the canal afore the moon rises . . ."

Mr. Dennit watched the trees sliding past.

"Suppose," he asked suddenly, "suppose Burton or Wallet is waiting."

"They wouldn't dare hang round here after dark."

The skiff shot suddenly into the open water of the canal and the girl stroked it west.

"We're about all right. I'll take you west a mile or so. Maybe we can catch a boat."

Even as she spoke, they heard ahead of them the toot of a brass horn. It was idly, softly made, as if the steersman were drowsy. It had no music, but to Mr. Dennit it sounded very lovely. And in a moment it came again. The girl rested, cocking her head.

"They're going west, about half a mile ahead."

The boat throbbed gently to her deep breathing. But instantly she began rowing, not with the same frantic speed, but with long steady strokes.

13

The moon rose behind them through a veil of mist, round and warm. As if to greet it, all along the shores small frogs began their peeping. A whippoorwill lifted its plaintive voice in the track of the towpath. And in a low-hanging tree on the south shore a tree toad swelled its throat and trilled as if its heart were aching. Tears came to Mr. Dennit's eyes.

He did not speak, but he watched the slow moonlight drawing the girl's features for him to see.

She was young. Her dark hair surrounded her cheeks and fell away over her rough woolen shirt in a damp curling mane. Her eyes were long and pointed and dark. In the sounds of the marsh night, handling her oars so strongly, she was beautiful as a wild creature is beautiful where it grows naturally. But Mr. Dennit, with the citizen's misplaced instinct, felt sorry for her. He was thinking of Tom's dark face as he talked to Benj about the girl, his hard eyes, his thin mouth.

"I'm so grateful," he began.

"Don't," she said. "I did it because I wanted to."

"But you don't want to live with those awful men!"

"I might as well. I like the swamp."

"Yes, but . . ."

She seemed to divine his thought.

"I like Tom. He's hard-bitted to you, mister. I don't deny it. But he's young. And he's powerful here."

"But," cried Mr. Dennit, "he'll treat you badly. He might beat you!"

He caught his breath.

She shrugged her square shoulders.

"A man has to break loose now and again. I guess I can watch out for myself, mister."

"I could take you back with me — find you a home," said Mr. Dennit desperately.

"I don't want a home. I'll find my own, that is."

Her voice hardened.

"Now you tend to yourself, mister. Don't bother about me."

Mr. Dennit felt humiliated.

"I want to do something for you."

"I'm grateful. But there's nothing."

"You 're one of them, I suppose," Mr. Dennit muttered.

"Yes, I am. What difference?"

"Why did you get me out?"

She lowered her eyes. She might have been blushing.

After a short hesitation she said, "You see, mister, me and Tom is getting married to-morrow. And I guess I 've got a kind of funny streak into me. I could n't a-bear thinking of you laying down under the boat to-morrow night when Benj leaves us."

She did not look at him. But Mr. Dennit felt his humiliation completed. He lowered his face.

"You must pardon me, miss. I 'm an inexperienced man. I did n't intend anything against your young man. And I made an awful mess of everything, or I would n't have given you all this trouble."

As she made no reply, he lifted his eyes. She was smiling.

"I don't mind, mister. I 'm proud to have done it, even to getting the better of Tom and Benj. I never seen nothing since I was born as brave as you getting down into that hole with a girl, and you could n't swim."

Mr. Dennit was glad his back was to the moon. He was flushing all over.

"I was just plain scared. I 'd have gone with anybody then."

She laughed aloud.

Round the bend ahead, they heard a man call from the boat.

"Did you hear that, George?"

"Yeanh. One of them shanty-boater girls."

"Well, lay into that black mule. This stretch makes a man uneasy."

The skiff rounded the bend. Just in front, a freight boat was creeping along. They could see the figure of the steersman outlined in black against the glow of the bow lantern. At the same instant the man heard the oars. He turned at them.

"Hey there!"

Mr. Dennit raised his hand.

"Hello! Will you take a passenger?"

"Who the hell are you?"

"Atwater Dennit. I got left behind by my packet."

The man swore. "Did you hear that, Bill?" he yelled at the driver.

The mules stopped, and the heavy old boat barged slowly forward with lessening way.

"Come up where I can look at you," directed the boater.

The girl rowed into the zone of the bow lantern.

"By eternal nation! It is him. Sure, you can get on. This is a Trumbull boat. *Western Cargo,* out of Rome. Me, I'm Vince Tucker."

Mr. Dennit caught the low rail. He turned to the girl.

"I'll say just once more how grateful I am."

"Don't, mister. Good night."

"Good night."

The skiff slid into darkness. Mr. Dennit went aft to confront the amazed boater.

"How'd you come to be left here, Mr. Dennit?"

"I went fishing."

A gaping hole of amazement fringed with yellow teeth opened in the steersman's beard.

"But who's the girl? How'd you find her?"

Mr. Dennit said, "She very kindly put me on this boat."

"I seen that," said the boater, and he swore to himself. "All right, you can go down. We'll be in Syracuse after sunup."

He waited until Mr. Dennit had vanished into the small cabin.

"George," he called softly as the mules took up their way. "George, did you hear that?"

"Yeanh."

"George, did you see that girl?"

"Yeanh? One of them shanty-women. They're a bum scrub for a man like you and me, I've heard."

"But, George, didn't you see her good?"

"Oh, shut up! I seen her. Don't bother a man that's sleepy."

"By god, she was a pretty piece," the steersman said to himself.

"I wonder how that clerk got across her, and what he was doing with her. Fishing? Hell!"

But Mr. Dennit never told — not even after he had delivered his money to Mr. Jones. It was his great adventure, and he preferred to keep it to himself.

THE OLD JEW'S TALE

I

THE old Jew clasped and unclasped his long hands. "It was a foggy night and morning like this, Dan," he said to the driver-boy, "when I first seen the Asiatic cholera on the canal. That was a bad time."

He leaned forward to close the stove draft a trifle.

"The cholera hit Albany along about the end of June, as I re-member — year of thirty-two. We'd been doing short hauling up the canal. I wasn't only about eighteen then and was pulling down full driver's pay for the first time. There hadn't been no sign of cholera above Albany, though it was commencing to hit New York bad and was doing terrible things in Albany, so people had a notion it might not travel up the Mohawk. The packet lines kept running steady out of Schenectady, but they weren't being traveled much.

"The boat I worked on was the *Pretty Western* and my captain was a man about sixty year old and a pretty tough article. He'd worked on the building of the canal; they said he'd touched off danged near every blast for the Lockport double flight. He'd been right in the mess of it, and now he'd got a boat to spend his life easy, he'd say. His name was Kruscome Shanks, and he was one of the regular old-timers. He was hauling for the Dennison Freight Lines; but the amount of strap he could swaller down and yet keep afloat was an extraordinary thing to see. I said he was a tough article.

"But I got along with him pretty good, because I was strong them days and good for pulling him out of the ructions he'd stir up in pretty near every bar he got into. He was a great hand for a wrassle. 'Ben,' he'd say, 'if a man ever sasses you or me or the

Pretty Western, spit in his eye and give him ganders.' He was like that himself."

The old Jew brooded awhile, his hands on his knees.

"We got a load of nails at Schenectady for Buffalo on July ninth. Loaded in the morning and was just ready to pull out when there come a man aboard, high and dandy in his dress, shiny boots, stick with silver onto it — he was a handsome-looking figger, and I stood leaning against the black mule (we hitched tandem in the early days) just to look at him. By grab, Dan, I could smell a scent onto him.

"I don't figger he was more 'n thirty-two, or maybe three; but at first sight you 'd hardly say he was over twenty-five, he looked that fresh-colored and smooth, and his eyes, which were dark, had a sort of pleasant, sleepy look to them when he 'd talk. But when you got closer, you seen different. His eyes was big, but they was n't easy, and there was a little sort of dimple in his face just under the nigh corner of his nose, and he had a way, too, of rolling back his upper lip when he swallowed, and showing his teeth. It looked like a smile until you took his weak points into combination.

"Of course, I did n't figger all this out right away. I was most mortal eager just to watch the way he dandled that stick. I notioned a gent like him was just about as fine a thing as a man would want to be. But a little later I commenced to change my mind; and after he 'd told what he wanted, he did n't cut no figger at all for a gentleman with Kruscome Shanks. It seemed he wanted passage through to Buffalo on our freighter for two people.

"Kruscome liked his comforts; so he says, 'If the price is all right, it 's all right by me. You got the whole deck and the stable on rainy nights.'

" 'That won't do,' says the stranger. 'I 'm bringing my wife with me.'

" 'Wife?' says Kruscome. 'Woman?'

" 'Yeanh,' says the gent. 'That means I 'll want the cabin. You two 'll take the stable.' He was cold in his talk. You could see he knowed what he wanted and expected to get it, too.

"'Like hell!' says Kruscome. 'Get them mules to going, Ben!' he yells at me; but the other says, 'Whoa!' — and a mule generally always stops when you say that to him, and I stopped too. I thought Kruscome was going to lay that gent across the rail and spank his doeskins; but he did n't. The gent just whispers into his ear, and afterward Kruscome put his finger in too, like he thought something was queer; and then he says, respectful, which was extraordinary, 'Mister,' he says, 'for that much money I 'd lock the Devil through to Heaven,' he says, grabbing hold of his beard. 'Go get your wife.'

"I thought the gent was a pretty handsome spark, but I was n't only a lad.

"Ten minutes later the gent comes back carrying his satchel bags, and back of him was a young woman wearing a veil. I thought she had a tidy body, but she seemed a mite poor in flesh. But I did n't get a chance to see nothing of her then, because they went right aboard and Kruscome yells at me and we hauled out.

"We 'd got off to a late start and we did n't do better than twenty mile that day. We tied up three hours out of Canajoharie. We had n't seen much traffic that day, but the men on the east boats we met looked kind of scared, and they all asked how things was going down the canal. There was n't any cholera yet and Kruscome told them, 'It 'll never get up above the locks. It 'll stay down in the valley. It travels by water, so it can't get uphill.' But one old feller said he thought the rats brought it, and it could go anywhere. But nobody really knowed.

2

"We did n't see nothing of our passengers all morning, but when they finally come out on deck Kruscome and me noticed that the gent had put on an old coat. It was a hot day and the mist showed still against the valley, and he looked sleepy and tired. But just after he come out a packet boat come up behind us. When we heard the horn, the gent did a queer thing. He pulled his hat down over his face and turned his back to the canal. He looked as if he wanted to get below, but as if he did n't want the packet boat to see him do it.

"The packet boat went by and nobody took no notice of us. There were n't a lot of folks on her anyway. When she got well ahead, the gent walked up and down again as free as a heron, but he kept a-looking back all the while; and even when we passed a freight boat he 'd kind of slouch down so a man could n't see his face.

"A little while after, his wife come out too, and most of the time she stayed with him; but me, being ahead with the mules, I did n't see her face. Only now she had her cloak off she looked somehow prettier. She was always a-looking out west, and while she did she 'd sort of draw up her innards under her and fetch a breath.

"Jeepers, Dan, she was a pretty gal! I don't guess she was better than eighteen year. You could see by her eyes that she was kind. Every time I looked at her, I could feel me getting all cluttered up inside, but by dang I could n't keep my eyes off her. Her hair was brown, kind of dark, but it looked like she 'd just learned to put it up. It would keep getting unloosed all the while, and she 'd pat it and try to look as if she 'd had that trouble with it right along. At supper that night she 'd talk to me and Kruscome, and even that old bullhead 'd loosen up and grin at her and tell her about the canal — only he rose-watered heavy, even telling about church, though the nearest he 'd ever come to one was jail. Her mouth had a way of jumping open when she 'd draw a sudden breath and was surprised, and that would keep any man talking just to see her do it. It was cute. And she did n't take no notice of his teeth, which was all gone but the dog teeth, having been knocked out, and his gums yeller with snuff-taking.

"Me, I just set listening to Kruscome lie and looking at her. Her husband did n't talk none, but kept playing to himself with some cards — some kind of game, I don't know what. She 'd throwed together a pretty meal, which would surprise you too, for she did n't look like anyone accustomed to cooking that I 'd seen. But

it tasted fine; and we ate and talked, Kruscome and me, and I bet
there ain't never been such a lying pair of canawlers inside of one
boat since this ditch was dug. Old Kruscome sat there at one end
of the table with his handkerchief stuck into his shirt, eating beans
with his knife, as if eating with a girl like her was a thing he'd
been brung up special to do. And every little bit he'd lean back
and wipe his beard and tell her another story. It almost made a
man ashamed to listen to him.

"But by holy, Dan, it was hard to see the way she coddled onto
her husband. Every time she'd say a word, she'd toss a look at
him to see what he was thinking. Most of the time he kept to his
plate, and he was fancy with his fork and cutlery — silver ones out
of his bag; but it looked to me like he had a dog's way of biting
his food. Then he sat back and sort of grinned, kind of hard, and
looked from her to me and Kruscome, just like he was figgering
accounts. I did n't like his look no more.

"Well, pretty soon she got talking how she and her husband —
she said their name was Marrow — had decided to go west, and how
they'd eloped together and this was their honeymoon; and she
looking at him with her eyes as big as posies. Gol darn, Dan, she
were n't only a gal!

"But right away Marrow looked hard, and broke in on the talk.
He said they'd come up from New York on the *Constellation* (a
fast boat for them days, Dan) and that there'd been a case of
cholera on board. Well, me and Kruscome had been so taken up
with her, we'd forgotten all about the cholera; and to hear the
word made Kruscome jump. But Marrow said right away that him
and her'd kept on deck all night, so there was n't no danger. He
said he'd heard things was bad in Albany, but it did n't seem
likely that the canal would get it. That sort of soothered Kruscome,
and anyway he did n't want to make a fuss before the gal. He
let it drop. It was n't every day he made that much money, anyhow.

"But we'd guess now and then why Marrow wanted to ship on a
freighter. Old Kruscome said to me when we went into the stable,

'He's a-running off with her, Ben; but it's my idee he's a rotten man for a gal to run off with.' I asked him what he was going to do about it. But he grunted, kind of, saying he had his money. It seemed he'd guessed why Marrow wanted to ship on a freighter, but he'd only guessed the half."

3

Old Benjamin nodded seriously. "Them nails made heavy hauling. We went slow. It was hot, and you could n't force the mules. Now and then when there was n't any packet boats on the line, Marrow and his wife'd get out on the towpath and walk a spell. It was pretty to see her hop off the boat, and him catching her and hugging her up a second. She'd laugh so's even the mules'd turn back an ear maybe; it was pretty to hear her laugh, Dan. I'd pretend I was n't watching, but I was a young lad then, and I could n't keep my eyes off her. Every time she'd get close to me, I'd commence to feel all stuffed up; and when she'd look at me I could n't look back. Only when she did n't I'd watch her all the while.

"Once she made to keep on walking with me, but he called her back aboard. But when we drawed through Utica the morning of the twelfth, he commenced to take less worry. He was n't afraid, he said, of anything's catching him now, except only the cholera. And then he laughed. He did n't pay much more attention to his wife; seemed like he got kind of cold to her; but she acted like she did n't notice it. And that day, as we were passing through Utica, we heard him cuss her for the first time and send her out of the cabin. She come out on the towpath and walked with me a spell, and she talked about where she come from. Even a lad like me could see she was worried, and I guessed she would have liked to cry some.

"She come from Boston. There was n't nobody in her family only her pa; and I guess, from what she said, he was strict in his notions about the idees of other people. I guess he'd been hard on her. But he must've known a thing or two, because when this

Marrow showed up he would n't have nothing to do with him —
turned him out. But Marrow managed to see her at some parties,
and the short of it was he got her to come away with him. They 'd
gone to New York, and she said he 'd married her there and then
come up north to Albany. He 'd told her he had interests in Ohio,
and that he 'd bought land there where they 'd settle and cut out
their home together in a new country — just the talk to fetch a
young gal over; and she 'd bit for it and run with him. But she
was n't sorry about it. There 's a lacing of ginger in New England
blood, Dan, only it don't show often.

"She must have stayed out with me for three miles or more, talking of how it was back to her home, wondering if the new cook
was turning out good, and who her friends 'd marry, and what
parties would be coming off; and me, I could n't say nothing but
'Yeanh,' and then she went back on board. After she 'd gone, I
walked along wondering things to myself — mostly how long it
would be before I got a boat of my own and would be making good
money like Kruscome. And then I got figgering how I 'd fit it
out, and what the colors would be in the cabin. But I was n't only
a lad them days, Dan.

4

"Along in the afternoon, when we was hauling through Rome,
old Kruscome says, 'There 's one thing, Ben, we 're past the cholera.
And danged if I 'll go east till it 's gone.' But it was a mysterious
disease, and in some places it come like a judgment.

"That night we tied up at Alverson's, beyond Rome. It was the
only house for a long stretch, and Alverson kept a stock of likker
and a store. It was a foggy night, and warm, and there were n't
any boats when we stopped, and nobody in Alverson's only the old
man and his two boys.

"Well, after supper we left the gal on the boat and we went for
an evening in the store. Marrow was chippered up and wearing
his dandy coat. He said now not even the cholera would catch up
with them, and right from the start he started to get drunk, and

he done it. He commenced talking after a while. He'd been east selling stock in a made-up transportation scheme; he'd forged letters to certain people, putting it on a personal-favor idea, and collected handsome. He was a slick speaker when he set out to be, even if he said it himself. But he found it too easy and aimed higher than he could shoot, and tried a bank. Already he'd seen quite a lot of the gal, for some people he'd milked had shown him around; but the bank he picked to start on belonged to her pa, who'd spotted his tricks right off the rudder. He set out to make things hot for Marrow, so Marrow had to pull out and take the gal along with him, and when he got far enough off he'd write and send her back if what money he'd asked for was sent to him. He figgered to make all around. The marriage wasn't by law; he'd fixed it up so's to handle her easy. He was real pleased with himself. He talked like he was letting us in on the world. Alverson and his boys didn't say nothing. They wasn't sociable, and so long as a man paid for his drinks, that was all they wanted. Kruscome just set with his mug on his knees looking at him.

"We sat around till after ten o'clock. It was pretty dark; there wasn't only one candle, and when that burnt out we sat by the light of the stove. It had grown pretty cool after dark and Alverson'd lit a light fire. You could see just the knees of us sitting round, or our hands when they hung down. When Marrow wasn't talking, it was just like the rest of us was listening.

"And then he commenced to sing, and I got to hating him worse. And between singing he'd drink some more, and then he'd say what he'd do with the gal, and he got confidential.

"Just then the door opened. She come in, and he waved his hand kind of wide and says, 'And there she stands, gents.' I could see she'd heard, she stood that still. She must've been looking around for us, but there wasn't a face she could see. I wanted bad to tell her something, but I didn't see that there was anything I could say, rightly. Marrow laughed, kind of hoarse in his throat, and says to her, 'Come in, Margaret.' And then, just as though he meant to do it, he teetered over onto his knees and his face come into the light, looking right at me. If I ever see a man surprised, it was him.

"He said, 'My God!'

"The cholera had took him — just when we thought we was by it. It's a nasty thing to see. Kruscome got up; I could see his feet walking. 'Get a light, Alverson,' he said; and then he says to me, 'Take Mrs. Marrow back to the boat, Ben.' And he says to her, 'Ben's all right. You go on back. We'll look out for him.'

"But she stood there, and I thought she hadn't heard him, so I took hold of her arm, and I could feel it very stiff. She didn't make no motion to take it away, but she says, 'I married him.' And the way she said it made me forget the way she made me feel, generally.

"Then Alverson come back with a new candle, and we seen Marrow good. It was plenty. Jeepers, Dan, you ain't got any idee the way the cholera messes a man when it takes him that way. He just set there, doubled onto his knees. I seen Alverson looking down from under his candle and he looked scared. 'Take him out,' he says. 'Take him out of here, the whole bunch of you,' he says. But we just kept on looking at Marrow. 'Get out of here,' says Alverson. 'Get out. Joe, get the shotgun and send 'em out. Send 'em out quick.'

"Old Kruscome let go of his beard then. 'All right,' he says. 'Grab his legs, Ben.' We carried him onto the boat. Alverson shut the door, but we heard him sloshing the floor and washing it, and we could smell the vinegar he was using.

"There was a heavy fog come down — heaviest I ever seen. Seemed like you could have buttered bread with it. We set Marrow down in the cabin on the floor. But it sure had him sudden; he died in about an hour, saying nothing at all. So we buried him alongside of the towpath, in the fog, me and Kruscome digging and her holding a lantern. It made just light enough to show us where to dig. She did n't say nothing all the while we was working, but maybe she said a prayer. I did n't think to do it at the time; and Kruscome was n't given to prayer, he was that tough.

"When we 'd put back the sods, we got onto the boat. She slept in the bunk and said she would n't mind for us to sleep in the cabin, but we did n't want to after watching him there."

5

The old Jew sucked his breath in through his pipe. It had gone out.

"Jeepers, Dan, but she was a pretty gal! She looked all white the next morning and her cheeks kind of flat. You could see she 'd been sleeping bad. But just the same she looked pretty. She did n't have no black clothes with her but a shawl, and she had that on, drawed tight in front of her.

"But she cooked us up some eggs and tea and set there looking out of the winder, and nothing to see there but the damn fog. The cabin was small enough when you could see the country through the winder, but with that fog it made you most afraid to touch things. She must have been worried. There she was, halfways to nowheres and hid out of sight in that fog at that, and a couple of boaters which anybody could see was n't delicate in their notions. But that did n't bother her. And because it did n't bother her, it did n't bother us.

"But I got to get along. It 'll be our turn outside pretty quick. . . .

"There at breakfast old Kruscome swallers down his tea and then sets looking at her. 'Well, Mrs. Marrow,' he says. (She had n't heard what Marrow had said about the marriage, so we guessed it was n't rightly our business to tell her.) 'Well,' says Kruscome, 'what 're you going to do?' She set still like she did n't hear good. So he says, 'We 'll get to Syracuse to-morrow — we might get in to-night — and I 'll put you onto a packet where I know the captain, and he 'll see you safe back to Albany.' Kruscome did n't say anything about the fare paid to Buffalo. That was Marrow's business, and he was dead anyhow. I did n't see rightly why he should.

"She set there studying awhile, and all the time I was hoping hard she'd decide to go on through with us. I was just a lad. She set there awhile. Then she says, 'I don't want to go back.' Kruscome sort of rose halfway off his chair. 'My God, gal,' he says. 'What can you do out here?'

"'I'm tired of Boston,' she says, and she looked tired. 'It'd be black misery there,' she says, though it struck me she looked pretty miserable right where she was. 'I figger I'll keep on how I was going. I've been looking in my husband's satchel bag. There's quite a lot of money — enough to take care of me,' she says, 'and there's a land title for a hundred acres out in Greebe County. I'll show it to you,' she says; and danged if it did n't look actual. That was the funny part. There was his faked stock, and right in among it that title deed. 'I'll be danged,' said Kruscome, 'I would n't have guessed it. The thing looks actual and true.'

"She looked at him kind of stary, and then she says a funny thing. 'Why of course,' she says, 'he told me all about it. That's where we're going to build. We planned on it.' I felt my mouth come open and I set still; but Kruscome seemed to catch on. 'Why surely,' he says, 'that's so. It ought to be good land. But it's hard for a woman to start alone.' 'Well,' she says, 'there's a gal I used to know in Boston went out there to Dayton last year and got married. I can see her,' she says. 'I don't want to give up now'— and Kruscome nodding and spitting in the sand box, just like he'd got it all loaded down and covered up. She turned to me like she wanted my idees, so I nodded my head like Kruscome, but, not chawing, I did n't spit; though I could n't figger it out, because she looked like crying. So Kruscome says, 'All right, Mrs. Marrow. I'd advise for you not to go out there, but you know best; and if you've got friends out there, I guess you won't be so bad off.'

"Kruscome and me went to get the mules out, and he says to

me, 'By dang, Ben, she's got a lot of stuffing into her for such a small-bellied gal!' We hauled along. The mules went slow and the fog hung onto me. Long about eight o'clock the girl got onto the towpath and walked, taking hold of my arm so it got stiff from my holding it just one way. She didn't say nothing and I didn't neither; but now and then I'd look at her and see the fog all shiny on her hair and skin. I guess we didn't pay much attention to anything — I just knowed a couple of boats passed us — until the towline jerked and danged near tossed the mules off the towpath. They went onto their knees right on the edge of the water, but I grabbed the towline and yanked their rear ends round and got 'em back. I knew what had happened. The boat had fouled the bank, and that was queer, with Kruscome such a good hand at steering. But it was queerer not to hear him swear.

"When I looked back, he wasn't on deck. I got on the boat, but there weren't a sign of him, except by the rudder-post. Then I see the cholera'd taken him. When the cramps hit him, he must have fell off. The bad cases went that way — not a holler.

"I went back and unhooked the mules and told the girl what had happened, so she come back and stood on the towpath while I waded, feeling for him with the pole. He didn't come up, and when I found him thirty feet back, he was drowned." . . .

6

The old Jew glanced at the window. "We went on after a while, letting the mules take their own gait on the towpath, which was a pretty slow one once they found I wasn't there to prod 'em, and her and me stayed on deck steering. She seemed pretty turned over. She'd taken an affection to old Kruscome, and I liked him pretty good myself.

"After a ways like this she went down into the cabin. Long about noon I stopped the mules and got some food cooked. She was lying on the bunk and I fetched her a cup of tea. I was scared that the cholera would take her too. It seemed like it had marked the old *Pretty Western;* and with that fog a man could think anything that come into his head. It hung on till late into the afternoon. I don't ever remember its hanging on that way in summer.

"She come on deck when it lifted and stayed with me till supper time. And then she cooked me supper. We did n't talk much, and she went to bed early.

"It was cloudy that night and come on to blow hard, so I slept in the cabin and I liked sleeping there. I could hear her move around in the bunk. And next day it cleared up; the mist went by eight o'clock and the sun came out warm. She walked back of the mules awhile, carrying my whip, though she did n't have the heft to use it without hurting herself. She 'd pinned up her skirts so they would n't drag and she had a handkerchief tied under her chin, and you 'd have thought she was an emigrant girl, only she was prettier than any one you ever seen. The color come back into her face from walking and once in a while she 'd wave back at me.

"It 's hard for two young folks like we were to keep sad, Dan. And there was the sun after that fog, and the wind over the oats, and the cattle shiny in the meadows, black and white and red. And I 'd fell in love with her, Dan, though I 'd hardly dasst to say it to myself. And it seemed something had come over her. I could see the change, but I did n't know then what it was. I only guessed. But I was a young lad then. I did n't know she was making herself feel happy. I did n't know folks like she was would n't maybe think the way I thought. But every time she waved back at me I could feel the blood coming up inside of me.

"When she got tired, I 'd swing the stern in and she 'd jump for the ladder and I 'd grab her when she 'd come on deck and haul her up. Every time I 'd figger I 'd kiss her the next time, but I never got around to it somehow. And she 'd stand close up to me, looking out ahead westward and taking in her breath sharp, like she 'd been running, and her eyes as big as if she saw things there. She was kind and gentle, and she 'd talk about what kind of a house she was going to build and would ask me about the barns.

She'd go so far as to write things down that I'd say to her when they took her fancy.

"And it was nice to see her setting at the cabin table, tapping her mouth with the end of the feather and then writing down in the book, putting curls onto the capitals. She wrote pretty. But I liked the traveling time better when she was getting off and on the boat, or just to watch her tromping after the mules. You see it was the first boat I'd had in charge and I felt good — real good. It seemed the boat was next to being mine."

He was silent for a space.

"We went through Syracuse and Rochester, but we did n't lay by. She'd buy what food we needed at the shore stores and I'd get food for the mules that way too. She got me to learn her how to steer, and she was good at it and I liked teaching her. After that we made better time and took turns driving the mules. I liked it, Dan. I figgered maybe I'd get a job from Dennison to run one of their boats — maybe this same one. I figgered after a while I'd ask her if she'd marry me. It seemed she would, to me. I was a big lad, stronger than most men. My beard had n't begun to grow, but even then I looked pretty well. I got figgering and figgering how I'd grab her and kiss her when she come aboard each time after driving the mules and then give her the proposition right there. But I did n't get around to it until we sighted Buffalo.

"Buffalo were n't no bigger than a village them days, though it had commenced to grow fast. But I seen the smoke about a mile out and I hollered to her we were coming in. She run right back and I swung the stern in and she come up and I grabbed her, and I did n't let go but just held onto her and looked down at her. She got a little red, but she looked right back at me, so's we both seemed looking right inside each other. And then she smiled that way she had, with the upper lip jumping up, and danged if I did n't kiss her. And when I'd done that, she took hold of me round the neck and kissed me back. And she said, 'You're a good boy, Ben. You've been good to me. I like you,' she said. 'I won't never forget you, Ben.' And I could n't find what I wanted to say to her then, Dan, because she wasn't thinking about it. And she jumped away and ran down into the cabin to change her clothes. I thought them mules would never get into Buffalo."

The old Jew got to his feet and went to the window to look at the passing meadows. "By Cripus, Dan, but she was a pretty gal!"

The driver-boy stared at the stove. The color had gone out of the draft. "What come of her, Ben?" he asked.

"Why," said the Jew, "she took her things ashore and I carried them down to the lake dock for her. There was a Toledo packet going out that afternoon and she got a cabin. The *Lucas Williams,* it was. I seen her situated in her cabin. And then she grabbed my hand and she said, 'You're a good boy, Ben,' just like she had before, and she put some money in my hand, and I put it in my pocket and then I went on shore. I got my receipt for the nails and took it to the Dennison office and turned over the boat, telling them about Kruscome. They signed me on as driver to another boat."

He drew a deep breath.

"Gol," said the driver-boy.

"Yeanh," said the Jew. "I guess we'd better get on deck."

THE END OF THE TOWPATH

I

IN his leather chair, with its high back, its wings, and its rolled arms, old Mark sat, gazing into the heart of an open fire. As he leaned back against the cushions, in his suit of pepper-and-salt, neatly pressed but fitting loosely, one hand caressing a meerschaum pipe whose stem was cradled in the corner of his mouth, Mark looked what he was, an old retired canal-boater of the sort who left the water for the land, who put money in the bank for their children and rum in the cellar for themselves, and who settled down to drink away their remaining years in a state of perpetual self-approbation that would not be denied.

But as Mark dozed by the hearth he felt afraid. He could not have told why, for the fire into which he gazed warmed him through and through. It was a premonition as indefinable as the vague warning of a dream; but it hung close about him and came between him and the fire until he grew uneasy from a sense of cold. . . .

An utter restfulness pervaded the room. The thin voice of the little black clock on the mantelpiece mingled, like a whispered gossip, with the sputtering of the fire and the more distant rocking of a chair. Through the breath of quiet the long ears of old Mark caught another sound, so soft as to be scarcely perceptible; yet it was this, surely, more than the hurried ticking of the clock, more than the warmth of the fire, more even than the sight of his stein, retired to a post of honor over the hearth, that caused him to gaze into the fire and dream. Although, from all appearances, old Mark was not the sort to dream by day or night, before or after drink, the quiet breathing of his grandchild in its mother's arms gripped his heart. He held his breath to hear it more clearly, as if he were afraid that it might stop. After a moment he relaxed and basked in his comfort, for such comfort was very good to have. . . . Everything about him — the house, the farm, the money in the bank — was his, all his, for him and his children — and now for his grandchild. He and Samson Hanks, his partner on the canal, had made it — had taken it — had murdered Harley's bank carrier back of Denslow's in Syracuse to get it. But it was all his now. Hanks was in jail, with something else against him, for forty years. He'd not dare talk where he was. The money would stay; they couldn't take it from him. Not even Samson could have it — until they let him out. . . . It was all his, the comfort and the warmth, all his. . . . And presently the feelings in him rose up even to his mouth, and he wanted to spit, so he placed his hands on the arms of his chair, cleared his throat, and drew himself pointedly toward the andirons.

"Pa," exclaimed a woman's voice, "you can't spit in the house!"

Mark fell back from his position and turned to glare at the door of the next room, where his daughter-in-law was putting the baby to bed. He swallowed audibly and threw his head back against the chair, puffing furiously as he did so at his meerschaum pipe. Inwardly, in the memory of his former slovenly, licentious life, he rebelled. Who was she, anyway, to tell him what to do? What right had she to law him? The old man fastened his eyes upon the stein and stared his questions defiantly, even as he submitted. His vitals dozed under the warmth of his supper, and he dozed with them. They had named the boy for him, too. . . .

When old Lu Harrigan, who used to cook for him on the *Cardine,* bore him his first bastard, dead, he had been mightly impressed, and when she bore him his second, John, whose first coherent impulse had been to claw his eyes, for the first time in his life he almost saw God. There had not been many such times in his experience. More often he saw the Devil quite clearly.

"Pa!" said his daughter-in-law. "Me and John's goin' over to Boonville to hear th' band. They've got a new brass piece that plays wonderful. Mind you sweep the hearth and put up the fender."

Hell's waters on her anyway! Always busting in where she was n't wanted. Mark looked round the back of his chair at her. John was helping her on with her coat. Involuntarily his heart swelled. Good-lookers they were, healthy as colts. He growled at them and turned back to the fire. John laughed cheerfully down in his chest and called a good night. After a minute, Mark heard the Ford rattling down the towpath above the house. He was alone, and again he felt afraid. If Hanks were to get out and come back one of these nights, he 'd have to face him with no one to help. And he was n't as young as he used to be. . . .

Why did he have to grow old? Those healthy young devils! Off on Saturday night for their own amusement while he had to stay home and mind the baby. They would n't even let him drink his rum any more — the doctor said it was bad for his heart. Damn the doctor! . . . It was that cursed woman mostly. She never let him do what he wanted. Why, if he did n't like the beans old Lu used to make for him, back on the canal, he 'd knock her down and lock her out of the cabin. She loved him for it — and learned to cook better.

He had n't bothered to marry Lu. She was his cook, like any man's cook, unless he had a wife. Lord! It was long ago since she had jumped the bucket. Wonderful, fine woman — tell your fortune on cards, too. Those evenings were pretty fine for him and Lu, and his partner Samson Hanks . . . Hanks! . . . Hanks had tried to come it dirty on him, to take Lu away from him. But he 'd fixed him proper for forty years . . . in jail . . . Auburn. Jeepers! If you stopped to think, it was nearly forty years ago; and Hanks would be getting out. . . . That would mean the end of all his comfort; for, as soon as Hanks was free, he 'd come back on him. And the forty years would be gone any time now. . . .

Mark got up and poked the fire. An old foxhound, toothless, dim-eyed, with flabby lips, rose from his corner and whimpered. Mark sat down and watched him. In a moment the dog whined again, and presently, from up on the towpath, the sound of foot-steps floated down through the white, night air. As he listened now, Mark knew why he had been afraid. The steps were slow and crunched deliberately on the frosty road; they paused for an instant opposite the house and then turned down the hill; they approached the porch and hesitated. Then the screen door and the front door opened and closed in order.

Mark sat rigid in his chair, his face expressionless. But the smoke sprang from his lips in tiny spurts, and, like the backfire of a gun, small rings popped out of the wide bowl of the pipe and wheeled into the fireplace. The hound, who had been standing close to Mark's chair, growled hoarsely . . . and Mark growled as hoarsely to him to be still.

2

The man who entered now walked with more assurance. Mark watched him as he drew a rocking-chair close to the hearth, and lowered his bearded face to the flames. The ragged fingers of the firelight ran over his features, plucking out the black lines for any to see. . . . Hanks. Leaning closer to the logs, he spat squarely on the nearest and cocked his head on one side to listen for the hiss.

"Hello," he said, "how be you?"

Mark sank deeper between the wings of his chair, his mouth pursed like a button about the pipestem, and he, too, listened for the hiss. The fire rewarded them with melodramatic suddenness.

"Hello," said Mark.

For a while neither spoke, and the thin voice of the clock seemed to whisper to the fire all manner of things about these two.

"It's gettin' kind of frosty," remarked Hanks, after a moment.

"Eanh," grunted Mark.

The fire entered the conversation with a loud report — at which the old hound rose and stretched himself and turned about several times on the rug, and settled down again with a deep sigh.

"It's a long time," said Hanks softly.

"Eanh," growled Mark, between puffs.

A long time . . . Samson Hanks, who was his partner in trade and in drink . . . Samson Hanks, who knew him as he knew himself . . . Samson Hanks, who had tried to take Lu Harrigan from his kitchen and his bed . . . dirty Samson Hanks had come back on him; and with him he had brought Mark an utter hopelessness, a sense of lost comfort, and quiet, and peace. . . . A long time since that rain-streaked night when he had found Samson lying on the dock, with his fingers about another man's throat, as dead in his drink as the other was drunk with death. Mark had stood looking down on them in the gray rain, thinking of Samson and Lu, and, if he could have blessed anything, he would have blessed the gray rain for running down his neck and driving him for shelter into Parker's oyster booth, where he met the water-front watchman and told him where to look. Forty years the judge gave Samson Hanks, forty years. . . . A long time. . . .

"Mark," continued Samson, in a monotonous tone, as if his speech had been prepared in the long, hot hours on the roads, "here we be — us two — me and you. You done me dirty then; I'll do you dirty now. I know where all this come from" — he looked about the room — "and so do you — you and me both. It would n't be so nice if I was to tell the people round about. It would n't be so nice if I was to tell your bastard boy and his girl where from. It would n't be so nice if I was to say how you and me got this money, neither. Perhaps they'd send us both back to jail, but you're older 'n me, and I'm kind of used to it."

Mark gazed straight before him, his round face expressionless, but his eyes were glassy as they caught the firelight.

Samson went on calmly. "Then, if you'd rather not, there's another way. Sure there is. Me and you used to get on good; we can now, I reckon. Settle down here and have the kids to wait on us. You can get me a chair like yourn, and me and you can set here and think. . . . Like old times."

He rubbed his hands and spat.

Mark glanced at him with a feeling of awe. It would n't be

easy to let him in, but there was nothing else to do. Nell would object, and so would John. It would n't have been so bad if Nell had n't been there. It did n't matter so much about John; but he would n't dare to let Nell know. Why the devil had John married her? . . . Upstairs the baby sneezed.

His grandchild! He 'd forgotten all about little Mark. He 'd been born right, and it was n't fair that all this should fall on to him when he 'd come up to be a man. Named for his grandpa, at that!

A sudden sweep of rage carried him to his feet, and he stood over Samson with his huge hands clinched till the stiff muscles in his hands and arms knotted themselves and bulged under the skin, and the hardened veins swelled above his cheeks. For an instant he wanted to feel the man's face under his foot; he wanted to bear down on it with all his weight, and stamp on it, and turn his heel right and left, and feel the flesh tearing underneath the nails. But Hanks was staring at the fire, and, after a minute, Mark's figure sagged into its usual slackness, and when he spoke his voice was slow.

"The kids 'll be comin' home pretty quick now. You 'd better quit 'fore they get back. I 'll have to talk to 'em. Then I 'll see you down to the lock, about supper time, Saturday, and tell you what."

Samson laughed; he could afford to, for the whip was in his hand. There was no hurry. For what he had waited forty years he could wait another week. All right, he 'd go.

Mark listened until his footsteps had died out in the distance; he walked to the far corner of the room to reload his pipe — Nell would n't let him keep the tobacco in sight; he grunted as he stooped over to scratch a match on the bricks and sat down again. He started the tobacco in huge, deliberate puffs. His mouth and chin had set as solidly as concrete. He had his back against the wall, but, old man as he was, he could still fight.

He felt suddenly very tired and helpless and old, and he slumped in his chair. After all, there was nothing he could fight with.

A Ford chattered in the yard, the doors banged open, and, in a gale of skirts, coats, and frosty air, Nell swooped upon him and kissed him soundly upon the back of his head. A burst of smoke exploded from his lips. He was disturbed and irritated. A childish petulance, a feeling of hopelessness, came over him; tears appeared in his eyes and trickled down his cheeks.

"Damn that foxhide's tail — always gettin' in my eyes," he stormed; and, without looking at them, he stamped off to bed.

3

During the ensuing days he found it impossible to decide whether to let Hanks come into his house and buy his silence, or to throw him away to spread his scandal. By Saturday morning his thoughts were as confused as ever. About four o'clock that afternoon he called Dan, the hound, to him, threw his loose black coat over his shoulders, picked up his stick, and, slapping his hat upon the top of his head, sallied forth into the sunlight for his daily walk.

It was a warm day, late in October, and the woods looked bare and brown against the vivid blue of the sky; but here and there the distant sheen of sunlight caught up a gleam of scarlet maple or a flash of yellow birch and threw the color forward, like pennons in a lost cause.

With the hound striding solemnly at his heels, Mark followed a trail through the woods, where it was warm, where the sunlight shot down in vivid streams, patterned by the naked branches of the trees. A breath of mist from the preceding night had crept up from the river valley, and now it loitered in the shady places, mysteriously enlarging all things with its dim web, until the bent figure of the old man walked as a giant in a magic forest.

Through this cloister of light and shade Mark climbed the slow rise of a hill and came suddenly into the open once more, and stood upon the summit, with the scent of the northwest wind in his nostrils and the gray clouds rolling overhead. Here, where the brown grass sang crisply all about him, he settled down, and the hound lay down at his feet.

From where he sat he could see the valley of the Black River winding northward for miles. The water shone with a purple light, and the wind plucked up a ripple in a gleam, dazzling as diamonds. The farmers were drawing in the corn, the teams plodding heavily, well set against the collars, while the tall bundles rose in the arms of the men and swung upward and over upon the racks with the regularity of automatons. He could hear the chugging of a gasoline-engine half a mile away, and even catch the whistle and the long sigh as the knives bit through the stalks and the fan blew the ensilage into the silo.

Upon his left, near the tops of the hills, the feed-canal ran just below him. He could trace its downward course across the divide to the beginning of the Lansing Kill, where it dropped through forty locks in ten miles, before it reached the Delta Basin, to move on slowly to the Erie Canal. From there, he remembered, the latter moved on, with all its docks at Rome and Utica and Syracuse, until it ran past Geneseo, all the way to Buffalo and the lakes. In his mind's eye he saw these cities, too, and followed the ghostly shadow of the towpath to their oyster booths and bars. While he mused, he thought the boats came out upon the water, laden down with heavy cargoes, and the steersmen leaned on the sweeps, while the great rudders brought them slowly round the bends; and one boat tripped its rope for another to pass, while the crews laughed and jollied in the passing. With the coming of night, lights shone suddenly at intervals along the banks, and he was privileged to climb their gang-walks aboard, to sit by the open grates in the cabins and smoke, to drink warm rum from the heavy steins and to sleep deep sleeps again, with the water gurgling close to his ear and the soft swish of water grass weaving him dreams. A great longing rose up in his heart to be again what he once had been. . . .

The sun was low upon the horizon when he awoke and raised his head. He looked down the canal, but it was empty; and he knew that he had dreamed — that the boats, the horses, and the men, that the canal, with its solitary companion towpath, had run to their end; and that he was alone upon the hill — a last, withered owl, perched by the hand of fate upon a dead branch in his dying tree.

He stood up and leaned upon his stick. The wind played about him, running supply through his hair, bending up the wide brim of his hat, and blowing his coat in loose flaps behind him. The last sunlight just reached him from the horizon, and shone on his figure without touching the hill. As he gazed upon the feed-canal flowing black and silent and desolate down to the shadowy lowlands, he breathed strongly; he cursed Hanks, his ancestors and descendants to the very gates of Hell, and, making his resolution with a blasphemy, slowly he returned — slowly, for he felt that his towpath was running surely to the end.

4

The young couple left immediately after supper to go as usual to town to hear the band. Sitting close by the fire, Mark waited for the rattle of the Ford to die away. Then he rose, and, once again putting on his coat and hat and taking up his stick, he went out of the house with the hound at his heels.

The wind had gained in strength; the clouds tumbled about the sky like blown bees. A cold, green twilight shone under the clouds, and the road was still visible. The far edges of the hills had changed from cobalt to black, and the river striped the valley like a mourning band.

Bracing himself against the wind, Mark made his way down the towpath until he reached a deserted lock below a small lagoon. He sat down on one of the gatebeams, waiting patiently, gazing into the black water at his feet. The gates of the lock had nearly rotted away; long fingers of moss felt along the beams and poked between the planks. Here and there water, bursting through, splashed into the pool with an incoherent jangle.

After a round half-hour had passed, the old hound growled, and Mark, looking up, discovered Samson Hanks close upon him, walking slow, with his head bent down and his hands in his pockets. Neither said a word as he took his place beside Mark and hung his feet over the edge of the lock. For several minutes they were silent. At length Samson leaned forward and spat into the water. Some imprisoned frogs scattered hurriedly, diving with sounding *chugs* and popping up in other places to gaze owlishly at the two figures above them.

"Well," said Hanks, "here we be. Have you told the young 'uns?"

"Oh, eanh," grunted Mark, "eanh. I reckon."

They said nothing more, but sat together like crows upon a limb.

As the night closed down upon them, except for one faint glimmer in the west, Mark rose heavily to his feet and leaned upon his stick. Hanks laughed a laugh of triumph, and sat still, drinking his victory. But the wind caught up his laugh and carried it over to the beech grove beyond the lagoon, where it echoed close to a great blue heron, dozing on one leg among the reeds. It started up with a crane's lazy flight and flapped over the men with a slow beating of wings. Hanks lifted his head to stare at it, and his gaze followed the bird until it was lost in the gathering night.

In the shadow behind him old Mark drew a deep breath and raised his arms above his head. For a moment his age vanished and he seemed again the canal-boater, with all the strength in his vast body poised. The staff descended in a short, sharp arc and struck full upon the nape of Hanks's neck. A brittle crack broke the stillness — then a heavy splash; and the frogs croaked and dove and reappeared, to examine a new prisoner that floated quietly, face downward, rocking gently and solemnly in the ripples. . . .

5

With a momentary feeling of triumph, old Mark stared into the lock. But a sudden, strange sensation swept him up in a whirling grasp, until he lost contact with the earth, and even ceased to notice the pressure of the dog against his legs. He fancied that he had been carried into the clouds, and the absurdity of their tumbling amused and dizzied him. He experienced an impossible desire to cry out, for the wind seemed to snatch all his breath away. In the next moment he found himself leaning on his stick beside the lock, with the old hound whimpering at his feet. He felt a dull pain in his side; but at the same time a sense of elation carried him on irresistibly. Once again he had triumphed, as he would have forty years before. What if anyone did find it floating there in the scum? Who was to know? . . .

As he turned homeward, he laughed softly in his chest; but, though he scarcely noticed it, he moved so slowly that the hound, walking before him, had to make frequent stops to let him catch up.

On entering the house he went into the sitting room, filled and lit his pipe, and started to settle down in his favorite chair. At that instant his eyes fell upon the old blue-and-white stein on the mantelpiece. Lord! He was just in the mood for some rum — warm rum — to quiet him down. The children were out; there was still some rum in the cellar; it was as simple as that. Damn the doctor! Damn his heart! . . .

The climb up from the cellar proved quite an undertaking, and he puffed and wheezed prodigiously. But in time he reached the landing and returned to the parlor. He placed the stein judiciously on the hearth, where it would warm slowly, and sat down in his chair with a deep sigh. The smoke curled lazily from his pipe; the firelight beat upon his round face until it grew red as his flannel undershirt; but he leaned back heedlessly and kept his eyes upon the rum. . . .

He'd done the thing well! It made him feel strong as a horse. And the look of that old stein made him think of Lu. He wished she could be with him to share his triumph. But perhaps it was just as well, for he was pretty thirsty. . . . Damn her big body! How she could drink! . . . He used to bet on her against Lige Thomas's woman when they got together at Denslow's in Syracuse, and he'd never lost a cent. . . .

Quite a hand himself, he was, at the same trick. He used to empty that stein at one pull. If you came to think of it, now, there was a frog in blue in the bottom. He used to pull up the frog's eyes out of the liquor first, then the rest of him. . . . He could do it now, though! If he had n't done for Samson, he 'd make a bet with him on it. . . . He 'd take it down anyway, just to show himself.

The old hound came to him as he bent forward and picked up the stein. It was n't so heavy, not such a big drink. . . . He 'd make it one better, drink it with his legs crossed. He did so, and the hound flopped down by him and rested his chin on the outstretched foot. Mark wiggled it appreciatively, and the dog's tail thumped the floor two or three times in response.

He took a few sips, just to get the knack again — then a long breath — then he drank in earnest. It felt warm, warm — just right. It would n't be hard, but where was that damned frog? . . .

Once more he felt a strange sensation of lost contacts, and his breathing troubled him. . . . This kind of thing made one breathe so eternally fast. . . . Where had that blasted frog gone to? He glanced into the darkness of the stein. . . . Jeepers! There were its eyes coming up through the rum, round as buttons. They looked bright — very bright; and the light from them came toward him until he thought he could feel it on his face, all round him.

He 'd done it! There lay the frog, clear and dry, fine old frog. He placed the stein on the floor rather unsteadily. . . . Eighty years, and he 'd taken it down cross-legged — no wonder he felt so tired. He must tell someone about it in the morning. . . .

His accomplishment stirred him so deeply that he looked for a place to spit. He must n't do it in the house, eh? He 'd like to have someone tell him that now! . . . The andirons looked good and hot. He 'd take the left one for luck. . . .

He braced himself carefully and judged the distance. Little drops of sweat formed on his forehead, and his eyes bulged above his cheeks like two glass marbles. . . . The left one for luck. . . . That was how it ought to be done! Hear it hiss! He 'd take a short rest, and then, by jeepers, he 'd get some more rum! He 'd set them a mark, he would. . . .

The fire glowed warmly about him as he sank back between the wings of his chair. The hound settled down again and rested his muzzle on Mark's outstretched foot. The old man's broad mouth and tight little chin were twisted together in a wide smile. The red lids closed over the protruding eyes; and his thin, quick breathing seemed to hold a three-cornered gossip with the muttering fire and the clock. . . .

After a while, without warning, the hound's chin slipped from old Mark's foot and struck the floor with a soft thud. And the fire and the thin voice of the clock talked to each other alone.

DUET IN SEPTEMBER

I

OLD John Adam and his wife, Eve, had arrived at the Indian summer of their lives. Very peaceful and still they looked, sitting side by side in their rockers on the front porch. The old man held a Syracuse newspaper crinkled on his knee; and his wife, with her Bible in her lap, was knitting him winter mittens in rose and gray.

It was a Sunday afternoon late in September, and the sunlight, slanting up the valley, under the high pine branches and the porch roof of their house on the hill, touched them with a mellow glow.

For a man and a woman of sixty-five and sixty, they looked young; for farmer-folk of any age beyond the twenties, their faces were strangely smooth, fresh-hued — John Adam's with an even tawny glow from collar band to hair; Eve's changeable to sunlight and shadow, the variable coloring of a woman who has an acute physical consciousness of the smallest detail of her surroundings. Her brown eyes, the vigor of her white hair, and the fresh redness of her mouth, always bending to the least course of her thoughts, combined in giving her an outward appearance of unquenchable vitality. Her slight body was as vibrant to the sway of her moods as it had been forty years ago. Even now, though her eyes bent downward to her Bible and her hands knitted even stitches in the pool of sunlight on her lap, she seemed aflutter under her quiet.

John Adam's youth was the antithesis of his wife's — he had learned the gift of calmness. There was a fine erectness to his shoulders — not the stiff straightness of a soldier's carriage, but an uprightness arising from genuine well-being. It showed in the unhurried gaze of his blue eyes, in the composure of his blunt-fingered hands, and in a sturdy humor which made his full lips compact, his apple-chin solid.

Their restful postures sorted well with the quiet of the afternoon. Their house and small farm, which was worked for them by a young married couple of the neighborhood, stood on the south side of the hill, well up from the road and commanding a wide view up and down valley, the Black River threading the bottomland, and almost at their doorstep the feed-canal, flowing by toward Boonville.

An intangible suggestion of mistiness overspread the river and the riverside fields, bringing the yellow of the stubble, the green of the meadows, the growing crimson patches on the hills, into one russet harmony through which the sun breathed level rays. Even the black surface of the water acquired coppery warmth in the autumnal heritage it reflected. The windless air smelled faintly of fallen leaves; it had the tang of drying pasture and the sweet musty perfume of barns harboring the harvests. The sight of cows winding beside their shadows out of forest-hidden swales with udders swinging to their burden awoke a feeling of the full increase and ripeness of the year.

John Adam might well have responded to such a feeling, temporally. He had passed his life boating on the canal, with Eve, since he was twenty-two. He had made money with his first boat and bought another; and with the two he had made a little more, which he had invested, here and there, on pork, on grain, on the new Black River mills below Lyons Falls, until he had laid up enough for himself and Eve to last them through their remaining days. He had felt that he was getting old, and that the canal had changed after the preposterous political graft of the Barge Canal had been put through; so they had come to this small farm, which he had accepted years before in payment for a debt and set aside as a nest for their old age.

It was not much of a farming country; but he did not expect to make money now. All he wanted was a quiet spot to stay in with Eve, where they could look down on the feed-canal, running below their porch, and along which, once in a while, they could still watch occasional boats bound for Syracuse with freights of sand. The boats they saw now were grubby and in poor repair. There was none of the rush and hurry of the lumber days — not a single raft — and no bright paint, or flowers in the cabin windows. Half the boaters were Italians or hard-faced New England foreigners with their cold, high, nasal talk. But he and Eve liked now and then to see the boats creeping along — blunt, heavy-set, a sluggish stubbornness about them that made the horses collar-sore if you did n't take care. They could sit in their chairs and look down and live over a year or two of their own canal time, whenever one went by. . . .

It might have been what they were doing this afternoon, the two of them, with their paper and book and knitting; for they had not said a word in all of an hour, and, though each made a pretense at reading, the eyes of each were staring away down the valley: John Adam's with an unwavering gaze; Eve's restlessly, under slightly trembling lids.

Then John Adam lifted his paper deliberately for reading. He folded the sheets to a certain column on the front page, and, having done so, he looked at Eve.

"You 're sure it 's him, Eve?"

"Yes."

Her mouth was tremulous, her eyes clouded; but she gave no sign of weeping, unless in the husky overtone of her voice. But then she always spoke with a soft slurring that made her words sweet.

John Adam was staring over the porch rail again. It was so peaceful, so still, out there over the valley. The shadows stole forth from under the trees, longer and longer, cool and soothing on the hot earth; and the tinkle of cowbells was the only sound in all the afternoon. How glad he was now that he had saved this place for himself and Eve, even if they had few friends roundabout (farmers and boaters seldom mixed very close in the first generation); it was just as well, perhaps. They might have learned about the boy; or, for that matter, about Eve and himself. Of course he and Eve had their marriage license, and all, as far as that went; but then the date on it was only four years earlier than the one on their oldest daughter's. . . .

His eyes wandered back up the river, up the hill, over the edge of the porch, back again to the column of news.

It was an Associated Press item, not very long, but given its position on the first page because it marked the latest advance in science in a certain phase of life — or, rather, death. The head-line explained it sufficiently: —

FIRST EXECUTION BY LETHAL GAS ACCOUNTED A SUCCESS

The two paragraphs were dated eight days before, a day earlier than the date of the paper, and reported from a city or town in Nevada of which neither John Adam nor Eve had ever heard. The script described in detail the manner of administering the gas, the mode of watching through a trapdoor of glass above the death-cell (for all the world like killing a beetle in a cyanide bottle), the number of minutes it took the man to die, the exact hour of his death, the comments of executioner, sheriff, prison physician; and at the very end the name of the criminal — Nicholas Adam, *alias* Adam Russ, convicted in a bank murder. There was nothing interesting to news readers about the criminal. His name was printed merely to add validity to the write-up.

John Adam had not read the paragraph aloud; they had seen it the day the paper arrived; and, characteristically, neither had mentioned it, though they knew that in time they must talk it out together.

John Adam crossed his legs, folded the paper over his knee. He took a pipe from his upper right waistcoat pocket and a buckskin pouch from his left hip pocket, and, placing the one in the other, methodically set about the preparation of his smoke. He was almost complacent. Even his wife could have discovered no sign of grief in him, beyond a slight tightness of his mouth and chin. He looked too healthy, too respectably well-to-do, in his striped trousers and light blue shirt, to be reading on a Sunday afternoon of his son's execution for murder.

Seeing him outwardly so undisturbed, Eve ventured a doubt.

"Of course," she said, "we have n't an awful lot to go by. We ain't heard from him in six months."

"That 's right. But then he wrote he was goin' to pull off a big 'business deal,' and that he 'd planned to change his name for a clean start. Did n't he?"

Eve dropped her eyes to the growing wrist of the mitten: purl two pink, knit one gray.

"Eanh."

"And he said his name was goin' to be Adam Russ, did n't he?"
Eve's voice was very low.

"Yes."

John Adam lit his pipe, pocketing the bowl and flame between his palms and regulating his motions with a sidelong glance along the stem. He tossed the match over the porch rail into the peony bushes and brought the pipe round to the other side of his mouth.

"We always knew Nick 'd turn out bad."

There was no bitterness, only a sort of phlegm, in his voice as he went on: "All our boys turned out bad. Joe and George and Frank, they died while you was havin' them. And John when he was six, after that time Nick knocked him off the cabin roof for not givin' him his pie. Remember?"

This calm, cruel catalogue of their failures — particularly hers, she said to herself — was too much for Eve.

"Well, there 's Nelly and Jane."

"Girls!"

"Yes, but . . ."

"What come of them? Nell married Joe Goudger and went to Iowa, and a year later Jane goes for a visit and marries a damned Dutchman — Hennsen, or something like that. They might have stayed here with us, seein' as how they 'll get what I 've got in the bank when we 're done with it. And most every year I 've got to loan them something besides. They was n't neither one of them as pretty as you was, anyway."

"I could n't help that," said Eve, a little maliciously, in spite of her ache. Then, when she looked at John Adam, so sturdy and well-seeming a man, she wondered if the girls were n't as pretty; and if not, why they were n't as pretty.

Suddenly a smile tugged at the corners of her mouth as she accepted the compliment. She could still blush, easily.

"John Adam."

John blew out a cloud of smoke.

"Why don't we go out to them?"

"You know we could n't stand it, Eve. You and me, we're too set in our ways here. There's no canal there, no hills, nothing but damn flats and big crops and hogs, and ditches instead of canals."

"You've never been there."

"Nor you neither. But I've heard about it out to Buffalo."

She agreed.

"I guess it is too far for us to go."

"Besides," said John, taking up her argument which he had previously trod underfoot, "we ain't certain about Nick. We'd have heard from Jane if it was. She always had a hankering for people in trouble. Probably why she married that — furriner."

"Not till to-morrow," said Eve, reckoning on her fingers, and echoing his hope. "Not even if she'd wrote a special delivery."

"Postmaster Emory might fetch it over from Boonville to-day, if she done that. Not that it makes much difference; Nick would n't never have to come back."

"I wish I'd known, though — only to write to him, maybe."

John stared away down the river road.

A farmer family was driving by in a buckboard — from Sunday visiting. The wife waved, and Eve waved back.

The woman in the carriage was young, and she remarked to her husband: —

"Ain't they peaceful and quiet, Hank? They're always like that. And she's purty for an old woman, too. I hope you an' me'll be like them."

"Eanh," he said, noncommittally.

2

Sunday afternoon. There was nothing for either of them to do. Chores: the man would tend to them. Pick-up supper: the woman would call them.

John Adam smoked on.

Eve was silent; that was one of the best things about her, John said to himself: she didn't bother you with talk all the time.

The feed-canal, winding along the sides of the hills, took him back to the first time he had seen her. . . .

Forty-two years ago; he had just bought his first boat. Before then he had driven for his uncle, Amos Gives, a close-fisted old man, who had never given him more than a third of his proper wages, but who, when he died, had left him enough money to buy the *Nancy Gives*.

It seemed like a day or two ago that he had made his first trip in the old boat. He was going up the Oswego after a load of early apples for Albany from the Jennings orchards just below Baldwinsville. He had tied up opposite the Jennings house, a hundred yards from the orchards, and climbed ashore while men brought the barrels on wagons and loaded them. His uncle had always freighted for Jennings, and the privilege had descended to him, as a matter of course, along with the boat and the two pairs of horses.

In spite of his elation at being a man of property, owning a well-fitted boat, with bunk space for four, and cabin done in blue and yellow, he felt restless. The *Nancy Gives* seemed to have all the trimmings, and the woodwork was as fine-grain maple as you could see on the Erie between Buffalo and Albany. In fact, it was a much handsomer boat than he had supposed.

Even the boy he had hired appeared to be uncommonly good with horses; and he had a rare gift for profanity. But John had a remote consciousness that something was lacking.

The scene was very clear to him still: the farm on a tongue of land thrust out into the river, with the towpath built up along the shore, the white house, the red barns, the two teams coming out in turn from under the twisted apple trees, the men — two of them heaving the barrels to the wagon boxes, two swinging them to the rail and rolling them into the pit on runners, and two more stowing them. They worked fast, in spite of the heat. Up along the towpath a row of willow trees spread out great branches that were trees in themselves and cast shade over the house and lower end of the orchard. And in this shaded corner his eyes had fallen on Eve, stooped over, picking up apples for table use and dropping them into her pink-checked apron, gathered basketwise in her left hand.

Mrs. Jennings had taken her out of a Methodist orphanage in Syracuse seven years before and had, after the necessary fee to the matron, adopted her as a maid of all work. John Adam had seen her on earlier occasions when his uncle had called for apple shipments; they had talked when she had had one Sunday evening off — he had done most of the talking — about the canal, and the easy indolent travel back and forth across the state, the great canal ports, Utica, Syracuse, Rochester, Albany, and Buffalo, and Rome, and the life in them. John had hinted of the liberty and the easy pleasures, aggrandizing his small stock of experiences with the experience of others, and growing amazingly in his own eyes in a sudden flood of self-belief.

Eve had listened, open-mouthed, her dark eyes clouded — as he grew to know them later — with the vagueness of new desire. Her own experience seemed so pitifully circumspect beside his half-imagined descriptions.

And now, as the apples rolled aboard the *Nancy* in their round-bellied barrels, he went over to her.

"Eve," he said.

She turned round on him quickly, coming upright in the same motion of her hips, with a swift grace.

"Oh, it 's you, John Adam."

"Eanh."

"Mr. Jennings said your uncle was dead. I 'm sorry."

"Eanh."

She had on a gingham sunbonnet to match her apron. Her hair, black then, was drawn down tight on each side along her cheeks, making, under the pink shade of the bonnet, a frame for her small, compact face, which gave it force. Her mouth was wide and red — it had n't changed a particle in all these years — and the sunlight fell at just the proper angle to throw a shadow on her eyes. Her arms, bare to the elbow, had caught up the apron against her breast; John Adam could see the brown down on the forearms. She looked so slight and light-footed under the harvested branches that she seemed incongruous, a belated bit of apple bloom.

"Eanh," he had repeated, gazing at her. "I 've got the *Nancy* now, for my own."

He struggled for words. He realized now what the *Nancy* lacked, he told himself: she wanted a woman aboard — particularly Eve — to look out for him and the boy. But he could not find out how to tell her.

Perhaps her rigid religious discipline under the angular tuition of Mrs. Jennings, and previously of the orphanage, had given Eve the power of divination, for she blushed. Perhaps, too, John had hinted more to her a year before than he could remember. At any rate, she put physically into action what he wanted to propose.

John could never forget her then; she always lived for him in that moment; she would beyond time.

The gnarled old tree had sent forth an immensely long arm that would have overbalanced it but for the posts set underneath, and this branch came low over their heads, screening them from canal and house. Eve raised her face, so that John could see her mouth in profile, and lifted her right arm. Just within reach an apple, which had been overlooked by the pickers, hung red and ripe amid the leaves, and a small ray of sunlight touched it so that the very look of it was sweet.

The girl pulled it off and took a generous bite and handed it to John Adam. He took it and looked back at her. She was watching him with eyes in which amusement, approval, trepidation, and desire strove against one another; but her betraying feature, her mouth, had suddenly grown tender.

John munched the apple, and found words.

"I 've got the boat now, Eve. Would you come with me?"

She laughed, all at once, tilting her head in the sun-dappled shade.

"Mrs. Jennings would n't let me go. The idea — why, it 's against her notions!"

But if John was slow to start anything, he had a great power of continuing.

"Well, why n't you run away with me? I 'll pay Mrs. Jennings what she thinks is due — though I guess she 's got pretty good int'rest out of you as an investment."

"Think you will, too?"

John kicked a bruised apple aside with the toe of his boot.

"Eanh."

" 'Run away'? You could n't hardly do *that* in a canal boat, John. I could n't do it, anyways; it 's so against all teaching! How do you think we could do it?"

"Why, I guess I could stop down the river about a mile; and if you 'll clip out of the house after dark and walk along down, I 'll wait — and then we 'll go on all night and make up for time I should have been traveling, so 's I could deny your bein' with me."

He tossed the core of the apple away.

She stared into his eyes a long minute, a dark brooding glance, which left him strangely at ease while her eyes were on him, but clogged his arteries when she turned away.

"Good-bye, Mr. Adam," she said. "I hope you 'll be back next fall. It 's a real pity your uncle died, I 'm sure."

She whirled with a flutter of her skirt and ran back to the house.

"I would n't let that worry you an awful lot," remarked a good-natured voice at his back.

"Gol'," said John to himself, and he wheeled about to find Mr. Jennings leaning over the snake fence bordering the orchard, arms folded on the top rail, gray hat on the back of his head, a straw drooping limply from one corner of his mouth. He grinned; so did John Adam.

"No," he replied, "I don't aim to let it bother me, a great lot."

"Well, you 're loaded now. Me and you 'd better settle up. You 'll be wanting to clear out for an evening's drag, I guess? Can't stay to supper? We 'd be glad to have you."

"No," said John, "I aim to get three hours of hauling yet to-day. How 's my draft?"

"Three foot eight. Maybe a mite more. But you 'll clear all right."

Jennings handed over the money and took his lading receipt. The boy was getting the team down the gangplank. They came out from under the half-hatch forward, sleepy and listless. John took his place at the rudder. The men who had stowed away the apples slipped the ropes from the mooring posts and tossed them aboard.

"All right," cried John.

"Giddup!" shouted the boy, brandishing a rope's end and letting loose all his profanity at the team.

The boat got under way without fuss and passed along beneath the cool avenue of willow branches. It was half an hour later that John Adam told the boy to pull up to mooring posts stuck inconsequentially beside the towpath in a deserted stretch. The boy was surprised, but willing enough. As the night was warm, John had him hitch the horses under a tree, to avoid delay in starting.

They ate supper and then sat on the deck together, the boy whistling, and, by some miracle, forbearing to ask questions.

Eve came aboard out of the darkness quite suddenly and with all the naturalness in the world. They hitched the horses back on the eveners and went on.

Eve spent an hour below, looking things over, and then she came up and sat at his feet on the space aft the cabin roof. They had n't talked at all; they had just looked at the stars; had seen the spidery web of bridge rails grow out of the darkness, pass in arched shadows over them; had gone by sleeping farms, windowless, with last tendrils of smoke just visible above the chimneys. It was so still, the water so smooth, the smell of waterside fields so fresh — and the land slid by so easily.

Only once in a while the boy would let out his string of patent profanity when John Adam let the boat in too close to the bank, because he was taking too long a look at Eve; and John had sworn back at the boy and threatened to fire him out of hand; and Eve had laughed, low, husky laughter which floated on with them.

So they had come into Syracuse on Sunday morning, with the bells all ringing for church, and the smell of the apple cargo heavy about their faces in the misty air. . . .

John Adam, on his porch, sucked long at his pipe, and took the smoke way down into his lungs. The taste of it was fine — old Warnick and Brown, No. 1, Heavy. Boaters smoked that tobacco. He had for forty-one years. He had lit his first pipeful that Sunday morning coming into Syracuse with Eve. Forty-one years — it had been almost a second woman to him. Not that he wanted one. There was Eve all the time, faithful, loving; they had eaten out of life together, as they had of the apple, she never changing to him although other men offered her higher pay.

The children — well, they had had hard luck; but he was never very keen about them; only boys, like Nick, and John before he died of his fall. Nick had got out of hand, somehow; John Adam had n't had time to take care of him himself; he 'd left him to Eve.

Then, ten years — no, eighteen, by Cripus, except for that last trip with ice for Coney Island they 'd taken ten years ago just to see the canal once more — eighteen years ago they 'd come to

this farm and settled down, and he had married Eve for the girls'
sake; not that there was any point in it. He'd had an idea Eve
hankered after it — she had queer hankerings in her; you could feel
them behind her eyes when they got soft, like rain clouds in a July
sky.

Nick was gone. High-handed about it, too — not a word but
for short, bad letters, half-spelled, once a year, perhaps. Eve had
'em somewhere. . . .

It was getting on in the afternoon. He could see the supper
smokes rising from chimneys here and there down the valley.

3

"John," Eve was saying, "do you think it's really so?"

"I reckon it must be, Eve."

Her one hope lay in a letter from Jane. Jane always had had a
soft spot for Nick; she'd know what had become of him; she was
softer-hearted than her mother. Eve had never been wholly able
to forgive Nick for causing little John's death — not that Nick
could have guessed what he was doing, being so young. But little
John had been her favorite child — John Adam, like his father,
and blue-eyed and light-haired; while Nick was dark, like herself.
She had been bitter against him for years; she had kept him off the
boat, out of sight as much as she could when they lay by in towns
and cities. She hated to acknowledge even to herself that he was
John Adam's favorite. John was not interested in the girls, both of
whom had lived; and she had given him three sons, dead before
they could come alive, and two more, one of whom had killed
the other and then gone off. It was her fault. One son, only,
had she given John Adam; and that one had been executed for a
common criminal (even if the arrangement of it was novel and interesting to the general public). John had never spoken about having no boys; but she could see his disappointment quite plainly.

But perhaps, she said to herself, the write-up in the paper was
all a rumor; perhaps Nick would come back alive, so that they
could make it all up to each other.

John Adam was looking at her. Without glancing at his face, she could tell it by the way he held his paper. Even if she was to blame with the children, she could still say he loved her. Perhaps her weakness lay there — she had loved him more than the children; they had been merely the necessary aftermath to her. . . .

She had gone on the canal with him as his cook willingly, body and soul to be his, and she had n't regretted it. She had found the life as he found it, indolent, full of effortless content. She had had him to herself, for years on end; and it had been easy to keep him happy, in spite of the occasional panics she 'd have that he was going to leave her. He never had. They 'd slid along quietly with the current. Theatres when they came to the cities, oyster suppers at the water-front booths, or dinners at choice places like Baggs Hotel in Utica, or Blossom's when they made a Sunday excursion to Canandaigua. They went sight-seeing twice in New York. And in between there were the long still days on the water with acquaintances passing now and then as you finished a sock — people you knew to speak to. Easy housekeeping; a grocery store almost every night when you tied up, fifty yards away. Nothing to do but see that the children did not fall off the cabin roof and remember to water the potted plants once a day. And always John Adam to show other women; he and she had set each other off well when they walked up a street or went aboard another boat for an evening's chat.

He had been proud of her; she had n't aged as quickly as most dark women did, and the children had done no harm. She had kept John tight to her, and she still had him. He was looking at her now, she knew it, with his far-away face, under which she had learned to read everything that mattered at all — just as she had read him that day in the Jennings orchard — think of it — more than thirty years ago!

Mrs. Jennings had behaved better than she might have supposed; though she did not know how far John Adam had gone in settling with her. Anyway, the old lady had called on her in the *Nancy*

in her best bombazine black dress and wished her luck with a look
which said: "You'll need it!"   As if John had ever been on the
point of turning her away!   He had given her everything she
wanted; had married her, even though she hadn't asked him,
cared to ask him.   There was no need of it on the canal.

But she could not deny to herself that she had wanted him to
marry her, even if she had not asked for it.   It had mostly taken
away from her the dread of impermanence in their old age.   Old
boaters were apt to take queer notions; she had seen some.

"Let's get married," he had said one day during a January
thaw, when they were wintering in Utica.   And they had done
it two weeks after.   He had been much more excited about it than
she, much more worried, almost comically.   There was nothing to
fluster them, the surrogate asked no questions.   There had been
no hitch in the church on Genesee Street; they had gone in John
and Eve, and had come out man and wife.   That was all there was
to it.   And a few years later they were settled on this farm, alone,
the children gone, Mr. and Mrs. Adam for an actual fact.

Almost immediately the canal had slipped into the background.
If it had not been for the feed-canal running by a little below
them, they might have forgotten their boating, what with John
and his farm and the two apple trees he was trying out for the
start of an orchard, and her with a whole house to look after: two
floors, running water, electric light, a telephone to jingle one awake,
a kitchen that had no fussy ventilator to mind, and no smell of
cargoes.

They had both longed time and again for the past; but the canal
had changed.   They had seen that on their last trip with ice for
Coney Island — starting in the spring with a chain of boats from
Alder Creek, leaving the horses at Rome for a tug which scattered
soot over them all the way to Albany, making rags of her new
frilled curtains, down the Hudson, into the East River, with its
horrid city water smells, out into the Sound behind another tug,
where waves came right over the pit and froze the ice solid, Negroes
unloading the ice, complaining of the cold against their feet.   Then

back into the harbor one morning, with mist over the great buildings, a load of fertilizer from New Jersey, home, peddling it up the Black River feeder; and not once on the whole trip had they seen one of their old acquaintances. That was the sad part of the old canal life. While you boated it, you lived like two people in a water-walled garden, and you saw people outside; and they saw you outside their gardens; and then the gardens passed. Acquaintances you had, any amount — the women had, but it was hard for a woman to find friends. But Eve had never thought about that.

Man and wife — out of their garden — and the children gone; she had never had much hold over them, had n't cared to. In all those years all she had brought John was herself; it was all he wanted, then. . . .

Nick was dead. In her heart she knew it; knew John Adam knew it. If only he did not realize how badly she had failed him, she would n't care, even now. And she could see by his paper that he was still looking at her. . . .

"Eve," he said, "there 's Emory."

A Ford sedan came over their bridge, the postmaster holding a special-delivery letter through the front window.

"I was into the post office to-day, and I see this had come for you; so I fetched it over. — No, thanks. I 've got to run right on to supper."

John went down and took it from him. The sun had already set; the cowbells tinkled as the cows left the barns. There was a faint salmon lining to the clouds on the western horizon, and a blue shadow of twilight was stealing down the river.

4

John Adam opened the letter. It was from Jane, and it enclosed a clipping of a newspaper article, similar to the one they had been reading.

" 'Poor Nick,' " John Adam read aloud. "I knew it was true, Eve."

He glanced farther down the sheet of pink note-paper.

"The rest of it's mostly 'poor Jane.' That Dutchman of hers, he's run off, and she wants cash to clear his debts."

He put the letter in his trousers pocket; Eve could find it there when he put on his work pants in the morning.

He stood at the foot of the steps, staring down the valley, down the canal — upright, square-shouldered, hearty-looking with his red cheeks and white hair; and Eve stared at his back, where the suspender straps crossed under his waistcoat.

She wanted to cry; but John always got irritable if she showed signs of it.

"I expect Jane'll come home."

"Eanh," she said.

"We ain't had much luck with 'em, Eve."

"There's Nelly."

"She ain't dead yet. You can't tell."

Eve dropped her eyes.

John sat down on the steps, his hands in his pockets, and started whistling — an old boat tune. It had become darker quickly. The surface of the canal looked like black velvet; the river you could hardly see. And the whole valley was still.

Then they heard a clink on the towpath, and, heaving against a towrope, a team came out from under their bridge. Slowly they went on, and a boat followed. A woman was by the rudder-sweep; Eve could catch the flutter of a light skirt. The woman was singing softly, with a queer accent, the words of the tune John was whistling — and the voice and the whistle fell into the same bar.

> "Lo-ow bridge! Everybody down!
> Lo-o-ow bridge! We're comin' to a town.
> Pretty soon we'll pass it, you and me,
> Boatin' by our lonely on the old E-rie."

She hadn't heard the song for months, for years. There was a wailing to the tune, a long-drawn melancholy, as the boat and the singer faded out of sight round a bend. The woman's voice had sounded young — as her own might have when she first kept house on the *Nancy Gives* — and the twilight had taken it away in a whisper. For the first time it came full upon Eve that she and John were old — old man and old wife — and that the canal had closed its lockgates on them.

They had no holding tie with it. The children had migrated or — died.

Her shoulders trembled as she bent over her lap.

John sighed, a sigh which turned into a snort, like a hound blowing his nostrils clear of an old scent.

He was looking down at his two infant apple trees.

"I wonder if that apple we've been watching's ripe yet. I ain't looked to see in some time."

He got up and went down over the patch of lawn, very erect, very sturdy, his head a light blur in the deep shadow. Eve stared after him miserably. When he turned round and looked at her she was conscious, suddenly, of how white her hair must show to him, seeing her against the dark house. She was still unable to think of her marriage in terms of a married woman.

"By gol', Eve," he was saying, "it come right off in my hand."

He brought it back to her on his palm, his arm outstretched.

"It's the first one we've raised, by Jeepers! We'll have an orchard yet, and you can practise up on that applejack you used to make."

Carefully he held it out to her. It was not a very big apple; but she took it and looked at it, smelled of it to please him.

"It smells sweet," she said.

"Taste it, Eve."

She had a bite.

"It tastes sweet."

She bit into it again.

"Here," said John Adam. "Let me have it. You can't eat it all, Eve."

He took it from her, munched it, got rid of a seed which he snapped over the porch rail.

"It's a good apple, Eve. It's real sweet."

AN HONEST DEAL

I

"There she is," said I. Finis Wilson, with a wave of his hand toward the mare. "Gentle, kind, the ideal horse." He ran his hand all over her, slapping her. "One hundred and thirty dollars, cash. I paid a hundred and ten for her."

The active little farmer looked her over for the seventh time, walked twice round her nervously, and asked, almost hopefully, "She ain't scared of the cars, you say?"

"No," said Mr. Wilson. "As far as the cars is concerned, she'd go to sleep with her tail on the rail. Would n't she, George?"

George was Finis Wilson's forty-year-old stableboy. He lifted a pair of soupy eyes from where he sat on a bucket and said, "I guess that's right."

"Sure," said Finis Wilson, "it's right."

"I'm glad to hear it," said the farmer, looking more worried as he fingered some bills in his pocket, "I'm aiming to use her hauling milk."

A wide grin overspread Mr. Wilson's thin features. He pulled the ends of his pale moustache together over his chin, then poked the farmer confidentially between the ribs.

"For a milk horse," he remarked, "that mare can do about everything but milk the cows."

The farmer thought a moment. "Make it a hundred," he suggested with the air of a man with bold decisions in his head.

"Sold!"

Mr. Wilson stretched out a long arm. The farmer counted the money into his palm, wetting his thumb and forefinger to feel each bill.

"I'll hitch her onto the back of your wagon," said Mr. Wilson.

The farmer climbed aboard and started his heavy team, and the thin mare shuffled off lazily behind.

Leaning against the barn, Mr. Wilson watched them disappear.

"George," he observed in his mild voice, "there was a sale."

"I guess that's right," said George.

"You was a witness," said Mr. Wilson. "I was strictly honest in all I told him."

"How about what she done at the depot?" asked the stableboy. He made a thrust with the dungfork with which he had emerged from the barn. Following the gesture, Finis Wilson saw a pair of wheels and splintered shafts piled up on a battered wagon box that lacked a spring and the rear axle.

"George, you'd ought to pay more attention," — he shook his head sombrely, — "or you won't never get to be a horse dealer. It was the engine give her that idee."

George set down the dungfork in order to scratch his head.

"I guess that's right, Mr. Wilson."

"It's a sensitive point, George; but if he gives her time she may outgrow even that notion about the engine."

"Yeanh."

"It was an honest deal," said Mr. Wilson. "I always make an honest deal, George, and if you paid more attention you'd see how I do it and you'd maybe be a successful horse trader yourself when you get to be a man. I've always been honest in trading. Of course, a man can make a little here and a little there by lying and cheating, but that's only small money. He's got to be honest to make a big profit. I'm honest, George. I've never been cheated in a trade to my knowledge. And no man has ever got the law onto me, either."

He slowly pulled the back of his hand across his lips, and a look of sadness crept into his eyes.

"Oncet in a while," he went on, "it's natural that a man don't understand me. The man that bought that black bitch just now may be one of them. But that's what an honest man has got to expect. I've found that out, and I'll tell you why it is, George.

It's because the horse himself is the sensitive point in a deal."

"Yeanh," said George, "I guess that's right."

He stood awhile staring after the thin stooped shoulders disappearing up the alley. Then he picked up the dungfork and flung its contents on the barnyard heap.

"I don't know a great lot," he observed to himself in a puzzled way, "but I'm real glad that's the last of *her*."

2

If horse traders have a reputation for being indolent men, it is probably because they are constantly overworking their imaginations. I. Finis Wilson was most familiar to his neighbors in the town of Ava, New York, when they saw him sitting on the porch of Mrs. Edna Brown's hotel, his cowhide boots on the rail and his head lolling against the back of the rocking-chair.

The hotel stood on the main street, which was an enlargement of the highway to Rome, and the porch offered him a perfect observation post from which to watch for strange horses entering the county. It was Finis Wilson's serious statement and pride that no horse had lived and died in upper Oneida County without having passed at least once through his barn on the wings of profit.

On the hotel porch, Finis nodded to one or two of the boarders and sat down to spend an hour till supper in pleasant meditation on the departure of the black mare. The stout man on his right spat leisurely into the ear of an open nasturtium and remarked, "I seen Whiter driving out with that black mare."

"Yeanh?"

"Yeanh."

The man saw no chance of securing figures, so he settled himself to a comfortable enjoyment of the shade and the slight breeze. The hum of bees in the nasturtium vines was lulling. He folded his hands over his paunch and gently rocked himself. Then, without warning, an idea occurred to him.

"Jeepers!" he exclaimed.

"Yeanh?"

"Did you see the mare the doctor drove in with this morning?"

Finis glanced sideways over his thin nose. "No," he said.

"There's a horse!"

"Yeanh?"

"Oh, gol! She's pretty."

Finis grunted.

"She's a dandy animal. He got her from a feller in Frankfort."

"Yeanh?"

"She's got quite a record for speed down there. She looks it. Bright bay. Bet she's a Morgan."

"Yeanh? There's quite a few breeds you see that color in."

The stout man was annoyed and blew out his cheeks, remarking, "Well, Finis, you'll have to look her over probably; but I hear she ain't for sale."

"Yeanh."

"It's too bad you didn't get the first profit onto her yourself," said the stout man.

Finis did not answer this. He removed his feet from the rail and ambled inside after his supper.

The stout man still looked annoyed. He turned to the traveling polish salesman.

"I'd hate to be the doctor," he said. "Once Finis sees that mare that doctor won't have no peace. It's too bad, at that. He's a nice boy; but he's just out of Harvard College, and doctors ain't got much sense in a money deal, anyhow."

The vendor of polishes puffed out his chest.

"I'm a pretty good hand at judging a man," he said, "and I shouldn't think your doctor'd have much to worry about getting cheated by that thin hayseed, if he's the one you're talking about."

The fat lids of the other's eyes seemed slowly to congeal as he gave the toes of his boots a noncommittal scrutiny.

"Well, maybe you're right, at that. Finis didn't go to no college; but he's never been cheated in a deal and he says he's never done no cheating into a deal, to the best of his knowledge. But then he's an ignorant man. Finis is kind of slow."

"Sure," said the salesman, affably. "Just what I said."

"Course Finis ain't got much polish," the fat man went on as if to himself, "but he always was kind of cute. He started out when he was thirteen. He took and sold Riddle's gray mare out of Riddle's back pasture lot to a bunch of gypsies for eighty dollars. Then he went around to Riddle with the money and bought that mare for twenty-five dollars. Riddle never went into the back lot to see if she was there. Finis knowed so much about her, he was glad to get that much. Nobody would n't have knowed a thing about it if them gypsies had n't come back the next week hollering that they 'd been cheated into buying a mare with the cold spavin for eighty dollars. That 's how Finis has always done. He 's kind of slow, so he aims to keep ahead of the other feller. But even then it was a fair deal, except for the gypsies, and we run them out of town."

The salesman shifted the conversation.

"Funny name he 's got. What did you say it was?"

The stout man unfolded his hands from his belly.

"I. Finis Wilson," he said dryly. "I. for Ira. His pa named him that after himself. He was his fourteenth child. His ma give him the other name."

3

When Finis Wilson emerged from supper to take his seat again on the porch in the cool of the evening, he was meditating on the stout man's description of the doctor's new mare. Before he could actually sit down, a thud of hoofs and a rattle of spokes sounded down the street and the doctor flashed past in his surrey, driving his regular horse — one that Finis had sold him when he first came to Ava in the spring. It had been a good sale, Finis remembered, but he had not made as large a profit as he might have, for he knew that most doctors needed two horses and he intended to preserve his patronage for the second also. Besides, the doctor had seemed too much of a nice boy, and was so frankly unaccustomed to horses that Finis had not found it in his heart to disillusion him in the first deal.

"We'll coax him a bit," he had said to George, "and gentle him some."

Finis watched the doctor out of sight. It occurred to him that his absence would afford a first-rate opportunity to examine the mare freely and see how well-founded the stout man's enthusiasm had been.

He made his way slowly down the street. Twilight had come in about the trunks of the overarching elms with a touch of dew and a scent of the meadows visible between the houses. Finis, strolling along with his hands in his pockets, nodded every now and then to villagers taking their ease on their front porches. At the corner of the doctor's cottage he paused to cut himself a chew. Having stowed it outside of his right molars, he wiped his lips with the back of his thumb, jerked the ends of his moustache, and disappeared behind the house.

In front of the stable door he found William Dewey, the doctor's man, polishing a new light single harness, whistling the while monotonously on three notes. Finis thought he was rubbing with unwonted enthusiasm. He leaned himself against the doorframe and crossed one leg before the other.

"Ain't seen you show so much grit at a job in a long while, Bill," he observed.

"Got to have a smart harness for a smart mare, Finis."

Bill breathed on the check buckle and rubbed it tenderly with his handkerchief. "Genuine sterling plate on them buckles, Finis. Doc bought it particular for his new mare."

"Yeanh, I heard he'd picked up a new horse somewheres. What's she like?"

"Like? Say, there ain't a horse in seven counties can touch her. She's won in Whitesboro every year for five. She's a genuine pure-bred Morgan. You could trade all the brutes you got in your barn, Finis, all for one horse, and I bet even you couldn't get a value equal to her."

"I been hearing she's fair to middling," Finis said.

"You don't believe it, by Cripus, but I'll fetch her out."

"Don't take the bother," said Finis politely, but his long nose twitched and a tingling came under the skin between his shoulders.

"No bother," said Bill from within the barn, with the note of a man who is willing to convince a friend of his stupidity.

Finis heard the light, quick steps of a horse affably backing out of a stall and approaching the door, but he managed to preserve his casual pose. Then a bright head came forth and the short ears pricked at him, and he saw her take a breath of his scent. In spite of himself, one hand came out of his pocket to stroke the delicate nostrils. It seemed to Finis that he had never come to a quicker understanding with a mare, and he began to realize that the doctor wasn't her natural owner.

But Bill pushed himself importantly between them and, taking the lead rope close to the halter, brought her out into the open. She was all Morgan, wide-chested, a hint of Arab about her head, high-crested, straight-legged, full-quartered. Finis felt cold little ripples of excitement doing circus acts with his heart. One look and she filled his eyes. It gave him genuine pain to know that she wasn't his. As Bill trotted her round in significant silence, Finis's hand came up and his lips ran over her good points as if to a buyer; his hand reached behind him for his showing whip. To sell such a horse would be a fitting climax to his long career. He saw himself at the Syracuse Fair turning down eight-hundred-dollar bids; he saw himself in a frock coat and yellow boots and a new gray hat; he heard comment about her on all sides, and his own voice saying, "Northern bred, mister. On my own farm. Four years old and a daisy. Ask anybody that comes from Ava." And all the time, too, he realized that she belonged to a college-bred doctor, no more than a boy, who had pink cheeks and next to no knowledge of the world and horses. If he had been a philosopher, he would have doubted God's existence; being Finis Wilson, he knew that it wasn't right and that he would have to do something about it.

So he said in his mild voice, "She's a pretty clever buggy proposition at that, Bill."

Bill came to a dead stop.

"Buggy proposition! I thought you knowed a horse!"

"Yeanh. Don't take it hard, Bill. She's past twelve. Let me look at her mouth. Get a lantern."

Bill sent a shuddering spit directly for the toes of Finis's boots, and led the mare into the barn without a word.

"You oughtn't to take it so hard, Bill."

"Twelve!" Bill's voice came cavernously from the barn. "She's rising five. Doc's uncle raised her on his own place."

"Well, a man's relative is apt to make that kind of a mistake in a gift."

Bill came out of the barn with a lantern and resumed his work on the harness. He kept a scornful silence, and after a few remarks Finis moseyed away to the main street.

He stopped to look in at the string of horses in his barn and said, "Trash!" bitterly.

His stableboy lifted his head out of the corner manger and looked at him sleepily.

"I guess that's right, Mr. Wilson."

"You shut up!" said Finis, with unexpected savageness.

4

If ever Finis Wilson desired anything in his life, it was the doctor's mare. He dreamed about her that night, and the first thing he saw in the morning after breakfast was the doctor driving her out of town on a distant call. The rate at which she took him past brought a grunt of admiration up out of the stout man.

"Didn't I tell you?" he demanded triumphantly of Finis.

Finis declined to answer.

"Something's soured into him," the stout man soliloquized aloud. "He'd ought to see the doctor."

He sat down and said to himself that it was too bad the doctor wasn't a sharper man.

But Finis went on to his barn, where he put George through three hours of misery at cleaning the stable. For his own occupation he sat on the grain bin in search of ideas. Little by little these settled in his stomach, and before dinner time Finis had acquired quite a pain. So he went round to the doctor's cottage. There was a string beside the door which he pulled, and a bell rang loudly just over his head. At the same moment the doctor himself opened the door.

"I saw you through the window," he explained. "Come in."

He led Finis into his consulting room. He was a young man with fresh-colored skin and inexperienced eyes. Finis peered up at him shrewdly from under his hat brim.

"Sit down," said the doctor.

"I don't know that it's serious, Doc. It's just that my dinner ain't been setting so good lately."

"Let's see your tongue," said the doctor. He had learned that his patients expected all the rituals of his office, and as a matter of fact they were as pleased to see the diploma framed on the wall as he was himself.

As long as he would have to pay, Finis extracted the last atom of service, pulse taking, thermometer, and all, and carefully pocketed the doctor's pills. Then, as a natural thing, he brought the conversation round to the mare.

"She's a likely-looking buggy horse," he said grudgingly. "I'm wondering if you and me couldn't make a deal onto her."

"Why, I don't know, Finis. I hadn't thought of selling her. You see, she was a gift. My uncle gave her to me for a wedding present."

Finis was properly startled.

"Yes," said the doctor. "I'm going out to Indiana next month to get married. I'd have gone out this spring, only I didn't have the money to. I've got enough now, though not much for a honeymoon."

He smiled, and blushed.

"Well, by gol, that's fine," said Finis. Then a sly look came into his eyes. "I'd give you two hundred dollars for that mare. That would give you quite a trip, now."

"Well, you know what she's worth, I guess. But I couldn't sell her. I wouldn't want to."

"I'll make it two-fifty, between friends, and I'll find you another horse, cheap," Finis offered.

The doctor appeared lost in thought. If he had felt of Finis's pulse at that moment he would have been professionally alarmed. But the thin dealer's only sign of excitement was the twisting of the ends of his long pale moustache together over his chin.

The doctor looked up.

"No, Finis, she's not for sale. She's too near the perfect horse for my work, though I guess she wouldn't go far outside of it."

"That's right, but she's kind of a clever article, you know."

"Just the same, I couldn't. Take two of those pills after every meal. They're a kind of physic. And they'll touch up your liver. Come around again in a day or two."

Finis sighed, paid, and went out. He made his way to his barn, where he found George feeding the horses their noon grain.

"George," he asked, "have you looked at that mare the doctor's got?"

"Yeanh."

"What do you think of her?"

"Well, she's kind of pretty," said George, trying to imitate his employer's accustomed manner.

"Kind of pretty! You poor, abandoned twerp. That mare's the finest piece of horse meat I've seen in this county in twenty years."

"Yeanh," George said meekly. "I guess that's right."

"Here," said Finis, suddenly taking the pill box from his pocket, "eat them. I just bought them off Doc and there ain't no point in throwing them away. They're good for the liver."

"Thanks," said George. Finis sat down on a box and filled an old corncob.

"George, I'd give a lot to buy that mare, but the danged fool won't sell. I offered him a good price, at that. What can a man do to buy a horse from a man that don't want to sell?"

"Give him some more money," said George.

"You shut up!" said Finis.

5

It was the source of infinite sorrow to Finis Wilson that George appeared to have offered the only possible way to deal with the doctor. But in the succeeding weeks he raised his price to four hundred dollars, with no effect. Two days later he had called at the doctor's office and narrated George's symptoms as his own. Since George had eaten all the pills at once, the symptoms were sufficiently peculiar to warrant Finis's appearance for several times more. "I feel like a horse taking a heavy load downhill on a high breeching. I can't get no comfort no more." It occurred to him that the symptoms also described his own state of mind.

But the doctor, while he retained his interest in Finis's digestion, would have none of the deal. "If he was n't such a danged fool," Finis complained, "he'd see I was offering him more than the mare is worth."

Finally Finis lost all sense of balance. He stopped the doctor in the middle of the main street as he was returning from a Sunday afternoon call, driving his old horse, and he said, "Doc, I honestly make you my last offer for that mare. I'll pay you five hundred dollars down for her — just as she is. Spot cash for the mare alone. You're leaving to go west for your wife, ain't you?"

The doctor drew a long breath. Five hundred dollars would not only furnish a honeymoon; there would be enough remaining to furnish the upstairs bedroom he had been writing Ermintrude about, which by correspondence they had planned in complete detail. But he preserved his presence of mind.

"Yes, I'm leaving on the evening train. I'll be walking down to the depot, Finis, and I'll let you know once for all then."

"I'll be on the hotel porch, Doc. I'll have the money in my pants pocket."

A great calm had settled over Finis's mind. He had tendered his limit — there was no more for him to do.

As for the doctor, he drove slowly home.

6

Now the doctor was very young, and perhaps he may be excused when it is remembered that a country practice, while more highly considered in the old days than it is now, did not bring in a great deal of money for the luxuries of life. Further, it must be remembered that the doctor was dealing with the slyest man in seven counties, according to repute. And third, and perhaps most important, was a point that even Finis had overlooked. Though he was practising in a village in upstate New York, and though he was planning to marry an Indiana girl, the doctor's blood was of the Yankiest New England strains. He came from Sandwich; and his name was Nickerson. This as a preliminary to destiny. . . .

As he turned into his yard, he looked at his watch and saw that he had an hour till train time. As he got down over the wheel, he made up his mind that he would not sell the mare — even for five hundred dollars. He was so relieved to have reached this decision that his faculties cleared from their dazzlement, and he became aware of his man, Bill, tears streaming from his eyes and strange noises issuing from his mouth.

"Cholera," was the doctor's first thought. "Liquor," his second. The third was a flash of fate. "The mare."

"Bill!"

Bill stared at him dimly. "She's just fetched her last kick," he said.

"What's the matter?"

"I come in after dinner and there she lay as big as a elephant that's going to litter," groaned Bill. "She'd got loose some way. She'd got her head in the grain bin and filled herself bowdacious full, and there she was kicking like a steam engine and roaring like Niagara Falls. I got a pill into her, but it was too late.

I done the best I could, Doc, honest. But it were n't no good at all."

The doctor looked in without a word and saw his mare on her back, all four legs in the air. It was all he needed to see. Though he was not much of a horseman, he began to appreciate the genuineness of Bill's sorrow when the latter said, "I been mighty close to prayer, Doc."

The doctor was dazed again, as if the five hundred dollars had bludgeoned him between the eyes. If he had only closed with Finis, he saw that the sorrow might still have been theirs, but the grief would have been the dealer's.

Then a light came to him, or it may have been the resurgence of the good New England blood that pioneered this great land of ours. He clapped Bill on the shoulder.

"Listen here, Bill. Borrow Mr. Smith's stone boat and his big team, and right after dark you take her round to Finis Wilson's. I'm leaving in three quarters of an hour for Indiana. I'm going to strike a deal with him."

All the world loves a horse, but there is no one in the world at all who does n't like even better to see a horse dealer trimmed and shaved. Bill looked as if he had been shown the way to hope.

"All right, Doc."

7

With one eye on the clock and the other on the window, the doctor packed his carpetbags with wedding clothes. It was getting late, and a shower that had been promising for some time was obscuring the sunset. By the time he reached the station it would be really dark.

He took up his bags and walked swiftly along the main street. Lights from the hotel windows showed Finis sitting on the steps. He got up.

"Doc?" he said. There was a hint of quaver in his voice.

The doctor spoke like a man who has reached a decision against his better judgment.

"I've decided to let you have her, Finis. She's yours for five hundred."

Finis handed a wad of bills to the doctor, who counted them carefully in the dim light.

"I'm an honest man," said Finis in a pained manner.

"It's best to be businesslike," said the young doctor; "it saves misunderstandings. I've told Bill to take the mare around to your barn in half an hour."

"Good," said Finis. "I'd thought to fetch her myself, but I guess it'll be better waiting for her. More exciting, so to speak."

He held out his hand, and, though his back was to the light, the doctor felt a twinge to see so plainly joy unalloyed on his thin face.

"Shake, Doc," said Finis. "And I'd take it kindly you and Bill wouldn't say nothing about this deal for a while."

"I won't," the doctor promised. "I'll be gone for a week."

The train whistled for the above-town crossing, and the doctor sprinted for the station.

Finis watched his fluttering coat tails, and he grinned and grinned. Then he took his own way to his stable. He went leisurely, drawing out his expectation to the last drop. If the doctor had been a keen man, he said to himself, he would have waited for another hundred dollars. And Finis knew that the hundred dollars would have been forthcoming.

"Well, George," he said to his henchman, "how be you?"

George got feebly up from his bed in the manger and rubbed his eyes.

"Not very good, Mr. Wilson. Some way I ain't been right since my inwards got a hold on them pills."

"Cheer up and feel better," said Finis with surprising boisterousness. "To-night I bought the doctor's mare. Here's a dollar for you to feel better on."

"Thanks," said George. "Shall I go fetch her?"

"She's to be delivered. Fix some straw in that box stall."

George got up and spread some bedding. It was hard for Finis to sit still, and in spite of himself he was unable to keep his eyes from the door. After a while George sat beside him. They said nothing, but the light of the lantern at their feet showed both their heads turned left and both jaws motionless to listen, and up above in the brown dark of the mow their great shadows also listened. Only Finis's hand was twisting together the ends of his long pale moustache.

"There's a stone boat coming down the alley," said George.

"What . . ."

Finis awoke like a shot to impending disaster. It was revealed to him in the form of Bill, a heavy team, and the four stiff legs of the mare, pointed to the single star showing dimly through the clouds.

Finis came to his feet, walked slowly out with the lantern in his hand, and stared down for a long time. A great and mastering rage was gathering in his breast, but words offered no outlet to it until Bill said with heavy seriousness, "I told Doc he had n't ought to sell, but he notioned your price was close to being a fair one."

Then Finis swore. He swore in a low-pitched monotony of sound, from which he emerged only once to demand from George the return of the dollar bill he had given him to celebrate the deal.

But George also was on the point of going mad. He stood in a corner with a dungfork, saying, "That doctor twerp got enough out of me already. He won't get nothing more."

"Cripus," said Finis suddenly. "He were n't only a boy by his looks."

"I thought you 'd understand," Bill chuckled, preparing to return the boat and team.

"Bill," said Finis, "don't say nothing about this."

Bill laughed unpleasantly.

"Five dollars," said Finis.

"A dollar a day," said Bill.

Finis sat down, and suddenly he was a man again. He was thinking.

"In all my life," he said sombrely, "I was n't never done on a deal. And I 'll be danged if I 'll let this boy-doctor do me. I would n't have, only I was too honest to suspicion him, Bill. I was honest, and here 's what come of it."

The lantern at his feet showed water dimming his sharp blue eyes.

"It 's tough," Bill said.

"I 've got to make a profit on this mare," said Finis in a low voice. "If I don't I 'll have to go to New York where folks is softer. But I 've got to make an honest profit. You see that, boys. If I don't, that pink young hellion is going to have the snort on me."

"Well," said Bill, "I 'll leave you think it out yourself."

He went away. For half an hour Finis clasped his head in thought.

Then he said, as if feeling his way toward something, "Westernville."

In the darkness of the barn George felt his jaw come open.

"Westernville," said Finis. "Westernville. . . . They 're a great bunch to play cards. . . . They 've got sporting notions. . . . Quite a lot of boaters over there. They always take a chance, the big bezabors. . . . Westernville."

He looked over his shoulders. There was sweat on his cheeks, and George saw that the ends of his moustache were knotted squarely.

"I 'll do an honest deal," said Finis loudly, "and make an honest profit, by Jeepers Cripus! George, you come from Westernville. Don't they play cards in the store real late on Sunday nights?"

"I guess that 's right," said George.

"Hitch up that white trotter to the buggy. I bought him for a stepper. By gander, I 'll get a chance to feel out his pulse now."

It took them a moment to get the snorting beast into the shafts. Finis climbed up with his whip, while George held the horse's head. Before George could get off the ground, the hind wheels had skidded into the main street.

8

It was the bride who finally, after three weeks' honeymoon, suggested that they return to Ava.

"You can't afford to lose your practice, Jonathan N.," she said.

With obvious reluctance the doctor agreed. Perhaps he had a New England conscience, and, now that the deal was over, perhaps it troubled him.

"We'll get in by the evening train," he said, "so our neighbors won't know we're back till the next morning. We'll fool them that way."

She looked at him adoringly.

"I think that's nice," she said.

So they packed up that night, after they had spent an evening together by the great cataract — an ideal spot for lovers, precluding speech. And they got on the train next morning on the long trip home. All day it seemed to Ermintrude that her husband was unduly absorbed in his own thoughts, but she supposed that he must be regulating them for their return to an arduous life, and she tried to be helpful by assuming a cheerful silence.

So they came back, and the doctor suggested that they get off on the wrong side of the train. She was the first to get down, and it did her good to see that they had been watching for her husband, for there was a man waiting there. He clapped her husband on the shoulder.

"Hullo, Doc," he said.

She saw that he was a lean man with long yellow moustaches, and that her husband was embarrassed. She wondered if it was because the lean man smelled so uncommonly of horses. But then she heard the doctor say, "Finis, I've been thinking over that deal we made, and I've been thinking maybe I took too much. Suppose I give you back a hundred."

She was worried and puzzled by her husband's troubled voice, and she turned appealing eyes on the thin man. He was grinning in a very friendly way at her and twisting together the ends of his pale moustache over his chin.

"Don't you bother, Doc," he replied in his mild voice. "I made a profit of a hundred dollars on that mare."

The bride heard her husband draw a long breath.

"Yeanh," said the horsy man, "I made a profit of a hundred dollars on that mare; and I done it honest, too. *I* never cheated a man in a deal."

The doctor seemed to wince — then he stuttered a question inaudible to his wife, and the horsy man laughed as if to himself.

"When that mare was delivered," he said, "I was surprised. But I said to myself, 'Of course the doc don't know about it — it's that bezabor Bill. It would be hard,' I said, 'if the doc was a loser just on account of accident. But,' I says, 'if I can make an honest profit and deal, I won't say nothing.' So I recollected that there was always late Sunday night card games over to Westernville, and that they was a sporting proposition over there. And I knowed for a fact that some of them would want that mare; so I hitched up my white trotter and went scooting over. It was muddy roads, but we got there inside of an hour and a half — which is some night driving, Doc; that horse is sure a dinger for night driving, Doc, and I could let him go cheap for a cash turnover."

The horsy man cocked his head, but as the doctor said nothing he went on. And as he went on his voice gained a little in excitement, and it seemed to the doctor's bride that she could see him all muddy bursting through the door and stopping the pinochle games, his blue eyes shining.

"I went into the store," said Finis, "and I says, 'Boys, drink.' And there wasn't one of them bezabors didn't step up. 'Boys,' says I, 'I'm an honest man, and I've come over to make an honest proposition to you. I've gone and bought the doctor's mare,' I says, 'and I've paid out five hundred dollars for her. That's a big price to get a profit on, and I wouldn't ask one of you to give it me. But I says to myself, "Them Westernville boys is sporting," and I figgered this way. I'll sell seven one-hundred-dollar tickets;

we'll put 'em in a hat when the cash has been delivered, and let anyone you say drawr.' Believe me or not, them bezabors made up that seven hundred dollars in about seven minutes. The keep drawred, and Jerry Bumstead was the lucky man. Them Irish canawlers is all lucky as the devil. He wanted to come back with me to collect the mare, so I took him. But when he seen the mare lying belly-up in the yard he certainly did cuss. I says, 'Jerry, I'm an honest man. I've never been cheated and I won't cheat you. This is an honest deal, so here's *your* hundred dollars back.'"

Finis was still grinning. All at once the doctor grinned back.

"Finis," he said, "I want you to meet Mrs. Nickerson."

Finis made a bow.

"Mam," he said, stowing his cud of tobacco well back and holding her hand in both of his, "you've married the smartest man in seven counties, barring only I. Finis Wilson. Can I carry your bag?"

THE SWAMPER

THEY said that he had lost his mind; at any rate he could not remember anything for very long. That was why he kept on as swamper for Amos Gives's Saloon for so many years. Any man who worked for Gives must have been a half-wit; and if old David got a free supper and breakfast out of the establishment, he got precious little more except the cussing Amos gave him every morning.

David (God help him!) used to come into the bar at five o'clock every morning — that was his regular hour; so there he was at sunrise on this first Saturday in May, unlocking the door with his key. He stopped on the porch and looked down the canal; the saloon was built on the wharf at the top of the hill, so that boaters could come right down the gang, as soon as they tied up, and walk through the bar door in three steps if they wanted to. This village was quite a place in 1879; three sawmills on the Black River, which ran past the foot of the town; and the town itself rising up the hill in two tiers of houses. The saloon and Widgeon's Hotel stood at the top. The canal licked along their foundations, and the road, coming over the bridge, ran on a level with the second-story windows. What with the mill-hands and the loggers that came in on Saturdays, and the farmers and the boaters, there must have been two thousand people here. And if you were sending a letter to any one of them, instead of "Hawkinsville" you wrote "Slab City, N. Y." on the envelope; and put "Oneida County" in the lower left corner, if you were particular. It really was quite a place: there were a tannery and four stores (dry goods and groceries) and three blacksmiths, and three churches, not counting the Lutheran Church across the canal at the top of the hill. It was just opposite the saloon, so that Mr. Ennory used to say that you could see Heaven and Hell in Slab City, right before your eyes, and doing a pretty good trade at that. And if William Durkin was round and drunk (he generally was) he would always want to know which was which.

So here was old David on the stoop of the saloon that morning on the first Saturday in May, 1879. There were three boats loading matched spruce boarding for Albany tied up at the wharf. He could hear the horses getting up in their stalls in the bows and rattling their halters. It was a warm morning, with a bit of mist on the river, and very still, so that the canal looked like black silk under the rising sun. David pulled out his pouch of Warnick and Brown, Heavy, and filled his pipe and lit it before opening the door. He looked feeble with his straggly gray hair and weak eyes, and his match shook so in his hand that the flame could hardly grab hold of the stick. But he sucked the smoke deep into him and then let it out in a long stream. It was the only smoke in boat or house.

When he went inside, he saw the bar was well enough, so he built a fire in the big chunk stove to take off the damp and another in the kitchen stove to heat water for Amos's shaving. Then he got his pail and mop and put a lot of water on the floor. After he had done that, he went up and knocked at Amos's door and came away, for Amos was a mean man in the early morning. David came downstairs and took the water back off the floor: that was what he called mopping.

He went out into the kitchen and sat down to wait till the water boiled. He couldn't hear Amos stamping round upstairs as usual, but that did not bother him. There was not a sound in the house; and David looked out of the window at the river valley. The mist floated along upstream on a level with the lowest houses, hiding the meadows; and as he sat there David began to hear cowbells tinkling on cows coming in from night pasture.

The sound was quite clear and full, as sound is in misty weather, and it kept breaking out at different parts all along the valley, until all the mist was ringing like one bell. He must have listened for quite a while, because all at once he heard the kettle boiling loud enough to make him jump and run for a pitcher, which he filled and took upstairs. He stopped at the door, but there wasn't a sound out of Amos, so he knocked again. As Amos did not swear, he opened the door and put the pitcher on the wash-hand-stand.

Then, thinking he would like to see what Amos looked like when he was asleep, he went over to the bed. The window was open a crack, and he could hear the cowbells quite clearly.

Amos Gives was lying on his side with his legs drawn up, and David looked at him awhile before he went downstairs and out on the stoop. He sat down in a chair and knocked out his pipe and put in another load. The sun had come in under the roof to warm him, so he shoved his hat back on his head, put his feet on the rail, and spat a good spit clear over the wharf into the canal.

He could see a boat drawn by a black team coming up round the bend from Boonville. The boat hung low in the water and the team were having heavy work bringing it up against the current. It would take them all of fifteen minutes to reach the wharf.

The town below was beginning to wake up. David could smell the rising breakfast smokes. On the road he heard a man shouting, and, a moment after, a four-horse team came out on the dock with a wagonload of lumber. They drew up opposite the last boat in the line, and the driver went aboard and pounded on the cabin door. At the same time four men appeared from the hotel and began listlessly to hand the lumber into the pit. The boarding was light — one man could handle it alone; so the four had made a line of points between which the boards were raised and lowered, like inchworms walking. The driver and the boater came over to the saloon.

" 'Lo, Dave," said the driver.

" 'Lo," said David.

"Mornin'," said the boater.

"Mornin'," said David.

The two men sat down, the boater removing a battered pipe-hat which he placed under his chair. David did not recognize him. He was a big man with a hearty complexion and a nose like an apple. He wore a dark green shirt without a tie under his loose yellow waistcoat, and his brown trousers just reached the tops of his cowhide shoes.

"Saloon open?" he asked loudly.

"No," said David.

A woman came out of the cabin of the second boat. She was tall, with hawk-like gray eyes, a strong chin, a fine full figure.

"Mornin', folks," she said.

"Mornin', mam," David replied for all of them.

He knocked out his pipe.

" 'Baccer?" asked the boater with the pipe-hat, offering his pouch.

"What kind?"

"Mechanic's Delight."

"Don't never smoke it. That's railroad tobaccer. Warnick and Brown's mine. I used to boat it," said David.

"Did you really?" asked the boater, slightly huffed. David looked too out-at-ends and weak and watery ever to have done anything.

"Eanh," said David. "I boated it."

"That's right," said the teamster. Then he leaned over to the boater.

"David's twirly," he said, indicating his head with his thumb. "Used to be a rich man hereabouts; had a boat of his own. Man of the community; always making money; trying for more. Thought he'd get it by marryin' his daughter to Uberfrau for more money. Didn't work. She ran away. Dave went to pieces; lost his money. Got twirly; look at him."

David listened with a critical cock to his head.

"That's right," he said.

"Poor man," said the woman, pityingly.

"Eanh," continued the teamster, putting flavor in his voice. "Went round by himself after she went off with the boater; he rotted inside, I guess, and went twirly. Been that way for ten years. She was a fine gal; lot of us tried for her. Now look at him; he's a sight to see. Swamps the barroom for two meals a day and sleeps in the mill barn, long side of my team — they're good 'uns. Twirly, but he's all right. Sort of mischeevous — like a chipmunk. Tell you all about his gal. Says she's a fine lady, now; claims he hears from her; claims she's comin' back to take care of him now he's old. Ain't it right, David?"

"Eanh," said the old man. "Gettin' kind of doddery, so she's a-coming back."

"I feel sorry for him," said the woman; "that's the truth. Poor old man!"

"Funny thing," said the boater.

The sun had come out very hot, and a small breeze rose to flick the water into ripples. The mist had burned away from the river; the meadows shone green here and there with new grass.

"Anne!" roared a man's voice from the second boat. "Where in hell is my shirt?"

The tall woman made a face and went back into the cabin. The teamster twisted himself in his chair to get at his handkerchief.

"Gol," he said. "There's Simms coming in with his boat."

David grunted.

"I seen it."

As the black team passed them, the boat slid in to the wharf.

"New team," said the teamster.

"Whoa!" yelled the man who was driving them. "Can't you stop when I tell you?"

The horses were quite ready to stop; they lowered their heads and seemed to let go of the muscles in their ears and flanks.

The man who was steering ran to the rail and flung a rope ashore which the driver caught and, as the boat ground against the wharf timbers, snubbed to a post. They drew in the bows and tied them. The man on the boat slid a broad gang to the wharf and lifted the roof of the bow compartment. It went up like a box trap, leaving a door open in the side of the boat; and the team went aboard for breakfast. The three men on the stoop could see them turn round and face the shore before the man lowered the trap. Then they heard the harness jingle as the team shook themselves.

"'Lo, Simms," said the teamster. "New team?"

"'Lo, George. Yes, they be. Cheap, too."

"Pretty good. How much?"

"Two fifty. Say . . ."

He came forward, an angular, middle-sized man with blue shirt and black hat, wearing a gossip's expression.

"Well?" asked the teamster.

"Got a passenger."

"Smells like fertilizer to me."

Simms lost his dramatic forward bend, then recovered.

"Yes," he said. "I'm peddling it. I've got a passenger, though."

"Where from?"

"Utica. She signed my cabin at Bentley's Oyster Booth and Bar."

"*She?*"

"I thought that'd fetch you," said Simms, smirking. "Yes, sir. A fancy woman. Gownds. Dresses. Powders in the morning. Got a New York hat. Took my cabin; and me and Henry slept with the horses. Turn about at the stove."

"What's she coming here for?" asked the boater with the pipe-hat.

"I don't know. Aims at business, she says."

"What in?"

"Aims to start a bar. She used to work at Bentley's, I hear."

"Not Amy Silverstone?" asked the boater with the pipe-hat.

"Yes, *sir*. I never seen her before. But that's her name. Swell and stylish and tiled with money. Fancy woman, she is."

"Well, I'll be dredged," exclaimed the boater with the pipe-hat. "What she'd want to come here for beats me. They give her a name on the Erie," he went on with a leer; "she ran a cook's agency. She had a name, all right. She did more than run the bar."

The man on the second boat came out of the cabin, followed by the tall woman.

"Guess I'll have a drink," he said. "Hot day. I'm dry."

"Mornin'," said David for all of them.

He sat up with importance.

"The bar ain't open."

"Oh hell," said the boater, and he sat down, while his cook sat down, too, a little way off from the men.

"Anne," he yelled at her, "go back and clean up! Think I'm paying you wages just to look at you?"

The tall woman tossed her head.

"You'd better look at me while you have the chance, Goudger."

"Git on back, dang you!"

"I'm no slave," said the tall woman. "It ain't hard for *me* to find work."

"Oh, all right."

"Speaking of bars," said the teamster, turning to Simms, "your passenger'll have a job getting Amos Gives's trade."

David coughed and gazed critically at the tiller of Simms's boat.

"No, she won't," he said.

The others slewed round at him.

"Kind of twirly," explained the teamster. "He don't mean harm."

They relaxed.

"I wish this damned saloon would open," said the man the cook called Goudger, plaintively. "I'm dry."

"It won't open," said David.

"Ha, ha, ha!" laughed Goudger. "That's a good 'un. Won't open on Saturday with the loggers coming in! Haa, haa! Wait till I tell Amos."

"You won't tell him," said David, and he spat.

"Why not?" said Simms, sarcastically. "Wouldn't you tell us why not, Dave?"

"Eanh, I reckon so. I'm goin' fishing."

They guffawed.

"Thinks Gives 'll let his swamper go fishing on Saturday!"

"*He* won't stop me," said David. "*He's* dead."

They fell silent and rather white.

The tall woman had laughed, shrilly. . . .

2

They stared uneasily at the windows behind them.

"What's wrong?" asked a woman's voice.

The men swung about to face the canal. Simms's passenger was coming on to the stoop. She was something to see. She had a short, plump figure, a wide mouth, and cool, affable blue eyes. Her brilliantly yellow hair was done up in curls at the back of her head. She wore a stiff, apple-green dress with full skirts, a short coat of the same color trimmed in scarlet, and a red and green hat beflowered with yellow pansies, which was drawn down tight on her head. Her plump pink hands came forth from the throats of her long yellow gloves, and the rings on her fingers threw glitters all over her breast. Her voice was hearty and had a cheerful lift to it.

"What's wrong?" she repeated.

The men had all been shaken pretty badly; but the teamster managed to explain, while the rest gaped at the woman. She gave the teamster her full attention, bending toward him with a suggestion of graciousness. As she listened, she composed her features to a proper expression of melancholy, so that little lines made themselves apparent under her rouge — particularly about her mouth and nostrils. Then she straightened up and gave them another shock.

"Of course, it's too bad," she said. "But it amounts to the same thing as evacuation of the premises, don't it? You see, I own it; it belongs to me; I bought it last month; and he was to move out to-day."

"*He* ain't going to dispute that," said David.

She gave him a fine smile; and they realized all at once that she had looks. There was something cool about her; they liked her.

"I guess, as Mr. Gives went out this way, I'll have to keep the bar closed to-day. But I'll open it Monday night. My name's Amy Silverstone and I'll be glad to see all you gents here then. From seven to eight all drinks is on the house. Now will somebody be so obliging as to fetch a doctor?"

She swept past them with a swagger of her full skirts.

"Fancy woman," said Simms, with pride in his voice.

The teamster went off for the doctor and Lawyer Gannet.

"By gol," said the boater with the pipe-hat, "you'd hardly think she had a name on the Erie, now, would you? Well, she has."

"I've heerd tell," said one of the men who had been unloading lumber, "I've heerd tell that she's the hardest drinker on the Big Ditch."

"That's right," said the boater. "To see her so *re*-fined and bold-looking, you'd hardly think it was so. But when she was into Bentley's she'd drink with any man who'd ask her; and she'd never say no. Lots of times a man would set himself up to drink her down under, but he allus gave way first. Jeepers! Half the time she'd take him off to bed, and then come down and start in drinking again, cold sober as your Sunday razor."

There was a general murmur in the group.

"It don't hardly seem true," said Goudger; "but I've heard plenty as had seen her say it was."

"She has her own partic'lar drink," said someone else.

"Eanh," said the boater with the pipe-hat. "She always drinks her own."

"She's a fancy woman, all right," said Simms. "Look at the cool way she took hold here. Old Dave had nothing on her."

"Hell!" growled Goudger. "Now I don't get no drink at all. Anne, you wash them dishes — hear me?"

He herded the tall woman off to the boat.

"What're you going to do now?" asked the boater with the pipe-hat.

"I'm going fishing," said David.

He got up slowly and went back down the hill through the town, walking stooped over, his tattered trousers dragging about his heels, his hat on the back of his head, his watery eyes peering from side to side.

The others could see puffs of smoke pop back past his ear now and then, until he disappeared into the mill barn.

"Funny thing," said the boater with the pipe-hat, dubiously.

3

David had the right of it all round: the saloon did not open; nobody told Gives; and he went fishing.

He got some cheese sandwiches at the hotel, and the cook gave him some bad potato cuttings in a bag. He walked a mile up the canal to Izzard's Cove and sat down on the towpath. When he had lighted his pipe, he baited a hand line with a piece of potato and threw the hook out into the water. Across from where he sat lay Izzard's old boat. It had been tied up there to the far shore for five years now, ever since the smallpox epidemic when they had isolated Izzard and his cook and driver in the setback. It was one of the few things David remembered perfectly. He had had to bring provisions up from the store every morning and leave them at the foot of the tree under which he now sat. Then he would go back a way while the cook or the driver would row slowly over in a boat and get them. After they had rowed back, David would return and give the news across the intervening water and ask about old Izzard.

Old Izzard had died; the others came out after three months and went away. Later on it got about that Izzard had not died of smallpox. But David put no stock in such rumors.

It was a gloomy spot in which to spend a holiday; but it was a great piece of water for carp, being the only setback for a mile each way. The heavy-headed fish ran in there out of the current and lay on their bellies on the bottom, nosing the rudder of Izzard's old boat. David could read the name on the stern of it — Lucius P. Izzard, *Boonville*.

It did not make much difference how the old devil had died; it

was good riddance, David said to himself. If it had n't been for Izzard, with his high national talk about the canal, David's daughter Molly would have married Uberfrau who owned the mill and had a fine house to live in, and David could have given up boating for a comfortable life. The old boar-hog! He'd snitched her right out from under his nose; and not hide nor hair had he heard of her since, in spite of his keeping up stories about her for the form of it. She was probably cooking it for some boater on the Erie, now. She might be married; David doubted it. She was too ignorant a girl to get away with a thing like that; she'd trust a gypsy with a twenty-dollar gold piece; she was that kind. Most likely she was dead. . . .

It had hit David hard, her going off like that — look at him now. He leaned over and looked into the water at himself, swamper of the Slab City Saloon.

Then he had a bite, and he settled down to fishing. . . .

4

On Sunday mornings, David usually got up pretty late. He had learned the news the night before: Lawyer Gannet had verified the fancy woman's statement; and the doctor had verified David's. He said that Gives had died of apoplexy. The saloon was in new hands.

That did not disturb David. He let himself into the bar — and then wrinkled his nose in disgust. Mrs. Silverstone had been busy. The bar was clean as a whistle; there were fresh calendar pictures tacked to the walls; the stove was blacked, and the cupola top had been painted with gilt; the bar and the floor were oiled down slick. Even the windows had been washed.

He counted four new spittoons along the bar, bright brass ones. "Cripus!" he snorted. "Jeepers Cripus!"

He spat on the side of the stove. He was outraged. He lifted his voice and shouted querulously, "Saaay! Who's been monkeying with my saloon?"

Someone stirred upstairs in Gives's bedroom; firm slippered steps advanced to the head of the stairs; a pair of feet appeared on the treads; and slowly Mrs. Silverstone came into view. The fancy woman had on a nightgown under a bright red wrapper, and her brilliant yellow hair dangled in curl papers, with a row of odd little metal pins along her forehead. David stepped back abashed. Her plump face was lathered and she carried a razor in her right hand.

Suddenly the lather crinkled and broke over her mouth, and she grinned. She came up to the old man with her buoyant walk, the swagger noticeable even without her flaunting skirts.

"Say, old man, how 'd you come in?"

If Mrs. Silverstone had been impressive in her giddy clothes, in this war regalia she was stunning. David took his eyes off the razor and some of his indignation gave way to timidity, for the exhilaration of the preceding day's events was wearing off. He held up the key and muttered surlily, "I 'm swamper into this saloon."

"Ah," said the fancy woman. "Be you really?"

She rested the knuckles of her right hand on her hip and leaned against the bar. It was an attitude calculated to please; but the razor and lather gave it an outlandish touch. David repeated with a slight whine, "I 'm swamper into this saloon."

"Well," said the fancy woman, "if you 're swamper here, clean up that spit before you 're fired."

David lifted hand and voice to protest, but he met the fancy woman's eye.

"Clean it up," she commanded.

"Eanh." He was abject.

When he had finished, the fancy woman told him to sit down.

"Now," she said, in a pleasanter voice. "You 're David, ain't you?"

"Eanh."

"You 're an old man, ain't you? You ain't much good for work."

David shuffled his feet and looked into his hat, which he had just thought of taking off. "I'm allowed pretty good with a mop," he said.

"Look here, old man. Who do you think cleaned up this filth to make it look like this? By Jeepers, I ought to know how you swamp if anybody does!"

"Yes, mam," said David. "I guess you do."

She was mollified, apparently, for she came over to the bench and sat down beside him. The sunlight played over the two of them from the east window, and the fancy woman's full figure in the scarlet wrapper made a great blob of color that the floor caught up in reflections about her feet. She wiped the lather from her lips with the back of her hand and pulled a cigar out of her pocket.

"Got a match?"

David lighted it for her. She crossed her legs, regardless of convention.

"Old man, you and me'd better talk business."

"Eanh," said David, scenting a turn in his favor and pulling out his pipe.

The fancy woman mouthed her cigar and puffed leisurely.

"Now," she began, "this ain't the first bar I've run. I know the trade; but I'll be eternally tarred if any bar of mine is going to look like this one did. I'm going to get all trade, mill-hands and the more *re*-fined — them as want to smell their likker. Now I'll try you out as a swamper, but you'll have to clean to suit *me*. No smooching in the corners, and the floors oiled every week. Hear me?"

"Eanh," said David.

"All *right*," said Mrs. Silverstone. "Now, I've got my own 'keep a-coming up from Utica, see? And he can handle any rumpus if I need help — which I generally don't. But I'll want you round for odd jobs. I won't have you looking like a junk heap, so I've got some clothes for you — new pants, shirt, and shoes. You'll sleep out back in the kitchen, and you'll get your meals, and two dollars a week extry. Take it or leave it."

"I guess I'll take it," said David, mustering his dignity. "Sold!"

The fancy woman smiled; she seemed to have a liking for the old man.

"You're pretty old, ain't you?"

"Middlin'," said David.

"What happened to make you swamp for such a cheap bar? They tell me you owned a boat, once."

David launched on his sorrows.

"That's right. Me and my datter used to boat it, up and down the Erie — Buffalo, Syracuse, New York a lot of times. I had a farm here, and a man to work it. But she went away on me. Sneaked out, she did." He put his hand to his eyes. "She was a purty little gal — black-haired she was, kind of soft-like. I was all tore up when she sneaked on me. Yes, mam, she went away, she did, and left me, a pore old man, and here I be a-swamping."

"Pore old man," echoed the fancy woman. "They tell you was mean to her."

"Mean? Me mean? Say, would she be writing to me every week if I was mean? Married to a pork dealer, she is; and she's coming back to look out after me, she writes. Would she do that if I was mean — her such a quiet little gal, and gentle, with no harsh ways?"

He sobbed at the recollection and pulled out a red cotton handkerchief to wipe his eyes. The fancy woman stared out of the window as if she had not heard.

"Mebbe I was mean," said David; "by her lights I might've been. But I done it for the best, and she won't hold against me. Say, you never seen her, did you, when you was on the Big Ditch? Molly, she was; a little black-haired girl; kind of trembly ways?"

"No," said Mrs. Silverstone. "I never did."

She stretched her plump figure, raising her arms over her head, so that the razor tossed swift glitters of sunlight between the beams. She yawned, got slowly to her feet, and went over to the bar, where she paused to examine something. David followed her.

"Nosey!" she said looking up at him with a grin. She paused, then spoke to him again. "See them bottles? That's my special mixture. The Delta Distill'ry puts it up for me; I have to have it, with all the drinking I have to do for sociability and business. Now I ain't mean. I don't grudge you a swaller now and then; but *that* stuff costs money, and if you touch it, by Cripus, I'll ride you for fair!"

David took a look at her and backed away.

"Now you set down till I've dressed," she said, tossing her cigar into one of the new spittoons, "and then I'll learn you to clean good."

"Yes, mam," said David.

He listened to her moving round in her room for a minute, then put on his hat and sneaked over to the bar with elaborate caution.

"Ride me?" he snorted. "The old rum-hugger!"

He found a loose cork in one of the bottles, and his watery eyes gleamed. Leaning over, with the sunlight coming along the bar to fall on the small bald patch on the top of his head and the end of his nose, he looked like a thieving chipmunk. He worked the cork out, raised the bottle to his mouth and, with a great effort, swallowed noiselessly.

A look of tearful surprise enshrouded his face. He replaced the bottle, hurried over to the spittoon, and emptied his mouth of the liquid.

Her particular mixture! The old scut!

He sat down again and watched the stairs with furtive eyes as the fancy woman began to descend. . . .

5

When he sat down on the stoop of the saloon on Monday evening, David smarted inwardly from the sarcasms of Mrs. Silverstone. He had done nothing right, according to her notions; and he objected, anyway, to being ordered round. It wasn't as if he had never swamped before. He had done it for years.

The new bartender had arrived to exasperate him further, for he regarded David as a personal slave. How could David dispute him? The man was a big, black-haired fellow with the forearms of a smith and the fists of a prize-fighter. He wore very tight clothes, a red waistcoat, and a top hat tilted to one side. He was almost as fancy as the fancy woman herself. It made David snarl to think of him. In spite of the good supper in his insides, he recalled Amos Gives almost with approval.

But he had new clothes on and a dollar of his wages in his pocket — the other dollar being on him and in him in the form of a new hat and two glasses of whiskey. His feelings were verging on exuberance. With the bar behind him opening for the first time under the new management, it was plain that he regarded himself as a figure of importance.

It was seven o'clock. The sunset had tinged some clouds above the canal with bright orange. Four boats were tied up at the wharf and a big lumber raft was in the making just below the bridge. The sounds and smells of cookery floated from the cabins of the boats; and in one of them a man was singing hoarsely. In the bar David could hear Mrs. Silverstone and the new 'keep putting on the finishing touches. Now and then one glass rang against another.

A man and a woman came off the end boat in the line. David recognized Goudger and his cook, the tall woman who had laughed hysterically at the news of Gives's death.

" 'Lo, Dave," said Goudger.

"Evenin'," said David.

"Bar open now, eh?"

"I reckon."

"I see they're a-keeping you on."

"They be," said David.

Goudger stroked the back of his neck, glanced at David, at the door, and tramped inside. The woman sat down on the chair next to David's.

"Evening, mam," he said.

She smiled.

Other men came to the stoop and spoke to David and went inside. David gave them all greeting with an air. You might
have thought, almost, that he was proprietor of the sal on. He
pushed his hat back on his head, hooked his thumbs through his
galluses, tilted his chair against the wall. He smoked incessantly.
" 'Lo," he said, and, "Evenin', Pete"; "Yes, it does seem like a
droughth coming on"; "Them new horses of Slinger's look fair
to middling, all right, but I 'll bet they 're over nine"; "Eanh, business is so-so. 'Course it ain't Saturday, but you wait."

They passed him, good-humoredly responsive to his comments.
The woman stayed at his side.

"No taste for likker, mam? Very good gin from the new Rome
distill'ry. Some prime whiskey."

The tall woman said nothing; but she smiled, a thin little smile,
whenever he spoke. She leaned forward in her chair, elbows on
knees, chin in hand, her eyes moody. David said to himself that
she was a fine specimen of a woman; he did n't remember seeing
many as good-looking. There was something bold about her, too.
She had a deep-fringed blue shawl over her shoulders and a straight
wool dress that managed to bring out her figure, here and there.

While he looked at the tall woman, who in turn stared down
the canal, David started to hear a voice murmur, "Pardon, David."

"Eh!"

"Beg pardon, Dave. Sorry to interrupt. Is thish th' saloon?"

The speaker swayed unsteadily on his feet and regarded the two
others with a vague earnestness. David grunted.

"My name 's Will'am Durkin, mam! Pleasure."

He turned to David.

"Say, Dave. What 's thish I hear about the fancy woman —
drinking with everybody all night long and not saying no or turning up her toes? Jeepers, that ain't in nature and I don't believe
it, do you, mam?"

The tall woman remained silent.

"I don't believe it can be done. Been tryin' it m'self for twenty-
two yearsh. B' Jeepers! I 'm a-goin' 'o see. I 'll set Pa's son again'
a wommin any day."

He bowed profoundly and elaborately to the tall woman, manœuvring his feet with skill.

"Beg — *hic* — pardon. Beg pardon, mam. Nothing pershonal."

The tall woman looked at his bottom waistcoat button for a minute and then looked back down the canal; and Durkin sighed and disappeared into the bar.

It grew dusky; then the darkness gathered under the stoop roof. Lights, which had already been lighted in the bar, shone past David and the tall woman, painting their faces with shadow.

The woman drew a deep breath.

"Eanh," said David.

It became quite dark — there were no stars and the canal flowed unseen save for two patches of water running through the light from the windows. Laughter echoed in the barroom; but on the stoop the sound of it was dim.

"So she gave you a job, did she?" asked the tall woman.

David drew himself forward on his chair. "Well, I said as how I'd swamped here so long the saloon was as much mine as it was hers."

He paused, but, as the woman had nothing to say, he went on: "She didn't give me no answer to that; so I struck her for bed and board and new clothes besides my pay."

"What'd she do?"

"Oh," said David, modestly, and he hitched his new trousers over his knees to ease the crease, "oh, she took it pretty good."

"I'm surprised," said the tall woman.

"Ain't you goin' in?" asked David, after a while.

"No."

Someone in the bar was singing "The Orphan Ballad Singers" in a long-drawn, nasal tenor.

> "Oh dreary, weary are our feet,
>   And weary, dreary is our way;
>   Through many a long and crowded street
>   We've wandered mournfully to-day.
>
>   My little sister, she is pale;
>   She is too tender and too young

To bear the autumn's sullen gale —
   And all day long the child has sung.

She was our mother's favorite child,
   Who loved her for her eyes so blue.
She is so delicate and mild,
   She cannot do what I can do.

She never met her father's eyes
   Although they were so like her own,
In some far-distant land he lies,
   A father to his child unknown. . . ."

A sentimental hush fell on the room behind them. The tall woman sighed. Old David hid his face in his hands.

"Say," he said suddenly between his fingers, "you ain't seen my datter on the Erie, has you? She was like that. A little, trembly gal, with black hair. She sneaked on me and I ain't seen her since."

The tall woman rested her chin on her fist.

"Don't you never hear from her?"

"Yes. Eanh. She writes. Says she's comin' back to take care of me now I'm old and doddery. But she's long coming. You ain't seen her on the Big Ditch, has you?"

"No," said the woman.

Bit by bit the laughter and clatter were resumed in the bar. It had grown damp and a little cooler. The tall woman shivered.

"Better go in," said David.

"I don't want to."

"Why not?"

He wasn't sure of the tall woman's answer, if she made any, for Mrs. Silverstone's hearty lifting laughter rang out just then.

David decided to remain with the tall woman. He had made a great impression, he told himself, and he did not want to have it spoiled by being ordered about if he went into the bar.

Goudger came out with another man reeling on his arm.

"Hello, David," they said.

"Hello. 'Lo, Bill."

"My namesh Will'am D-durkin," said Goudger's companion with high seriousness. "You're David, if thatsh y-you."

"You're drunk," said David scornfully.

"My shame ish open 'o all men," admitted William, collapsing onto a chair. "My glorioush nation! That fancy woman *can* d-drink! My hat'sh off to her."

The boater with the pipe-hat appeared in the door.

"It sure is," he said. . . . "I just saw George putting it in the stove."

"Bye-bye hat," apostrophized William Durkin. "Nev' mind. The woman wash too much for me. I got to believe about her now. But it ain't in nature. She'sh been too much for more men than me. She drinksh with them all."

"That's right," said Goudger. "She does it with all that steps up to her and never turns a hair. Them that's seen her in Bentley's says she'll go on that way all night. She uses her own whiskey. She's got her own partic'lar drink."

"I've seen her in Bentley's," said the boater with the pipe-hat. "And it ain't no lie."

"Jeepersh," said William. "I wish I knowed how she did it."

The tall woman had moved away when Goudger came out. Now she rejoined them. David grinned at her.

"I know," he said to Durkin.

"How?"

"I've drunk her partic'lar drink. I tried it yesterday when she was upstairs getting dressed," he added with an air of importance.

"What wash it?" asked Durkin. "Old Jam-maicy?"

"Cold tea," said David.

"I don't believe it," said Goudger.

"The old man's right," said the tall woman. "I *know*."

"How do you know, Anne?" asked Goudger.

"I worked for her in Utica," said the tall woman. "She got her claws on me when I first come to Utica, and she left her marks on me. My God!"

"I got you through her agency," said Goudger. "What're you kicking about?"

"You're one of the marks, God help you," said the tall woman in a flat voice.

"I think you're a jackass," said Goudger.

He guided William back into the bar.

"So you know her, too?" said the boater in the pipe-hat.

"I got a taste of her this morning," said David. "She thinks she knows the whole damned world."

"She dang near does," said the boater.

"I know her," said the tall woman. "We came from the same part of the state, only she came earlier than I did."

"Thinks she knows the whole damned world," repeated David. "Bossed me round. Bossed me round ragged. . . ."

"She took a fancy to me," went on the tall woman, "because we've got the same name."

"Listen," said the boater with the pipe-hat. "She drinks tea. . . ."

"She's a devil," said the tall woman.

"Listen here, David," said the boater. "You know where them bottles of hers is kept?"

"Eanh. At this end of the bar. They've got the same label as the three-hundred-per-cent Delta Special Whiskey, and that's right alongside."

"Well," said the boater. "Let's play a joke on her. I'll get some of the boys to keep the 'keep busy and you shift the bottles when he ain't watching. Then I'll drink with her, by Cripus!"

"Ha, ha!" laughed the tall woman. "That would be some joke."

"I'll bet that'll take the fancy out of her," said the boater.

David got slowly to his feet.

"Bossed me at swamping, hey? All right."

He and the boater with the pipe-hat went into the bar.

6

The bar was crammed with men, amazement on their faces, staring, a few even forgetting to drink. Tobacco smoke swayed back and forth to the wind of loud conversation. Lamps, in brackets on the walls, looked dim behind it. The strength of it was stifling.

At the bar the 'keep was hustling. His face was crimson, his brow sweaty; only the deftness of his big hands held him abreast of the demands for more liquor. Slab City was drinking itself under.

At the far end of the room, the fancy woman sat beside a table. Her face beamed and she scattered laughter on all and sundry. The essence of good humor shone on her cheeks and forehead. She wore a bright yellow dress, cut square at the bosom and very low; and a black ribbon was plaited in her brilliant yellow hair. Her fingers blazed with rings, and about her neck were so many necklaces and lockets that they clinked to her movements.

A teamster was sitting opposite to her, drinking turn about, he with a bottle of whiskey, she with her own bottle slung in a little wicker basket at her waist. The rest looked on over their glasses; she had not declined a drink all evening; and here she was, the most sober in the room. Her attentions were impartial — but they all liked her; and as the evening progressed universal opinion pronounced her handsomer.

The teamster got up from the table, unsteadily, holding the back of his chair with fumbling hands. There was a look of disappointment in his face; but he managed a grin in answer to the fancy woman's good-natured laughter.

At the back of the room, the boater with the pipe-hat was holding a conference with Goudger and five or six others. After a minute or two, the group descended on the bar, noisily demanding mixed drinks, until the 'keep's hands flew like a sleight-of-hand artist's. Under cover of their roaring, David slunk behind the bar. He found three bottles of the "mixture" and replaced them with the Delta Special.

Laughing loudly, the others took their seats.

"Work it?" they asked David.

"Easy," he said, his eyes gleaming like a squirrel's.

The boater with the pipe-hat got up and went over to Mrs. Silverstone.

"I ain't seen you for a year. You've sure got things fixed up slick."

"Why, it's Mr. Greenshawl, ain't it? I'm real glad to see you. You come this way regular?"

"Pretty regular."

"Set down, set down," said the fancy woman. "What'll you have?"

"Delta Special."

"You was always a hard drinker," chuckled the fancy woman. "Joe!" she called the barkeep. "Bring a special for Mr. Greenshawl, and some of my mixture."

The barkeep brought them, taking the corks out deftly on the way.

"Here's how," said Greenshawl.

A silence had fallen on the room. Something in the boater's attitude, perhaps, had warned them that something was up. Perhaps it was the sudden stillness of the men who had just been roaring for the 'keep's attention.

"Here's how," echoed the fancy woman, her finger curled as she lifted her glass.

Greenshawl gulped his, and closed his eyes for an instant. When he opened them, he saw Mrs. Silverstone's glass as empty as his own.

"Strong likker," he said, shaking his head.

"Yes," said she, "I like it pretty well myself. But I generally stick to my own mixture."

He could not see a flicker on her face. She filled her glass and held it to the light; and her hand was steady. He began to mistrust David.

"Drawing lumber?" asked the fancy woman.

"Eanh," said Greenshawl, putting his pipe-hat under his chair.

"A good haul!" she said, and drank again.

"Good trade for you!" said Greenshawl, and as he drank he rested his elbow on the table.

"He's feeling it a'ready," whispered the man on David's right. "And she's cold sober."

"She's so bung full of tea," said the man on his left, "she's got to get oiled first. Wait for the end of this glass."

They waited. From between them David stared at the fancy woman with a sudden horror.

"You ain't such a quick drinker as you used to be, Greenshawl," she was saying.

He mustered a laugh.

"Getting older," he said.

"That's right," she agreed. "I ain't the hand I used to be, myself. If it wasn't for the mixture I make, I'd have to give it up."

"She's like rock-ballast," said the man on David's right.

David was afraid. The tall woman was standing in the doorway.

"She's commencing to sweat," said the man on his left.

A dull brick red had flooded the fancy woman's cheeks. They grew darker swiftly. But her attitude of self-possession remained unshaken. . . .

Greenshawl groped for his hat and rose unsteadily with the last glass of his bottle held before him.

"Mrs. Silverstone," he said shakily, "you're solid! I'll drink to you, and proud to do it."

She got to her feet and grinned. But there was a stiffness in her lips that made it hard for her to speak. And the dark red of her cheeks had flushed her whole face and breast.

"I can take a joke," she said, "as well as the next."

She stood quite steady and raised her right hand to her mouth to blow a kiss, without noticing the empty bottle still clenched in it. As her hand came opposite her chin, her fingers relaxed and let the bottle smash on the floor. She tottered suddenly and regained her balance with an effort.

Then she fell. For an instant, in the dead stillness, the tobacco smoke swung lower from the ceiling.

"What in hell?" cried the barkeep, running over to her. The others crowded round. The barkeep bent over her. All at once he reached out his hand and laid it on her breast. Nobody said anything. It came upon them that she was dead.

She had fallen backwards with her arms flung up over her head, and her yellow dress caught the light about their feet. She had on red stockings and red-heeled shoes. The swagger was all gone out of her clothes. She looked as if someone had dropped an over-large bouquet of geraniums and marigolds to the floor, where they had been stepped on.

Old David whimpered as he looked at her.

The tall woman came in. She pushed the men aside and stared down at the fancy woman.

"I used to think," she said, "that woman wore a wig."

She squatted down.

"I'm going to find out."

"What the hell?" said the barkeep; but he did not stop her.

The tall woman laid her hand on Mrs. Silverstone's hair and pulled gently, and then tugged. Mrs. Silverstone's mouth fell open.

"If it wash a wig," said William Durkin, "it would come off."

The tall woman parted the hair with her fingers. It showed black at the roots.

"She dyed it," said the tall woman.

"How did it happen?" asked the barkeep.

"It was a joke, that's all," said Goudger.

"Who done it?"

"David," said two or three. "He shifted the bottles."

The barkeep snarled.

"You dirty little twirk, you've done us out of two soft jobs."

"She oughtn't to run a saloon," whined David, "if she can't drink her own likker."

"You shut up."

"I guess maybe we ought to pick her off the floor," said the bar-keep. He and Greenshawl carried her up to her room.

"I'm going to get out of here to-night," exclaimed Goudger. "Anne!"

The tall woman came over to him. She stopped on the porch where David had sat down again. The old man cowered when she spoke.

"She's dead, all right."

David moaned.

"You damned fool," said Goudger, "that was a hell of a joke to play on a woman. Why, she might've been your datter for all you know."

He went aboard his boat, lit a lantern, and started getting his team out on the towpath. He hung the lantern in the bow.

"Lucky I finished loading this lumber Saturday," he growled. "Hurry up, Anne."

The tall woman followed, leaving David bent over his knees on the porch steps. He looked up in time to see the tall woman pass under the lantern light, her profile clearly etched against the planking.

"Take me along, Mr. Goudger."

"Hell, no," said Goudger.

"I could steer."

"I don't want you along."

The tall woman spoke out of the darkness of the stern.

"Poor old man."

The horses started, and little by little the lantern dwindled.

7

The men in the saloon trooped out on the stoop. One of them, who had overhead Goudger's remark, taunted David.

"That was some joke of yourn; why, it might've been your daughter. She had black hair."

"No, no," cried David.

The barkeep came out.

"It's a funny thing," he remarked. "She come from this part of the state."

"Oh Lord!" whimpered David.

"I just found a paper upstairs," said the 'keep. "Silverstone ain't any name of hers. She was Molly," — he held the paper to the light of the window, — "Molly Johnson, and she came from hereabouts."

"That lets you out, Dave," said a teamster — with a forced laugh.

"She was a fancy woman," said Greenshawl, taking off his pipe-hat and wiping his forehead.

"She's dead," said another.

David had risen to his feet. His hands jumped and fluttered as he tried to fill his pipe. His face was quite white in the light from the windows.

"'We come from the same part of the state'. . . 'We've got the same name,'" he repeated the tall woman's words.

"Molly," he said.

He began to sob with the braying noise of a small boy.

The barkeep stared at him with scornful pity.

"Say, you didn't kill your datter. She ain't your datter. What're you crying about?"

"No, no," cried David. "But I seen her."

He started off down the towpath after Goudger's boat, stooped over, at his slow walk.

"Pore Dave," said the teamster; "he's twirly, but he don't mean harm."

Greenshawl put on his pipe-hat.

"It's a funny thing," he said, dubiously.

IT COMES AT TWILIGHT

I

IT was a fine farm.

On one side of the road the old white farmhouse stood in its maple grove, its long porch offering a view far up the valley. From one of the rockers, on a Sunday afternoon, Walter Pruyn could look over his meadows and pastures for half a mile and read the crops as far as his neighbor's fence. Up the hill ran his pasture land, dotted with sculptured barberries and thorns. As the land lay, curving to the small runnels of the brooks, with its wood lots, and trees marking the boundary fences, and the Oriskany Valley like a great cleft, one had a feeling for the structure of the earth.

Across the road the barns made an open-sided square around the yard. The cattle barn stood parallel to the road, and in summer afternoons its roof lifted a back against the sun. On the lower side, at right angles, stood the small barn, used now for machinery and Pruyn's Ford car. On the upper side, parallel to the small barn, was a henhouse with a loft over it, in which were stored relics of the farm's early life. Just above the henhouse the old oast-house reared itself like a monument on its small knoll. Time was when the side of Paris Hill, like the Oriskany Valley, raised hops. Chenango beer! A stack of hop-poles, disused for several years, stood like an Indian wigwam in the middle of the five-acre piece. Pruyn had often thought of buzzing them for stove wood, but they still stood there.

The red buildings were placed close together opposite the house — the space between the corners was no wider than was needed for the passage of a load of hay. For the educated reader, they

made a page of history. The small barn had been Pruyn's grand-
father's cattle barn, and the henhouse had been used for horses.
Pruyn remembered how he had helped the carpenters heave up the
rafters for the big barn. He had been in his young manhood —
a year before his father died, two years before he married.

He and his wife had raised a family here, as he himself had been
raised: two girls and a boy. The oldest girl worked in Utica, in
a lawyer's office. The second had married out west. The boy
was linesman with Niagara-Hudson. The farm had paid for
their start, and, if they chose to live away, it was all right. The
farm paid for their parents.

Pruyn stood for a moment in the late spring afternoon looking it
all over. The old orchard that skirted the road just below the
house had put forth a few early blossoms. The bees among them
made moving sparks in the sunset. It was still and peaceful; but
there was a distinct chill in the air, a hint of frost. He trusted that
it would n't freeze.

Beyond the whistle of a sparrow up the hill, the only sound was
the steady rasp of the barn broom where Randall was cleaning up.
He was glad of Randall, a good worker; they had taken him from
the State School nine years ago, or nearly ten.

Pruyn pulled his hand across his fresh-shaven chin. He had
not thought of it till this moment. In a month, Randall's parole
would be over. He wondered if the boy would choose to stay on
with them. He hoped so — he was a good honest worker, steady,
slow with horses, perhaps, but quite reliable. A man would never
suspect now that he was out on parole.

In the house he heard Mabel bustling back and forth. As far
as a man could make out, she had been ready twenty minutes ago.
He grinned tolerantly. It was the first party they had gone to in
a long time, and there was still plenty of time left.

From the barn came the rumble of the cattle door's closing, and
in an instant Randall started across the barnyard toward him. He
slouched a little in his walk — a middle-sized young man in his
twenties, with a tangle of brown hair. He looked tired. Plough-

ing was over. They had oats to seed and corn to plant, nothing more, to bring the summer in.

"You'd better go to bed early, Randall. We've had a hard day."

"Yes, Mr. Pruyn."

He spoke slowly in a very low voice. Odd trick; it had been hard to learn to hear him the first year. He raised his eyes. They were piercing black. He said, "I set a trap in under the barn for that skunk."

"All right, Randall. Maybe we'll have to get him out to-morrow."

"He might get in to-night."

The boy was excited. Pruyn couldn't think of him except as a boy, as he had first come to them, shy, furtive, afraid, but on his mettle. Living with him all these years, a man could see no change beyond his increasing weight and strength. Sometimes his strength would make a man uneasy if he stopped to look at the small features.

"He won't get in to-night," Pruyn said. "You'd better get to sleep."

The boy always took his word. Now his eyes filmed over with a vacant, far-away look, like a June haze. He sat down on the steps and his hands hung limply over his knees. The door opened behind them to let out Mrs. Pruyn, a small white-haired woman, wrapped in a dark loose coat.

"I'm all ready, Pa."

2

The boy sat alone on the steps, watching the dust settle on the road. They had gone to the church party down in the bottom of the valley. The sound of the car was a drone, that became steadily fainter, until the drone of the bees crept through it. The boy's eyes shifted to the bright, glancing specks. They were becoming fewer and fewer as the night cold preceded the dusk.

The side of the valley on which the farm lay was picked out by the setting sun, but on the opposite hill a soft blueness was being born. The boy saw it taking shape. It began with a shadow by the willows along the creek, a queerly meaningless veil cast upon the living brightness of the water. Then it began to move. It started westward up the sloping ground, mastering the spots of darkness behind buildings and fences, creeping slowly from farm to farm, with a visible motion which the boy could see if he watched closely, as he could see the visible march of time in the minute hand of a clock.

He did not feel the cold, but his back straightened as if it had been touched, and he raised his clouded eyes.

The sun hung just above the hill on which the college stood, red and golden, like a burst flower in the hollow of the clouds. He could see the hilltop clearly, the etched outlines of the trees in leaf, the roof of a building, the brittle gold atop the chapel spire. As he watched, he saw the gold as a spark, afloat above the pool of shadow in the valley; and for a space, as the dusk lay against the hillside, the world ceased to move. The bees in their own orchard were quiet, but the sound of their wings lingered in his ears as though he heard the earth breathing.

The spark from the chapel spire caught a reflection in his eyes. He thought of the Pruyns going down to the church party. There would be bright lights there; he loved bright lights. He was grateful to the Pruyns; he was proud of the work he did for them. They had never left him before, but he did not mind. They were kind to him. When they came back he would like to have a surprise for them. They had given him the only place to live in he had ever known. He remembered the School vaguely. It was the place he had come from on parole. He did not understand the meaning of the word; but, as nearly as he had been able to discover, it was a kind of job to do that lasted a long time. Mr. Pruyn talked of it sometimes. Mrs. Pruyn mentioned it once in a while in the evenings as she sat mending in the corner, her rocker squeaking faintly for each stitch. He said it sometimes to himself when he was tired. But he would like to have something for them, something he had done out of his own head. They were gone down where the shadow lay, and he must wait up for them.

His eyes turned into the valley once more and he saw that another change had begun. The shadow was growing. He saw that the shadows of the trees that lay aslant the hills were moving. As they came, they traced the contour of the fields, slowly, over dips and rises, now barely creeping, now leaping a ditch with a slight forward dart. He watched them a long time before he understood.

They were coming toward him; they were marching on the farm; they were creeping from cover to cover, like the stealing shapes of men.

There was something that he should remember. It began to hammer at his head with little taps, like the light taps of a metalworker's hammer — something about going indoors.

Indoors — he could remember that. He could not remember what it was. Something about going indoors. It made a phrase that repeated itself, and his uncertain recollection saw a face. It was the time when he remembered faces.

This was the face of a middle-aged man with a pointed brown beard, and he saw it against a white wall. The man wore eyeglasses upon a narrow nose, and the gold clasp there caught a spark. He would hear, if he listened, what the bearded lips were saying. They were speaking so slowly, so carefully. He could almost see a word: "Indoors." His hands clenched.

At the back of his head he heard a report, like a rifle shot, and his eyes were cut by the flash, as quick, soundless, and incomprehensible as the flash that precedes a dream in early sleep. He was standing still at the end of the porch, his hands grasping the railing, his hunched shoulders prickling with sweat, his black eyes peering through his thick hair at the hilltop across the valley.

The sun had set, but long arms of light reached among the clouds, and like a black, engulfing wave the darkness was surrounding him. His eyes sought for the spark on the chapel spire; but it had been extinguished. There were only the red arms of light far off like towering flames. The spark was gone.

With it was gone the image of the bearded face. He tried to remember one word, but it was gone. . . .

He stood quite still. The darkness lay upon the farm without stars, with utter breathlessness, raising a wall of stillness between him and the peepers way down by the creek. He was hemmed in.

He felt powerless to move. He could not even reach out with his hands to the porch rail. He could only try to remember.

The face came again, bearded; but the beard was rounded and grizzled, and below it he saw a red checked shirt, and above it a weathered skin and shrewd eyes that mocked him. He concentrated carefully, for the face was talking. He could hear it quite clearly. It said, "If you want to get a skunk out of a hole, take a fire in a can and smoke him out."

He gave a little cry as his fear left him. He had remembered. It was all right if somebody only told him. It always had been all right. His mind became active. He remembered the Pruyns, as if they were back beside him on the porch, ready to set out, and he wanted to give them a present. He would get out the skunk and have it dead. It had been after the hens. Mr. Pruyn would be glad to have it dead.

He moved suddenly, surprised to find himself able to walk. He felt his way into the house. Mrs. Pruyn had left a candle burning on the kitchen table. He stood still, looking round. He saw his shadow on the wall, and he felt himself accompanied.

On the table stood a lard pail. He stepped over to it and looked inside. There was a little lard left, so with a spoon he transferred it painstakingly to a saucer. Then he went out to the woodshed and gathered chips.

He filled the pail and brought it back to the kitchen. He made a wad of paper and lit it with the candle. Then he fed small chips to it till they caught. A little blaze sprang up toward his face, catching sparks in his eyes. His cheeks were glistening.

He put on the larger chips and they smouldered, making smoke. He had done it right, the first time.

The fire threw heat against his hand that held the pail, but he did not heed it. He knew his way in darkness. There was a loose clapboard at the corner of the lower end of the barn, and this the skunk had squeezed past to make his nest, for there was no cement floor there, but a clear space under the loft.

Carefully setting down his pail, he stretched out on his belly and peered into the dark hole. It was silent. The cows beyond had lain down for the night. Only the peepers cried far down in the dark valley, with their voice of fear, of love, of hate, of jubilation.

Then he heard a slight clink, a scuffle; and a fearful smell poured out at him. The skunk had heard him there, and trapped itself. His heart pounded exultantly. He did not mind the smell, or the smart in his eyes. He reached the bucket into the hole as far as he could and backed away.

He must get a club.

He remembered the barn broom and hurried round to the cattle door. He pulled, and it slid on its track, rumblingly. He knew in the darkness exactly where he had left the broom, but he paused. There was a tension in the thick stable air. He could feel that the cattle were restless. Suddenly, all about him, a jangle of bells broke out as the cows raised their hind quarters and heaved themselves up. Then it was still once more. He had a moment's doubt, but he smelled the skunk on his sleeve and the man's face took shape before his eyes. The bearded lips said, "He'll come out as slick as butter."

A cowbell clinked. As he reached the handle of the broom, he heard the cow nearest him shift her weight. "So, boss," he said. But she was looking. He could tell that she was looking, and he had not heard his own voice. He stood still on the runway, and even through the thick soles of his boots he could feel the troughs in the cement. The man's face was gone and he was alone in darkness.

The darkness seemed to have acquired motion. He could not feel it against his lips, but it had a taste, sharp and dry and old, and it breathed. It pushed against him with a suffocating power;

and because he could not feel it, he could make no move to throw it off. His eyes ached with staring.

There was a moment of utter quiet. He turned to the cattle door. But the darkness made him no opening. His chest heaved. He could hear his own breathing, and the blood in him roared like a river.

And then all along the stanchions he saw lights. They came slowly into being, always in pairs, to right and left, and all were turned toward him, but the darkness remained. And then they were shut out, like a wind against a candle. But they came on again faintly, and he saw reproach in them. If one had but blinked, he could have moved, but they froze him where he stood, and they stared with an eternal lambency. There was no single face to aid him.

One of the horses snorted and jerked against his halter rope.

Then, reaching along the runway, he saw his shadow outlined dimly and he broke into a run. His boots pounded on the cement, shocking every nerve in his body and shooting dancing lights against his eyes. When his feet struck the barnyard dirt, the silence fell, and in the black pit of the barn behind him a sigh went up.

But he did not hear it. He ran round the barn, a black shape in the blackness, holding the broom above his head. He turned the corner, and his face came into light, flushed hot, with lips everted, and mad eyes.

The earth at the loose clapboard beamed red. Little blades of grass, groping for sunlight, showed black needle-points. The light was tremulous.

A spider was reeling in his web, and, while the boy stared down with laboring chest, the insect loosened the last knot and scuttled off.

His eyes followed it. At the very edge of the darkness, he saw a small hole picked in the ground at the edge of the foundation. And from it, one behind the other, issued ants. They held white eggs in their hands. They came endlessly, orderly. At the doorway stood a single ant pointing the way to a mullein stalk. Here at the corner stood another, pointing in turn to a stone in the mud, on the far side of the red light, where the little dribble of the yard trough passed between the barns. On the stone still another ant was standing. He was pointing out a straw stalk that crossed the dribble, and on the stalk the boy saw unbroken the hurrying procession. He squatted down to see them closely. They came and came, passing the very soles of his boots.

He heard the rustle of hay and the squeak of frightened voices, and a troop of rats dropped down from a crevice in the foundation of the barn and fled across to the meadow. He could see their whiskers, tight back with horror, the undulating ripple their backs made, the red coals of their eyes, and as the last one passed him he heard the chatter of teeth.

He looked and he saw straight into the hole, as if he looked through a tunnel into the centre of the earth, and there was a great red glow. Chaff curled and blew golden specks like lighted fountains. A tongue of fire felt its way along the clapboard and withdrew, and the noiselessness of its disappearance was complete, and the boy suddenly made out the brown beams of the barn like the bones.

The draft was established and the flame fled inward, and the boy heard the voice of the fire.

He did not move when he heard it; he was squatting on his hams, one hand drooping over his knees, the fingers of the other limply touching the handle of the broom. But the firelight, lapping over him, put life into his crouched figure, put life into his shadow that reached farther and farther behind him with every breath until it caught the wall of the small barn and mounted the clapboards to squat there in gigantic profile.

The fire roared in its small corner with a sudden gust. The stillness of the night on the buildings was mastered; the flames had burst through the floor boards of the mow and were reeling over the chaff toward the shallow layer of hay; and in the dim tabernacle their voices found echoes.

Knotholes and cracks along the walls became apparent. A riffle of wings sounded from the cupola, and a pair of pigeons, one dark, one white, rose above the roof and began an eccentric ascent; and behind them the first ejaculation of smoke burst like a monstrous flower.

The boy still squatted. His small eyes made feral coals searching the heart of the fire. His shadow against the wall crouched in utter fascination, a worshiper bent down. In his mind the buildings and the farmyard and the trees along the road began to assume stature with the mounting of the fire until they towered over the entire earth. The old red barns and the white house and the orchard trees acquired the dignity of ages. The night became a time of splendor. And the boy's shadow expressed genius.

His soul was absorbed.

Then a cow bellowed.

The sound was the sound of imprisoned life, blatant with the horror of fire.

When he heard it, the boy came to his feet and stepped from the corner, and the shadow against the wall of the small barn was gone forever.

The night closed down upon him, and he was small and fearful. He stood motionless, his face turned against the blackness. He was afraid.

Then a calf bawled. A cow bellowed back. The two voices merged and the cry issued from the barn and went across the valley over the roofs of the farms, over the tops of the trees.

An impulse started the boy's feet, and his hands were made aware of their commission.

He understood. He remembered the Pruyns. There was one thing left for him to do.

He went into the cattle barn.

Red lights showed in the cracks of the walls, revealing the double row of backs, bony and still. Not a tail twitched. But the sound of burning was harsh above their heads, and a parade of smoke passed along the ceiling to the doors.

The boy went down the double rows of stanchions. As each clicked open, the cow whirled and lumbered for the door. The click of their hoofs on the cement was flurried and quick.

He had to head the calves the right way and kick them to make them run, for at the touch of his hands their contrariness reared up in them.

But the bull's eyes were blind with madness. His broad neck was low and his curved nostrils shuddered. He struck the door-post with his shoulder, slid sideways, righted himself, and charged against the night.

The boy could now see plainly the whole length of the barn. He slipped in beside the first horse and caught the halter-rope. His fingers gripped the end and yanked it loose. He would have to lead the horse.

The horse was docile and stood beside him with just a perceptible tremor that came down the rope to the boy's hand. He decided to take the horses to the orchard across the road, and he led the first one there and let it go. He came back for the second, and that one, too, went easily. The third was shifting its weight nervously in the stall and almost wrenched him beneath its hoofs as it reared back, but his arms were strong enough to hold it, and it took comfort from his hands, and he turned it for the orchard and let it go. The fourth was yanking against the halter-rope and snorting when he entered the stall. He stroked its neck and whispered, "Shh, shh," at it and got it free. It made a commotion in the orchard when it reached the fence, and all four beasts raised their tails and shuddered; and as he looked over his shoulder on his way back for the last horse he clearly saw their faces watching him.

At the barn door, smoke poured over him, and inside there was a red glow, and the heat was in the smoke, and the black rump of the horse seemed a little spot in the heart of the combustion.

He leaped back and stood trembling.

From behind him in the henhouse came a shrill cacophony of horror. A hen had wakened and looked through the window at the end of the roost and given word. The others joined her shrieks and the stout Plymouth Rock rooster felt his bones turned into jelly as he crowed and led the way through the door.

Outside they were reduced to silence, and the trembling boy heard a sigh rise from the odd horse's lips. The odd horse was an old retainer, gray-muzzled, bony, of no use in the world, beyond, perhaps, some garden cultivating. But the sigh it gave, like a last resignation, urged the boy in. He got quickly to its side and found it quite quiet. He had to fight for his breath in the smoke. He wrenched loose the halter-rope; but the horse did not back. He yanked the halter. "Back! Back!" But there was no movement. He might have yanked a block of iron. He laid his hand against the horse's wet shoulder, and he found it hard and lifeless. He yanked again and kicked the brute's knees. But the horse had lost all sense of pain. He yelled and struck the horse's nose, but his voice was lost in the mounting roar above them.

The fire was untrammeled. It had mastered the wood as well as the chaff and straw. In the heart of the deep organ-blast it poured upwards was an almost unctuous note. And through it all came the snap of sparks, like the bite of brittle teeth, along the rafters.

Choking smoke crammed into the boy's mouth. He yelled again and wept. The horse would not budge; it stood insensate as a sacrifice, waiting the actual touch of flame to make its writhing.

The boy broke out of the stall and lay down on the cement run for sweet air. It flowed along the floor from the doorway, in a cool dispassionate stream. As he lay there, the boy remembered a face at last. It was the face of an old man seen against the blackness as a stable burned. The boy could see it clearly, red in the flames, white-haired, clean-shaven, cold-eyed, with an even-tempered mouth. The mouth was saying, "Cover his eyes." The boy did not remember himself. He saw instead a small boy grasped fast in the man's hand, forced to look on, but watching the cold face above him.

He remembered some cement bags by the door and crawled for one. He came creeping back on hands and knees along the gutter until his elbow struck the old horse's heels, and he crept into the stall. But the horse still stood like iron.

Breathing a last deep breath, he pulled himself up beside the horse's free head and pulled the bag over it. He took the horse's ear in his hand, and the beast moved to the touch, placidly; and side by side they issued from the barn.

All the land was alight.

The flames mounted in a tower above the cupola. They bathed the walls of the barn as the two walked through the yard, and blistering heat came after them.

The flames on the wall flowed tipsily up and down and made short leaps into the night and jumped back again. The trees had lost all natural color and become scarlet towers. And where the monstrous shadow had crouched against the smaller barn a new fire had taken hold.

But the two went placidly to the orchard, and the boy took off the bag.

With the old horse among them, the four others whirled and fled. They went aimlessly round and round, and the boy, looking on from the bars, realized that they would run away.

In the bright light by the fence another face came to him, an Irish face, with eyes full of melancholy, saying, "Leave a lantern for them to bide by." He went into the house. The candle still burned, half down, and with it he found and lit the barn lantern and took it to the lower end of the orchard and set it in the grass. As he approached the horses quieted, gathered round him, and he left them head to head, drawing comfort from the light.

Now he was alone with the fire. The three barns burned together. On the big barn, the flames had eaten out the clapboards and made evident the studding and the rafters. A pile of smoke rolled up from them until it made a cloud against the clouds; and in the heart of it fountains of chaff sparks played and whirled away where the smoke took them.

He huddled down on the porch and watched the flames still rise. He had long since lost his sense of hearing. The roar of the fire had gone on forever. All his life he had heard it. He could not shut it out. Even when he closed his eyes he felt the heat against his lids and opened them again.

His face was crusted black with soot, channeled here and there with sweat and crying, and it looked dead, as if it too had felt the teeth of fire.

The two barns now were burning as hot as the big barn, and flames had vaulted the twenty feet to the oast house. They had burned through the near wall and in a moment they were roaring out of the ventilator at the top. The oast-house seemed to rise from its foundations to the pull of the fire. The flames shrieked in it and it lifted and fell apart, broken all around; a gush of embers was emptied in the air and, flying over, struck a dead branch in a maple, and a miniature fire was born.

The crackle and spit were lost in the rush of the oast-house; now they were audible again. The big barn's heavy timbers made a skeleton, outlasting the smaller barns.

Away across the valley, where the boy looked, he could see the windows of all houses reflecting red light. They had a kind of unwinking stare, menacing him. In the hush that lay upon the valley he heard at last the screaming of the village siren. He listened, but he could not hear the smaller sirens of the fire trucks, though he knew that they must come. And the siren continued its unearthly cry. In it he seemed to read the hatred of all people for the man who sets a fire. He huddled down. He had no friends, not even the Pruyns, any longer.

He went into the house, thinking to save himself, and set two plates upon the kitchen table and cut a piece of bread and broke it, and broke a plate and overset two chairs and put the candle on the floor in a corner and blew it out.

Then he went out on the porch and huddled down again. But now the road all the way to the village was alight with the lamps of cars, pointing like eyes at him, and close at hand the searchlights of the fire trucks, their roaring motors and their blistering sirens. He could not bear it. He went into the house.

Through the windows he saw the trucks line up and run a hose to the spring and wet the trees. There was nothing they could do but keep the house. People on foot came streaming up the road and stood around. They moved aimlessly back and forth, and their voices made a drone. Some pointed here and there. Some laughed.

But he saw only the big barn's rafters raise their ends, as the rooftree weakened, and one by one dive down into the seething pit. And he burst out crying.

The fire chief and four others entered the house with a flashlight. They found him there.

3

How did the fire start, they wanted to know. Blinking against the light, ugly and uncertain, he told them how two men had forced a supper from him, how they had tried to steal things from the house, how he had managed to throw them out, and how in vengeance they had set fire to the barn. A halting story, and he cried. He could not see their faces, only their bodies, black shapes against the windows. His own working face was the only one in the room. He heard one man laugh. He told them how, single-handed, he had saved the cattle and the horses, and he pointed to the window in proof. A neighbor and his boys were leading the horses up the road to his own barn. The same man repeated his laugh. He clenched his fists and cried that it was true.

But they said, "Begin again."

He shook his fists at them. He said to look at the chairs, and his low voice became shrill. But they did not believe him.

"Get out!" he shouted.

But the chief came toward him.

"Get out! I'll get a gun!"

Without warning he sprang back from the kitchen and caught up Pruyn's gun in the parlor. He heard a scuffling and a cry. And the man who had laughed fled out with the flashlight, slamming the door, leaving his four comrades in the half-dark, dim shapes against the windows, trying to break out. Himself, he laughed. He stole in, raising the gun. He felt a man beside him and swung the muzzle round. The hammer clicked and the gun was wrenched away and he felt himself go down.

The flashlight was recalled, and they found the fire chief sitting on the boy. The man was sniffing and saying, "He stinks of skunk.". . .

The troopers came and brought him out, and the crowd forgot the fire and milled round to see the man who had set it. He lifted his hands to fend the faces off, but they pressed closer. The troopers dragged him off to a car, and there he saw Mr. Pruyn, stony-faced. Pruyn remembered the skunk-trap. He broke down and told the truth.

They waited there, then, a little quiet group, till the fire burned flat on the ground and the ashes came into view; and then, with one trooper holding his arm, they slipped away down into the valley, where they heard the peepers still singing.

But behind him he had heard a boy laugh and make a joke about paroles, and he wondered what kind of thing a parole might be.

THE DEVIL'S FANCY

I

To Set the Warp

"I SHOULD like to have it done in time for Christmas. Do you think that's possible, Mrs. Ferris?"

"Yes. I think I can get it done." She looked up from the brittle piece of paper. "My mother used to be a famous weaver, and she taught me when I was a girl. But my fingers lost the knack of it since she died. It will take longer. And then this is a strange pattern."

The Squire stood back to the hearth. His hands were in his breeches pockets, drawing up his deerskin coat.

"It's just a notion." His red face was embarrassed. His wife had suggested the errand to him that morning; and he could not explain himself easily. . . . His wife had said at breakfast, "Frank, I'm worried about Mrs. Ferris. Everybody knows she has almost no money, and she has no relatives to go to. She wouldn't consent to living with us, and we can't offer her work in the house. Can't you think of something for her, some way of making a — a living?" He had racked his brains all morning. It was only in the afternoon, when a case of a disputed boundary had been brought before him, and he had had occasion to go upstairs for the lot survey, that he had chanced upon this old paper. As he read it he had remembered Mrs. Ferris's early reputation as a weaver; duplicating this special pattern would allow him to offer her a price that would not seem like charity. He was glad that they had already agreed on the price. He could easily afford it, and it might start her off on a decent living. If he bought one, Manners and Grigby were sure to buy from her. . . .

He said, "We used to have one like it, and the other day Mrs. Thomas mentioned it to me. I should like to get her one. They are almost unique, you know. I have n't seen a bedspread like it, ever."

He looked down at the widow uneasily. As she stood in front of him, her lace cap came barely to the second button of his shirt. In the warm room, his nostrils caught the fragrance of her hair. She could n't be more than thirty, thirty-five — she had her figure still, and except for her hands her skin was like a girl's. Her eyes disturbed him, when she lifted them to his. They were dark and pointed at the outer corners. Whenever she allowed the heavy lids to droop, a queer slyness came upon them.

She was saying, "This means a great deal to me, Squire. You understand that. I have been looking for something to do. I am very grateful."

He buttoned his coat brusquely.

"I 'm grateful to you, Mrs. Ferris."

She gave him her hand and stood in the door to see him down the path.

He said, "It 's begun to snow."

"I don't see any."

A flake had rested on the dark coil of her hair. She laughed when she saw the direction of his gaze.

"No wonder I did n't see it."

"Good night, Mrs. Ferris."

"Good night, Squire."

After the Squire's back had disappeared into the shadows down the street, Mrs. Ferris returned to her cabin, closed the door behind her, and drew the latch. The days had been getting noticeably shorter lately. Though it was only six o'clock now, it seemed quite dark. It might be the snow.

She stood with her husband's heavy watch in her hand. The firelight behind her gave a bare suggestion of her figure through her black dress. The Squire had guessed her to be under thirty-five. She smiled to herself while she stood there: the Squire was an open man — any woman with half an eye could read him. Then she caught a quick breath; walked to the window to draw the dull blue curtains. The snow was drifting down now steadily. The road outside was powdered. No ruts showed. She drew the curtains with a snap, and turned back to the room. She was grateful to the Squire; she could not tell him half how grateful; but she could at least do him his spread.

The rough log walls of the cabin caught shadows from the hearth. It was a soundly built house, small, but big enough for her. She had been lucky to get it so cheap after her husband's death. It was one of the only five in the neighborhood, too, that boasted a glass sash.

She had been living in it three months now, and it savored strongly of her possession. Barely furnished, it was neat and clean. The puncheon floor had a white shine, the stone hearth glistened. Her copper winked in the firelight. And the rough walls themselves were disguised. She had made a closet from a shelf with bright blue cotton curtains, and she had a blue coverlet for the built-in bunk and a curtain that drew round it on cord. She had fashioned the frame herself. The door, of double boards with a stout bar, was let into the right-hand corner of the front wall. In the other corner stood her table, bearing a candle in a brass stick and the four volumes of her husband's Bible. A shelf above it carried her china and two wineglasses of deep red that had belonged to her mother. Her only chair had a place under the window, between table and door. Two stools occupied the corners of the hearth. To the left of the hearth was the bed, to the right, along the end wall, a stepladder led to the loft.

When she had lit her candle she took it to the ladder, tucked her skirts up to her knees, and mounted slowly. Her legs were slim as a girl's in their rough blue wool stockings. She climbed lightly.

For a while the room remained unoccupied. The fire snapped brightly under the singing kettle. From the board ceiling the sound of her footsteps came quietly. After a few moments, she dragged something across the floor and then let it down the steps, one step at a time. Her back bent as she came down, crouching after it, the weight on her arms drawing her dress tight on her rounded back. She left it at the foot of the ladder and mounted again for her candle. Finally she dragged the loom to a place in front of the chair, where she dusted it carefully.

She rose at last, pink-cheeked from her exertions, sat down, and took up the paper the Squire had left.

In faded ink at the top was written "The Devil's Fancy." It was a strange pattern; she had heard of it from her mother, but she had never seen a completed example. She followed the directions painstakingly, her forehead puckered, but she could not make a picture of it in her mind. She would have to wait until she had the thread. The Squire had left her the money to buy it with, and she knew that the tavern store had had a supply of white for over a year. Luckily the Squire had asked for the pattern in plain white. To-morrow she would begin.

She rose, barred the door, and leisurely made ready for bed.

As she went to the spring for water in the morning, her step had a lightness that had been absent for months. The snow was scarcely half an inch deep; it must have stopped just after she went to bed; and after the clearing a heavy frost had fallen, so that in the dawn all the woods shone softly with a creamy texture. A little later it would be etched in glass. After that the woods would emerge in their winter's bareness; but by then she would be at work.

The frost crackled under her boots; the trail was hard. Mouse tracks made lace through the frost. The roaring burst of a grouse made a fountain spray in a bush just ahead. Then the woods fell silent.

The spring had a crust of ice which she broke with the bottom of her bucket. When she turned back to the road, she saw a finger of smoke in the tavern chimney. It mounted straight, without wavering. There seemed no air in the world, only the cold, and she breathed deep.

Her cheeks were bright pink when she came out again from breakfast, a shawl about her shoulders, and made for the store. The corporal's wife got the thread and accepted the money with some surprise.

"I'm weaving something for the Squire," the widow explained. Mrs. Beardsley's round face looked sharply at her.

"We saw the Squire coming out of your house last night," she said. But her tone left the explanation its face value and nothing more. The widow smiled, and her eyelids drooped. It was a question of change. Mrs. Beardsley went into the tavern. The widow moved to the calendar on the wall. November 3, 1809. Five years — she had come here with her husband in 1804. He had had consumption, and he had spent all their money looking for gold he had expected to find among the infinite tangle of roots. Poor Dore. She could see the forest beyond the window. He had left her practically nothing. She had sold her house to the Manners', and moved into the cabin. There were no relatives for her to go back East to. And a woman in her position, unless she had money, had either to marry at once or to open her house. She waited impatiently for the thread. The Squire had given her a chance at money.

Mrs. Beardsley was getting change beyond the door. The widow caught snatches of the corporal's slow talk. Fat old mountain, he never could bring himself to get out of his chair until bedtime, and he was grumbling at having to. His wife waited patiently. Once in a while she said, "Get up, John. She's waiting."

"Quilting money! Think of that. Well, the Squire knows what he wants."

He chuckled.

His wife said, "She's been too high and don't-touch-me for the boys; but a squire's something else again."

"Shut up, Nance. If she wasn't you'd want to run her out of here. She ain't your class. That's what."

"Well, give the money."

The widow took the change quietly and returned to her own cabin. She was glad to get back. It had become a refuge to her. A refuge from the wilderness — there was the kettle singing. A refuge from the immediate past — for here she shut out whom she pleased; she was under the Squire's protection. A refuge for her heart — everything was her own; only her husband's watch remained.

The sunlight streaming through the window dimmed the fire. She put her shawl on a hook and took the thread to the loom, the hanks twisted into ropes.

As she sat down under the window, the sunlight found copper in her dark hair. Her back was slender and young as she bent for the slip of paper.

The Devil's Fancy

The warp is laid on regularly till the seventh row; then, and every third row thereafter, a double twist should be used. . . .

The letters had a small tremor, but they were clear to read if she kept her eyes close to them.

As she read, she smelled the ancientness of the paper, as if it were dusty. Her eyes blurred with the fine letters, but her fingers set the warp quickly.

2

To Run the Woof

Her hands had recovered their old skill more readily than she had dared to hope. The bone shuttle that had been her mother's, worn smooth by her mother's fingers to an old yellow lustre, flew nimbly from hand to hand.

She was by herself now more than ever since her husband died. In the daytime, people passing her window could see her seated before the loom; and one warmer day the farmer who brought her provisions surprised her singing softly. He told his wife about it.

"What was she singing?"

"I don't know. Just a tune, I guess."

"Poor dear. Mrs. Beardsley said she was weaving for the Squire. I'm glad."

Indeed, in the first flush of gratitude, she sang. There had been no escape from life before; and once the cabin had been fitted over, there had been nothing to occupy her thoughts as she sat alone. The women had not called. Few had time; and those in the village thought her a notch too high and dandy for their taste. They did not understand.

But weaving takes the hands and the eyes and the energies of all the body; it occupies the mechanical side of the brain, and leaves the heart idle.

"The Devil's Fancy." The directions were mechanical things to follow. The pattern would not show until the end, for the spread was woven in two separate widths, which must be joined in the end, leaving the complete impression formed only at the last stitch.

As her hands flew in their directed flight, she began unconsciously to live her life over. The first touch of the completed weave on her knees stirred recollections.

She remembered the old place on the Hudson, just below Albany. The meadows before the house sloped to the river's edge; the drive from the wharf wound through them, following a half circle in and out of shrubbery. She remembered the hot scent of clover and the drone of bees, and the long grass that covered her when she lay down.

The house, with its square front to the river, stood on a knoll among elm trees. Behind were the stables; then, farther back, the farmhouse and the barns. At night the cattle came with a bell or two among them and the dog at their heels, barking now and then.

There was no smell of clover here, and the dogs barked like

wild things. They let the cattle run loose — there were no fences. Only the Squire's place bore any resemblance to a farm, and his two barns were built of logs.

She had not seen a black face in four years.

There had been black servants on the old place near Albany. She thought of her old nurse, and smiled. She could hear her soft voice with the note of shrillness calling at supper time, "Cor-nelia, Cornel-ia!" rising on the last syllable; then came her own belated rush home; the black hand in her hair; the warm house smell; and the voice saying like a lament, "You little wild girl."

Early days, when she had had her run of the place, and watched her mother at a dinner party from her perch on the stairs. Dark-haired and wistful, her mother sat at the foot of the table, saying little; but her head bent graciously to her guests. And just under the top of the door she could see her father's heavy hands carving, — the hands she was afraid of, — his deep, righteous voice booming while the guests listened. He lived well; he took care of his family, his beasts, and his servants; he satisfied the demands of the whole great place; but he never seemed to have seen the hunger in her mother's eyes. They were honest eyes, and to Cornelia the hunger showed openly.

The smart of her father's hand, even in memory, made her stir uneasily; and then in the silent cabin her laugh came huskily among the silent things. She straightened on her chair and looked round. No snow to-day, no sound. Yes — she heard what had made her look up: the snuffle of oxen, and a sleigh piled high with wood for the tavern.

She bent again to the paper. "Lock the thread twice." Her hands performed it. The sleigh runners creaked on the dry snow — it was getting colder. Her ears caught the ticking of her hus-band's watch. She drew her knees from under the weave and went across the cabin to see the time. Past eleven — dinner time. She went to the hearth and raked the coals. She had mixed the corn batter at breakfast and Dimble had brought her a venison steak as a gift. She covered the pan's lid with a mound of coals, put the steak on a fork, brought milk from the north corner, laid her single place at the table. . . .

After her meal, she went out for a short walk. Her fingers had the rhythm of weaving now, and she did not want to leave; but she knew that if she had no exercise her eyes and back would give out.

All the time she walked, she was aware of an anxiety to return. She took a path off the main street, a short cut to the Squire's place, but it followed the creek and made pretty walking. All the still pools were crusted over with clear black ice, and underneath she could see the bubbles pressed out flat and slipping by.

She came out at last on the Squire's fields. He had more than a hundred acres cleared round his buildings; no stump meadows showed between her and the rambling low log barns. The creek divided the buildings, leaving the house by itself under its maples. It was the handsomest log house in the county — two square buildings joined by a long hall. From each of the great chimneys smoke rose steadily into the clear noon air.

The widow stood quite still, holding the shawl round her with her left hand. Her eyes made out the Squire's figure, tramping in from the wood lot. The door opened and his wife came out and put her arms round him and pulled him in. The door closed, but an extra volume of smoke sprang from the chimney.

Standing by herself under the trees, the widow could imagine the scene in the big room — the cries and questions, the throwing on of the extra log, the Squire sitting down to warm himself before his dinner. Her warm mouth curved slowly; her smile had something secretive. She was grateful to the Squire; but she could imagine him seated there with his family. He was the handsomest man she had ever seen.

After a while she slipped homeward to her work. The farther she went from the clearing the more eagerly she walked. She must not take so long a recess again.

The cabin was as she had left it. She paused only to throw

more wood on the fire. When she felt the thread again her fingers seemed to move of their own accord. She seemed to feel again the sting of her father's hand. . . .

The continuity of her mental review of her life did not surprise her; she was hardly aware of it. But as the weaving progressed it became increasingly vivid.

So far there had been no repetition in the design; its progression gave no hint of the finished pattern.

She had been alone so many months; but she realized that she had never understood freedom before. Even on the old place above the Hudson there had been restraints, not so much from her father as from her mother's hungry eyes.

She remembered her own first taste of life. A new superintendent had come with his family. One of them had been a boy slightly older than she, perhaps fifteen — she could not be sure; but his light brown hair and brown eyes, bent over her on that afternoon in the tall swaying riverside grass, were clearer than the firelight. They brought back the dusty grass sighing in a light wind, the touch of cloud shadows they could not see, the smell of his body.

They had taken long jaunts together after the cows which he had to bring to milking every evening and morning. And one day the old nurse had found them together. He had gone away then. . . .

She remembered her schooling with her sister, under the little schoolmaster, and her household learning under her mother's teaching.

She remembered her sister's illness with the cholera, the terror on the farm, and her mother's dying of it.

Her father had told her in the hall outside her mother's door and she had gone to her room crying.

Thereafter she had ruled the house. Those were days when young men came and she had new dresses. She could see herself standing before the long glass, and her old nurse, thin and wrinkled,

stroking her bare white body with black hands. Her eyes closed
an instant as she weaved, and her breath stopped, her lips parted
slightly. . . .

Day by day the woven piece crept down over her knees. Her
eyes followed the words on the old paper, and her fingers made
the twists.

Snow came steadily, now, every day. Outside the window, the
cabins showed roofs shawled in snow, and the road was a silent
single sleigh track. It was still the great route westward, but
wagons never came, and the sleighs came less than every week.

Sometimes, as she weaved, the widow looked for the pattern
under her fingers; but even if she looked long she could see nothing
beyond the appearance of snow. There were knots that made an
irregular design like snowflakes, and in the heart of them there
was movement, but those that showed seemed stationary.

Yet in the quiet cabin, with only the watch ticking and the fire
sparking to the kettle, the review of her life continued.

It vaguely excited her now. As the second week in December
ended, she felt growing impatience for the completion of her task.

She remembered her father's dying when she was nineteen,
and her life alone for two years on the farm, her money handled
by a guardian. Two years later Dore Ferris had appeared; two
months later, in spite of her guardian's disapproval, they had
married. Then had begun years of wandering through the west.

Her husband had been a consumptive, full of impractical ro-
manticism. Her life became a perpetual movement from town
to town, rides through the wilderness, nights in taverns, until
they settled here in Chloe.

She had been a good wife, patient under his household domineer-
ing; she had been faithful; she had not complained of the gradual
dissipation of her money on his visionary schemes. She had been
a great deal alone, for she had no gift for making friends of
women, and she had always been careful of the men. Men alone
out here had lost all sense of trust. Reading their eyes, she could

never blame them. She wanted to comfort them; but she did not know how, for she must be as careful as they. She had only in those years to recollect her teaching, her father's voice, and her mother's grace. . . .

But her mood had changed with the weaving. She had been living her life again; she had brought herself to the weaving; but the prelude had changed, — not in facts, but in a manner of reading them, — and her heart was uneasy.

Their possessions had dwindled when she came with her husband to Chloe. The Squire had met them in the village; he had been a friend of her husband's family, — or, rather, his wife had, — and they had seen a good deal of him. She had learned to recognize him by the smell of his deerskin coat, which was strong with Virginia tobacco; she could tell it was he even before she had opened the door.

It had been fortunate for her that he had taken such an interest in them; without him she would have been helpless now — she would have been compelled to accept a man, instead of having her freedom.

And her freedom was dear to her — the motion of the weaving in the quiet, the peacefulness, no longer fear in her loneliness.

The second half of the spread moved steadily over her knees. The warm touch of it reminded her of her mother sitting at the same loom, weaving, and teaching her daughters. Her mother had been extraordinarily fine at weaving — for there was no necessity for her doing it. But she took joy in it; and now, in the end cabin in the village of Chloe, her daughter began to understand. They had tried various patterns; but, as far back as she could remember, the widow could think of none that interested her so, or that, she knew instinctively, would so have satisfied her mother. She often wondered nowadays why it was called "the Devil's Fancy."

As she neared the end of the second piece, Christmas was in the offing. Several of her neighbors had brought her invitations to a Christmas Eve dinner; the Manners' had asked her, and the

Squire, and the Beardsleys, and Farmer Dimble. But she realized that to finish it by Christmas morning she must work late Christmas Eve.

More snow had fallen. On her daily walks she now wore snowshoes, unless she elected to take the road.

She preferred the woods, the swamps round the Squire's field. Once she had met him and they had talked together by the bole of a straight hemlock, their breaths making a single cloud — she in her shabby old beaver jacket and cap and muff, he with the sheepswool coat open over his throat, his hair damp from chopping, holding his pipe in an enormous red mitten.

"Can't you come to Christmas Eve supper, Mrs. Ferris? We'd be glad to see you."

"If you want your present, I can't."

"I want it for the morning. But not that bad."

She smiled quietly.

"It's my first business deal," she said. "I don't want to break it."

He smiled in his turn.

"Come if you get it done, though — promise."

"Yes."

"Good."

He paused.

"If you don't come, I won't expect it till Christmas morning. I'll come then."

"I'll have it done before midnight, anyway — if you're late in the village."

He looked down at her without answering.

She always made him restless. He could slip over and get it and have it ready for Christmas morning. She was looking into the dark places of the swamp. She was slim as a willow. She had changed, he said to himself, subtly. She seemed asleep, with awakening just under her lids; as now and then he had seen his wife in the morning dusk when they were first married.

He said bluffly, "Don't wait up."

She watched him going with his long strides. . . .

She had seen him again and been able then surely to promise
him the spread.

On Christmas Eve at noon she finished the weaving.

3

To Join the Weave

The village street was banked in snow to the cabin eaves.
Trenches had been hollowed out to the doors, and the window
lights shone redly through funnels.

Mrs. Ferris got up from her own supper, cleared away the dishes,
and stood for a moment in her door, looking down the street.
The road was a single track. They had had their first heavy
winter storm, but old Beardsley at the tavern prophesied good
weather. There might still be travelers.

The cold bit her cheeks and she stepped back into the warm
cabin. She had had her fire going hard all day for many days
now; the walls had been heated through and gave out now a
pleasant woods smell that mingled with the smell of the bacon
flitch hung behind the chimney. The walls were bright with the
glow of the fire; it lit the kettles with red eyes, it caught shadows in
the window curtains, and it enveloped the figure of the widow
with an appearance of warmth and aliveness, even though she was
standing still in the middle of the room.

She looked slim, almost girlish, in her dark cloth dress. She
was thinking of the Squire, as he had looked that day under
the hemlock tree with the hesitation in his eyes. Her own eyes
were half closed, her head was bent.

Suddenly her chin flashed up and she swung toward the table
cupboard with a slight lifting of her skirts. The motion made
a warm wind in the cabin that caused the candle flames to flicker
and spout thin tongues of smoke.

In an instant she was seated in her chair with the ends of the
two halves of the spread on her knees and the threaded bone
needle in her right hand. She leaned forward to the table, drew

the paper of directions toward her, turned it over to the last paragraph. "To join the weave." She put together the two inside corners and her needle made a stitch. The candles drew evenly again, the fire burned quietly on its bed of red coals, the air in the cabin grew still.

The widow worked steadily, smiling to think how nearly done her task was. The weaving was beautifully accomplished, no false threads, no twists overtight; it was smooth, knowing work.

Little by little the halves came together. The weaving had been like a betrothal — the meeting of the thread, the speeches of the weaving, each half separately; now the marriage, and the whole to be completed.

As the halves came together, the widow began to see the meaning of the pattern. It was still outside, and inside it was peaceful, but the color mounted steadily to her cheeks, flushing her bosom, her throat, as it came. She breathed quickly. She could see now, instead of in bits as she had followed it through the weaving, her whole life before her. She saw the hunger again in her mother's eyes, she heard the righteousness in her father's voice, she saw the boy's face in the grass over her head, and the faces of all the men she had ever met, one by one. She saw the eddy of water meeting in two streams, the thrust of wind in the heart of snow, the welding of flames on a single stick. And her heart became swollen in her breast.

She smelled the scent of Virginia tobacco, and saw the Squire's face, and felt sorrowful and glad. She heard a jingle of bits coming down the road. But she did not hear and she did not see. The blood was in her head and her eyes swam.

"It's hot," she said to herself, and she untied the lace at the front of her dress, opening it over her breast. Then, still holding the half-finished spread, she rose and drew the curtains and placed the candles on the windowsill to gain additional light from their reflections.

The palms of her hands were hot and slippery. She worked

hurriedly; the needle seemed to leap to its appointed stitches. The Squire might come.

Once she looked up to see her husband's watch, and her heart sank. It was midnight. A glance at the window showed snow beginning. It was falling steadily, flake on flake, soundlessly, against the opacity of the night. But as she stared she seemed to see farther and farther, smaller and smaller flakes, until she saw the wind coming, and the flakes whirled before it and made a pattern.

She glanced at the work in her hands and saw that she had taken the last stitch. And she sat quite still while a hand knocked on her door. . . .

It knocked again.

She rose a little breathlessly, and said, "Come in."

The latch lifted; the door hesitated, as if the hand expected a bar; then it swung wide.

The man who stepped into the room and closed the door behind him had snow on his wide hat and black coat. He removed the hat and said, "Good evening."

He was young, scarcely twenty, with thin smooth cheeks and merry dark eyes. And as he met her stare the relief she had seen there first dawned gradually into complete delight.

"I saw the open window, and the candle, you know. So I took a chance."

He unbuttoned his coat, then hesitated; and gradually she understood.

The color drained from her face.

He said hurriedly, "I may have been mistaken."

She looked at him again.

"Where are you from?"

"Ohio. I did n't think I'd get through this winter, but I took a chance. I just came in, you see, and there was nobody to talk to at the tavern, and I saw your open window."

"Yes."

He was merely a boy, an eager boy.

"I saw the candle, and you know it looked like Christmas."
He laughed suddenly. "So it is. Merry Christmas."

She smiled, and the lids drooped on her eyes.

"As a matter of fact, I'd just stopped work."

She folded the spread, looking at him over the edge as she did so.
He became apprehensive once more.

"I'm sorry," he began.

She took the candle from the window and drew the curtains.
As she passed him to bar the door, he caught the smell of her hair.
He was young and ill at ease. He bent over the spread.

"Lord, that's beautiful weaving. What's the pattern?"

She smiled again secretively. She understood completely. The
pattern had been woven in her and she had never known.

"It's called the Devil's Fancy."

He stood awkwardly following her movements. She laughed.
"You can hang your coat there."

NINETY

I

GEORGE STALLION sat at the head of the breakfast table and glanced along the bowed heads of his progeny. The early sunlight coming past his shoulders made a haze in the fringe of his patriarchal beard and cast his broad shadow over the dishes. His hooked nose and black eyebrows and fierce black eyes proclaimed him undisputed master of his family. He sat erect, broad-shouldered as his sons and grandsons, pink-cheeked as his granddaughters. He scarcely seemed old, until you noticed the taut skin on his forehead: it was ivory-colored, like his beard.

He drained his cup slowly, letting the coffee lie for a moment about his teeth to get the full benefit of the sugar. Then he leaned back to watch his family finishing the meal. His oldest daughter, a woman of sixty-odd now, held the foot of the board, under a crocheted work cap of blue chenille. He drew in his breath and waited while she filled her husband's cup. Just as the coffee reached the lip, he cleared his throat, a rumbling that started in his chest and brought up the heads of the family with it.

"Where's Belle?" he demanded.

His voice held a deep harshness and had a trick of hovering just beyond his lips, as though it were waiting to strike one.

Judy's fat hands jumped and the coffee slopped into the saucer; and the old man grinned under his beard.

"My gracious, Pa!" she said. "You make a person start!"

He covered his amusement with a scowl.

"Where is she?" he shouted. "Laying abed, the lazy slut. By Jeepers, she ought to be hided! I'll do it one of these days."

"No, she ain't, Pa," said Judy. "She's minding Pearl. Poor Pearl," she went on, lowering her glance properly, "she takes it harder than most."

"What do you know about it?" the old man growled.

Judy was childless. Consequently she liked to have opinions on bearing children.

"Well, she's young, you know, Pa. Men don't rightly understand such things," she said to her sister, who discreetly avoided answering.

The old man took hold of the end of his beard and peered at her from under thinly lashed lids.

"Don't eh? Well, gal, when you was born, there wasn't no doctor could get through the snow here, so me and Mrs. Dustin brung you into open air. You was just about as fat as you be now, Judy, and a dang sight redder, and you jumped and squawked like you did now, when I slapped your bottom."

Judy flushed and became silent.

"Cripus!" the old man grumbled. "Your ma didn't go to bed just to have a baby. She got up next morning, and the morning after she was milking again — seven cows, good milkers at that. Pearl's a lazy."

Pearl's young husband glared at him angrily, then scraped back his chair and got up to leave the room.

"John!" roared the old man. "Say 'Excuse me.' Just because I got to tell Judy a thing or two, you don't need to get uppity."

The young man stopped surlily.

"I ain't going to listen to your talk."

"All right. All right. You don't have to. If you don't like it, you can get out and take Pearl. But you ain't going to do that. You haven't got the grit. So you wait till I give you morning's orders. You hitch up the grays and haul manure on to the south meadow. That's good work for you now. It'll keep your feet warm."

John took his hat from a nail and slapped it on to his head. He slammed the door. The old man chuckled.

"Notional squirt. You'd think the both of them was having children."

He turned to Judy's husband.

"How 're you coming with the potatoes, Arnold?"

Arnold rinsed the coffee round and round in his cup and drained off the last drop.

"Pretty good, Pa. I won't promise, but we ought to have them in this afternoon."

"All right," said the old man. "You and Joe 'd better keep after them. This weather ain't going to hold a lot longer. We'll have killing frost next week, I believe."

"I reckon," said Arnold, his Adam's apple fluttering in his thin neck after the hot drink.

The old man turned to his oldest grandsons. "You and Ben better get into the east lot and commence cutting pole wood. Them maples needs clearing thin, and they'll do for stove wood. Jim 's choring in the barn. I'll want the bays on the buckboard, Jim, about ten o'clock."

"All right, Gramp."

The men trooped out and the women got up to go about their work. The old man watched them go: twelve of them; all his blood, or married to it. He believed in keeping them under his roof. They got a good home, he got cheap labor. It worked both ways. It was lucky he had them broken in, though, or they'd be fighting among themselves all day. He had them buffaloed all right.

He swung his chair round and put his feet on another and leaned back. Judy was taking off the dishes. She did it quietly. The old man liked an after-breakfast snooze now that he was getting older. He liked to feel the warmth creeping into the sunlight on his back. Pretty soon he began to nod.

"Why, Grampa! Ain't you shamed? Sleepin' to-day."

He lifted his handsome old head and glanced over his shoulder. The hard eyes gleamed and his beard moved over his mouth.

"Morning, Belle."

"Many happy returns of the day," she said. Her voice was fresh and full-throated, much like her grandmother's. She came up to him and kissed him, and he put his arm round her waist and drew her to his lap and petted her. He liked to feel her waist snug in his arm and yielding to it. The other women of the family he kissed as a matter of course; he enjoyed kissing his youngest granddaughter.

She poked his head back with the heel of her hand and smiled at him. Her face was extraordinarily like his — a little finer-featured, but with the same thick brows and black eyes. He always softened to her.

"You old surl," she laughed. "You been teasing Judy."

"Won't hurt her, Belle. She's in too good flesh for being healthy."

"You talk like an old woman, Grampa. You're getting doddery."

He slapped her a good whack.

"I'll leather you, Belle, if you don't look out. There ain't any doubt I could do it."

He peered at her sideways, his tongue in his cheek.

"When I get to doddering, Belle, I'll go down to the barn and hang me."

"Doddery old man," she repeated. "What're you going to do to-day? Sit in the shade and sleep, probably."

"Maybe I will, at that. I'm turned ninety; and I've seen a lot and done a lot. More 'n you'll ever get in your head, Belle."

"I wouldn't doubt it."

"Don't sass," he growled, pinching her. "Look at what I've done. You're just a sort of incidental piece on the side. Your grandma and me come here having nothing. It was hard living, but we made a good farm. I've made money. I boated it. I made money on pork. I'm still making money, Belle. I could buy out half the people round here. . . . Most of the new people hold their land just as long as I want 'em to. I'll bet I could buy out some of the Adamses across the river, even if they are city people. The old folks round here died out or had to move. Only George Stallion hung on and made things pay. He can't be beat."

She patted his head and he lowered it toward her.

"Getting bald, Grampa."

He snorted.

"You little chippy, you, you don't care a hoot. I reckon I'll go to town. I want to see Francis at the bank. Then I'll ride out to Whister's and see about closing the mortgage. I could use his beech lot this fall, and his north pasture'll come in handy for us next summer."

"Don't be too hard on him, Grampa. He's a man likely to get mad."

His eyes lighted.

"He can't bother me, Belle. I've handled worse'n him. I'd like to see him act up once. If I can handle the Stallion family, I oughtn't to have no bother with a twerk like him."

"Well, I don't care what you do to him. But don't get tired. There's the party to-night, you know."

He grunted.

"Look here, gal. I'm ninety, but that ain't nothing. There's no dry rot into me."

"No," she said. "You never gave yourself the chance to get dry inside."

His head butted her shoulder.

"That's right. . . . Who's coming to this party?"

"Why, there's the Melvins and Kittleses and Crystals, and George and Nancy Lane, and the minister; he's bringing along Mrs. Bridgeman and her sister from Utica, Mrs. Kurty. She belongs to the Sisters of Grace."

"She better not try any fancy religion on me," he growled.

Belle kept hold of her fourth finger and looked down at him from the corners of her black eyes.

"There's all the neighbors, of course, coming to eighteen, and the Garvins, and the Salters, and Erwin Saunders."

The old man glanced at her quickly. He had felt a tremor in her, barely noticeable; but Belle had wedged in the name neatly, and she went on to the end of her list. He said nothing. But he kept mouthing the name to himself. A rising young man in the town, Erwin Saunders was.

"Well," he said when she had finished, "it's quite a collection, though we could get along without the minister, and the weeds he'll bring. By grab, Belle, a man can't get no pleasure dancing with a woman that's thinking about God and altar cloths."

She caught his head against her breast, forcing his beard up against his nose until he sneezed. He shoved her away.

"Get out. Get your breakfast and do some work. I've got to get in town. Where's Jim? Where's the bays? By Jeepers, I'll give him a belting. It's way after ten."

"Two minutes," said Belle.

"Where's my coat? Judy!"

His daughter came into the room, hung the coat over the nearest chair, went out without a word.

"Stewing in her own grease," grunted the old man. "She'd better watch out. Some day she'll get drowned that way."

Belle helped him on with his coat and brought him his hat. Through the door they could hear the bays stamping in the barn-yard and tossing the bits on their tongues.

The old man caught his granddaughter in one arm, where he could look straight into her eyes.

"Belle, do you like this Erwin Saunders twerk?"

"Eanh."

"A lot?"

"Eanh."

"A great lot?"

"Eanh."

She looked back at him frankly.

"We're going to get married this winter."

She kissed him suddenly, pushing her lips through his beard. He held her a second; then stepped away and gazed down at her, smoothing his moustache, rumbling to himself.

She grinned at him with a square mouth, like a man.

"What're you going to do about it, Grampa?"

He went on stroking out the hairs with meticulous care.

"I thought you'd pick a man, Belle. I never figured you'd cotton to a — a sody clerk."

He yanked his hat over his eyes and stamped out to the waiting team. Belle walked to the door and watched him out of sight.

2

The team was trotting smartly, making play against the reins. The old man was sitting forward over his crossed knees, his eyes abstractedly fixed on the horses' ears. He was brooding about Belle.

He'd seen Erwin Saunders round the farm a good deal lately, but he'd never thought he would get Belle. The boy was right enough, as far as he knew, and he was making more or less money; he'd inherit his father's store. But for Belle to fall in love with him was hard. He wasn't of the tough old stock that Belle was. More than any of his children or grandchildren, she took after the old man. Well, she might make something of the Saunders family. Stallion knew better than to fight it out with her. He'd let it slide along. He'd take it out on Whister. He didn't like the man, or his wife either — strait-laced Baptist, with her tight hair and·pinched-in stomach. He'd given the man time once before to pay the interest; but he wouldn't now. He wanted that north pasture anyway.

People would say he acted mean. Let them talk. He as good as owned a lot of them. If they talked, they'd do it quiet.

He shook out the reins a bit, and the team lengthened out. It was hot, with the still, scented heat of the Indian summer, with a faint haze on the Black River bottom. He crossed the canal and entered the shadowed cool of the woods. It felt good. Down there on the right was the Garvin place. Nice folks, the Garvins were. Mrs. Garvin was a pretty girl when they settled there; she was a pretty woman now. There was the oldest boy coming down to get the mail. Well-set-up youngster, more of a Stallion than some of his own. . . . The old man grinned and waved, and the boy waved back with the same grin.

Some might have noticed; but that was the last one, anyhow, and nobody said anything. It hadn't made any difference. Garvin knew better than to raise a fuss.

The team held a steady pace. It was a little past eleven when he left the order for the groceries and crossed the street to the bank. There he found Mr. Francis in his office and he went in and sat down.

"Morning, Joe."

"Morning, George."

They grinned at each other. The bank president was old, but smooth-shaven, plump, and dressed in a suitable dark suit, with a bunch of fobs dangling from his watch chain.

"Many happy returns, George. Glad to see you so healthy. You and me are getting along, George, getting along."

Stallion puffed his cheeks angrily.

"You're ten years younger than I be, Joe. Getting along! Why, when I look round and see all the young twitter-twitts hanging round this town Saturday nights, my innards twist on me. They think they've seen things and talk a lot; but they don't know nothing."

"Well. . . ."

"Well, hell! By dang, I could pick any one of them up and hold him over my head and set him down in a corner if I went to wrastle with him."

"I guess you could, George. But they're all right. They make money. They're a pretty steady lot."

"So're stones. What of their making money? You and me went and took ours, Joe."

"Now I wouldn't say that, George," said the bank president, lowering his voice and rubbing his knees. "I wouldn't say just that."

"You don't like to let the other fellow know he's beat," Stallion said. "That's part of your business. When I hit a man, I let him know it."

He stretched and grinned, his white beard jumping up from his waistcoat. The bank president winked.

"I bet you, George."

"Sure, Joe, you ought to know it."

"Well, *you* don't."

Stallion chuckled.

"Better not let me catch on, Joe."

"I won't," promised the bank president.

"What I come in here for, Joe, was to make sure the interest was overdue on the Whister mortgage. Where's the papers?"

"I don't need to look. Whister didn't pay up last May."

Stallion grunted.

"Aiming to close it?"

"Eanh."

"That man's got a bad temper, George. You better let us handle it. We'll smooth it out."

"I bet you would. But I don't want it smoothed. I don't like him. He's been bothering me right along about fences. Never keeps 'em up. I killed one of his cows last July that got into the barley and sold her to the butcher. He tried to collect. Claimed my fences was down."

"He might bust out. He's got a bit of mad in him, George."

"I know it — that's part of it. It's my birthday. I'm going to have fun watching him. I can look out for him."

He gnarled his lump of a fist and looked it over.

"Coming to my party, Joe?"

"Surely."

"Just a bit of a shindy."

"What time?"

"Oh, about seven."

He got up and went over to the door and laid his hand on the knob.

"Say, Joe, does Erwin Saunders deposit here?"

"Yes, he does."

"How much is he worth?"

"Well, it ain't exactly right for me — "

"Cripus, Joe, I know that and all the rest of it. Belle wants to marry him."

The banker looked up.

"Well, I'll be — "

"Eanh, so 'll I."

"I can't give you exact figures, but I'd say it was round eight thousand. Quite a lot for a young man like him. His uncle left him some, you know."

Old George blew up against his moustache.

"Well, that'd have been the only thing I might have raised a fuss on. It's too bad."

"I wouldn't have guessed it," said the banker.

"See you to-night, then, Joe."

"Surely."

3

He picked up his groceries and went down to the shed where he had left the team. On the street he met two members of the Ladies' Aid Society, walking with a friend. They were looking for contributions for their Christmas fund and incidentally getting signatures to a resolution against liquor and noxious drugs, drawn up by the society after a speech on the same subject. George gave them a dollar, because he knew that there was no way out of it; and for them to get less out of him than they hoped for would be more bitter in their mouths than to get nothing at all. But when they handed him the resolution against liquor and tobacco, he took a chew out of his pocket and got it rolling from side to side before he answered.

"Now why do you ladies want me to sign that-there?" he asked.

The two Ladies' Aiders exchanged a glance and introduced their companion, a formality which their eagerness for his contribution had led them unconsciously to avoid. She was a small woman, wrinkled about the under side of her chin, with pinched nostrils and a pinched hat, but with the holy light of battle in her eyes.

"Mrs. Kurty, know Mr. Stallion," they said, and stepped aside in tacit acknowledgment of her superior gifts. Mrs. Kurty had written the resolution and delivered the address. She was that most unfortunate of human combinations, a church worker and a widow.

At the first glimpse of her, George Stallion felt the old devil climbing up in him, and his eyes became sombre.

Mrs. Kurty bustled right up to the point.

"Everybody knows you, Mr. Stallion. You're a leading townsman."

"Never lived in a town in my life," said George.

"That don't matter," she said. "The community looks up to you."

"Never asked 'em to, mam. Mostly they call me a dirty skunk, when me or my boys ain't round."

"Your signature would mean a lot."

"I never could write very good, mam. Generally I blot the S."

Mrs. Kurty screwed a smile into one corner of her mouth, but she set her chin at the same time and shifted her attack.

"We need your name, Mr. Stallion," she began.

He simulated surprise.

"Why, I thought these ladies was married proper."

The Ladies' Aiders threw up their chins and turned their backs. A dull red made small spots high up in each of Mrs. Kurty's cheeks.

"You're a credit to the town, ain't you?" Her voice was sharp. "You're an evil man to say such a thing to three unprotected women."

His mouth laughed silently under his beard, but his eyes remained speculative and sad. Mrs. Kurty pressed her elbows in tight against her sides.

"It's men like you spoil the nation," she cried shrilly. "You set a bad example; you drink, you smoke and chew, and practise all kinds of filthy vice."

"Eanh," he said. "I tried gumming snuff for a year or two when I was a lad."

"And look at you now. A shameless reprobate! A sight for all people. Walking the town in a man's shape."

"That's right," he agreed. "Now, mam, seeing you're the opposite — "

"I thank God for it," she broke in.

"Why don't you go look in a mirror?"

She stamped her foot.

"It isn't the face and figure God will look at — it's the soul inside."

"Well, that never gave me no trouble."

"No, you old rascal! I'll bet it didn't. I can see it in your eye. Why, in all your ninety years you talk about, did you ever find the Saviour?"

"Didn't know he was lost, mam."

He spat affably at a late grasshopper perched on the sidewalk, and walked off.

He felt pretty well when he got the team out of the shed and started back. The bays looked nice trotting out of town; and he nodded to people as he met them. He hadn't felt so well in a long time. He hadn't been so quick at answering. It had done him good to button up that Kurty woman. That meant something; she had studied her oats even if she hadn't eaten them. It wasn't the same as trompling on fat Judy. Well, he'd go over and up the other side of the river and drop in on Whister and tell him the mortgage was closed. He'd timed things about right. He ought to get there as Whister was coming in to dinner. He'd be feeling savage.

He touched up the horses, keeping them just under a gallop, and the fellies muttered in the sand and glanced merrily. The old man's nostrils widened to the stinging smell of sweat. Well, it wouldn't hurt them going home.

The Whister farm was a nice place, small, set back in a shallow arm of the river valley, with a brook running through the far end of the barnyard. It looked neat — the white house under the pine, the gray barns, the woodshed partly stocked and smelling of bark; but it all looked bare, too. The late zinnias and asters had a lean appearance and were too widely spaced. Still, with a human woman in the house, it would pick up fast. He had thought of it with Belle living there — before she had decided on that sody clerk.

He swung the horses neatly through the gate, drove them to the brook to let them wet their muzzles, turned them, and glanced about from under his thick brows. A few chickens were scratching round the barn doors, and a cat was taking a noon nap curled up on the gatepost.

"Whister!" roared the old man. "Hey, Whister!"

After a minute, the door on the kitchen stoop opened, and a short heavy-set man stepped out, with his shirt sleeves still rolled up, his wrists red from hot water, and a comb in his hand.

"Hullo," he said. His eyes wandered over the barnyard and fastened themselves on some invisible object just above the sky line. "What do you want?" he asked in a heavy voice.

Stallion chewed on his whiskers.

"Did n't you hear me coming in?"

"Eanh."

"Why did n't you come out, then?" he roared.

"Did n't see as there was any call to do that."

The vague shape of a woman appeared inside the door. Whister handed her the comb and came out to the wagon. He walked stiffly. When he reached the shoulder of the nigh horse, he turned his gray eyes impersonally on the old man's face.

"What do you want?"

Stallion grunted and glanced round the place.

"It 's a good farm, ain't it?"

"If that 's what you wanted to say, I 'd better get in to lunch."

He turned partly round.

"Whister!"

The team jerked their heads. The man stopped.

"How about that interest?"

Stallion spoke loudly, and out of the corner of his eye he saw the woman come through the door.

"When do you want it?"

"It 's overdue."

"Well?"

"Five months."

"I'll pay you next month."

"No, you won't."

The woman drew in her breath sharply and stepped down beside her husband. She was a well-built woman, thin but strong. There was a quiet heat in her eyes.

"Why can't he?"

"I'm going to foreclose."

He let himself back on the seat and waited for an explosion, his black eyes jumping from one to the other.

"You wouldn't do that," said the woman. "We'll pay next month."

"I want the money to-day."

"We can borrow," said the woman. "Henry could bring it round to-morrow, maybe."

Stallion's hard old eyes looked her over without expression.

"I said to-day."

"I don't see how Henry could get it."

"That ain't my bother."

He hadn't expected them to take it this way. He thought they'd break out at him.

"Henry could get it round by nine in the morning, maybe."

"Twelve to-night, and that's all."

The husband's dull gray eyes followed the peregrinations of an ant along the rail fence. It climbed the post and waved its horns at the cat, and the tip of the cat's tail twitched twice.

"Listen — " said the woman.

Suddenly he turned on her.

"Shut up, Anne."

His forearms hardened across his chest; and the devil danced in the old man's eyes.

"I ain't never liked you, Stallion. I don't want to talk with you. Get the hell out of here."

Stallion got to his feet, then climbed easily down over the wheel.

"Ordering me off my own place, hey?"

"It ain't yourn yet. Get out."

"Going to put me off?"

He walked up to Whister and stared down at him. His full size became apparent then; his heavy chest muscled low from lifting, his great curved shoulders, and his mallet hands just swinging by his thighs.

Whister dropped his hands from his chest, but the woman caught his arm.

"Don't hit him, Henry." She snatched a hank of hair from her thin intense face. "Don't hit him, Henry. He's an old man."

Stallion laughed hoarsely.

"Come inside the house, Henry. He's an old man. You'd kill him if you hit him."

Her husband's eyes wavered to hers.

"Get out of here," she said. "Henry won't whip you. Don't bother us."

Stallion threw back his head and laughed.

"Crawl back of your woman, Whister! You hairless dry-gut."

"Get inside, Henry," the woman said.

"You get out of here, Stallion. I'll give you three minutes to get off. Then I'll put you off; by God, I will."

He trudged into the house behind his wife and shut the door. For a minute Stallion could hear their voices talking rapidly. He pulled his heavy silver watch from his pocket and stood where he was, shifting his glance occasionally to the door. He waited five minutes, climbed deliberately into the wagon, and walked the team out of the barnyard.

He drove home slowly. Now and then he would slap the reins on the rumps of the horses and chuckle. He'd scared the man's insides out. There weren't any two ways about it. He'd stayed two minutes longer than he'd been allowed. Old? That was just to let Whister crawl out. Old? Why, he didn't show more than fifty of his years — he didn't feel that many. No, by Cripus! He'd have knocked the man as stiff as a peavy, and both of them knew it. Old? What did she mean anyhow? But the man had crawled, belly-washed himself. The old man laughed till the team laid back their ears, and then he spanked them with the reins till they cantered.

Belle met him at the door.

"How'd you get along, Grampa?"

He kissed her and grinned.

"Good."

4

After lunch the women cleared the dining room and parlor, and the men helped them set up a table of planks and sawhorses to run round two sides of the dining room, and rigged a four-by-six platform beside the front door for the fiddler to sit on.

The old man poked round and gave multitudinous orders about the cider, rum, and whiskey. Then he went upstairs and had Belle brush out his black coat and trousers while he greased his black Sunday boots. Finally, when he could think of nothing else to do, he picked up the weekly paper and sat down on the front porch.

It was a soft afternoon, with the haze heavy over the valley; the woods to the north gray and almost leafless, the balsams blue-black in the swamps; and the smell of rotting grass and leaves sweet and lazing. Down in the maple lot, the axes of his two grandsons chopped with dull, hollow-sounding strokes in the heavy air. He could see the gray team hauling manure in the south meadow, the iron wheels sinking in and pulling up clods once in a while as the team started the wagon; then the horses dozy while John tossed out the forkfuls right and left, and then drawing ahead another wagon length.

Off to the right a section of the canal showed between the trees. Every now and then a boat went by with its cargo of sand, the mules having an easy time pulling with the current, the driver cracking his snake whip out of principle. Next week Barton would bring his boat up to get the potatoes.

The old man put his feet on the rail and dozed. He hadn't

felt so spry in a long time, but he might as well take it easy. What if Whister's woman had called him old? There was n't much meaning in years — a hook a lazy man used to hang his harness on. If it was n't for his birthday, he 'd be doing his lick of work along with the boys. Joe Francis at the bank was ten years younger than he was, but he looked older. George could remember when Joe was the only man he knew who could give him a real tussle at a wrestle. Now he could put him down with one hand. Years did n't mean anything. Damn Whister's woman. . . .

While he sat there, with the hot dim afternoon sun picking out the clean lights and shadows in his face and silvering his beard, Belle came out on the porch, an uneasy pucker between her brows. The old man glanced up sleepily.

"Pearl 's worse," she told him.

He grunted.

"Doctor Briggs is coming to the party, ain't he?"

"Eanh, Grampa."

"Don't you worry, Belle. He can look her over then. She ain't due for three days anyhow."

"I don't guess there 's any point sending for him right away," she half agreed. Now that the old man had shown himself un-worried, she felt easier herself. "But I think the baby 'll come early."

He grunted again.

"You women all get the wrong notion. There ain't nothing queer in dropping a child. It 's seeing yourself growing into him after-ward that 's queer."

She leaned against an upright and stared toward the canal.

"I wonder will it be a boy," she said.

"Pearl 's likely to have one. These soft, easy-crying gals is apt to have boys."

"I 'd want a boy," she said.

"Then you 'll have girls," he said. "You 're that mean you 'd fool yourself, Belle, if you could n't find anybody else to fool."

He chuckled and pretended to snore.

"There's somebody coming down the towpath," she said. "He's turning in here. He's got a pack on him. I'll bet it's Harvey Cannywhacker."

The old man sat up, banging his feet on the floor, and craned his neck round her.

"It is, at that. By dang, I'd wanted a good cigar!"

A whistled rendering of "The Irish Washerwoman," high and unmusical, approached slowly, and then a small black hat drawn low over a pair of small sharp eyes appeared round the corner of the house, and a man came up the steps under a large brown pack.

"Hullo, George. Hullo, Belle."

He dumped the pack and wiped his forehead with a red cotton handkerchief.

" 'Lo, Harvey," said the old man. "Set down."

Belle smiled and went into the house.

"Got a good cigar?"

"Got some rolled in my pocket, George. Have one?"

"Eanh."

The little man sat down, and they lit up and blew clouds under the roof of the porch.

"Hot," said the old man.

"Kind of sweaty."

"Been up the canal?"

"Forestport. Coming down now. Did n't sell so good this time."

"You can roll me eight dozen," said the old man. "I'm having a party to-night."

"Eanh?"

"You'd better stay. We'll put you up."

"All right. I guess I'll commence rolling. It's a good haul for me to make. Cigar peddling's dropping off. Too many stores coming into the country."

The peddler pulled up a small table, opened his bag, and began rolling. His hands worked rapidly back and forth, sifting on the filling, whipping up the leaves, and rolling the wrapping on tight with the balls of the thumbs.

"Eanh," said the old man. "Eanh. I'm having a party to-night."

"What's the celebration?"

"Birthday. Ninety. Ninety just."

"Well, I'd never have guessed it. Why, it don't seem ten years when I used to see you raising ructions all over the canal."

The old man grinned under his beard.

"I used to raise a lot of hell. Still do, Harvey."

"Gol," said the peddler. "I believe it. . . . Ninety years," he went on, "is a long time. It's a long time, George. You're lucky not to feel it."

The old man stretched.

"Years don't mean anything," he said, irritably. "My pa was eighty when he got jammed in the number-four lock out of Albany. He was drunk then. He wasn't old."

"Well, a man goes on until he finds he's an old man."

"Eanh?"

"Then he is old, and he can't help it."

The old man swore.

"A man learns it all to once," said Harvey. "He goes along till he sees him coming back at himself, like a circle, and he knows he's old, and he can't help it. It's a sad thing."

"Cripus," said George. "Years ain't anything."

They shifted the conversation. They talked about the canal and the early Black River country; the great pine forests, nearly gone; only one of them left, twenty-two feet round the butt, down on the Hebner place. And they spoke of how the wolves used to come down in winter on the gray snow at night. How they found Arnon Marcy one morning up in a tree, frozen solid, his arms locked round the limb over his head, his legs scissored on the limb he sat on, and the circling tracks underneath. How he fought Dwight Wilkins above the Lansing Kill gorge for an hour and a half and whipped him. How they saw a triple rainbow once on the Hudson. How the horse cholera ravaged the canal, and how George broke oxen during that winter so that his spring ploughing would n't have to wait. Full lives, full lives. . . .

"Pa said I was the first boy born on the Erie Canal," George said. "Sometimes I wished I 'd stayed on to it."

After a while he fell asleep, a great bulk of a man in the rocking-chair, with only the white hairs about his mouth stirring. And the little peddler's hands went on rolling cigars and making stacks of them in the afternoon shadow.

5

By eight o'clock the parlor was full of neighbors and friends and people who were scared to say no. But everyone had a good time who went to a party at George Stallion's. There was good food and good drink, and anybody danced that liked to, and no-body danced that did n't. Even the family themselves had a good time. For then they realized that the old tyrant was something of a celebrity, who was liked or admired or hated; and they shared a little of his power. His sons and grandsons told proud stories of his agility and strength, and the women said laughingly that he was an old bear of a man, and managed to look as if he were just the opposite. Even Judy, who saw and heard open-mouthed ad-miration of her cookery all round her, softened and volunteered that he was the heartiest eater in the family. When there were other people to show his points to, they were all proud of him; and they had a right to be.

He stood in the wide door between the dining room and parlor. On one side, a vista of the table running round two walls of the room, with candles on it, red, waxy-looking ones that sputtered continually, a pie every yard to the inch, and cup cakes, coffee cakes, and fried cakes, fruit, glasses, knives, forks, plates, syrup, candies — a glittering sight. On the other side of him the cider keg, cradled conveniently in a sawhorse, the bung driven and the spigot set. Round the walls, decorations of evergreen and vibur-num berries and here and there a little early bittersweet. His sons and daughters on his left, beyond them the grandchildren, man and wife, except for unmarried Jim at the end of the line, and Belle on the old man's right. The guests came in to him and Belle, offering congratulations, and then moved down the family, laughing, talking, exchanging gossip, receipts, prescriptions, jokes.

Old George, standing in the wide door, dominated them all. His roaring voice boomed out over their heads. He stood straight, without bending toward his guests. His black coat and trousers, his flaming red waistcoat, made a shock of color which hung in every man's eyes as long as he remained in the room. His massive head towered above them, red-cheeked, white-bearded, the black eyes gleaming under the heavy black brows.

"Regular old rip-hell," Garvin said to his wife. "He don't miss a thing."

Mrs. Garvin nodded reminiscently.

At the other side of the room John was helping Martin, the fiddler, on to the platform. An old man, too, with a smooth high forehead and white hair hanging on his ears, and a yellow skin so clear it looked like gold. He had St. Vitus's dance in his legs, but the melody of all the world in his fingers. And he sat down, wrapping his legs round the legs of the chair to hold them still, and he fiddled with the strings. Then he looked across at old George and a smile passed between them. Martin had fiddled for the wedding of every member of the family, for every birth-day party here, thirty-seven of them. He swallowed in his lean throat and whistled, a high call, like the call of killdeer on the river beaches. "Turkey in the Straw." Old Stallion led out Belle and they headed the dance. He crossed partners with Mrs. Garvin, she with Erwin Saunders. In between, as they clapped the time, he felt the blood in his heavy palms, felt it run up his arms and bring his head to life. His feet lifted of their own accord, and he stamped. Old? Old? Jeepers! When he looked at Mrs. Garvin, she blushed. Old!

At the end of the dance, some of the older couples sat down to talk or went into the downstairs bedroom to play cribbage. But

Stallion footed two more. Then he climbed up beside Martin and called for a quadrille. Martin had ripped open his shirt collar, but his fingers were hungry for the strings.

The tune, quick, sweet, shrill. Old George Stallion's booming voice in the first change.

"First four right. . . ."

Belle was not dancing. Probably upstairs with Pearl.

"And left. . . ."

By grab, the doctor was n't there either. Probably upstairs, too. Pearl raising a fuss. She was n't a Stallion. John looked sort of peaked. The young rascal was worried. Served him right for marrying such a pale-tempered girl just because she had yellow hair.

"Ladies change. . . ."

Martin's legs twitching, toes clawing for the rungs. Same thing as the stringhalt. Regular old war horse, though.

"*And* promenade. . . ."

He liked to see the faces going by. Getting their color now. They 'd be hungry. He 'd raised a sweat himself. It was like old times. The best birthday he could remember in a long while. He had n't felt so well . . . he felt like a colt on grass. Old? Cripus! What was Cannywhacker talking about? Old all to once. A man coming back at himself. Buttery, fooling notion.

" 'L' a man left. . . ."

He clapped his hands for the second change. Here came Joe Francis with his business, bank look, still puffing from that first reel. Yes, eanh, he 'd told Whister to pay that night or it was going to be closed. If Joe did n't get the interest in the morning, he could go ahead with the papers. No fuss about it. Whister had belly-washed.

"First four forward. . . ."

Kill him if he hit him, hey? He was sound as a nut. That did n't bother him.

"Cross over and sashay. . . ."

He was tough as a nut.

"Cross back. . . ."

He could hear his voice filling the room, the fiddle's high notes just squirting through it. There went Arnold grinning at him. Best man of any his girls had married. Good man, Arnold was. Worked hard. Not as hard as he had, though.

"Balance four. . . ."

And the third change.

"Twice over." And so to the fourth change. "Then side. . . ."

He could see Judy bringing the eatables into the dining room. She always did well with a party.

"First couple lead up to the right and four hands around. . . ."

It was queer the doctor had n't come down. John had left, too. Well, what of it? He felt good; he 'd never felt better. By holy! He wished he was dancing instead of calling.

"Lead up to the next, and right, and left. . . ."

They 'd want to eat at the end of this.

"Then balance all. . . ."

He clapped again and shouted for the winder.

"Forward all. . . ."

His great voice bellowed. Harvey over there was smoking cigars he 'd sold. Foxy twerk!

"Ladies to the right. . . ."

The tune was picking up.

"All jig. . . ."

"Forward and back. . . ."

Now he 'd send them out to eat. The folks were coming out of the card room. The minister looked as if he 'd been losing again. That was n't more 'n right. He had you by the neck on Sundays.

He stamped his feet and roared at them, his face hot and red, his beard thrust out, his head thrown back, his thumbs caught in the armholes of his red waistcoat.

"Gents pass partners and then promenade to your seats."

He laughed down at them. He liked them there, with the devil coming up in them, tasting at the hell in themselves. It made him feel good.

"That means get along into the other room and eat and drink, and there's plenty of both."

He jumped to the floor and stood for an instant with them all round him.

And then he saw Harvey Cannywhacker move away from the stairs, and fat Judy's face with a woman's smile on it, and John behind looking queer and sort of uppish, and the doctor with the merits of profession sitting on him smooth, and Belle last, carrying a blanket.

"Get out of the way, please, folks," said Judy, and came bustling to him, breathless. He was thirsty and hungry.

"What's all this?" he demanded. "What's all the fuss? We're just going to eat. What're you busting in for?"

He glanced over the others and saw Harvey's sharp eyes watching him from the stairs. What was it all about?

"Folks," cried Judy in her high voice, "I guess you all know Pa's ninety to-day. Ninety! And he's hearty as a four-year-old. We've wished him many happy returns. We've give him presents. But Pearl and John've gone and got a surprise party for him."

She beckoned to Belle, raised her voice.

"They've got him a great-grandchild!"

A universal cooing broke from the women. The men found themselves strangely and suddenly outside the circle.

"It's a boy. One of the finest it's been my privilege—"said the doctor.

"We've named him George," said John, proudly. "Me and Pearl had it all figured out."

Belle undid a corner of the blanket and held it out to the old man. He glanced at it curiously—just a fleshy red ball; he'd seen the identical same thing lots of times. Belle pushed it into his arms. He held it, staring down at it, holding his beard in out of the way against his waistcoat. Nose wiggled like a pig's. He'd seen the same thing lots of times. All this fuss . . .

"We've named it George," repeated John. "Me and Pearl had it all figured out — George Stallion!"

"Well, Grampa," said Belle, looking up at him saucily, "now I guess you *are* an old man."

Suddenly Stallion's jaw dropped and vacuous astonishment clouded his eyes like an old man's. Old . . . It was what Harvey had said. Coming back at himself. Yes, he could look at the whole circle. There he was himself, and there was Judy, and there was John, and here again was George Stallion. His voice whistled in his beard.

"God! Am I that old?"

He handed the bundle back. He gazed round at the people. They laughed at him, clawed at his hands, laughed. Little by little they edged toward the dining room.

"A toast!" cried the minister. "I'll give you a toast."

Judy hustled the baby away, the doctor following her. The others had gone into the dining room. And Martin had fallen asleep in the midst of the noise.

George Stallion was alone. He ran his finger over his teeth.

"Old."

Old man. He walked to the front door. Kicked at it. Then he stepped outside. It was still, glassy still. And the moon was growing white before the frost. He could smell it.

He stepped down toward the barn. A man was coming in from the road. Whister. But he didn't seem to recognize him.

"Get out of my way."

"Anne sent me up, Stallion. . . ."

"Get out of my way."

The man stepped in front of him again. Almost mechanically he pulled back his fist.

6

They drank the toast.

"The grandson, George Stallion."

They took it back a generation.

"The mother, Pearl Stallion."

The minister had a way of calling toasts. He was a master hand.

"The father, John Stallion."

John was proud.

"George Stallion. The great-grandfather. George Stallion —
God bless him!"

They drank it down, clapped their hands, shouted his name.

"Where is he?" Belle asked suddenly in a bit of quiet. "Where's
Grampa?"

A man's shoes scraped hesitantly through the front door. He
was white-mouthed. He had an ugly red patch which was growing
blue on his jaw.

"I seen him," he said. "He was going to the barn. He knocked
me down."

They stared at him. The cigar peddler came in. The light
picked out his black eyes and straggly black hair.

"Stallion's dead. He's hung himself."

At their low sigh, the fiddler awoke with a start, and, seeing their
white faces looking toward him, smiled apologetically and began
to play "The Irish Washerwoman."

"My God," Whister said. "I was going to pay him the interest.
I was bringing it up. What'll I do with it now?"

"You'd better give it to me," said the banker.

Belle burst out crying.